Classic Mystery and
Detective Stories

Classic Mystery and Detective Stories

Copyright © 2020 Bibliotech Press
All rights reserved

ISBN: 978-1-64729-536-2

Robert Louis Stevenson et al

Classic Mystery and Detective Stories

The present edition is a reproduction of previous publication of this classic work. Minor typographical errors may have been corrected without note; however, for an authentic reading experience the spelling, punctuation, and capitalization have been retained from the original text.

ISBN: 978-1-64799-536-2

TABLE OF CONTENTS

ROBERT LOUIS STEVENSON

THE PAVILION ON THE LINKS

I

I was a great solitary when I was young. I made it my pride to keep aloof and suffice for my own entertainment; and I may say that I had neither friends nor acquaintances until I met that friend who became my wife and the mother of my children. With one man only was I on private terms; this was R. Northmour, Esquire, of Graden Easter, in Scotland. We had met at college; and though there was not much liking between us, nor even much intimacy, we were so nearly of a humor that we could associate with ease to both. Misanthropes, we believed ourselves to be; but I have thought since that we were only sulky fellows. It was scarcely a companionship, but a co-existence in unsociability. Northmour's exceptional violence of temper made it no easy affair for him to keep the peace with anyone but me; and as he respected my silent ways, and let me come and go as I pleased, I could tolerate his presence without concern. I think we called each other friends.

When Northmour took his degree and I decided to leave the university without one, he invited me on a long visit to Graden Easter; and it was thus that I first became acquainted with the scene of my adventures. The mansion house of Graden stood in a bleak stretch of country some three miles from the shore of the German Ocean. It was as large as a barrack; and as it had been built of a soft stone, liable to consume in the eager air of the seaside, it was damp and draughty within and half ruinous without. It was impossible for two young men to lodge with comfort in such a dwelling. But there stood in the northern part of the estate, in a wilderness of links and blowing sand hills, and between a plantation and the sea, a small pavilion or belvedere, of modern design, which was exactly suited to our wants; and in this hermitage, speaking little, reading much, and rarely associating except at meals, Northmour and I spent four tempestuous winter months. I might have stayed longer; but one March night there sprung up between us a dispute, which rendered my departure necessary. Northmour spoke hotly, I remember, and I suppose I must have made some tart rejoinder. He leaped from his chair and grappled me; I had to fight, without exaggeration, for my life; and it was only

1

with a great effort that I mastered him, for he was near as strong in body as myself, and seemed filled with the devil. The next morning, we met on our usual terms; but I judged it more delicate to withdraw; nor did he attempt to dissuade me.

It was nine years before I revisited the neighborhood. I traveled at that time with a tilt-cart, a tent, and a cooking stove, tramping all day beside the wagon, and at night, whenever it was possible, gypsying in a cove of the hills, or by the side of a wood. I believe I visited in this manner most of the wild and desolate regions both in England and Scotland; and, as I had neither friends nor relations, I was troubled with no correspondence, and had nothing in the nature of headquarters, unless it was the office of my solicitors, from whom I drew my income twice a year. It was a life in which I delighted; and I fully thought to have grown old upon the march, and at last died in a ditch.

It was my whole business to find desolate corners, where I could camp without the fear of interruption; and hence, being in another part of the same shire, I bethought me suddenly of the Pavilion on the Links. No thoroughfare passed within three miles of it. The nearest town, and that was but a fisher village, was at a distance of six or seven. For ten miles of length, and from a depth varying from three miles to half a mile, this belt of barren country lay along the sea. The beach, which was the natural approach, was full of quicksands. Indeed I may say there is hardly a better place of concealment in the United Kingdom. I determined to pass a week in the Sea-Wood of Graden Easter, and making a long stage, reached it about sundown on a wild September day.

The country, I have said, was mixed sand hill and links; links being a Scottish name for sand which has ceased drifting and become more or less solidly covered with turf. The pavilion stood on an even space: a little behind it, the wood began in a hedge of elders huddled together by the wind; in front, a few tumbled sand hills stood between it and the sea. An outcropping of rock had formed a bastion for the sand, so that there was here a promontory in the coast line between two shallow bays; and just beyond the tides, the rock again cropped out and formed an islet of small dimensions but strikingly designed. The quicksands were of great extent at low water, and had an infamous reputation in the country. Close in shore, between the islet and the promontory, it was said they would swallow a man in four minutes and a half; but there may have been little ground for this precision. The district was alive with rabbits, and haunted by gulls which made a continual piping about the pavilion. On summer days the outlook was bright and even gladsome; but at sundown in September, with a high wind, and a heavy surf rolling in close along the links, the place told of nothing but dead mariners and sea disaster. A ship beating to windward on the horizon, and a huge truncheon of wreck half buried in the sands at my feet, completed the innuendo of the scene.

2

The pavilion—it had been built by the last proprietor, Northmour's uncle, a silly and prodigal virtuoso—presented little signs of age. It was two stories in height, Italian in design, surrounded by a patch of garden in which nothing had prospered but a few coarse flowers; and looked, with its shuttered windows, not like a house that had been deserted, but like one that had never been tenanted by man. Northmour was plainly from home; whether, as usual, sulking in the cabin of his yacht, or in one of his fitful and extravagant appearances in the world of society, I had, of course, no means of guessing. The place had an air of solitude that daunted even a solitary like myself; the wind cried in the chimneys with a strange and wailing note; and it was with a sense of escape, as if I were going indoors, that I turned away and, driving my cart before me, entered the skirts of the wood.

The Sea-Wood of Graden had been planted to shelter the cultivated fields behind, and check the encroachments of the blowing sand. As you advanced into it from coastward, elders were succeeded by other hardy shrubs; but the timber was all stunted and bushy; it led a life of conflict; the trees were accustomed to swing there all night long in fierce winter tempests; and even in early spring, the leaves were already flying, and autumn was beginning, in this exposed plantation. Inland the ground rose into a little hill, which, along with the islet, served as a sailing mark for seamen. When the hill was open of the islet to the north, vessels must bear well to the eastward to clear Graden Ness and the Graden Bullers. In the lower ground, a streamlet ran among the trees, and, being dammed with dead leaves and clay of its own carrying, spread out every here and there, and lay in stagnant pools. One or two ruined cottages were dotted about the wood; and, according to Northmour, these were ecclesiastical foundations, and in their time had sheltered pious hermits.

I found a den, or small hollow, where there was a spring of pure water; and there, clearing away the brambles, I pitched the tent, and made a fire to cook my supper. My horse I picketed farther in the wood where there was a patch of sward. The banks of the den not only concealed the light of my fire, but sheltered me from the wind, which was cold as well as high.

The life I was leading made me both hardy and frugal. I never drank but water, and rarely eat anything more costly than oatmeal; and I required so little sleep, that, although I rose with the peep of day, I would often lie long awake in the dark or starry watches of the night. Thus in Graden Sea-Wood, although I fell thankfully asleep by eight in the evening I was awake again before eleven with a full possession of my faculties, and no sense of drowsiness or fatigue. I rose and sat by the fire, watching the trees and clouds tumultuously tossing and fleeing overhead, and hearkening to the wind and the rollers along the shore; till at length, growing weary of inaction, I quitted the den, and strolled toward the borders of the wood. A young moon, buried in mist, gave a

3

faint illumination to my steps; and the light grew brighter as I walked forth into the links. At the same moment, the wind, smelling salt of the open ocean and carrying particles of sand, struck me with its full force, so that I had to bow my head.

When I raised it again to look about me, I was aware of a light in the pavilion. It was not stationary; but passed from one window to another, as though some one were reviewing the different apartments with a lamp or candle. I watched it for some seconds in great surprise. When I had arrived in the afternoon the house had been plainly deserted; now it was as plainly occupied. It was my first idea that a gang of thieves might have broken in and be now ransacking Northmour's cupboards, which were many and not ill supplied. But what should bring thieves at Graden Easter? And, again, all the shutters had been thrown open, and it would have been more in the character of such gentry to close them. I dismissed the notion, and fell back upon another. Northmour himself must have arrived, and was now airing and inspecting the pavilion.

I have said that there was no real affection between this man and me; but, had I loved him like a brother, I was then so much more in love with solitude that I should none the less have shunned his company. As it was, I turned and ran for it; and it was with genuine satisfaction that I found myself safely back beside the fire. I had escaped an acquaintance; I should have one more night in comfort. In the morning, I might either slip away before Northmour was abroad, or pay him as short a visit as I chose.

But when morning came, I thought the situation so diverting that I forgot my shyness. Northmour was at my mercy; I arranged a good practical jest, though I knew well that my neighbor was not the man to jest with in security; and, chuckling beforehand over its success, took my place among the elders at the edge of the wood, whence I could command the door of the pavilion. The shutters were all once more closed, which I remember thinking odd; and the house, with its white walls and green venetians, looked spruce and habitable in the morning light. Hour after hour passed, and still no sign of Northmour. I knew him for a sluggard in the morning; but, as it drew on toward noon, I lost my patience. To say the truth, I had promised myself to break my fast in the pavilion, and hunger began to prick me sharply. It was a pity to let the opportunity go by without some cause for mirth; but the grosser appetite prevailed, and I relinquished my jest with regret, and sallied from the wood.

The appearance of the house affected me, as I drew near, with disquietude. It seemed unchanged since last evening; and I had expected it, I scarce knew why, to wear some external signs of habitation. But no: the windows were all closely shuttered, the chimneys breathed no smoke, and the front door itself was closely padlocked. Northmour, therefore, had entered by the back; this was the

4

natural, and indeed, the necessary conclusion; and you may judge of my surprise when, on turning the house, I found the back door similarly secured.

My mind at once reverted to the original theory of thieves; and I blamed myself sharply for my last night's inaction. I examined all the windows on the lower story, but none of them had been tampered with; I tried the padlocks, but they were both secure. It thus became a problem how the thieves, if thieves they were, had managed to enter the house. They must have got, I reasoned, upon the roof of the outhouse where Northmour used to keep his photographic battery; and from thence, either by the window of the study or that of my old bedroom, completed their burglarious entry.

I followed what I supposed was their example; and, getting on the roof, tried the shutters of each room. Both were secure; but I was not to be beaten; and, with a little force, one of them flew open, grazing, as it did so, the back of my hand. I remember, I put the wound to my mouth, and stood for perhaps half a minute licking it like a dog, and mechanically gazing behind me over the waste links and the sea; and, in that space of time, my eye made note of a large schooner yacht some miles to the northeast. Then I threw up the window and climbed in.

I went over the house, and nothing can express my mystification. There was no sign of disorder, but, on the contrary, the rooms were unusually clean and pleasant. I found fires laid, ready for lighting; three bedrooms prepared with a luxury quite foreign to Northmour's habits, and with water in the ewers and the beds turned down; a table set for three in the dining-room; and an ample supply of cold meats, game, and vegetables on the pantry shelves. There were guests expected, that was plain; but why guests, when Northmour hated society? And, above all, why was the house thus stealthily prepared at dead of night? and why were the shutters closed and the doors padlocked?

I effaced all traces of my visit, and came forth from the window feeling sobered and concerned.

The schooner yacht was still in the same place; and it flashed for a moment through my mind that this might be the "Red Earl" bringing the owner of the pavilion and his guests. But the vessel's head was set the other way.

II

I returned to the den to cook myself a meal, of which I stood in great need, as well as to care for my horse, whom I had somewhat

5

neglected in the morning. From time to time I went down to the edge of the wood; but there was no change in the pavilion, and not a human creature was seen all day upon the links. The schooner in the offing was the one touch of life within my range of vision. She, apparently with no set object, stood off and on or lay to, hour after hour; but as the evening deepened, she drew steadily nearer. I became more convinced that she carried Northmour and his friends, and that they would probably come ashore after dark; not only because that was of a piece with the secrecy of the preparations, but because the tide would not have flowed sufficiently before eleven to cover Graden Floe and the other sea quags that fortified the shore against invaders.

All day the wind had been going down, and the sea along with it; but there was a return toward sunset of the heavy weather of the day before. The night set in pitch dark. The wind came off the sea in squalls, like the firing of a battery of cannon; now and then there was a flaw of rain, and the surf rolled heavier with the rising tide. I was down at my observatory among the elders, when a light was run up to the masthead of the schooner, and showed she was closer in than when I had last seen her by the dying daylight. I concluded that this must be a signal to Northmour's associates on shore; and, stepping forth into the links, looked around me for something in response.

A small footpath ran along the margin of the wood, and formed the most direct communication between the pavilion and the mansion house; and, as I cast my eyes to that side, I saw a spark of light, not a quarter of a mile away, and rapidly approaching. From its uneven course it appeared to be the light of a lantern carried by a person who followed the windings of the path, and was often staggered, and taken aback by the more violent squalls. I concealed myself once more among the elders, and waited eagerly for the newcomer's advance. It proved to be a woman; and, as she passed within half a rod of my ambush, I was able to recognize the features. The deaf and silent old dame, who had nursed Northmour in his childhood, was his associate in this underhand affair.

I followed her at a little distance, taking advantage of the innumerable heights and hollows, concealed by the darkness, and favored not only by the nurse's deafness, but by the uproar of the wind and surf. She entered the pavilion, and, going at once to the upper story, opened and set a light in one of the windows that looked toward the sea. Immediately afterwards the light at the schooner's masthead was run down and extinguished. Its purpose had been attained, and those on board were sure that they were expected. The old woman resumed her preparations; although the other shutters remained closed, I could see a glimmer going to and fro about the house; and a gush of sparks from one chimney after another soon told me that the fires were being kindled.

Northmour and his guests, I was now persuaded, would come

6

ashore as soon as there was water on the floe. It was a wild night for boat service; and I felt some alarm mingle with my curiosity as I reflected on the danger of the landing. My old acquaintance, it was true, was the most eccentric of men; but the present eccentricity was both disquieting and lugubrious to consider. A variety of feelings thus led me toward the beach, where I lay flat on my face in a hollow within six feet of the track that led to the pavilion. Thence, I should have the satisfaction of recognizing the arrivals, and, if they should prove to be acquaintances, greeting them as soon as they landed.

Some time before eleven, while the tide was still dangerously low, a boat's lantern appeared close in shore; and, my attention being thus awakened, I could perceive another still far to seaward, violently tossed, and sometimes hidden by the billows. The weather, which was getting dirtier as the night went on, and the perilous situation of the yacht upon a lee shore, had probably driven them to attempt a landing at the earliest possible moment.

A little afterwards, four yachtsmen carrying a very heavy chest, and guided by a fifth with a lantern, passed close in front of me as I lay, and were admitted to the pavilion by the nurse. They returned to the beach, and passed me a third time with another chest, larger but apparently not so heavy as the first. A third time they made the transit; and on this occasion one of the yachtsmen carried a leather portmanteau, and the others a lady's trunk and carriage bag. My curiosity was sharply excited. If a woman were among the guests of Northmour, it would show a change in his habits, and an apostasy from his pet theories of life, well calculated to fill me with surprise. When he and I dwelt there together, the pavilion had been a temple of misogyny. And now, one of the detested sex was to be installed under its roof. I remembered one or two particulars, a few notes of daintiness and almost of coquetry which had struck me the day before as I surveyed the preparations in the house; their purpose was now clear, and I thought myself dull not to have perceived it from the first.

While I was thus reflecting, a second lantern drew near me from the beach. It was carried by a yachtsman whom I had not yet seen, and who was conducting two other persons to the pavilion. These two persons were unquestionably the guests for whom the house was made ready; and, straining eye and ear, I set myself to watch them as they passed. One was an unusually tall man, in a traveling hat slouched over his eyes, and a highland cape closely buttoned and turned up so as to conceal his face. You could make out no more of him than that he was, as I have said, unusually tall, and walked feebly with a heavy stoop. By his side, and either clinging to him or giving him support—I could not make out which—was a young, tall, and slender figure of a woman. She was extremely pale; but in the light of the lantern her face was so marred by strong and changing shadows, that she might equally well have been as ugly as sin or as beautiful as I afterwards found her to be.

7

When they were just abreast of me, the girl made some remark which was drowned by the noise of the wind.

"Hush!" said her companion; and there was something in the tone with which the word was uttered that thrilled and rather shook my spirits. It seemed to breathe from a bosom laboring under the deadliest terror; I have never heard another syllable so expressive; and I still hear it again when I am feverish at night, and my mind runs upon old times. The man turned toward the girl as he spoke; I had a glimpse of much red beard and a nose which seemed to have been broken in youth; and his light eyes seemed shining in his face with some strong and unpleasant emotion.

But these two passed on and were admitted in their turn to the pavilion.

One by one, or in groups, the seamen returned to the beach. The wind brought me the sound of a rough voice crying, "Shove off!" Then, after a pause, another lantern drew near. It was Northmour alone.

My wife and I, a man and a woman, have often agreed to wonder how a person could be, at the same time, so handsome and so repulsive as Northmour. He had the appearance of a finished gentleman; his face bore every mark of intelligence and courage; but you had only to look at him, even in his most amiable moment, to see that he had the temper of a slaver captain. I never knew a character that was both explosive and revengeful to the same degree; he combined the vivacity of the south with the sustained and deadly hatreds of the north; and both traits were plainly written on his face, which was a sort of danger signal. In person, he was tall, strong, and active; his hair and complexion very dark; his features handsomely designed, but spoiled by a menacing expression.

At that moment he was somewhat paler than by nature; he wore a heavy frown; and his lips worked, and he looked sharply round him as he walked, like a man besieged with apprehensions. And yet I thought he had a look of triumph underlying all, as though he had already done much, and was near the end of an achievement.

Partly from a scruple of delicacy—which I dare say came too late—partly from the pleasure of startling an acquaintance, I desired to make my presence known to him without delay.

I got suddenly to my feet, and stepped forward.

"Northmour!" said I.

I have never had so shocking a surprise in all my days. He leaped on me without a word; something shone in his hand; and he struck for my heart with a dagger. At the same moment I knocked him head over heels. Whether it was my quickness, or his own uncertainty, I know not; but the blade only grazed my shoulder, while the hilt and his fist struck me violently on the mouth.

I fled, but not far. I had often and often observed the capabilities of the sand hills for protracted ambush or stealthy advances and retreats; and, not ten yards from the scene of the scuffle, plumped down again upon the grass. The lantern had fallen and gone out. But what was my astonishment to see Northmour slip at a bound into the pavilion, and hear him bar the door behind him with a clang of iron!

He had not pursued me. He had run away. Northmour, whom I knew for the most implacable and daring of men, had run away! I could scarce believe my reason; and yet in this strange business, where all was incredible, there was nothing to make a work about in an incredibility more or less. For why was the pavilion secretly prepared? Why had Northmour landed with his guests at dead of night, in half a gale of wind, and with the floe scarce covered? Why had he sought to kill me? Had he not recognized my voice? I wondered. And, above all, how had he come to have a dagger ready in his hand? A dagger, or even a sharp knife, seemed out of keeping with the age in which we lived; and a gentleman landing from his yacht on the shore of his own estate, even although it was at night and with some mysterious circumstances, does not usually, as a matter of fact, walk thus prepared for deadly onslaught. The more I reflected, the further I felt at sea. I recapitulated the elements of mystery, counting them on my fingers: the pavilion secretly prepared for guests; the guests landed at the risk of their lives and to the imminent peril of the yacht; the guests, or at least one of them, in undisguised and seemingly causeless terror; Northmour with a naked weapon; Northmour stabbing his most intimate acquaintance at a word; last, and not least strange, Northmour fleeing from the man whom he had sought to murder, and barricading himself, like a hunted creature, behind the door of the pavilion. Here were at least six separate causes for extreme surprise; each part and parcel with the others, and forming all together one consistent story. I felt almost ashamed to believe my own senses.

As I thus stood, transfixed with wonder, I began to grow painfully conscious of the injuries I had received in the scuffle; skulked round among the sand hills; and, by a devious path, regained the shelter of the wood. On the way, the old nurse passed again within several yards of me, still carrying her lantern, on the return journey to the mansion house of Graden. This made a seventh suspicious feature in the case. Northmour and his guests, it appeared, were to cook and do the cleaning for themselves, while the old woman continued to inhabit the big empty barrack among the policies. There must surely be great cause for secrecy, when so many inconveniences were confronted to preserve it.

So thinking, I made my way to the den. For greater security, I trod out the embers of the fire, and lighted my lantern to examine the wound upon my shoulder. It was a trifling hurt, although it bled somewhat freely, and I dressed it as well as I could (for its position made it difficult to reach) with some rag and cold water from the spring. While I was thus busied, I mentally declared war against

9

Northmour and his mystery. I am not an angry man by nature, and I believe there was more curiosity than resentment in my heart. But war I certainly declared; and, by way of preparation, I got out my revolver, and, having drawn the charges, cleaned and reloaded it with scrupulous care. Next I became preoccupied about my horse. It might break loose, or fall to neighing, and so betray my camp in the Sea-Wood. I determined to rid myself of its neighborhood; and long before dawn I was leading it over the links in the direction of the fisher village.

III

For two days I skulked round the pavilion, profiting by the uneven surface of the links. I became an adept in the necessary tactics. These low hillocks and shallow dells, running one into another, became a kind of cloak of darkness for my inthralling, but perhaps dishonorable, pursuit.

Yet, in spite of this advantage, I could learn but little of Northmour or his guests.

Fresh provisions were brought under cover of darkness by the old woman from the mansion house. Northmour, and the young lady, sometimes together, but more often singly, would walk for an hour or two at a time on the beach beside the quicksand. I could not but conclude that this promenade was chosen with an eye to secrecy; for the spot was open only to seaward. But it suited me not less excellently; the highest and most accidented of the sand hills immediately adjoined; and from these, lying flat in a hollow, I could overlook Northmour or the young lady as they walked.

The tall man seemed to have disappeared. Not only did he never cross the threshold, but he never so much as showed face at a window; or, at least, not so far as I could see; for I dared not creep forward beyond a certain distance in the day, since the upper floors commanded the bottoms of the links; and at night, when I could venture further, the lower windows were barricaded as if to stand a siege. Sometimes I thought the tall man must be confined to bed, for I remembered the feebleness of his gait; and sometimes I thought he must have gone clear away, and that Northmour and the young lady remained alone together in the pavilion. The idea, even then, displeased me.

Whether or not this pair were man and wife, I had seen abundant reason to doubt the friendliness of their relation. Although I could hear nothing of what they said, and rarely so much as glean a decided expression on the face of either, there was a distance, almost a stiffness, in their bearing which showed them to be either unfamiliar or at

10

enmity. The girl walked faster when she was with Northmour than when she was alone; and I conceived that any inclination between a man and a woman would rather delay than accelerate the step. Moreover, she kept a good yard free of him, and trailed her umbrella, as if it were a barrier, on the side between them. Northmour kept sidling closer; and, as the girl retired from his advance, their course lay at a sort of diagonal across the beach, and would have landed them in the surf had it been long enough continued. But, when this was imminent, the girl would unostentatiously change sides and put Northmour between her and the sea. I watched these maneuvers, for my part, with high enjoyment and approval, and chuckled to myself at every move.

On the morning of the third day, she walked alone for some time, and I perceived, to my great concern, that she was more than once in tears. You will see that my heart was already interested more than I supposed. She had a firm yet airy motion of the body, and carried her head with unimaginable grace; every step was a thing to look at, and she seemed in my eyes to breathe sweetness and distinction.

The day was so agreeable, being calm and sunshiny, with a tranquil sea, and yet with a healthful piquancy and vigor in the air, that, contrary to custom, she was tempted forth a second time to walk. On this occasion she was accompanied by Northmour, and they had been but a short while on the beach, when I saw him take forcible possession of her hand. She struggled, and uttered a cry that was almost a scream. I sprung to my feet, unmindful of my strange position; but, ere I had taken a step, I saw Northmour bareheaded and bowing very low, as if to apologize; and dropped again at once into my ambush. A few words were interchanged; and then, with another bow, he left the beach to return to the pavilion. He passed not far from me, and I could see him, flushed and lowering, and cutting savagely with his cane among the grass. It was not without satisfaction that I recognized my own handiwork in a great cut under his right eye, and a considerable discoloration round the socket.

For some time the girl remained where he had left her, looking out past the islet and over the bright sea. Then with a start, as one who throws off preoccupation and puts energy again upon its mettle, she broke into a rapid and decisive walk. She also was much incensed by what had passed. She had forgotten where she was. And I beheld her walk straight into the borders of the quicksand where it is most abrupt and dangerous. Two or three steps farther and her life would have been in serious jeopardy, when I slid down the face of the sand hill, which is there precipitous, and, running halfway forward, called to her to stop.

She did so, and turned round. There was not a tremor of fear in her behavior, and she marched directly up to me like a queen. I was barefoot, and clad like a common sailor, save for an Egyptian scarf round my waist; and she probably took me at first for some one from the fisher village, straying after bait. As for her, when I thus saw her face to face, her eyes set steadily and imperiously upon mine, I was filled with admiration and astonishment, and thought her even more beautiful than I had looked to find her. Nor could I think enough of one who, acting with so much boldness, yet preserved a maidenly air that was both quaint and engaging; for my wife kept an old-fashioned precision of manner through all her admirable life—an excellent thing in woman, since it sets another value on her sweet familiarities.

"What does this mean?" she asked.

"You were walking," I told her, "directly into Graden Floe."

"You do not belong to these parts," she said again. "You speak like an educated man."

"I believe I have a right to that name," said I, "although in this disguise."

But her woman's eye had already detected the sash.

"Oh!" she said; "your sash betrays you."

"You have said the word betray," I resumed. "May I ask you not to betray me? I was obliged to disclose myself in your interest; but if Northmour learned my presence it might be worse than disagreeable for me."

"Do you know," she asked, "to whom you are speaking?"

"Not to Mr. Northmour's wife?" I asked, by way of answer.

She shook her head. All this while she was studying my face with an embarrassing intentness. Then she broke out—

"You have an honest face. Be honest like your face, sir, and tell me what you want and what you are afraid of. Do you think I could hurt you? I believe you have far more power to injure me! And yet you do not look unkind. What do you mean—you, a gentleman—by skulking like a spy about this desolate place? Tell me," she said, "who is it you hate?"

"I hate no one," I answered; "and I fear no one face to face. My name is Cassilis—Frank Cassilis. I lead the life of a vagabond for my own good pleasure. I am one of Northmour's oldest friends; and three nights ago, when I addressed him on these links, he stabbed me in the shoulder with a knife."

"It was you!" she said.

"Why he did so," I continued, disregarding the interruption, "is more than I can guess, and more than I care to know. I have not many friends, nor am I very susceptible to friendship; but no man shall drive me from a place by terror. I had camped in the Graden Sea-Wood ere he came; I camp in it still. If you think I mean harm to you or yours, madame, the remedy is in your hand. Tell him that my camp is in the Hemlock Den, and to-night he can stab me in safety while I sleep."

With this I doffed my cap to her, and scrambled up once more among the sand hills. I do not know why, but I felt a prodigious sense of injustice, and felt like a hero and a martyr; while as a matter of fact, I

12

had not a word to say in my defense, nor so much as one plausible reason to offer for my conduct. I had stayed at Graden out of a curiosity natural enough, but undignified; and though there was another motive growing in along with the first, it was not one which, at that period, I could have properly explained to the lady of my heart.

Certainly, that night, I thought of no one else; and, though her whole conduct and position seemed suspicious, I could not find it in my heart to entertain a doubt of her integrity. I could have staked my life that she was clear of blame, and, though all was dark at the present, that the explanation of the mystery would show her part in these events to be both right and needful. It was true, let me cudgel my imagination as I pleased, that I could invent no theory of her relations to Northmour; but I felt none the less sure of my conclusion because it was founded on instinct in place of reason, and, as I may say, went to sleep that night with the thought of her under my pillow.

Next day she came out about the same hour alone, and, as soon as the sand hills concealed her from the pavilion, drew nearer to the edge, and called me by name in guarded tones. I was astonished to observe that she was deadly pale, and seemingly under the influence of strong emotion.

"Mr. Cassilis!" she cried; "Mr. Cassilis!"

I appeared at once, and leaped down upon the beach. A remarkable air of relief overspread her countenance as soon as she saw me.

"Oh!" she cried, with a hoarse sound, like one whose bosom had been lightened of a weight. And then, "Thank God you are still safe!" she added; "I knew, if you were, you would be here." (Was not this strange? So swiftly and wisely does Nature prepare our hearts for these great lifelong intimacies, that both my wife and I had been given a presentiment on this the second day of our acquaintance. I had even then hoped that she would seek me; she had felt sure that she would find me.) "Do not," she went on swiftly, "do not stay in this place. Promise me that you sleep no longer in that wood. You do not know how I suffer; all last night I could not sleep for thinking of your peril."

"Peril!" I repeated. "Peril from whom? From Northmour?"

"Not so," she said. "Did you think I would tell him after what you said?"

"Not from Northmour?" I repeated. "Then how? From whom? I see none to be afraid of."

"You must not ask me," was her reply, "for I am not free to tell you. Only believe me, and go hence—believe me, and go away quickly, quickly, for your life!"

An appeal to his alarm is never a good plan to rid oneself of a spirited young man. My obstinacy was but increased by what she said, and I made it a point of honor to remain. And her solicitude for my safety still more confirmed me in the resolve.

13

"You must not think me inquisitive, madame," I replied, "but, if Graden is so dangerous a place, you yourself perhaps remain here at some risk."

She only looked at me reproachfully.

"You and your father—" I resumed; but she interrupted me almost with a gasp.

"My father! How do you know that?" she cried.

"I saw you together when you landed," was my answer; and I do not know why, but it seemed satisfactory to both of us, as indeed it was truth. "But," I continued, "you need have no fear from me. I see you have some reason to be secret, and, you may believe me, your secret is as safe with me as if I were in Graden Floe. I have scarce spoken to anyone for years; my horse is my only companion, and even he, poor beast, is not beside me. You see, then, you may count on me for silence. So tell me the truth, my dear young lady, are you not in danger?"

"Mr. Northmour says you are an honorable man," she returned, "and I believe it when I see you. I will tell you so much; you are right: we are in dreadful, dreadful danger, and you share it by remaining where you are."

"Ah!" said I; "you have heard of me from Northmour? And he gives me a good character?"

"I asked him about you last night," was her reply. "I pretended," she hesitated, "I pretended to have met you long ago, and spoken to you of him. It was not true; but I could not help myself without betraying you, and you had put me in a difficulty. He praised you highly."

"And—you may permit me one question—does this danger come from Northmour?" I asked.

"From Mr. Northmour?" she cried. "Oh, no, he stays with us to share it."

"While you propose that I should run away?" I said. "You do not rate me very high."

"Why should you stay?" she asked. "You are no friend of ours."

I know not what came over me, for I had not been conscious of a similar weakness since I was a child, but I was so mortified by this retort that my eyes pricked and filled with tears, as I continued to gaze upon her face.

"No, no," she said, in a changed voice; "I did not mean the words unkindly."

"It was I who offended," I said; and I held out my hand with a look of appeal that somehow touched her, for she gave me hers at once, and even eagerly. I held it for awhile in mine, and gazed into her eyes. It was she who first tore her hand away, and, forgetting all about her request and the promise she had sought to extort, ran at the top of her speed, and without turning, till she was out of sight. And then I knew that I loved her, and thought in my glad heart that she—she herself—

14

was not indifferent to my suit. Many a time she has denied it in after days, but it was with a smiling and not a serious denial. For my part, I am sure our hands would not have lain so closely in each other if she had not begun to melt to me already. And, when all is said, it is no great contention, since, by her own avowal, she began to love me on the morrow.

And yet on the morrow very little took place. She came and called me down as on the day before, upbraided me for lingering at Graden, and, when she found I was still obdurate, began to ask me more particularly as to my arrival. I told her by what series of accidents I had come to witness their disembarkation, and how I had determined to remain, partly from the interest which had been awakened in me by Northmour's guests, and partly because of his own murderous attack. As to the former, I fear I was disingenuous, and led her to regard herself as having been an attraction to me from the first moment that I saw her on the links. It relieves my heart to make this confession even now, when my wife is with God, and already knows all things, and the honesty of my purpose even in this; for while she lived, although it often pricked my conscience, I had never the hardihood to undeceive her. Even a little secret, in such a married life as ours, is like the rose leaf which kept the princess from her sleep.

From this the talk branched into other subjects, and I told her much about my lonely and wandering existence; she, for her part, giving ear, and saying little. Although we spoke very naturally, and latterly on topics that might seem indifferent, we were both sweetly agitated. Too soon it was time for her to go; and we separated, as if by mutual consent, without shaking hands, for both knew that, between us, it was no idle ceremony.

The next, and that was the fourth day of our acquaintance, we met in the same spot, but early in the morning, with much familiarity and yet much timidity on either side. While she had once more spoken about my danger—and that, I understood, was her excuse for coming— I, who had prepared a great deal of talk during the night, began to tell her how highly I valued her kind interest, and how no one had ever cared to hear about my life, nor had I ever cared to relate it, before yesterday. Suddenly she interrupted me, saying with vehemence—

"And yet, if you knew who I was, you would not so much as speak to me!"

I told her such a thought was madness, and, little as we had met, I counted her already a dear friend; but my protestations seemed only to make her more desperate.

"My father is in hiding!" she cried.

"My dear," I said, forgetting for the first time to add "young lady," "what do I care? If I were in hiding twenty times over, would it make one thought of change in you?"

15

"Ah, but the cause!" she cried, "the cause! It is"—she faltered for a second—"it is disgraceful to us!"

IV

This was my wife's story, as I drew it from her among tears and sobs. Her name was Clara Huddlestone: it sounded very beautiful in my ears; but not so beautiful as that other name of Clara Cassilis, which she wore during the longer and, I thank God, the happier portion of her life. Her father, Bernard Huddlestone, had been a private banker in a very large way of business. Many years before, his affairs becoming disordered, he had been led to try dangerous, and at last criminal, expedients to retrieve himself from ruin. All was in vain; he became more and more cruelly involved, and found his honor lost at the same moment with his fortune. About this period, Northmour had been courting his daughter with great assiduity, though with small encouragement; and to him, knowing him thus disposed in his favor, Bernard Huddlestone turned for help in his extremity. It was not merely ruin and dishonor, nor merely a legal condemnation, that the unhappy man had brought upon his head. It seems he could have gone to prison with a light heart. What he feared, what kept him awake at night or recalled him from slumber into frenzy, was some secret, sudden, and unlawful attempt upon his life. Hence, he desired to bury his existence and escape to one of the islands in the South Pacific, and it was in Northmour's yacht, the "Red Earl," that he designed to go. The yacht picked them up clandestinely upon the coast of Wales, and had once more deposited them at Graden, till she could be refitted and provisioned for the longer voyage. Nor could Clara doubt that her hand had been stipulated as the price of passage. For, although Northmour was neither unkind, nor even discourteous, he had shown himself in several instances somewhat overbold in speech and manner.

I listened, I need not say, with fixed attention, and put many questions as to the more mysterious part. It was in vain. She had no clear idea of what the blow was, nor of how it was expected to fall. Her father's alarm was unfeigned and physically prostrating, and he had thought more than once of making an unconditional surrender to the police. But the scheme was finally abandoned, for he was convinced that not even the strength of our English prisons could shelter him from his pursuers. He had had many affairs in Italy, and with Italians resident in London, in the latter years of his business; and these last, as Clara fancied, were somehow connected with the doom that threatened him. He had shown great terror at the presence of an Italian seaman on board the "Red Earl," and had bitterly and repeatedly accused

16

Northmour in consequence. The latter had protested that Beppo (that was the seaman's name) was a capital fellow, and could be trusted to the death; but Mr. Huddlestone had continued ever since to declare that all was lost, that it was only a question of days, and that Beppo would be the ruin of him yet.

I regarded the whole story as the hallucination of a mind shaken by calamity. He had suffered heavy loss by his Italian transactions; and hence the sight of an Italian was hateful to him, and the principal part in his nightmare would naturally enough be played by one of that nation.

"What your father wants," I said, "is a good doctor and some calming medicine."

"But Mr. Northmour?" objected Clara. "He is untroubled by losses, and yet he shares in this terror."

I could not help laughing at what I considered her simplicity.

"My dear," said I, "you have told me yourself what reward he has to look for. All is fair in love, you must remember; and if Northmour foments your father's terrors, it is not at all because he is afraid of any Italian man, but simply because he is infatuated with a charming English woman."

She reminded me of his attack upon myself on the night of the disembarkation, and this I was unable to explain. In short, and from one thing to another, it was agreed between us that I should set out at once for the fisher village, Graden Wester, as it was called, look up all the newspapers I could find, and see for myself if there seemed any basis of fact for these continued alarms. The next morning, at the same hour and place, I was to make my report to Clara. She said no more on that occasion about my departure; nor, indeed, did she make it a secret that she clung to the thought of my proximity as something helpful and pleasant; and, for my part, I could not have left her, if she had gone upon her knees to ask it.

I reached Graden Wester before ten in the forenoon; for in those days I was an excellent pedestrian, and the distance, as I think I have said, was little over seven miles; fine walking all the way upon the springy turf. The village is one of the bleakest on that coast, which is saying much: there is a church in the hollow; a miserable haven in the rocks, where many boats have been lost as they returned from fishing; two or three score of stone houses arranged along the beach and in two streets, one leading from the harbor, and another striking out from it at right angles; and, at the corner of these two, a very dark and cheerless tavern, by way of principal hotel.

I had dressed myself somewhat more suitably to my station in life, and at once called upon the minister in his little manse beside the graveyard. He knew me, although it was more than nine years since we had met; and when I told him that I had been long upon a walking tour, and was behind with the news, readily lent me an armful of

17

newspapers, dating from a month back to the day before. With these I sought the tavern, and, ordering some breakfast, sat down to study the "Huddlestone Failure."

It had been, it appeared, a very flagrant case. Thousands of persons were reduced to poverty; and one in particular had blown out his brains as soon as payment was suspended. It was strange to myself that, while I read these details, I continued rather to sympathize with Mr. Huddlestone than with his victims; so complete already was the empire of my love for my wife. A price was naturally set upon the banker's head; and, as the case was inexcusable and the public indignation thoroughly aroused, the unusual figure of £750 was offered for his capture. He was reported to have large sums of money in his possession. One day, he had been heard of in Spain; the next, there was sure intelligence that he was still lurking between Manchester and Liverpool, or along the border of Wales; and the day after, a telegram would announce his arrival in Cuba or Yucatan. But in all this there was no word of an Italian, nor any sign of mystery.

In the very last paper, however, there was one item not so clear. The accountants who were charged to verify the failure had, it seemed, come upon the traces of a very large number of thousands, which figured for some time in the transactions of the house of Huddlestone; but which came from nowhere, and disappeared in the same mysterious fashion. It was only once referred to by name, and then under the initials "X.X."; but it had plainly been floated for the first time into the business at a period of great depression some six years ago. The name of a distinguished royal personage had been mentioned by rumor in connection with this sum. "The cowardly desperado"— such, I remember, was the editorial expression—was supposed to have escaped with a large part of this mysterious fund still in his possession.

I was still brooding over the fact, and trying to torture it into some connection with Mr. Huddlestone's danger, when a man entered the tavern and asked for some bread and cheese with a decided foreign accent.

"Siete Italiano?" said I.

"Si, Signor," was his reply.

I said it was unusually far north to find one of his compatriots; at which he shrugged his shoulders, and replied that a man would go anywhere to find work. What work he could hope to find at Graden Wester, I was totally unable to conceive; and the incident struck so unpleasantly upon my mind, that I asked the landlord, while he was counting me some change, whether he had ever before seen an Italian in the village. He said he had once seen some Norwegians, who had been shipwrecked on the other side of Graden Ness and rescued by the lifeboat from Cauldhaven.

"No!" said I; "but an Italian, like the man who has just had bread and cheese."

18

"What?" cried he, "yon black-avised fellow wi' the teeth? Was he an I-talian? Weel, yon's the first that ever I saw, an' I dare say he's like to be the last."

Even as he was speaking, I raised my eyes, and, casting a glance into the street, beheld three men in earnest conversation together, and not thirty yards away. One of them was my recent companion in the tavern parlor; the other two, by their handsome sallow features and soft hats, should evidently belong to the same race. A crowd of village children stood around them, gesticulating and talking gibberish in imitation. The trio looked singularly foreign to the bleak dirty street in which they were standing and the dark gray heaven that overspread them; and I confess my incredulity received at that moment a shock from which it never recovered. I might reason with myself as I pleased, but I could not argue down the effect of what I had seen, and I began to share in the Italian terror.

It was already drawing toward the close of the day before I had returned the newspapers to the manse, and got well forward on to the links on my way home. I shall never forget that walk. It grew very cold and boisterous; the wind sung in the short grass about my feet; thin rain showers came running on the gusts; and an immense mountain range of clouds began to arise out of the bosom of the sea. It would be hard to imagine a more dismal evening; and whether it was from these external influences, or because my nerves were already affected by what I had heard and seen, my thoughts were as gloomy as the weather.

The upper windows of the pavilion commanded a considerable spread of links in the direction of Graden Wester. To avoid observation, it was necessary to hug the beach until I had gained cover from the higher sand hills on the little headland, when I might strike across, through the hollows, for the margin of the wood. The sun was about setting; the tide was low, and all the quicksands uncovered; and I was moving along, lost in unpleasant thought, when I was suddenly thunderstruck to perceive the prints of human feet. They ran parallel to my own course, but low down upon the beach, instead of along the border of the turf; and, when I examined them, I saw at once, by the size and coarseness of the impression, that it was a stranger to me and to those of the pavilion who had recently passed that way. Not only so; but from the recklessness of the course which he had followed, steering near to the most formidable portions of the sand, he was evidently a stranger to the country and to the ill-repute of Graden beach.

Step by step I followed the prints; until, a quarter of a mile farther, I beheld them die away into the southeastern boundary of Graden Floe. There, whoever he was, the miserable man had perished. One or two gulls, who had, perhaps, seen him disappear, wheeled over his sepulcher with their usual melancholy piping. The sun had broken through the clouds by a last effort, and colored the wide level of quicksands with a dusky purple. I stood for some time gazing at the spot, chilled and disheartened by my own reflections, and with a strong and commanding consciousness of death. I remember wondering how long the tragedy had taken, and whether his screams had been audible at the pavilion. And then, making a strong resolution, I was about to tear myself away, when a gust fiercer than usual fell upon this quarter of the beach, and I saw, now whirling high in air, now skimming lightly across the surface of the sands, a soft, black, felt hat, somewhat conical in shape, such as I had remarked already on the heads of the Italians.

I believe, but I am not sure, that I uttered a cry. The wind was driving the hat shoreward, and I ran round the border of the floe to be ready against its arrival. The gust fell, dropping the hat for awhile upon the quicksand, and then, once more freshening, landed it a few yards from where I stood. I seized it with the interest you may imagine. It had seen some service; indeed, it was rustier than either of those I had seen that day upon the street. The lining was red, stamped with the name of the maker, which I have forgotten, and that of the place of manufacture, Venedig. This (it is not yet forgotten) was the name given by the Austrians to the beautiful city of Venice, then, and for long after, a part of their dominions.

The shock was complete. I saw imaginary Italians upon every side; and for the first, and, I may say, for the last time in my experience, became overpowered by what is called a panic terror. I knew nothing, that is, to be afraid of, and yet I admit that I was heartily afraid; and it was with sensible reluctance that I returned to my exposed and solitary camp in the Sea-Wood.

There I eat some cold porridge which had been left over from the night before, for I was disinclined to make a fire; and, feeling strengthened and reassured, dismissed all these fanciful terrors from my mind, and lay down to sleep with composure.

How long I may have slept it is impossible for me to guess; but I was awakened at last by a sudden, blinding flash of light into my face. It woke me like a blow. In an instant I was upon my knees. But the light had gone as suddenly as it came. The darkness was intense. And, as it was blowing great guns from the sea, and pouring with rain, the noises of the storm effectually concealed all others.

It was, I dare say, half a minute before I regained my self-possession. But for two circumstances, I should have thought I had been awakened by some new and vivid form of nightmare. First, the flap of my tent, which I had shut carefully when I retired, was now unfastened; and, second, I could still perceive, with a sharpness that excluded any theory of hallucination, the smell of hot metal and of burning oil. The conclusion was obvious. I had been awakened by some one flashing a bull's-eye lantern in my face. It had been but a flash, and away. He had seen my face, and then gone. I asked myself the object of so strange a proceeding, and the answer came pat. The man, whoever

20

he was, had thought to recognize me, and he had not. There was another question unresolved; and to this, I may say, I feared to give an answer; if he had recognized me, what would he have done?

My fears were immediately diverted from myself, for I saw that I had been visited in a mistake; and I became persuaded that some dreadful danger threatened the pavilion. It required some nerve to issue forth into the black and intricate thicket which surrounded and overhung the den; but I groped my way to the links, drenched with rain, beaten upon and deafened by the gusts, and fearing at every step to lay my hand upon some lurking adversary. The darkness was so complete that I might have been surrounded by an army and yet none the wiser, and the uproar of the gale so loud that my hearing was as useless as my sight.

For the rest of that night, which seemed interminably long, I patrolled the vicinity of the pavilion, without seeing a living creature or hearing any noise but the concert of the wind, the sea, and the rain. A light in the upper story filtered through a cranny of the shutter, and kept me company till the approach of dawn.

V

With the first peep of day, I retired from the open to my old lair among the sand hills, there to await the coming of my wife. The morning was gray, wild, and melancholy; the wind moderated before sunrise, and then went about, and blew in puffs from the shore; the sea began to go down, but the rain still fell without mercy. Over all the wilderness of links there was not a creature to be seen. Yet I felt sure the neighborhood was alive with skulking foes. The light that had been so suddenly and surprisingly flashed upon my face as I lay sleeping, and the hat that had been blown ashore by the wind from over Graden Floe, were two speaking signals of the peril that environed Clara and the party in the pavilion.

It was, perhaps, half-past seven, or nearer eight, before I saw the door open, and that dear figure come toward me in the rain. I was waiting for her on the beach before she had crossed the sand hills.

"I have had such trouble to come!" she cried. "They did not wish me to go walking in the rain."

"Clara," I said, "you are not frightened!"

"No," said she, with a simplicity that filled my heart with confidence. For my wife was the bravest as well as the best of women; in my experience, I have not found the two go always together, but with her they did; and she combined the extreme of fortitude with the most endearing and beautiful virtues.

21

I told her what had happened; and, though her cheek grew visibly paler, she retained perfect control over her senses.

"You see now that I am safe," said I, in conclusion. "They do not mean to harm me; for, had they chosen, I was a dead man last night."

She laid her hand upon my arm.

"And I had no presentiment!" she cried.

Her accent thrilled me with delight. I put my arm about her, and strained her to my side; and, before either of us was aware, her hands were on my shoulders and my lips upon her mouth. Yet up to that moment no word of love had passed between us. To this day I remember the touch of her cheek, which was wet and cold with the rain; and many a time since, when she has been washing her face, I have kissed it again for the sake of that morning on the beach. Now that she is taken from me, and I finish my pilgrimage alone, I recall our old loving kindnesses and the deep honesty and affection which united us, and my present loss seems but a trifle in comparison.

We may have thus stood for some seconds—for time passes quickly with lovers—before we were startled by a peal of laughter close at hand. It was not natural mirth, but seemed to be affected in order to conceal an angrier feeling. We both turned, though I still kept my left arm about Clara's waist; nor did she seek to withdraw herself; and there, a few paces off upon the beach, stood Northmour, his head lowered, his hands behind his back, his nostrils white with passion.

"Ah! Cassilis!" he said, as I disclosed my face.

"That same," said I; for I was not at all put about.

"And so, Miss Huddlestone," he continued slowly, but savagely, "this is how you keep your faith to your father and to me? This is the value you set upon your father's life? And you are so infatuated with this young gentleman that you must brave ruin, and decency, and common human caution—"

"Miss Huddlestone—" I was beginning to interrupt him, when he, in his turn, cut in brutally—

"You hold your tongue," said he; "I am speaking to that girl."

"That girl, as you call her, is my wife," said I; and my wife only leaned a little nearer, so that I knew she had affirmed my words.

"Your what?" he cried. "You lie!"

"Northmour," I said, "we all know you have a bad temper, and I am the last man to be irritated by words. For all that, I propose that you speak lower, for I am convinced that we are not alone."

He looked round him, and it was plain my remark had in some degree sobered his passion. "What do you mean?" he asked.

I only said one word: "Italians."

He swore a round oath, and looked at us, from one to the other.

"Mr. Cassilis knows all that I know," said my wife.

"What I want to know," he broke out, "is where the devil Mr. Cassilis comes from, and what the devil Mr. Cassilis is doing here. You say you are married; that I do not believe. If you were, Graden Floe would soon divorce you; four minutes and a half, Cassilis. I keep my private cemetery for my friends."

"It took somewhat longer," said I, "for that Italian."

He looked at me for a moment half daunted, and then, almost civilly, asked me to tell my story. "You have too much the advantage of me, Cassilis," he added. I complied of course; and he listened, with several ejaculations, while I told him how I had come to Graden: that it was I whom he had tried to murder on the night of landing; and what I had subsequently seen and heard of the Italians.

"Well," said he, when I had done, "it is here at last; there is no mistake about that. And what, may I ask, do you propose to do?"

"I propose to stay with you and lend a hand," said I.

"You are a brave man," he returned, with a peculiar intonation.

"I am not afraid," said I.

"And so," he continued, "I am to understand that you two are married? And you stand up to it before my face, Miss Huddlestone?"

"We are not yet married," said Clara; "but we shall be as soon as we can."

"Bravo!" cried Northmour. "And the bargain? D——n it, you're not a fool, young woman; I may call a spade a spade with you. How about the bargain? You know as well as I do what your father's life depends upon. I have only to put my hands under my coat tails and walk away, and his throat would be cut before the evening."

"Yes, Mr. Northmour," returned Clara, with great spirit; "but that is what you will never do. You made a bargain that was unworthy of a gentleman; but you are a gentleman for all that, and you will never desert a man whom you have begun to help."

"Aha!" said he. "You think I will give my yacht for nothing? You think I will risk my life and liberty for love of the old gentleman; and then, I suppose, be best man at the wedding, to wind up? Well," he added, with an odd smile, "perhaps you are not altogether wrong. But ask Cassilis here. He knows me. Am I a man to trust? Am I safe and scrupulous? Am I kind?"

"I know you talk a great deal, and sometimes, I think, very foolishly," replied Clara, "but I know you are a gentleman, and I am not the least afraid."

He looked at her with a peculiar approval and admiration; then, turning to me, "Do you think I would give her up without a struggle, Frank?" said he. "I tell you plainly, you look out. The next time we come to blows—"

"Will make the third," I interrupted, smiling.

"Aye, true; so it will," he said. "I had forgotten. Well, the third time's lucky."

"The third time, you mean, you will have the crew of the 'Red Earl' to help," I said.

"Do you hear him?" he asked, turning to my wife.

"I hear two men speaking like cowards," said she. "I should despise myself either to think or speak like that. And neither of you believe one word that you are saying, which makes it the more wicked and silly."

"She's a trump!" cried Northmour. "But she's not yet Mrs. Cassilis. I say no more. The present is not for me."

Then my wife surprised me.

"I leave you here," she said suddenly. "My father has been too long alone. But remember this: you are to be friends, for you are both good friends to me."

She has since told me her reason for this step. As long as she remained, she declares that we two would have continued to quarrel; and I suppose that she was right, for when she was gone we fell at once into a sort of confidentiality.

Northmour stared after her as she went away over the sand hill.

"She is the only woman in the world!" he exclaimed with an oath. "Look at her action."

I, for my part, leaped at this opportunity for a little further light.

"See here, Northmour," said I; "we are all in a tight place, are we not?"

"I believe you, my boy," he answered, looking me in the eyes, and with great emphasis. "We have all hell upon us, that's the truth. You may believe me or not, but I'm afraid of my life."

"Tell me one thing," said I. "What are they after, these Italians? What do they want with Mr. Huddlestone?"

"Don't you know?" he cried. "The black old scamp had carbonari funds on a deposit—two hundred and eighty thousand; and of course he gambled it away on stocks. There was to have been a revolution in the Tridentino, or Parma; but the revolution is off, and the whole wasp's nest is after Huddlestone. We shall all be lucky if we can save our skins."

"The carbonari!" I exclaimed; "God help him indeed!"

"Amen!" said Northmour. "And now, look here: I have said that we are in a fix; and, frankly, I shall be glad of your help. If I can't save Huddlestone, I want at least to save the girl. Come and stay in the pavilion; and, there's my hand on it, I shall act as your friend until the old man is either clear or dead. But," he added, "once that is settled, you become my rival once again, and I warn you—mind yourself."

"Done!" said I; and we shook hands.

"And now let us go directly to the fort," said Northmour; and he began to lead the way through the rain.

VI

We were admitted to the pavilion by Clara, and I was surprised by the completeness and security of the defenses. A barricade of great strength, and yet easy to displace, supported the door against any violence from without; and the shutters of the dining-room, into which I was led directly, and which was feebly illuminated by a lamp, were even more elaborately fortified. The panels were strengthened by bars and crossbars; and these, in their turn, were kept in position by a system of braces and struts, some abutting on the floor, some on the roof, and others, in fine, against the opposite wall of the apartment. It was at once a solid and well-designed piece of carpentry; and I did not seek to conceal my admiration.

"I am the engineer," said Northmour. "You remember the planks in the garden? Behold them?"

"I did not know you had so many talents," said I.

"Are you armed?" he continued, pointing to an array of guns and pistols, all in admirable order, which stood in line against the wall or were displayed upon the sideboard.

"Thank you," I returned; "I have gone armed since our last encounter. But, to tell you the truth, I have had nothing to eat since early yesterday evening."

Northmour produced some cold meat, to which I eagerly set myself, and a bottle of good Burgundy, by which, wet as I was, I did not scruple to profit. I have always been an extreme temperance man on principle; but it is useless to push principle to excess, and on this occasion I believe that I finished three quarters of the bottle. As I eat, I still continued to admire the preparations for defense.

"We could stand a siege," I said at length.

"Ye—es," drawled Northmour; "a very little one, per—haps. It is not so much the strength of the pavilion I misdoubt; it is the double danger that kills me. If we get to shooting, wild as the country is, some one is sure to hear it, and then—why then it's the same thing, only different, as they say: caged by law, or killed by carbonari. There's the choice. It is a devilish bad thing to have the law against you in this world, and so I tell the old gentleman upstairs. He is quite of my way of thinking."

"Speaking of that," said I, "what kind of person is he?"

"Oh, he!" cried the other; "he's a rancid fellow, as far as he goes. I should like to have his neck wrung to-morrow by all the devils in Italy. I am not in this affair for him. You take me? I made a bargain for missy's hand, and I mean to have it too."

"That, by the way," said I. "I understand. But how will Mr. Huddlestone take my intrusion?"

"Leave that to Clara," returned Northmour.

25

I could have struck him in the face for his coarse familiarity; but I respected the truce, as, I am bound to say, did Northmour, and so long as the danger continued not a cloud arose in our relation. I bear him this testimony with the most unfeigned satisfaction; nor am I without pride when I look back upon my own behavior. For surely no two men were ever left in a position so invidious and irritating.

As soon as I had done eating, we proceeded to inspect the lower floor. Window by window we tried the different supports, now and then making an inconsiderable change; and the strokes of the hammer sounded with startling loudness through the house. I proposed, I remember, to make loop-holes; but he told me they were already made in the windows of the upper story. It was an anxious business, this inspection, and left me down-hearted. There were two doors and five windows to protect, and, counting Clara, only four of us to defend them against an unknown number of foes. I communicated my doubts to Northmour, who assured me, with unmoved composure, that he entirely shared them.

"Before morning," said he, "we shall all be butchered and buried in Graden Floe. For me, that is written."

I could not help shuddering at the mention of the quicksand, but reminded Northmour that our enemies had spared me in the wood.

"Do not flatter yourself," said he. "Then you were not in the same boat with the old gentleman; now you are. It's the floe for all of us, mark my words."

I trembled for Clara; and just then her dear voice was heard calling us to come upstairs. Northmour showed me the way, and, when he had reached the landing, knocked at the door of what used to be called My Uncle's Bedroom, as the founder of the pavilion had designed it especially for himself.

"Come in, Northmour; come in, dear Mr. Cassilis," said a voice from within.

Pushing open the door, Northmour admitted me before him into the apartment. As I came in I could see the daughter slipping out by the side door into the study, which had been prepared as her bedroom. In the bed, which was drawn back against the wall, instead of standing, as I had last seen it, boldly across the window, sat Bernard Huddlestone, the defaulting banker. Little as I had seen of him by the shifting light of the lantern on the links, I had no difficulty in recognizing him for the same. He had a long and sallow countenance, surrounded by a long red beard and side-whiskers. His broken nose and high cheek-bones gave him somewhat the air of a Kalmuck, and his light eyes shone with the excitement of a high fever. He wore a skull-cap of black silk; a huge Bible lay open before him on the bed, with a pair of gold spectacles in the place, and a pile of other books lay on the stand by his side. The green curtains lent a cadaverous shade to his cheek; and, as he sat propped on pillows, his great stature was painfully hunched, and his

26

head protruded till it overhung his knees. I believe if he had not died otherwise, he must have fallen a victim to consumption in the course of but a very few weeks.

He held out to me a hand, long, thin, and disagreeably hairy.

"Come in, come in, Mr. Cassilis," said he. "Another protector—ahem!—another protector. Always welcome as a friend of my daughter's, Mr. Cassilis. How they have rallied about me, my daughter's friends! May God in heaven bless and reward them for it!"

I gave him my hand, of course, because I could not help it; but the sympathy I had been prepared to feel for Clara's father was immediately soured by his appearance, and the wheedling, unreal tones in which he spoke.

"Cassilis is a good man," said Northmour; "worth ten."

"So I hear," cried Mr. Huddlestone eagerly; "so my girl tells me. Ah, Mr. Cassilis, my sin has found me out, you see! I am very low, very low; but I hope equally penitent. We must all come to the throne of grace at last, Mr. Cassilis. For my part, I come late indeed; but with unfeigned humility, I trust."

"Fiddle-de-dee!" said Northmour roughly.

"No, no, dear Northmour!" cried the banker. "You must not say that; you must not try to shake me. You forget, my dear, good boy, you forget I may be called this very night before my Maker."

His excitement was pitiful to behold; and I felt myself grow indignant with Northmour, whose infidel opinions I well knew, and heartily despised, as he continued to taunt the poor sinner out of his humor of repentance.

"Pooh, my dear Huddlestone!" said he. "You do yourself injustice. You are a man of the world inside and out, and were up to all kinds of mischief before I was born. Your conscience is tanned like South American leather—only you forgot to tan your liver, and that, if you will believe me, is the seat of the annoyance."

"Rogue, rogue! bad boy!" said Mr. Huddlestone, shaking his finger. "I am no precisian, if you come to that; I always hated a precisian; but I never lost hold of something better through it all. I have been a bad boy, Mr. Cassilis; I do not seek to deny that; but it was after my wife's death, and you know, with a widower, it's a different thing: sinful—I won't say no; but there is a gradation, we shall hope. And talking of that—Hark!" he broke out suddenly, his hand raised, his fingers spread, his face racked with interest and terror. "Only the rain, bless God!" he added, after a pause, and with indescribable relief.

For some seconds he lay back among the pillows like a man near to fainting; then he gathered himself together, and, in somewhat tremulous tones, began once more to thank me for the share I was prepared to take in his defense.

"One question, sir," said I, when he had paused. "Is it true that you have money with you?"

He seemed annoyed by the question, but admitted with reluctance that he had a little.

"Well," I continued, "it is their money they are after, is it not? Why not give it up to them?"

"Ah!" replied he, shaking his head, "I have tried that already, Mr. Cassilis; and alas! that it should be so, but it is blood they want."

"Huddlestone, that's a little less than fair," said Northmour. "You should mention that what you offered them was upward of two hundred thousand short. The deficit is worth a reference; it is for what they call a cool sum, Frank. Then, you see, the fellows reason in their clear Italian way; and it seems to them, as indeed it seems to me, that they may just as well have both while they're about it—money and blood together, by George, and no more trouble for the extra pleasure."

"Is it in the pavilion?" I asked.

"It is; and I wish it were in the bottom of the sea instead," said Northmour; and then suddenly—"What are you making faces at me for?" he cried to Mr. Huddlestone, on whom I had unconsciously turned my back. "Do you think Cassilis would sell you?"

Mr. Huddlestone protested that nothing had been further from his mind.

"It is a good thing," retorted Northmour in his ugliest manner. "You might end by wearying us. What were you going to say?" he added, turning to me.

"I was going to propose an occupation for the afternoon," said I. "Let us carry that money out, piece by piece, and lay it down before the pavilion door. If the carbonari come, why, it's theirs at any rate."

"No, no," cried Mr. Huddlestone; "it does not, it cannot, belong to them! It should be distributed pro rata among all my creditors."

"Come now, Huddlestone," said Northmour, "none of that."

"Well, but my daughter," moaned the wretched man.

"Your daughter will do well enough. Here are two suitors, Cassilis and I, neither of us beggars, between whom she has to choose. And as for yourself, to make an end of arguments, you have no right to a farthing, and, unless I'm much mistaken, you are going to die."

It was certainly very cruelly said; but Mr. Huddlestone was a man who attracted little sympathy; and, although I saw him wince and shudder, I mentally indorsed the rebuke; nay, I added a contribution of my own.

"Northmour and I," I said, "are willing enough to help you to save your life, but not to escape with stolen property."

He struggled for awhile with himself, as though he were on the point of giving way to anger, but prudence had the best of the controversy.

"My dear boys," he said, "do with me or my money what you will. I leave all in your hands. Let me compose myself."

And so we left him, gladly enough I am sure.

The last that I saw, he had once more taken up his great Bible, and with tremulous hands was adjusting his spectacles to read.

VII

The recollection of that afternoon will always be graven on my mind. Northmour and I were persuaded that an attack was imminent; and if it had been in our power to alter in any way the order of events, that power would have been used to precipitate rather than delay the critical moment. The worst was to be anticipated; yet we could conceive no extremity so miserable as the suspense we were now suffering. I have never been an eager, though always a great, reader; but I never knew books so insipid as those which I took up and cast aside that afternoon in the pavilion. Even talk became impossible, as the hours went on. One or other was always listening for some sound, or peering from an upstairs window over the links. And yet not a sign indicated the presence of our foes.

We debated over and over again my proposal with regard to the money; and had we been in complete possession of our faculties, I am sure we should have condemned it as unwise; but we were flustered with alarm, grasped at a straw, and determined, although it was as much as advertising Mr. Huddlestone's presence in the pavilion, to carry my proposal into effect.

The sum was part in specie, part in bank paper, and part in circular notes payable to the name of James Gregory. We took it out, counted it, inclosed it once more in a dispatch box belonging to Northmour, and prepared a letter in Italian which he tied to the handle. It was signed by both of us under oath, and declared that this was all the money which had escaped the failure of the house of Huddlestone. This was, perhaps, the maddest action ever perpetrated by two persons professing to be sane. Had the dispatch box fallen into other hands than those for which it was intended, we stood criminally convicted on our own written testimony; but, as I have said, we were neither of us in a condition to judge soberly, and had a thirst for action that drove us to do something, right or wrong, rather than endure the agony of waiting. Moreover, as we were both convinced that the hollows of the links were alive with hidden spies upon our movements, we hoped that our appearance with the box might lead to a parley, and, perhaps, a compromise.

It was nearly three when we issued from the pavilion. The rain had taken off; the sun shone quite cheerfully. I had never seen the gulls fly so close about the house or approach so fearlessly to human beings.

On the very doorstep one flapped heavily past our heads, and uttered its wild cry in my very ear.

"There is an omen for you," said Northmour, who like all freethinkers was much under the influence of superstition. "They think we are already dead."

I made some light rejoinder, but it was with half my heart; for the circumstance had impressed me.

A yard or two before the gate, on a patch of smooth turf, we set down the dispatch box; and Northmour waved a white handkerchief over his head. Nothing replied. We raised our voices, and cried aloud in Italian that we were there as ambassadors to arrange the quarrel, but the stillness remained unbroken save by the seagulls and the surf. I had a weight at my heart when we desisted; and I saw that even Northmour was unusually pale. He looked over his shoulder nervously, as though he feared that some one had crept between him and the pavilion door.

"By God," he said in a whisper, "this is too much for me!"

I replied in the same key: "Suppose there should be none, after all!"

"Look there," he returned, nodding with his head, as though he had been afraid to point.

I glanced in the direction indicated; and there, from the northern quarter of the Sea-Wood, beheld a thin column of smoke rising steadily against the now cloudless sky.

"Northmour," I said (we still continued to talk in whispers), "it is not possible to endure this suspense. I prefer death fifty times over. Stay you here to watch the pavilion; I will go forward and make sure, if I have to walk right into their camp."

He looked once again all round him with puckered eyes, and then nodded assentingly to my proposal.

My heart beat like a sledge hammer as I set out walking rapidly in the direction of the smoke; and, though up to that moment I had felt chill and shivering, I was suddenly conscious of a glow of heat all over my body. The ground in this direction was very uneven; a hundred men might have lain hidden in as many square yards about my path. But I who had not practiced the business in vain, chose such routes as cut at the very root of concealment, and, by keeping along the most convenient ridges, commanded several hollows at a time. It was not long before I was rewarded for my caution. Coming suddenly on to a mound somewhat more elevated than the surrounding hummocks, I saw, not thirty yards away, a man bent almost double, and running as fast as his attitude permitted, along the bottom of a gully. I had dislodged one of the spies from his ambush. As soon as I sighted him, I called loudly both in English and Italian; and he, seeing concealment was no longer possible, straightened himself out, leaped from the gully, and made off as straight as an arrow for the borders of the wood. It was none of my business to pursue; I had learned what I wanted—that we

30

were beleaguered and watched in the pavilion; and I returned at once, and walked as nearly as possible in my old footsteps, to where Northmour awaited me beside the dispatch box. He was even paler than when I had left him, and his voice shook a little.

"Could you see what he was like?" he asked.

"He kept his back turned," I replied.

"Let us get into the house, Frank. I don't think I'm a coward, but I can stand no more of this," he whispered.

All was still and sunshiny about the pavilion, as we turned to reenter it; even the gulls had flown in a wider circuit, and were seen flickering along the beach and sand hills; and this loneliness terrified me more than a regiment under arms. It was not until the door was barricaded that I could draw a full inspiration and relieve the weight that lay upon my bosom. Northmour and I exchanged a steady glance; and I suppose each made his own reflections on the white and startled aspect of the other.

"You were right," I said. "All is over. Shake hands, old man, for the last time."

"Yes," replied he, "I will shake hands; for, as sure as I am here, I bear no malice. But, remember, if, by some impossible accident, we should give the slip to these blackguards, I'll take the upper hand of you by fair or foul."

"Oh," said I, "you weary me!"

He seemed hurt, and walked away in silence to the foot of the stairs, where he paused.

"You do not understand," said he. "I am not a swindler, and I guard myself; that is all. I may weary you or not, Mr. Cassilis, I do not care a rush; I speak for my own satisfaction, and not for your amusement. You had better go upstairs and court the girl; for my part, I stay here."

"And I stay with you," I returned. "Do you think I would steal a march, even with your permission?"

"Frank," he said, smiling, "it's a pity you are an ass, for you have the makings of a man. I think I must be fey to-day; you cannot irritate me even when you try. Do you know," he continued softly, "I think we are the two most miserable men in England, you and I? we have got on to thirty without wife or child, or so much as a shop to look after—poor, pitiful, lost devils, both! And now we clash about a girl! As if there were not several millions in the United Kingdom! Ah, Frank, Frank, the one who loses his throw, be it you or me, he has my pity! It were better for him—how does the Bible say?—that a millstone were hanged about his neck and he were cast into the depth of the sea. Let us take a drink," he concluded suddenly, but without any levity of tone.

I was touched by his words, and consented. He sat down on the table in the dining-room, and held up the glass of sherry to his eye.

31

"If you beat me, Frank," he said, "I shall take to drink. What will you do, if it goes the other way?"

"God knows," I returned.

"Well," said he, "here is a toast in the meantime: 'Italia irredenta!'"

The remainder of the day was passed in the same dreadful tedium and suspense. I laid the table for dinner, while Northmour and Clara prepared the meal together in the kitchen. I could hear their talk as I went to and fro, and was surprised to find it ran all the time upon myself. Northmour again bracketed us together, and rallied Clara on a choice of husbands; but he continued to speak of me with some feeling, and uttered nothing to my prejudice unless he included himself in the condemnation. This awakened a sense of gratitude in my heart, which combined with the immediateness of our peril to fill my eyes with tears. After all, I thought—and perhaps the thought was laughably vain—we were here three very noble human beings to perish in defense of a thieving banker.

Before we sat down to table, I looked forth from an upstairs window. The day was beginning to decline; the links were utterly deserted; the dispatch box still lay untouched where we had left it hours before.

Mr. Huddlestone, in a long yellow dressing gown, took one end of the table, Clara the other; while Northmour and I faced each other from the sides. The lamp was brightly trimmed; the wine was good; the viands, although mostly cold, excellent of their sort. We seemed to have agreed tacitly; all reference to the impending catastrophe was carefully avoided; and, considering our tragic circumstances, we made a merrier party than could have been expected. From time to time, it is true, Northmour or I would rise from table and make a round of the defenses; and, on each of these occasions, Mr. Huddlestone was recalled to a sense of his tragic predicament, glanced up with ghastly eyes, and bore for an instant on his countenance the stamp of terror. But he hastened to empty his glass, wiped his forehead with his handkerchief, and joined again in the conversation.

I was astonished at the wit and information he displayed. Mr. Huddlestone's was certainly no ordinary character; he had read and observed for himself; his gifts were sound; and, though I could never have learned to love the man, I began to understand his success in business, and the great respect in which he had been held before his failure. He had, above all, the talent of society; and though I never heard him speak but on this one and most unfavorable occasion, I set him down among the most brilliant conversationalists I ever met.

He was relating with great gusto, and seemingly no feeling of shame, the maneuvers of a scoundrelly commission merchant whom he had known and studied in his youth, and we were all listening with an odd mixture of mirth and embarrassment, when our little party was brought abruptly to an end in the most startling manner.

A noise like that of a wet finger on the window pane interrupted Mr. Huddlestone's tale; and in an instant we were all four as white as paper, and sat tongue-tied and motionless round the table.

"A snail," I said at last; for I had heard that these animals make a noise somewhat similar in character.

"Snail be d——d!" said Northmour. "Hush!"

The same sound was repeated twice at regular intervals; and then a formidable voice shouted through the shutters the Italian word, "Traditore!"

Mr. Huddlestone threw his head in the air; his eyelids quivered; next moment he fell insensible below the table. Northmour and I had each run to the armory and seized a gun. Clara was on her feet with her hand at her throat.

So we stood waiting, for we thought the hour of attack was certainly come; but second passed after second, and all but the surf remained silent in the neighborhood of the pavilion.

"Quick," said Northmour; "upstairs with him before they come."

VIII

Somehow or other, by hook and crook, and between the three of us, we got Bernard Huddlestone bundled upstairs and laid upon the bed in My Uncle's Room. During the whole process, which was rough enough, he gave no sign of consciousness, and he remained, as we had thrown him, without changing the position of a finger. His daughter opened his shirt and began to wet his head and bosom; while Northmour and I ran to the window. The weather continued clear; the moon, which was now about full, had risen and shed a very clear light upon the links; yet, strain our eyes as we might, we could distinguish nothing moving. A few dark spots, more or less, on the uneven expanse were not to be identified; they might be crouching men, they might be shadows; it was impossible to be sure.

"Thank God," said Northmour, "Aggie is not coming to-night."

Aggie was the name of the old nurse; he had not thought of her until now; but that he should think of her at all was a trait that surprised me in the man.

We were again reduced to waiting. Northmour went to the fireplace and spread his hands before the red embers, as if he were cold. I followed him mechanically with my eyes, and in so doing turned my back upon the window. At that moment a very faint report was audible from without, and a ball shivered a pane of glass, and buried

33

itself in the shutter two inches from my head. I heard Clara scream; and though I whipped instantly out of range and into a corner, she was there, so to speak, before me, beseeching to know if I were hurt. I felt that I could stand to be shot at every day and all day long, with such remarks of solicitude for a reward; and I continued to reassure her, with, the tenderest caresses and in complete forgetfulness of our situation, till the voice of Northmour recalled me to myself.

"An air gun," he said. "They wish to make no noise."

I put Clara aside, and looked at him. He was standing with his back to the fire and his hands clasped behind him; and I knew by the black look on his face, that passion was boiling within. I had seen just such a look before he attacked me, that March night, in the adjoining chamber; and, though I could make every allowance for his anger, I confess I trembled for the consequences. He gazed straight before him; but he could see us with the tail of his eye, and his temper kept rising like a gale of wind. With regular battle awaiting us outside, this prospect of an internecine strife within the walls began to daunt me.

Suddenly, as I was thus closely watching his expression and prepared against the worst, I saw a change, a flash, a look of relief, upon his face. He took up the lamp which stood beside him on the table, and turned to us with an air of some excitement.

"There is one point that we must know," said he. "Are they going to butcher the lot of us, or only Huddlestone? Did they take you for him, or fire at you for your own beaux yeux?"

"They took me for him, for certain," I replied. "I am near as tall, and my head is fair."

"I am going to make sure," returned Northmour; and he stepped up to the window, holding the lamp above his head, and stood there, quietly affronting death, for half a minute.

Clara sought to rush forward and pull him from the place of danger; but I had the pardonable selfishness to hold her back by force.

"Yes," said Northmour, turning coolly from the window, "it's only Huddlestone they want."

"Oh, Mr. Northmour!" cried Clara; but found no more to add; the temerity she had just witnessed seeming beyond, the reach of words.

He, on his part, looked at me, cocking his head, with a fire of triumph in his eyes; and I understood at once that he had thus hazarded his life, merely to attract Clara's notice, and depose me from my position as the hero of the hour. He snapped his fingers.

"The fire is only beginning," said he. "When they warm up to their work, they won't be so particular."

A voice was now heard hailing us from the entrance. From the window we could see the figure of a man in the moonlight; he stood motionless, his face uplifted to ours, and a rag of something white on his extended arm; and as we looked right down upon him, though he was a good many yards distant on the links, we could see the moonlight glitter on his eyes.

He opened his lips again, and spoke for some minutes on end, in a key so loud that he might have been heard in every corner of the pavilion, and as far away as the borders of the wood. It was the same voice that had already shouted, "Traditore!" through the shutters of the dining-room; this time it made a complete and clear statement. If the traitor "Oddlestone" were given up, all others should be spared; if not, no one should escape to tell the tale.

"Well, Huddlestone, what do you say to that?" asked Northmour, turning to the bed.

Up to that moment the banker had given no sign of life, and I, at least, had supposed him to be still lying in a faint; but he replied at once, and in such tones as I have never heard elsewhere, save from a delirious patient, adjured and besought us not to desert him. It was the most hideous and abject performance that my imagination can conceive.

"Enough," cried Northmour; and then he threw open the window, leaned out into the night, and in a tone of exultation, and with a total forgetfulness of what was due to the presence of a lady, poured out upon the ambassador a string of the most abominable raillery both in English and Italian, and bade him be gone where he had come from. I believe that nothing so delighted Northmour at that moment as the thought that we must all infallibly perish before the night was out.

Meantime, the Italian put his flag of truce into his pocket, and disappeared, at a leisurely pace, among the sand hills.

"They make honorable war," said Northmour. "They are all gentlemen and soldiers. For the credit of the thing, I wish we could change sides—you and I, Frank, and you, too, missy, my darling—and leave that being on the bed to some one else. Tut! Don't look shocked! We are all going post to what they call eternity, and may as well be above board while there's time. As far as I am concerned, if I could first strangle Huddlestone and then get Clara in my arms, I could die with some pride and satisfaction. And as it is, by God, I'll have a kiss!"

Before I could do anything to interfere, he had rudely embraced and repeatedly kissed the resisting girl. Next moment I had pulled him away with fury, and flung him heavily against the wall. He laughed loud and long, and I feared his wits had given way under the strain; for even in the best of days he had been a sparing and a quiet laugher.

"Now, Frank," said he, when his mirth was somewhat appeased, "it's your turn. Here's my hand. Good-bye, farewell!" Then, seeing me stand rigid and indignant, and holding Clara to my side—"Man!" he broke out, "are you angry? Did you think we were going to die with all the airs and graces of society? I took a kiss; I'm glad I did it; and now you can take another if you like, and square accounts."

35

I turned from him with a feeling of contempt which I did not seek to dissemble.

"As you please," said he. "You've been a prig in life; a prig you'll die."

And with that he sat down in a chair, a rifle over his knee, and amused himself with snapping the lock; but I could see that his ebullition of light spirits (the only one I ever knew him to display) had already come to an end, and was succeeded by a sullen, scowling humor.

All this time our assailants might have been entering the house, and we been none the wiser; we had in truth almost forgotten the danger that so imminently overhung our days. But just then Mr. Huddlestone uttered a cry, and leaped from the bed.

I asked him what was wrong.

"Fire!" he cried. "They have set the house on fire!"

Northmour was on his feet in an instant, and he and I ran through the door of communication with the study. The room was illuminated by a red and angry light. Almost at the moment of our entrance, a tower of flame arose in front of the window, and, with a tingling report, a pane fell inward on the carpet. They had set fire to the lean-to outhouse, where Northmour used to nurse his negatives.

"Hot work," said Northmour. "Let us try in your old room."

We ran thither in a breath, threw up the casement, and looked forth. Along the whole back wall of the pavilion piles of fuel had been arranged and kindled; and it is probable they had been drenched with mineral oil, for, in spite of the morning's rain, they all burned bravely. The fire had taken a firm hold already on the outhouse, which blazed higher and higher every moment; the back door was in the center of a red-hot bonfire; the eaves we could see, as we looked upward, were already smoldering, for the roof overhung, and was supported by considerable beams of wood. At the same time, hot, pungent, and choking volumes of smoke began to fill the house. There was not a human being to be seen to right or left.

"Ah, well!" said Northmour, "here's the end, thank God!"

And we returned to My Uncle's Room. Mr. Huddlestone was putting on his boots, still violently trembling, but with an air of determination such as I had not hitherto observed. Clara stood close by him, with her cloak in both hands ready to throw about her shoulders, and a strange look in her eyes, as if she were half hopeful, half doubtful of her father.

"Well, boys and girls," said Northmour, "how about a sally? The oven is heating; it is not good to stay here and be baked; and, for my part, I want to come to my hands with them, and be done."

"There's nothing else left," I replied.

And both Clara and Mr. Huddlestone, though with a very different intonation, added, "Nothing."

As we went downstairs the heat was excessive, and the roaring of the fire filled our ears; and we had scarce reached the passage before the stairs window fell in, a branch of flame shot brandishing through the aperture, and the interior of the pavilion became lighted up with that dreadful and fluctuating glare. At the same moment we heard the fall of something heavy and inelastic in the upper story. The whole pavilion, it was plain, had gone alight like a box of matches, and now not only flamed sky high to land and sea, but threatened with every moment to crumble and fall in about our ears.

Northmour and I cocked our revolvers. Mr. Huddlestone, who had already refused a firearm, put us behind him with a manner of command.

"Let Clara open the door," said he. "So, if they fire a volley, she will be protected. And in the meantime stand behind me. I am the scapegoat; my sins have found me out."

I heard him, as I stood breathless by his shoulder, with my pistol ready, pattering off prayers in a tremulous, rapid whisper; and, I confess, horrid as the thought may seem, I despised him for thinking of supplications in a moment so critical and thrilling. In the meantime, Clara, who was dead white but still possessed her faculties, had displaced the barricade from the front door. Another moment, and she had pulled it open. Firelight and moonlight illuminated the links with confused and changeful luster, and far away against the sky we could see a long trail of glowing smoke.

Mr. Huddlestone, filled for the moment with a strength greater than his own, struck Northmour and myself a back-hander in the chest; and while we were thus for the moment incapacitated from action, lifting his arms above his head like one about to dive, he ran straight forward out of the pavilion.

"Here am I!" he cried—"Huddlestone! Kill me, and spare the others!"

His sudden appearance daunted, I suppose, our hidden enemies; for Northmour and I had time to recover, to seize Clara between us, one by each arm, and to rush forth to his assistance, ere anything further had taken place. But scarce had we passed the threshold when there came near a dozen reports and flashes from every direction among the hollows of the links. Mr. Huddlestone staggered, uttered a weird and freezing cry, threw up his arms over his head, and fell backward on the turf.

"Traditore! Traditore!" cried the invisible avengers.

And just then a part of the roof of the pavilion fell in, so rapid was the progress of the fire. A loud, vague, and horrible noise accompanied the collapse, and a vast volume of flame went soaring up to heaven. It must have been visible at that moment from twenty miles out at sea, from the shore at Graden Wester, and far inland from the peak of Graystiel, the most eastern summit of the Caulder Hills.

Bernard Huddlestone, although God knows what were his obsequies, had a fine pyre at the moment of his death.

IX

I should have the greatest difficulty to tell you what followed next after this tragic circumstance. It is all to me, as I look back upon it, mixed, strenuous, and ineffectual, like the struggles of a sleeper in a nightmare. Clara, I remember, uttered a broken sigh and would have fallen forward to earth, had not Northmour and I supported her insensible body. I do not think we were attacked: I do not remember even to have seen an assailant; and I believe we deserted Mr. Huddlestone without a glance. I only remember running like a man in a panic, now carrying Clara altogether in my own arms, now sharing her weight with Northmour, now scuffling confusedly for the possession of that dear burden. Why we should have made for my camp in the Hemlock Den, or how we reached it, are points lost forever to my recollection. The first moment at which I became definitely sure, Clara had been suffered to fall against the outside of my little tent, Northmour and I were tumbling together on the ground, and he, with contained ferocity, was striking for my head with the butt of his revolver. He had already twice wounded me on the scalp; and it is to the consequent loss of blood that I am tempted to attribute the sudden clearness of my mind.

I caught him by the wrist.

"Northmour," I remember saying, "you can kill me afterwards. Let us first attend to Clara."

He was at that moment uppermost. Scarcely had the words passed my lips, when he had leaped to his feet and ran toward the tent; and the next moment, he was straining Clara to his heart and covering her unconscious hands and face with his caresses.

"Shame!" I cried. "Shame to you, Northmour!"

And, giddy though I still was, I struck him repeatedly upon the head and shoulders.

He relinquished his grasp, and faced me in the broken moonlight.

"I had you under, and I let you go," said he; "and now you strike me! Coward!"

"You are the coward," I retorted. "Did she wish your kisses while she was still sensible of what you wanted? Not she! And now she may be dying; and you waste this precious time, and abuse her helplessness. Stand aside, and let me help her."

He confronted me for a moment, white and menacing; then suddenly he stepped aside.

"Help her then," said he.

I threw myself on my knees beside her, and loosened, as well as I was able, her dress and corset; but while I was thus engaged, a grasp descended on my shoulder.

"Keep your hands off her," said Northmour, fiercely. "Do you think I have no blood in my veins?"

"Northmour," I cried, "if you will neither help her yourself, nor let me do so, do you know that I shall have to kill you?"

"That is better!" he cried. "Let her die also, where's the harm? Step aside from that girl! and stand up to fight."

"You will observe," said I, half rising, "that I have not kissed her yet."

"I dare you to," he cried.

I do not know what possessed me; it was one of the things I am most ashamed of in my life, though, as my wife used to say, I knew that my kisses would be always welcome were she dead or living; down I fell again upon my knees, parted the hair from her forehead, and, with the dearest respect, laid my lips for a moment on that cold brow. It was such a caress as a father might have given; it was such a one as was not unbecoming from a man soon to die to a woman already dead.

"And now," said I, "I am at your service, Mr. Northmour."

But I saw, to my surprise, that he had turned his back upon me.

"Do you hear?" I asked.

"Yes," said he, "I do. If you wish to fight, I am ready. If not, go on and save Clara. All is one to me."

I did not wait to be twice bidden; but, stooping again over Clara, continued my efforts to revive her. She still lay white and lifeless; I began to fear that her sweet spirit had indeed fled beyond recall, and horror and a sense of utter desolation seized upon my heart. I called her by name with the most endearing inflections; I chafed and beat her hands; now I laid her head low, now supported it against my knee; but all seemed to be in vain, and the lids still lay heavy on her eyes.

"Northmour," I said, "there is my hat. For God's sake bring some water from the spring."

Almost in a moment he was by my side with the water.

"I have brought it in my own," he said. "You do not grudge me the privilege?"

"Northmour," I was beginning to say, as I laved her head and breast; but he interrupted me savagely.

"Oh, you hush up!" he said. "The best thing you can do is to say nothing."

I had certainly no desire to talk, my mind being swallowed up in concern for my dear love and her condition; so I continued in silence to do my best toward her recovery, and, when the hat was empty,

39

returned it to him, with one word—"More." He had, perhaps, gone several times upon this errand, when Clara reopened her eyes.

"Now," said he, "since she is better, you can spare me, can you not? I wish you a good night, Mr. Cassilis."

And with that he was gone among the thicket. I made a fire, for I had now no fear of the Italians, who had even spared all the little possessions left in my encampment; and, broken as she was by the excitement and the hideous catastrophe of the evening, I managed, in one way or another—by persuasion, encouragement, warmth, and such simple remedies as I could lay my hand on—to bring her back to some composure of mind and strength of body.

Day had already come, when a sharp "Hist!" sounded from the thicket. I started from the ground; but the voice of Northmour was heard adding, in the most tranquil tones: "Come here, Cassilis, and alone; I want to show you something."

I consulted Clara with my eyes, and, receiving her tacit permission, left her alone, and clambered out of the den. At some distance off I saw Northmour leaning against an elder; and, as soon as he perceived me, he began walking seaward. I had almost overtaken him as he reached the outskirts of the wood.

"Look," said he, pausing.

A couple of steps more brought me out of the foliage. The light of the morning lay cold and clear over that well-known scene. The pavilion was but a blackened wreck; the roof had fallen in, one of the gables had fallen out; and, far and near, the face of the links was cicatrized with little patches of burned furze. Thick smoke still went straight upward in the windless air of the morning, and a great pile of ardent cinders filled the bare walls of the house, like coals in an open grate. Close by the islet a schooner yacht lay to, and a well-manned boat was pulling vigorously for the shore.

"The 'Red Earl'!" I cried. "The 'Red Earl' twelve hours too late!"

"Feel in your pocket, Frank. Are you armed?" asked Northmour.

I obeyed him, and I think I must have become deadly pale. My revolver had been taken from me.

"You see, I have you in my power," he continued. "I disarmed you last night while you were nursing Clara; but this morning—here—take your pistol. No thanks!" he cried, holding up his hand. "I do not like them; that is the only way you can annoy me now."

He began to walk forward across the links to meet the boat, and I followed a step or two behind. In front of the pavilion I paused to see where Mr. Huddlestone had fallen; but there was no sign of him, nor so much as a trace of blood.

"Graden Floe," said Northmour.

He continued to advance till we had come to the head of the beach.

"No farther, please," said he. "Would you like to take her to Graden House?"

"Thank you," replied I; "I shall try to get her to the minister at Graden Wester."

The prow of the boat here grated on the beach, and a sailor jumped ashore with a line in his hand.

"Wait a minute, lads!" cried Northmour; and then lower and to my private ear, "You had better say nothing of all this to her," he added.

"On the contrary!" I broke out, "she shall know everything that I can tell."

"You do not understand," he returned, with an air of great dignity. "It will be nothing to her; she expects it of me. Good-by!" he added, with a nod.

I offered him my hand.

"Excuse me," said he. "It's small, I know; but I can't push things quite so far as that. I don't wish any sentimental business, to sit by your hearth a white-haired wanderer, and all that. Quite the contrary: I hope to God I shall never again clap eyes on either one of you."

"Well, God bless you, Northmour!" I said heartily.

"Oh, yes," he returned.

He walked down the beach; and the man who was ashore gave him an arm on board, and then shoved off and leaped into the bows himself. Northmour took the tiller; the boat rose to the waves, and the oars between the tholepins sounded crisp and measured in the morning air.

They were not yet half way to the "Red Earl," and I was still watching their progress, when the sun rose out of the sea.

One word more, and my story is done. Years after, Northmour was killed fighting under the colors of Garibaldi for the liberation of the Tyrol.

RUDYARD KIPLING

MY OWN TRUE GHOST STORY

As I came through the Desert thus it was—
As I came through the Desert.

The City of Dreadful Night.

Somewhere in the Other World, where there are books and pictures and plays and shop windows to look at, and thousands of men who spend their lives in building up all four, lives a gentleman who writes real stories about the real insides of people; and his name is Mr. Walter Besant. But he will insist upon treating his ghosts—he has published half a workshopful of them—with levity. He makes his ghost-seers talk familiarly, and, in some cases, flirt outrageously, with the phantoms. You may treat anything, from a Viceroy to a Vernacular Paper, with levity; but you must behave reverently toward a ghost, and particularly an Indian one.

There are, in this land, ghosts who take the form of fat, cold, pobby corpses, and hide in trees near the roadside till a traveler passes. Then they drop upon his neck and remain. There are also terrible ghosts of women who have died in child-bed. These wander along the pathways at dusk, or hide in the crops near a village, and call seductively. But to answer their call is death in this world and the next. Their feet are turned backward that all sober men may recognize them. There are ghosts of little children who have been thrown into wells. These haunt well curbs and the fringes of jungles, and wail under the stars, or catch women by the wrist and beg to be taken up and carried. These and the corpse ghosts, however, are only vernacular articles and do not attack Sahibs. No native ghost has yet been authentically reported to have frightened an Englishman; but many English ghosts have scared the life out of both white and black.

Nearly every other Station owns a ghost. There are said to be two at Simla, not counting the woman who blows the bellows at Syree dâk-bungalow on the Old Road; Mussoorie has a house haunted of a very lively Thing; a White Lady is supposed to do night-watchman round a house in Lahore; Dalhousie says that one of her houses "repeats" on autumn evenings all the incidents of a horrible horse-and-precipice accident; Murree has a merry ghost, and, now that she has been swept by cholera, will have room for a sorrowful one; there are Officers'

42

Quarters in Mian Mir whose doors open without reason, and whose furniture is guaranteed to creak, not with the heat of June but with the weight of Invisibles who come to lounge in the chairs; Peshawur possesses houses that none will willingly rent; and there is something—not fever—wrong with a big bungalow in Allahabad. The older Provinces simply bristle with haunted houses, and march phantom armies along their main thoroughfares.

Some of the dâk-bungalows on the Grand Trunk Road have handy little cemeteries in their compound—witnesses to the "changes and chances of this mortal life" in the days when men drove from Calcutta to the Northwest. These bungalows are objectionable places to put up in. They are generally very old, always dirty, while the khansamah is as ancient as the bungalow. He either chatters senilely, or falls into the long trances of age. In both moods he is useless. If you get angry with him, he refers to some Sahib dead and buried these thirty years, and says that when he was in that Sahib's service not a khansamah in the Province could touch him. Then he jabbers and mows and trembles and fidgets among the dishes, and you repent of your irritation.

In these dâk-bungalows, ghosts are most likely to be found, and when found, they should be made a note of. Not long ago it was my business to live in dâk-bungalows. I never inhabited the same house for three nights running, and grew to be learned in the breed. I lived in Government-built ones with red brick walls and rail ceilings, an inventory of the furniture posted in every room, and an excited snake at the threshold to give welcome. I lived in "converted" ones—old houses officiating as dâk-bungalows—where nothing was in its proper place and there wasn't even a fowl for dinner. I lived in second-hand palaces where the wind blew through open-work marble tracery just as uncomfortably as through a broken pane. I lived in dâk-bungalows where the last entry in the visitors' book was fifteen months old, and where they slashed off the curry-kid's head with a sword. It was my good luck to meet all sorts of men, from sober traveling missionaries and deserters flying from British Regiments, to drunken loafers who threw whisky bottles at all who passed; and my still greater good fortune just to escape a maternity case. Seeing that a fair proportion of the tragedy of our lives out here acted itself in dâk-bungalows, I wondered that I had met no ghosts. A ghost that would voluntarily hang about a dâk-bungalow would be mad of course; but so many men have died mad in dâk-bungalows that there must be a fair percentage of lunatic ghosts.

In due time I found my ghost, or ghosts rather, for there were two of them. Up till that hour I had sympathized with Mr. Besant's method of handling them, as shown in "The Strange Case of Mr. Lucraft and Other Stories." I am now in the Opposition.

We will call the bungalow Katmal dâk-bungalow. But that was

the smallest part of the horror. A man with a sensitive hide has no right to sleep in dâk-bungalows. He should marry. Katmal dâk-bungalow was old and rotten and unrepaired. The floor was of worn brick, the walls were filthy, and the windows were nearly black with grime. It stood on a bypath largely used by native Sub-Deputy Assistants of all kinds, from Finance to Forests; but real Sahibs were rare. The khansamah, who was nearly bent double with old age, said so.

When I arrived, there was a fitful, undecided rain on the face of the land, accompanied by a restless wind, and every gust made a noise like the rattling of dry bones in the stiff toddy palms outside. The khansamah completely lost his head on my arrival. He had served a Sahib once. Did I know that Sahib? He gave me the name of a well-known man who has been buried for more than a quarter of a century, and showed me an ancient daguerreotype of that man in his prehistoric youth. I had seen a steel engraving of him at the head of a double volume of Memoirs a month before, and I felt ancient beyond telling.

The day shut in and the khansamah went to get me food. He did not go through the, pretense of calling it "khana"—man's victuals. He said "ratub," and that means, among other things, "grub"—dog's rations. There was no insult in his choice of the term. He had forgotten the other word, I suppose.

While he was cutting up the dead bodies of animals, I settled myself down, after exploring the dâk-bungalow. There were three rooms, beside my own, which was a corner kennel, each giving into the other through dingy white doors fastened with long iron bars. The bungalow was a very solid one, but the partition walls of the rooms were almost jerry-built in their flimsiness. Every step or bang of a trunk echoed from my room down the other three, and every footfall came back tremulously from the far walls. For this reason I shut the door. There were no lamps—only candles in long glass shades. An oil wick was set in the bathroom.

For bleak, unadulterated misery that dâk-bungalow was the worst of the many that I had ever set foot in. There was no fireplace, and the windows would not open; so a brazier of charcoal would have been useless. The rain and the wind splashed and gurgled and moaned round the house, and the toddy palms rattled and roared. Half a dozen jackals went through the compound singing, and a hyena stood afar off and mocked them. A hyena would convince a Sadducee of the Resurrection of the Dead—the worst sort of Dead. Then came the ratub—a curious meal, half native and half English in composition—with the old khansamah babbling behind my chair about dead and gone English people, and the wind-blown candles playing shadow-bo-peep with the bed and the mosquito-curtains. It was just the sort of dinner and evening to make a man think of every single one of his past sins, and of all the others that he intended to commit if he lived.

Sleep, for several hundred reasons, was not easy. The lamp in the bathroom threw the most absurd shadows into the room, and the wind was beginning to talk nonsense.

Just when the reasons were drowsy with blood-sucking I heard the regular—"Let-us-take-and-heave-him-over" grunt of doolie-bearers in the compound. First one doolie came in, then a second, and then a third. I heard the doolies dumped on the ground, and the shutter in front of my door shook. "That's some one trying to come in," I said. But no one spoke, and I persuaded myself that it was the gusty wind. The shutter of the room next to mine was attacked, flung back, and the inner door opened. "That's some Sub-Deputy Assistant," I said, "and he has brought his friends with him. Now they'll talk and spit and smoke for an hour."

But there were no voices and no footsteps. No one was putting his luggage into the next room. The door shut, and I thanked Providence that I was to be left in peace. But I was curious to know where the doolies had gone. I got out of bed and looked into the darkness. There was never a sign of a doolie. Just as I was getting into bed again, I heard, in the next room, the sound that no man in his senses can possibly mistake—the whir of a billiard ball down the length of the slates when the striker is stringing for break. No other sound is like it. A minute afterwards there was another whir, and I got into bed. I was not frightened—indeed I was not. I was very curious to know what had become of the doolies. I jumped into bed for that reason.

Next minute I heard the double click of a cannon and my hair sat up. It is a mistake to say that hair stands up. The skin of the head tightens and you can feel a faint, prickly, bristling all over the scalp. That is the hair sitting up.

There was a whir and a click, and both sounds could only have been made by one thing—a billiard ball. I argued the matter out at great length with myself; and the more I argued the less probable it seemed that one bed, one table, and two chairs—all the furniture of the room next to mine—could so exactly duplicate the sounds of a game of billiards. After another cannon, a three-cushion one to judge by the whir, I argued no more. I had found my ghost and would have given worlds to have escaped from that dâk-bungalow. I listened, and with each listen the game grew clearer. There was whir on whir and click on click. Sometimes there was a double click and a whir and another click. Beyond any sort of doubt, people were playing billiards in the next room. And the next room was not big enough to hold a billiard table!

Between the pauses of the wind I heard the game go forward— stroke after stroke. I tried to believe that I could not hear voices; but that attempt was a failure.

Do you know what fear is? Not ordinary fear of insult, injury or death, but abject, quivering dread of something that you cannot see— fear that dries the inside of the mouth and half of the throat—fear that makes you sweat on the palms of the hands, and gulp in order to keep

45

the uvula at work? This is a fine Fear—a great cowardice, and must be felt to be appreciated. The very improbability of billiards in a dâk-bungalow proved the reality of the thing. No man—drunk or sober—could imagine a game at billiards, or invent the spitting crack of a "screw-cannon."

A severe course of dâk-bungalows has this disadvantage—it breeds infinite credulity. If a man said to a confirmed dâk-bungalow-haunter:—"There is a corpse in the next room, and there's a mad girl in the next but one, and the woman and man on that camel have just eloped from a place sixty miles away," the hearer would not disbelieve because he would know that nothing is too wild, grotesque, or horrible to happen in a dâk-bungalow.

This credulity, unfortunately, extends to ghosts. A rational person fresh from his own house would have turned on his side and slept. I did not. So surely as I was given up as a bad carcass by the scores of things in the bed because the bulk of my blood was in my heart, so surely did I hear every stroke of a long game at billiards played in the echoing room behind the iron-barred door. My dominant fear was that the players might want a marker. It was an absurd fear; because creatures who could play in the dark would be above such superfluities. I only know that that was my terror; and it was real.

After a long, long while the game stopped, and the door banged. I slept because I was dead tired. Otherwise I should have preferred to have kept awake. Not for everything in Asia would I have dropped the door-bar and peered into the dark of the next room.

When the morning came, I considered that I had done well and wisely, and inquired for the means of departure.

"By the way, khansamah," I said, "what were those three doolies doing in my compound in the night?"

"There were no doolies," said the khansamah.

I went into the next room and the daylight streamed through the open door. I was immensely brave. I would, at that hour, have played Black Pool with the owner of the big Black Pool down below.

"Has this place always been a dâk-bungalow?" I asked.

"No," said the khansamah. "Ten or twenty years ago, I have forgotten how long, it was a billiard room."

"A how much?"

"A billiard room for the Sahibs who built the Railway. I was khansamah then in the big house where all the Railway-Sahibs lived, and I used to come across with brandy-shrab. These three rooms were all one, and they held a big table on which the Sahibs played every evening. But the Sahibs are all dead now, and the Railway runs, you say, nearly to Kabul."

"Do you remember anything about the Sahibs?"

"It is long ago, but I remember that one Sahib, a fat man and always angry, was playing here one night, and he said to me:—'Mangal

Khan, brandy-pani do,' and I filled the glass, and he bent over the table to strike, and his head fell lower and lower till it hit the table, and his spectacles came off, and when we—the Sahibs and I myself—ran to lift him he was dead. I helped to carry him out. Aha, he was a strong Sahib! But he is dead and I, old Mangal Khan, am still living, by your favor."

That was more than enough! I had my ghost—a first-hand, authenticated article. I would write to the Society for Psychical Research—I would paralyze the Empire with the news! But I would, first of all, put eighty miles of assessed crop land between myself and that dâk-bungalow before nightfall. The Society might send their regular agent to investigate later on.

I went into my own room and prepared to pack after noting down the facts of the case. As I smoked I heard the game begin again,— with a miss in balk this time, for the whir was a short one.

The door was open and I could see into the room. Click—click! That was a cannon. I entered the room without fear, for there was sunlight within and a fresh breeze without. The unseen game was going on at a tremendous rate. And well it might, when a restless little rat was running to and fro inside the dingy ceiling-cloth, and a piece of loose window-sash was making fifty breaks off the window-bolt as it shook in the breeze!

Impossible to mistake the sound of billiard balls! Impossible to mistake the whir of a ball over the slate! But I was to be excused. Even when I shut my enlightened eyes the sound was marvelously like that of a fast game.

Entered angrily the faithful partner of my sorrows, Kadir Baksh.

"This bungalow is very bad and low-caste! No wonder the Presence was disturbed and is speckled. Three sets of doolie-bearers came to the bungalow late last night when I was sleeping outside, and said that it was their custom to rest in the rooms set apart for the English people! What honor has the khansamah? They tried to enter, but I told them to go. No wonder, if these Oorias have been here, that the Presence is sorely spotted. It is shame, and the work of a dirty man!"

Kadir Baksh did not say that he had taken from each gang two annas for rent in advance, and then, beyond my earshot, had beaten them with the big green umbrella whose use I could never before divine. But Kadir Baksh has no notions of morality.

There was an interview with the khansamah, but as he promptly lost his head, wrath gave place to pity, and pity led to a long conversation, in the course of which he put the fat Engineer-Sahib's tragic death in three separate stations—two of them fifty miles away. The third shift was to Calcutta, and there the Sahib died while driving a dog-cart.

If I had encouraged him the khansamah would have wandered all through Bengal with his corpse.

I did not go away as soon as I intended. I stayed for the night, while the wind and the rat and the sash and the window-bolt played a ding-dong "hundred and fifty up." Then the wind ran out and the billiards stopped, and I felt that I had ruined my one genuine, hall-marked ghost story.

Had I only stopped at the proper time, I could have made anything out of it.

That was the bitterest thought of all!

THE SENDING OF DANA DA

When the Devil rides on your chest, remember the chamar. —
Native Proverb.

Once upon a time some people in India made a new heaven and a new earth out of broken teacups, a missing brooch or two, and a hair brush. These were hidden under bushes, or stuffed into holes in the hillside, and an entire civil service of subordinate gods used to find or mend them again; and everyone said: "There are more things in heaven and earth than are dreamed of in our philosophy." Several other things happened also, but the religion never seemed to get much beyond its first manifestations; though it added an air-line postal dak, and orchestral effects in order to keep abreast of the times, and stall off competition.

This religion was too elastic for ordinary use. It stretched itself and embraced pieces of everything that medicine men of all ages have manufactured. It approved and stole from Freemasonry; looted the Latter-day Rosicrucians of half their pet words; took any fragments of Egyptian philosophy that it found in the Encyclopædia Britannica; annexed as many of the Vedas as had been translated into French or English, and talked of all the rest; built in the German versions of what is left of the Zend Avesta; encouraged white, gray, and black magic, including Spiritualism, palmistry, fortune-telling by cards, hot chestnuts, double-kerneled nuts and tallow droppings; would have adopted Voodoo and Oboe had it known anything about them, and showed itself, in every way, one of the most accommodating arrangements that had ever been invented since the birth of the sea.

48

When it was in thorough working order, with all the machinery down to the subscriptions complete, Dana Da came from nowhere, with nothing in his hands, and wrote a chapter in its history which has hitherto been unpublished. He said that his first name was Dana, and his second was Da. Now, setting aside Dana of the New York Sun, Dana is a Bhil name, and Da fits no native of India unless you accept the Bengali Dé as the original spelling. Da is Lap or Finnish; and Dana Da was neither Finn, Chin, Bhil, Bengali, Lap, Nair, Gond, Romaney, Magh, Bokhariot, Kurd, Armenian, Levantine, Jew, Persian, Punjabi, Madrasi, Parsee, nor anything else known to ethnologists. He was simply Dana Da, and declined to give further information. For the sake of brevity, and as roughly indicating his origin, he was called "The Native." He might have been the original Old Man of the Mountains, who is said to be the only authorized head of the Teacup Creed. Some people said that he was; but Dana Da used to smile and deny any connection with the cult; explaining that he was an "independent experimenter."

As I have said, he came from nowhere, with his hands behind his back, and studied the creed for three weeks; sitting at the feet of those best competent to explain its mysteries. Then he laughed aloud and went away, but the laugh might have been either of devotion or derision.

When he returned he was without money, but his pride was unabated. He declared that he knew more about the things in heaven and earth than those who taught him, and for this contumacy was abandoned altogether.

His next appearance in public life was at a big cantonment in Upper India, and he was then telling fortunes with the help of three leaden dice, a very dirty old cloth, and a little tin box of opium pills. He told better fortunes when he was allowed half a bottle of whisky; but the things which he invented on the opium were quite worth the money. He was in reduced circumstances. Among other people's he told the fortune of an Englishman who had once been interested in the Simla creed, but who, later on, had married and forgotten all his old knowledge in the study of babies and Exchange. The Englishman allowed Dana Da to tell a fortune for charity's sake, and, gave him five rupees, a dinner, and some old clothes. When he had eaten, Dana Da professed gratitude, and asked if there were anything he could do for his host—in the esoteric line.

"Is there anyone that you love?" said Dana Da. The Englishman loved his wife, but had no desire to drag her name into the conversation. He therefore shook his head.

"Is there anyone that you hate?" said Dana Da. The Englishman said that there were several men whom he hated deeply.

"Very good," said Dana Da, upon whom the whisky and the

opium were beginning to tell. "Only give me their names, and I will dispatch a Sending to them and kill them."

Now a Sending is a horrible arrangement, first invented, they say, in Iceland. It is a thing sent by a wizard, and may take any form, but most generally wanders about the land in the shape of a little purple cloud till it finds the sendee, and him it kills by changing into the form of a horse, or a cat, or a man without a face. It is not strictly a native patent, though chamars can, if irritated, dispatch a Sending which sits on the breast of their enemy by night and nearly kills him. Very few natives care to irritate chamars for this reason.

"Let me dispatch a Sending," said Dana Da; "I am nearly dead now with want, and drink, and opium; but I should like to kill a man before I die. I can send a Sending anywhere you choose, and in any form except in the shape of a man."

The Englishman had no friends that he wished to kill, but partly to soothe Dana Da, whose eyes were rolling, and partly to see what would be done, he asked whether a modified Sending could not be arranged for—such a Sending as should make a man's life a burden to him, and yet do him no harm. If this were possible, he notified his willingness to give Dana Da ten rupees for the job.

"I am not what I was once," said Dana Da, "and I must take the money because I am poor. To what Englishman shall I send it?"

"Send a Sending to Lone Sahib," said the Englishman, naming a man who had been most bitter in rebuking him for his apostasy from the Teacup Creed. Dana Da laughed and nodded.

"I could have chosen no better man myself," said he. "I will see that he finds the Sending about his path and about his bed."

He lay down on the hearthrug, turned up the whites of his eyes, shivered all over, and began to snort. This was magic, or opium, or the Sending, or all three. When he opened his eyes he vowed that the Sending had started upon the warpath, and was at that moment flying up to the town where Lone Sahib lives.

"Give me my ten rupees," said Dana Da, wearily, "and write a letter to Lone Sahib, telling him, and all who believe with him, that you and a friend are using a power greater than theirs. They will see that you are speaking the truth."

He departed unsteadily, with the promise of some more rupees if anything came of the Sending.

The Englishman sent a letter to Lone Sahib, couched in what he remembered of the terminology of the creed. He wrote: "I also, in the days of what you held to be my backsliding, have obtained enlightenment, and with enlightenment has come power." Then he grew so deeply mysterious that the recipient of the letter could make neither head nor tail of it, and was proportionately impressed; for he fancied that his friend had become a "fifth rounder." When a man is a "fifth rounder" he can do more than Slade and Houdin combined.

Lone Sahib read the letter in five different fashions, and was beginning a sixth interpretation, when his bearer dashed in with the news that there was a cat on the bed. Now, if there was one thing that Lone Sahib hated more than another it was a cat. He rated the bearer for not turning it out of the house. The bearer said that he was afraid. All the doors of the bedroom had been shut throughout the morning, and no real cat could possibly have entered the room. He would prefer not to meddle with the creature.

Lone Sahib entered the room gingerly, and there, on the pillow of his bed, sprawled and whimpered a wee white kitten, not a jumpsome, frisky little beast, but a sluglike crawler with its eyes barely opened and its paws lacking strength or direction—a kitten that ought to have been in a basket with its mamma. Lone Sahib caught it by the scruff of its neck, handed it over to the sweeper to be drowned, and fined the bearer four annas.

That evening, as he was reading in his room, he fancied that he saw something moving about on the hearthrug, outside the circle of light from his reading lamp. When the thing began to myowl, he realized that it was a kitten—a wee white kitten, nearly blind and very miserable. He was seriously angry, and spoke bitterly to his bearer, who said that there was no kitten in the room when he brought in the lamp, and real kittens of tender age generally had mother cats in attendance.

"If the Presence will go out into the veranda and listen," said the bearer, "he will hear no cats. How, therefore, can the kitten on the bed and the kitten on the hearthrug be real kittens?"

Lone Sahib went out to listen, and the bearer followed him, but there was no sound of Rachel mewing for her children. He returned to his room, having hurled the kitten down the hillside, and wrote out the incidents of the day for the benefit of his coreligionists. Those people were so absolutely free from superstition that they ascribed anything a little out of the common to agencies. As it was their business to know all about the agencies, they were on terms of almost indecent familiarity with manifestations of every kind. Their letters dropped from the ceiling—unstamped—and spirits used to squatter up and down their staircases all night. But they had never come into contact with kittens. Lone Sahib wrote out the facts, noting the hour and the minute, as every psychical observer is bound to do, and appending the Englishman's letter because it was the most mysterious document and might have had a bearing upon anything in this world or the next. An outsider would have translated all the tangle thus: "Look out! You laughed at me once, and now I am going to make you sit up."

Lone Sahib's coreligionists found that meaning in it; but their translation was refined and full of four-syllable words. They held a sederunt, and were filled with tremulous joy, for, in spite of their

51

familiarity with all the other worlds and cycles, they had a very human awe of things sent from ghostland. They met in Lone Sahib's room in shrouded and sepulchral gloom, and their conclave was broken up by a clinking among the photo frames on the mantelpiece. A wee white kitten, nearly blind, was looping and writhing itself between the clock and the candlesticks. That stopped all investigations or doubtings. Here was the manifestation in the flesh. It was, so far as could be seen, devoid of purpose, but it was a manifestation of undoubted authenticity.

They drafted a round robin to the Englishman, the backslider of old days, adjuring him in the interests of the creed to explain whether there was any connection between the embodiment of some Egyptian god or other (I have forgotten the name) and his communication. They called the kitten Ra, or Toth, or Shem, or Noah, or something; and when Lone Sahib confessed that the first one had, at his most misguided instance, been drowned by the sweeper, they said consolingly that in his next life he would be a "bounder," and not even a "rounder" of the lowest grade. These words may not be quite correct, but they express the sense of the house accurately.

When the Englishman received the round robin—it came by post—he was startled and bewildered. He sent into the bazaar for Dana Da, who read the letter and laughed. "That is my Sending," said he. "I told you I would work well. Now give me another ten rupees."

"But what in the world is this gibberish about Egyptian gods?" asked the Englishman.

"Cats," said Dana Da, with a hiccough, for he had discovered the Englishman's whisky bottle. "Cats and cats and cats! Never was such a Sending. A hundred of cats. Now give me ten more rupees and write as I dictate."

Dana Da's letter was a curiosity. It bore the Englishman's signature, and hinted at cats—at a Sending of cats. The mere words on paper were creepy and uncanny to behold.

"What have you done, though?" said the Englishman; "I am as much in the dark as ever. Do you mean to say that you can actually send this absurd Sending you talk about?"

"Judge for yourself," said Dana Da. "What does that letter mean? In a little time they will all be at my feet and yours, and I, oh, glory! will be drugged or drunk all day long."

Dana Da knew his people.

When a man who hates cats wakes up in the morning and finds a little squirming kitten on his breast, or puts his hand into his ulster pocket and finds a little half-dead kitten where his gloves should be, or opens his trunk and finds a vile kitten among his dress shirts, or goes for a long ride with his mackintosh strapped on his saddle-bow and shakes a little sprawling kitten from its folds when he opens it, or goes out to dinner and finds a little blind kitten under his chair, or stays at home and finds a writhing kitten under the quilt, or wriggling among his boots, or hanging, head downward, in his tobacco jar, or being mangled by his terrier in the veranda—when such a man finds one kitten, neither more nor less, once a day in a place where no kitten rightly could or should be, he is naturally upset. When he dare not murder his daily trove because he believes it to be a manifestation, an emissary, an embodiment, and half a dozen other things all out of the regular course of nature, he is more than upset. He is actually distressed. Some of Lone Sahib's coreligionists thought that he was a highly favored individual; but many said that if he had treated the first kitten with proper respect—as suited a Toth-Ra Tum-Sennacherib Embodiment—all his trouble would have been averted. They compared him to the Ancient Mariner, but none the less they were proud of him and proud of the Englishman who had sent the manifestation. They did not call it a Sending because Icelandic magic was not in their programme.

After sixteen kittens—that is to say, after one fortnight, for there were three kittens on the first day to impress the fact of the Sending, the whole camp was uplifted by a letter—it came flying through a window—from the Old Man of the Mountains—the head of all the creed—explaining the manifestation in the most beautiful language and soaking up all the credit of it for himself. The Englishman, said the letter, was not there at all. He was a backslider without power or asceticism, who couldn't even raise a table by force of volition, much less project an army of kittens through space. The entire arrangement, said the letter, was strictly orthodox, worked and sanctioned by the highest authorities within the pale of the creed. There was great joy at this, for some of the weaker brethren seeing that an outsider who had been working on independent lines could create kittens, whereas their own rulers had never gone beyond crockery—and broken at that—were showing a desire to break line on their own trail. In fact, there was the promise of a schism. A second round robin was drafted to the Englishman, beginning: "Oh, Scoffer," and ending with a selection of curses from the rites of Mizraim and Memphis and the Commination of Jugana; who was a "fifth rounder," upon whose name an upstart "third rounder" once traded. A papal excommunication is a billet-doux compared to the Commination of Jugana. The Englishman had been proved under the hand and seal of the Old Man of the Mountains to have appropriated virtue and pretended to have power which, in reality, belonged only to the supreme head. Naturally the round robin did not spare him.

He handed the letter to Dana Da to translate into decent English. The effect on Dana Da was curious. At first he was furiously angry, and then he laughed for five minutes.

"I had thought," he said, "that they would have come to me. In another week I would have shown that I sent the Sending, and they

53

would have discrowned the Old Man of the Mountains who has sent this Sending of mine. Do you do nothing. The time has come for me to act. Write as I dictate, and I will put them to shame. But give me ten more rupees."

At Dana Da's dictation the Englishman wrote nothing less than a formal challenge to the Old Man of the Mountains. It wound up: "And if this manifestation be from your hand, then let it go forward; but if it be from my hand, I will that the Sending shall cease in two days' time. On that day there shall be twelve kittens and thenceforward none at all. The people shall judge between us." This was signed by Dana Da, who added pentacles and pentagrams, and a crux ansata, and half a dozen swastikas, and a Triple Tau to his name, just to show that he was all he laid claim to be.

The challenge was read out to the gentlemen and ladies, and they remembered then that Dana Da had laughed at them some years ago. It was officially announced that the Old Man of the Mountains would treat the matter with contempt; Dana Da being an independent investigator without a single "round" at the back of him. But this did not soothe his people. They wanted to see a fight. They were very human for all their spirituality. Lone Sahib, who was really being worn out with kittens, submitted meekly to his fate. He felt that he was being "kittened to prove the power of Dana Da," as the poet says.

When the stated day dawned, the shower of kittens began. Some were white and some were tabby, and all were about the same loathsome age. Three were on his hearthrug, three in his bathroom, and the other six turned up at intervals among the visitors who came to see the prophecy break down. Never was a more satisfactory Sending. On the next day there were no kittens, and the next day and all the other days were kittenless and quiet. The people murmured and looked to the Old Man of the Mountains for an explanation. A letter, written on a palm leaf, dropped from the ceiling, but everyone except Lone Sahib felt that letters were not what the occasion demanded. There should have been cats, there should have been cats—full-grown ones. The letter proved conclusively that there had been a hitch in the psychic current which, colliding with a dual identity, had interfered with the percipient activity all along the main line. The kittens were still going on, but owing to some failure in the developing fluid, they were not materialized. The air was thick with letters for a few days afterwards. Unseen hands played Glück and Beethoven on finger-bowls and clock shades; but all men felt that psychic life was a mockery without materialized kittens. Even Lone Sahib shouted with the majority on this head. Dana Da's letters were very insulting, and if he had then offered to lead a new departure, there is no knowing what might not have happened.

But Dana Da was dying of whisky and opium in the Englishman's go-down, and had small heart for new creeds.

54

"They have been put to shame," said he. "Never was such a Sending. It has killed me."

"Nonsense," said the Englishman, "you are going to die, Dana Da, and that sort of stuff must be left behind. I'll admit that you have made some queer things come about. Tell me honestly, now, how was it done?"

"Give me ten more rupees," said Dana Da, faintly, "and if I die before I spend them, bury them with me." The silver was counted out while Dana Da was fighting with death. His hand closed upon the money and he smiled a grim smile.

"Bend low," he whispered. The Englishman bent.

"Bunnia—mission school—expelled—box-wallah (peddler)—Ceylon pearl merchant—all mine English education—outcasted, and made up name Dana Da—England with American thought-reading man and—and—you gave me ten rupees several times—I gave the Sahib's bearer two-eight a month for cats—little, little cats. I wrote, and he put them about—very clever man. Very few kittens now in the bazaar. Ask Lone Sahib's sweeper's wife."

So saying, Dana Da gasped and passed away into a land where, if all be true, there are no materializations and the making of new creeds is discouraged.

But consider the gorgeous simplicity of it all!

IN THE HOUSE OF SUDDHOO

A stone's throw out on either hand
From that well-ordered road we tread,
And all the world is wild and strange;
Churel and ghoul and Djinn and sprite
Shall bear us company to-night,
For we have reached the Oldest Land
Wherein the Powers of Darkness range.

—*From the Dusk to the Dawn.*

The house of Suddhoo, near the Taksali Gate, is two storied, with four carved windows of old brown wood, and a flat roof. You may recognize it by five red handprints arranged like the Five of Diamonds on the whitewash between the upper windows. Bhagwan Dass, the bunnia, and a man who says he gets his living by seal-cutting live in the lower story with a troop of wives, servants, friends, and retainers. The two upper rooms used to be occupied by Janoo and Azizun and a little black-and-tan terrier that was stolen from an Englishman's house and given to Janoo by a soldier. To-day, only Janoo lives in the upper rooms. Suddhoo sleeps on the roof generally, except when he sleeps in the street. He used to go to Peshawar in the cold weather to visit his son, who sells curiosities near the Edwardes' Gate, and then he slept under a real mud roof. Suddhoo is a great friend of mine, because his cousin had a son who secured, thanks to my recommendation, the post of head messenger to a big firm in the Station. Suddhoo says that God will make me a Lieutenant-Governor one of these days. I daresay his prophecy will come true. He is very, very old, with white hair and no teeth worth showing, and he has outlived his wits—outlived nearly everything except his fondness for his son at Peshawar. Janoo and Azizun are Kashmiris, Ladies of the City, and theirs was an ancient and more or less honorable profession; but Azizun has since married a medical student from the Northwest and has settled down to a most respectable life somewhere near Bareilly. Bhagwan Dass is an extortionate and an adulterator. He is very rich. The man who is supposed to get his living by seal cutting pretends to be very poor. This lets you know as much as is necessary of the four principal tenants in the house of Suddhoo. Then there is Me, of course; but I am only the chorus that comes in at the end to explain things. So I do not count.

Suddhoo was not clever. The man who pretended to cut seals was the cleverest of them all—Bhagwan Dass only knew how to lie—except Janoo. She was also beautiful, but that was her own affair.

Suddhoo's son at Peshawar was attacked by pleurisy, and old Suddhoo was troubled. The seal-cutter man heard of Suddhoo's anxiety and made capital out of it. He was abreast of the times. He got a friend in Peshawar to telegraph daily accounts of the son's health. And here the story begins.

Suddhoo's cousin's son told me, one evening, that Suddhoo wanted to see me; that he was too old and feeble to come personally, and that I should be conferring an everlasting honor on the House of Suddhoo if I went to him. I went; but I think, seeing how well off Suddhoo was then, that he might have sent something better than an ekka, which jolted fearfully, to haul out a future Lieutenant-Governor to the City on a muggy April evening. The ekka did not run quickly. It was full dark when we pulled up opposite the door of Ranjit Singh's Tomb near the main gate of the Fort. Here was Suddhoo and he said that by reason of my condescension, it was absolutely certain that I should become a Lieutenant-Governor while my hair was yet black. Then we talked about the weather and the state of my health, and the wheat crops, for fifteen minutes, in the Huzuri Bagh, under the stars.

Suddhoo came to the point at last. He said that Janoo had told him that there was an order of the Sirkar against magic, because it was feared that magic might one day kill the Empress of India. I didn't know anything about the state of the law; but I fancied that something interesting was going to happen. I said that so far from magic being discouraged by the Government it was highly commended. The greatest officials of the State practiced it themselves. (If the Financial Statement isn't magic, I don't know what is.) Then, to encourage him further, I said that, if there was any jadoo afoot, I had not the least objection to giving it my countenance and sanction, and to seeing that it was clean jadoo—white magic, as distinguished from the unclean jadoo which kills folk. It took a long time before Suddhoo admitted that this was just what he had asked me to come for. Then he told me, in jerks and quavers, that the man who said he cut seals was a sorcerer of the cleanest kind; that every day he gave Suddhoo news of his sick son in Peshawar more quickly than the lightning could fly, and that this news was always corroborated by the letters. Further, that he had told Suddhoo how a great danger was threatening his son, which could be removed by clean jadoo; and, of course, heavy payment. I began to see exactly how the land lay, and told Suddhoo that I also understood a little jadoo in the Western line, and would go to his house to see that everything was done decently and in order. We set off together; and on the way Suddhoo told me that he had paid the seal cutter between one hundred and two hundred rupees already; and the jadoo of that night would cost two hundred more. Which was cheap, he said, considering the greatness of his son's danger; but I do not think he meant it.

The lights were all cloaked in the front of the house when we arrived. I could hear awful noises from behind the seal cutter's shop front, as if some one were groaning his soul out. Suddhoo shook all over, and while we groped our way upstairs told me that the jadoo had begun. Janoo and Azizun met us at the stair head, and told us that the jadoo work was coming off in their rooms, because there was more space there. Janoo is a lady of a freethinking turn of mind. She whispered that the jadoo was an invention to get money out of Suddhoo, and that the seal cutter would go to a hot place when he died. Suddhoo was nearly crying with fear and old age. He kept walking up and down the room in the half light, repeating his son's name over and over again, and asking Azizun if the seal cutter ought not to make a reduction in the case of his own landlord. Janoo pulled me over to the shadow in the recess of the carved bow-windows. The boards were up, and the rooms were only lit by one tiny oil lamp. There was no chance of my being seen if I stayed still.

Presently, the groans below ceased, and we heard steps on the staircase. That was the seal cutter. He stopped outside the door as the terrier barked and Azizun fumbled at the chain, and he told Suddhoo to blow out the lamp. This left the place in jet darkness, except for the red glow from the two huqas that belonged to Janoo and Azizun. The seal cutter came in, and I heard Suddhoo throw himself down on the floor

57

and groan. Azizun caught her breath, and Janoo backed on to one of the beds with a shudder. There was a clink of something metallic, and then shot up a pale blue-green flame near the ground. The light was just enough to show Azizun, pressed against one corner of the room with the terrier between her knees; Janoo, with her hands clasped, leaning forward as she sat on the bed; Suddhoo, face down, quivering, and the seal cutter.

I hope I may never see another man like that seal cutter. He was stripped to the waist, with a wreath of white jasmine as thick as my wrist round his forehead, a salmon-colored loin-cloth round his middle, and a steel bangle on each ankle. This was not awe-inspiring. It was the face of the man that turned me cold. It was blue-gray in the first place. In the second, the eyes were rolled back till you could only see the whites of them; and, in the third, the face was the face of a demon—a ghoul—anything you please except of the sleek, oily old ruffian who sat in the daytime over his turning-lathe downstairs. He was lying on his stomach with his arms turned and crossed behind him, as if he had been thrown down pinioned. His head and neck were the only parts of him off the floor. They were nearly at right angles to the body, like the head of a cobra at spring. It was ghastly. In the center of the room, on the bare earth floor, stood a big, deep, brass basin, with a pale blue-green light floating in the center like a night-light. Round that basin the man on the floor wriggled himself three times. How he did it I do not know. I could see the muscles ripple along his spine and fall smooth again; but I could not see any other motion. The head seemed the only thing alive about him, except that slow curl and uncurl of the laboring back muscles. Janoo from the bed was breathing seventy to the minute; Azizun held her hands before her eyes; and old Suddhoo, fingering at the dirt that had got into his white beard, was crying to himself. The horror of it was that the creeping, crawly thing made no sound—only crawled! And, remember, this lasted for ten minutes, while the terrier whined, and Azizun shuddered, and Janoo gasped and Suddhoo cried.

I felt the hair lift at the back of my head, and my heart thump like a thermantidote paddle. Luckily, the seal cutter betrayed himself by his most impressive trick and made me calm again. After he had finished that unspeakable crawl, he stretched his head away from the floor as high as he could, and sent out a jet of fire from his nostrils. Now I knew how fire—spouting is done—I can do it myself—so I felt at ease. The business was a fraud. If he had only kept to that crawl without trying to raise the effect, goodness knows what I might not have thought. Both the girls shrieked at the jet of fire, and the head dropped, chin down on the floor, with a thud; the whole body lying then like a corpse with its arms trussed. There was a pause of five full minutes after this, and the blue-green flame died down. Janoo stooped to settle one of her anklets, while Azizun turned her face to the wall and took the terrier in her arms. Suddhoo put out an arm mechanically to Janoo's huqa, and she slid it across the floor with her foot. Directly above the body and on the wall were a couple of flaming portraits, in stamped paper frames, of the Queen and the Prince of Wales. They looked down on the performance, and, to my thinking, seemed to heighten the grotesqueness of it all.

Just when the silence was getting unendurable, the body turned over and rolled away from the basin to the side of the room, where it lay stomach up. There was a faint "plop" from the basin—exactly like the noise a fish makes when it takes a fly—and the green light in the center revived.

I looked at the basin, and saw, bobbing in the water the dried, shriveled, black head of a native baby—open eyes, open mouth and shaved scalp. It was worse, being so very sudden, than the crawling exhibition. We had no time to say anything before it began to speak.

Read Poe's account of the voice that came from the mesmerized dying man, and you will realize less than one half of the horror of that head's voice.

There was an interval of a second or two between each word, and a sort of "ring, ring, ring," in the note of the voice like the timbre of a bell. It pealed slowly, as if talking to itself, for several minutes before I got rid of my cold sweat. Then the blessed solution struck me. I looked at the body lying near the doorway, and saw, just where the hollow of the throat joins on the shoulders, a muscle that had nothing to do with any man's regular breathing, twitching away steadily. The whole thing was a careful reproduction of the Egyptian teraphin that one reads about sometimes; and the voice was as clever and as appalling a piece of ventriloquism as one could wish to hear. All this time the head was "lip-lip-lapping" against the side of the basin, and speaking. It told Suddhoo, on his face again whining, of his son's illness and of the state of the illness up to the evening of that very night. I always shall respect the seal cutter for keeping so faithfully to the time of the Peshawar telegrams. It went on to say that skilled doctors were night and day watching over the man's life; and that he would eventually recover if the fee to the potent sorcerer, whose servant was the head in the basin, were doubled.

Here the mistake from the artistic point of view came in. To ask for twice your stipulated fee in a voice that Lazarus might have used when he rose from the dead, is absurd. Janoo, who is really a woman of masculine intellect, saw this as quickly as I did. I heard her say "Ash nahin! Fareib!" scornfully under her breath; and just as she said so, the light in the basin died out, the head stopped talking, and we heard the room door creak on its hinges. Then Janoo struck a match, lit the lamp, and we saw that head, basin, and seal cutter were gone. Suddhoo was wringing his hands and explaining to anyone who cared to listen, that, if his chances of eternal salvation depended on it, he could not raise another two hundred rupees. Azizun was nearly in hysterics in the corner; while Janoo sat down composedly on one of the beds to discuss the probabilities of the whole thing being a bunao, or "make-up."

I explained as much as I knew of the seal cutter's way of jadoo; but her argument was much more simple:—"The magic that is always demanding gifts is no true magic," said she. "My mother told me that the only potent love spells are those which are told you for love. This seal cutter man is a liar and a devil. I dare not tell, do anything, or get anything done, because I am in debt to Bhagwan Dass the bunnia for two gold rings and a heavy anklet. I must get my food from his shop. The seal cutter is the friend of Bhagwan Dass, and he would poison my food. A fool's jadoo has been going on for ten days, and has cost Suddhoo many rupees each night. The seal cutter used black hens and lemons and mantras before. He never showed us anything like this till to-night. Azizun is a fool, and will be a pur dahnashin soon. Suddhoo has lost his strength and his wits. See now! I had hoped to get from Suddhoo many rupees while he lived, and many more after his death; and behold, he is spending everything on that offspring of a devil and a she-ass, the seal cutter!"

Here I said: "But what induced Suddhoo to drag me into the business? Of course I can speak to the seal cutter, and he shall refund. The whole thing is child's talk—shame—and senseless."

"Suddhoo is an old child," said Janoo. "He has lived on the roofs these seventy years and is as senseless as a milch goat. He brought you here to assure himself that he was not breaking any law of the Sirkar, whose salt he ate many years ago. He worships the dust off the feet of the seal cutter, and that cow devourer has forbidden him to go and see his son. What does Suddhoo know of your laws or the lightning post? I have to watch his money going day by day to that lying beast below."

Janoo stamped her foot on the floor and nearly cried with vexation; while Suddhoo was whimpering under a blanket in the corner, and Azizun was trying to guide the pipe-stem to his foolish old mouth.

Now the case stands thus. Unthinkingly, I have laid myself open to the charge of aiding and abetting the seal cutter in obtaining money under false pretenses, which is forbidden by Section 420 of the Indian Penal Code. I am helpless in the matter for these reasons, I cannot inform the police. What witnesses would support my statements? Janoo refuses flatly, and Azizun is a veiled woman somewhere near Bareilly—lost in this big India of ours. I dare not again take the law into my own hands, and speak to the seal cutter; for certain am I that, not only would Suddhoo disbelieve me, but this step would end in the poisoning of Janoo, who is bound hand and foot by her debt to the bunnia. Suddhoo is an old dotard; and whenever we meet mumbles my idiotic joke that the Sirkar rather patronizes the Black Art than otherwise. His son is well now; but Suddhoo is completely under the influence of the seal cutter, by whose advice he regulates the affairs of his life. Janoo watches daily the money that she hoped to wheedle out of Suddhoo taken by the seal cutter, and becomes daily more furious and sullen.

She will never tell, because she dare not; but, unless something happens to prevent her, I am afraid that the seal cutter will die of cholera—the white arsenic kind—about the middle of May. And thus I shall have to be privy to a murder in the house of Suddhoo.

HIS WEDDED WIFE

Cry "Murder!" in the market-place, and each
Will turn upon his neighbor anxious eyes
That ask:—"Art thou the man?" We hunted Cain
Some centuries ago, across the world,
That bred the fear our own misdeeds maintain
To-day.

—*Vibart's Moralities.*

Shakespeare says something about worms, or it may be giants or beetles, turning if you tread on them too severely. The safest plan is never to tread on a worm—not even on the last new subaltern from Home, with his buttons hardly out of their tissue paper, and the red of sappy English beef in his cheeks. This is the story of the worm that turned. For the sake of brevity, we will call Henry Augustus Ramsay Faizanne, "The Worm," although he really was an exceedingly pretty boy, without a hair on his face, and with a waist like a girl's, when he came out to the Second "Shikarris" and was made unhappy in several ways. The "Shikarris" are a high-caste regiment, and you must be able to do things well—play a banjo, or ride more than little, or sing, or act—to get on with them.

The Worm did nothing except fall off his pony, and knock chips out of gate posts with his trap. Even that became monotonous after a time. He objected to whist, cut the cloth at billiards, sang out of tune, kept very much to himself, and wrote to his Mamma and sisters at Home. Four of these five things were vices which the "Shikarris" objected to and set themselves to eradicate. Everyone knows how subalterns are, by brother subalterns, softened and not permitted to be ferocious. It is good and wholesome, and does no one any harm, unless tempers are lost; and then there is trouble. There was a man once—but that is another story.

The "Shikarris" shikarred The Worm very much, and he bore everything without winking. He was so good and so anxious to learn, and flushed so pink, that his education was cut short, and he was left to his own devices by everyone except the Senior Subaltern who continued to make life a burden to The Worm. The Senior Subaltern meant no harm; but his chaff was coarse, and he didn't quite understand where to stop. He had been waiting too long for his Company; and that always sours a man. Also he was in love, which made him worse.

One day, after he had borrowed The Worm's trap for a lady who never existed, had used it himself all the afternoon, had sent a note to The Worm, purporting to come from the lady, and was telling the Mess all about it, The Worm rose in his place and said, in his quiet, ladylike voice:—"That was a very pretty sell; but I'll lay you a month's pay to a month's pay when you get your step, that I work a sell on you that you'll remember for the rest of your days, and the Regiment after you when you're dead or broke." The Worm wasn't angry in the least, and the rest of the Mess shouted. Then the Senior Subaltern looked at The Worm from the boots upward, and down again and said: "Done, Baby." The Worm took the rest of the Mess to witness that the bet had been taken, and retired into a book with a sweet smile.

Two months passed, and the Senior Subaltern still educated The Worm, who began to move about a little more as the hot weather came on. I have said that the Senior Subaltern was in love. The curious thing is that a girl was in love with the Senior Subaltern. Though the Colonel said awful things, and the Majors snorted, and married Captains looked unutterable wisdom, and the juniors scoffed, those two were engaged.

The Senior Subaltern was so pleased with getting his Company and his acceptance at the same time that he forgot to bother The Worm. The girl was a pretty girl, and had money of her own. She does not come into this story at all.

One night, at beginning of the hot weather, all the Mess, except The Worm who had gone to his own room to write Home letters, were sitting on the platform outside the Mess House. The Band had finished playing, but no one wanted to go in. And the Captains' wives were there also. The folly of a man in love is unlimited. The Senior Subaltern had been holding forth on the merits of the girl he was engaged to, and the ladies were purring approval, while the men yawned, when there was a rustle of skirts in the dark, and a tired, faint voice lifted itself.

"Where's my husband?"

I do not wish in the least to reflect on the morality of the "Shikarris"; but it is on record that four men jumped up as if they had been shot. Three of them were married men. Perhaps they were afraid that their wives had come from Home unbeknownst. The fourth said that he had acted on the impulse of the moment. He explained this afterwards.

Then the voice cried: "Oh Lionel!" Lionel was the Senior Subaltern's name. A woman came into the little circle of light by the candles on the peg tables, stretching out her hands to the dark where the Senior Subaltern was, and sobbing. We rose to our feet, feeling that things were going to happen and ready to believe the worst. In this bad, small world of ours, one knows so little of the life of the next man— which, after all, is entirely his own concern—that one is not surprised when a crash comes. Anything might turn up any day for anyone. Perhaps the Senior Subaltern had been trapped in his youth. Men are crippled that way occasionally. We didn't know; we wanted to hear; and the Captains' wives were as anxious as we. If he had been trapped, he was to be excused; for the woman from nowhere, in the dusty shoes and gray traveling dress, was very lovely, with black hair and great eyes full of tears. She was tall, with a fine figure, and her voice had a running sob in it pitiful to hear. As soon as the Senior Subaltern stood up, she threw her arms round his neck, and called him "my darling" and said she could not bear waiting alone in England, and his letters were so short and cold, and she was his to the end of the world, and would he forgive her? This did not sound quite like a lady's way of speaking. It was too demonstrative.

Things seemed black indeed, and the Captains' wives peered under their eyebrows at the Senior Subaltern, and the Colonel's face set like the Day of Judgment framed in gray bristles, and no one spoke for a while.

Next the Colonel said, very shortly: "Well, sir?" and the woman sobbed afresh. The Senior Subaltern was half choked with the arms round his neck, but he gasped out: "It's a d——d lie! I never had a wife in my life!" "Don't swear," said the Colonel. "Come into the Mess. We must sift this clear somehow," and he sighed to himself, for he believed in his "Shikarris," did the Colonel.

We trooped into the anteroom, under the full lights, and there we saw how beautiful the woman was. She stood up in the middle of us all, sometimes choking with crying, then hard and proud, and then holding out her arms to the Senior Subaltern. It was like the fourth act of a tragedy. She told us how the Senior Subaltern had married her when he was Home on leave eighteen months before; and she seemed to know all that we knew, and more too, of his people and his past life. He was white and ashy gray, trying now and again to break into the torrent of her words; and we, noting how lovely she was and what a criminal he looked, esteemed him a beast of the worst kind. We felt sorry for him, though.

I shall never forget the indictment of the Senior Subaltern by his wife. Nor will he. It was so sudden, rushing out of the dark, unannounced, into our dull lives. The Captains' wives stood back; but their eyes were alight, and you could see that they had already convicted and sentenced the Senior Subaltern. The Colonel seemed five years older. One Major was shading his eyes with his hand and watching the woman from underneath it. Another was chewing his mustache and smiling quietly as if he were witnessing a play. Full in the open space in the center, by the whist tables, the Senior Subaltern's terrier was hunting for fleas. I remember all this as clearly as though a photograph were in my hand. I remember the look of horror on the Senior Subaltern's face. It was rather like seeing a man hanged; but much more interesting. Finally, the woman wound up by saying that the Senior Subaltern carried a double F.M. in tattoo on his left shoulder. We all knew that, and to our innocent minds it seemed to clinch the matter. But one of the Bachelor Majors said very politely: "I presume that your marriage certificate would be more to the purpose?"

That roused the woman. She stood up and sneered at the Senior Subaltern for a cur, and abused the Major and the Colonel and all the rest. Then she wept, and then she pulled a paper from her breast, saying imperially: "Take that! And let my husband—my lawfully wedded husband—read it aloud—if he dare!"

There was a hush, and the men looked into each other's eyes as the Senior Subaltern came forward in a dazed and dizzy way, and took the paper. We were wondering, as we stared, whether there was anything against any one of us that might turn up later on. The Senior Subaltern's throat was dry; but, as he ran his eye over the paper, he broke out into a hoarse cackle of relief, and said to the woman: "You young blackguard!"

But the woman had fled through a door, and on the paper was written: "This is to certify that I, The Worm, have paid in full my debts to the Senior Subaltern, and, further, that the Senior Subaltern is my debtor, by agreement on the 23d of February, as by the Mess attested, to the extent of one month's Captain's pay, in the lawful currency of the India Empire."

Then a deputation set off for The Worm's quarters and found him, betwixt and between, unlacing his stays, with the hat, wig, serge dress, etc., on the bed. He came over as he was, and the "Shikarris" shouted till the Gunners' Mess sent over to know if they might have a share of the fun. I think we were all, except the Colonel and the Senior Subaltern, a little disappointed that the scandal had come to nothing. But that is human nature. There could be no two words about The Worm's acting. It leaned as near to a nasty tragedy as anything this side of a joke can. When most of the Subalterns sat upon him with sofa cushions to find out why he had not said that acting was his strong point, he answered very quietly: "I don't think you ever asked me. I used to act at Home with my sisters." But no acting with girls could account for The Worm's display that night. Personally, I think it was in bad taste. Besides being dangerous. There is no sort of use in playing with fire, even for fun.

The "Shikarris" made him President of the Regimental Dramatic Club; and, when the Senior Subaltern paid up his debt, which he did at once, The Worm sank the money in scenery and dresses. He was a good Worm; and the "Shikarris" are proud of him. The only drawback is that he has been christened "Mrs. Senior Subaltern"; and, as there are now two Mrs. Senior Subalterns in the Station, this is sometimes confusing to strangers.

Later on, I will tell you of a case something like this, but with all the jest left out and nothing in it but real trouble.

A. CONAN DOYLE

A CASE OF IDENTITY

"My dear fellow," said Sherlock Holmes, as we sat on either side of the fire in his lodgings at Baker Street, "life is infinitely stranger than anything which the mind of man can invent. We would not dare to conceive the things which are really mere commonplaces of existence. If we could fly out of that window hand in hand, hover over this great city, gently remove the roofs, and peep in at the queer things which are going on, the strange coincidences, the plannings, the cross-purposes, the wonderful chains of events, working through generations, and leading to the most outré results, it would make all fiction, with its conventionalities and foreseen conclusions, most stale and unprofitable."

"And yet I am not convinced of it," I answered. "The cases which come to light in the papers are, as a rule, bald enough, and vulgar enough. We have in our police reports realism pushed to its extreme limits, and yet the result is, it must be confessed, neither fascinating nor artistic."

"A certain selection and discretion must be used in producing a realistic effect," remarked Holmes. "This is wanting in the police report, where more stress is laid perhaps upon the platitudes of the magistrate than upon the details, which to an observer contain the vital essence of the whole matter. Depend upon it, there is nothing so unnatural as the commonplace."

I smiled and shook my head. "I can quite understand your thinking so," I said. "Of course, in your position of unofficial adviser and helper to everybody who is absolutely puzzled, throughout three continents, you are brought in contact with all that is strange and bizarre. But here"—I picked up the morning paper from the ground—"let us put it to a practical test. Here is the first heading upon which I come. 'A husband's cruelty to his wife.' There is half a column of print, but I know without reading it that it is all perfectly familiar to me. There is, of course, the other woman, the drink, the push, the blow, the bruise, the unsympathetic sister or landlady. The crudest of writers could invent nothing more crude."

"Indeed your example is an unfortunate one for your argument," said Holmes, taking the paper, and glancing his eye down it. "This is

66

the Dundas separation case, and, as it happens, I was engaged in clearing up some small points in connection with it. The husband was a teetotaler, there was no other woman, and the conduct complained of was that he had drifted into the habit of winding up every meal by taking out his false teeth and hurling them at his wife, which you will allow is not an action likely to occur to the imagination of the average story teller. Take a pinch of snuff, doctor, and acknowledge that I have scored over you in your example."

He held out his snuffbox of old gold, with a great amethyst in the center of the lid. Its splendor was in such contrast to his homely ways and simple life that I could not help commenting upon it.

"Ah!" said he, "I forgot that I had not seen you for some weeks. It is a little souvenir from the King of Bohemia, in return for my assistance in the case of the Irene Adler papers."

"And the ring?" I asked, glancing at a remarkable brilliant which sparkled upon his finger.

"It was from the reigning family of Holland, though the matter in which I served them was of such delicacy that I cannot confide it even to you, who have been good enough to chronicle one or two of my little problems."

"And have you any on hand just now?" I asked with interest.

"Some ten or twelve, but none which present any features of interest. They are important, you understand, without being interesting. Indeed I have found that it is usually in unimportant matters that there is a field for the observation, and for the quick analysis of cause and effect which gives the charm to an investigation. The larger crimes are apt to be the simpler, for the bigger the crime, the more obvious, as a rule, is the motive. In these cases, save for one rather intricate matter which has been referred to me from Marseilles, there is nothing which presents any features of interest. It is possible, however, that I may have something better before very many minutes are over, for this is one of my clients, or I am much mistaken."

He had risen from his chair, and was standing between the parted blinds, gazing down into the dull, neutral-tinted London street. Looking over his shoulder, I saw that on the pavement opposite there stood a large woman with a heavy fur boa round her neck, and a large curling red feather in a broad-brimmed hat which was tilted in a coquettish Duchess-of-Devonshire fashion over her ear.

From under this great panoply she peeped up in a nervous, hesitating fashion at our windows, while her body oscillated backward and forward, and her fingers fidgeted with her glove buttons. Suddenly, with a plunge, as of the swimmer who leaves the bank, she hurried across the road, and we heard the sharp clang of the bell.

"I have seen those symptoms before," said Holmes, throwing his cigarette into the fire. "Oscillation upon the pavement always means an affaire de coeur. She would like advice, but is not sure that the matter is not too delicate for communication. And yet even here we may discriminate. When a woman has been seriously wronged by a man, she no longer oscillates, and the usual symptom is a broken bell wire. Here we may take it that there is a love matter, but that the maiden is not so much angry as perplexed or grieved. But here she comes in person to resolve our doubts."

As he spoke, there was a tap at the door, and the boy in buttons entered to announce Miss Mary Sutherland, while the lady herself loomed behind his small black figure like a full-sailed merchantman behind a tiny pilot boat. Sherlock Holmes welcomed her with the easy courtesy for which he was remarkable, and having closed the door, and bowed her into an armchair, he looked her over in the minute and yet abstracted fashion which was peculiar to him.

"Do you not find," he said, "that with your short sight it is a little trying to do so much typewriting?"

"I did at first," she answered, "but now I know where the letters are without looking." Then, suddenly realizing the full purport of his words, she gave a violent start, and looked up with fear and astonishment upon her broad, good-humored face. "You've heard about me, Mr. Holmes," she cried, "else how could you know all that?"

"Never mind," said Holmes, laughing, "it is my business to know things. Perhaps I have trained myself to see what others overlook. If not, why should you come to consult me?"

"I came to you, sir, because I heard of you from Mrs. Etherege, whose husband you found so easily when the police and everyone had given him up for dead. Oh, Mr. Holmes, I wish you would do as much for me. I'm not rich, but still I have a hundred a year in my own right, besides the little that I make by the machine, and I would give it all to know what has become of Mr. Hosmer Angel."

"Why did you come away to consult me in such a hurry?" asked Sherlock Holmes, with his finger tips together, and his eyes to the ceiling.

Again a startled look came over the somewhat vacuous face of Miss Mary Sutherland. "Yes, I did bang out of the house," she said, "for it made me angry to see the easy way in which Mr. Windibank—that is, my father—took it all. He would not go to the police, and he would not go to you, and so at last, as he would do nothing, and kept on saying that there was no harm done, it made me mad, and I just on with my things and came right away to you."

"Your father?" said Holmes. "Your stepfather, surely, since the name is different."

"Yes, my stepfather. I call him father, though it sounds funny, too, for he is only five years and two months older than myself."

"And your mother is alive?"

"Oh, yes; mother is alive and well. I wasn't best pleased, Mr. Holmes, when she married again so soon after father's death, and a

68

man who was nearly fifteen years younger than herself. Father was a plumber in the Tottenham Court Road, and he left a tidy business behind him, which mother carried on with Mr. Hardy, the foreman; but when Mr. Windibank came he made her sell the business, for he was very superior, being a traveler in wines. They got four thousand seven hundred for the good-will and interest, which wasn't near as much as father could have got if he had been alive."

I had expected to see Sherlock Holmes impatient under this rambling and inconsequential narrative, but, on the contrary, he had listened with the greatest concentration of attention.

"Your own little income," he asked, "does it come out of the business?"

"Oh, no, sir. It is quite separate, and was left me by my Uncle Ned in Auckland. It is in New Zealand stock, paying four and half per cent. Two thousand five hundred pounds was the amount, but I can only touch the interest."

"You interest me extremely," said Holmes. "And since you draw so large a sum as a hundred a year, with what you earn into the bargain, you no doubt travel a little, and indulge yourself in every way. I believe that a single lady can get on very nicely upon an income of about sixty pounds."

"I could do with much less than that, Mr. Holmes, but you understand that as long as I live at home I don't wish to be a burden to them, and so they have the use of the money just while I am staying with them. Of course that is only just for the time. Mr. Windibank draws my interest every quarter, and pays it over to mother, and I find that I can do pretty well with what I earn at typewriting. It brings me twopence a sheet, and I can often do from fifteen to twenty sheets in a day."

"You have made your position very clear to me," said Holmes. "This is my friend, Doctor Watson, before whom you can speak as freely as before myself. Kindly tell us now all about your connection with Mr. Hosmer Angel."

A flush stole over Miss Sutherland's face, and she picked nervously at the fringe of her jacket. "I met him first at the gasfitters' ball," she said. "They used to send father tickets when he was alive, and then afterwards they remembered us, and sent them to mother. Mr. Windibank did not wish us to go. He never did wish us to go anywhere. He would get quite mad if I wanted so much as to join a Sunday School treat. But this time I was set on going, and I would go, for what right had he to prevent? He said the folk were not fit for us to know, when all father's friends were to be there. And he said that I had nothing fit to wear, when I had my purple plush that I had never so much as taken out of the drawer. At last, when nothing else would do, he went off to France upon the business of the firm; but we went, mother and I, with

69

Mr. Hardy, who used to be our foreman, and it was there I met Mr. Hosmer Angel."

"I suppose," said Holmes, "that when Mr. Windibank came back from France, he was very annoyed at your having gone to the ball?"

"Oh, well, he was very good about it. He laughed, I remember, and shrugged his shoulders, and said there was no use denying anything to a woman, for she would have her way."

"I see. Then at the gasfitters' ball you met, as I understand, a gentleman called Mr. Hosmer Angel?"

"Yes, sir. I met him that night, and he called next day to ask if we had got home all safe, and after that we met him—that is to say, Mr. Holmes, I met him twice for walks, but after that father came back again, and Mr. Hosmer Angel could not come to the house any more."

"No?"

"Well, you know, father didn't like anything of the sort. He wouldn't have any visitors if he could help it, and he used to say that a woman should be happy in her own family circle. But then, as I used to say to mother, a woman wants her own circle to begin with, and I had not got mine yet."

"But how about Mr. Hosmer Angel? Did he make no attempt to see you?"

"Well, father was going off to France again in a week, and Hosmer wrote and said that it would be safer and better not to see each other until he had gone. We could write in the meantime, and he used to write every day. I took the letters in the morning, so there was no need for father to know."

"Were you engaged to the gentleman at this time?"

"Oh, yes, Mr. Holmes. We were engaged after the first walk that we took. Hosmer—Mr. Angel—was a cashier in an office in Leadenhall Street—and—"

"What office?"

"That's the worst of it, Mr. Holmes; I don't know."

"Where did he live, then?"

"He slept on the premises."

"And you don't know his address?"

"No—except that it was Leadenhall Street."

"Where did you address your letters, then?"

"To the Leadenhall Street Post Office, to be left till called for. He said that if they were sent to the office he would be chaffed by all the other clerks about having letters from a lady, so I offered to typewrite them, like he did his, but he wouldn't have that, for he said that when I wrote them they seemed to come from me, but when they were typewritten he always felt that the machine had come between us. That will just show you how fond he was of me, Mr. Holmes, and the little things that he would think of."

"It was most suggestive," said Holmes. "It has long been an

axiom of mine that the little things are infinitely the most important. Can you remember any other little things about Mr. Hosmer Angel?"

"He was a very shy man, Mr. Holmes. He would rather walk with me in the evening than in the daylight, for he said that he hated to be conspicuous. Very retiring and gentlemanly he was. Even his voice was gentle. He'd had the quinsy and swollen glands when he was young, he told me, and it had left him with a weak throat and a hesitating, whispering fashion of speech. He was always well dressed, very neat and plain, but his eyes were weak, just as mine are, and he wore tinted glasses against the glare."

"Well, and what happened when Mr. Windibank, your stepfather, returned to France?"

"Mr. Hosmer Angel came to the house again, and proposed that we should marry before father came back. He was in dreadful earnest, and made me swear, with my hands on the Testament, that whatever happened I would always be true to him. Mother said he was quite right to make me swear, and that it was a sign of his passion. Mother was all in his favor from the first, and was even fonder of him than I was. Then, when they talked of marrying within the week, I began to ask about father; but they both said never to mind about father, but just to tell him afterwards and mother said she would make it all right with him. I didn't quite like that, Mr. Holmes. It seemed funny that I should ask his leave, as he was only a few years older than me; but I didn't want to do anything on the sly, so I wrote to father at Bordeaux, where the company has its French offices, but the letter came back to me on the very morning of the wedding."

"It missed him, then?"

"Yes, sir, for he had started to England just before it arrived."

"Ha! that was unfortunate. Your wedding was arranged, then, for the Friday. Was it to be in church?"

"Yes, sir, but very quietly. It was to be at St. Saviour's, near King's Cross, and we were to have breakfast afterwards at the St. Pancras Hotel. Hosmer came for us in a hansom, but as there were two of us, he put us both into it, and stepped himself into a four-wheeler, which happened to be the only other cab in the street. We got to the church first, and when the four-wheeler drove up we waited for him to step out, but he never did, and when the cabman got down from the box and looked, there was no one there! The cabman said that he could not imagine what had become of him, for he had seen him get in with his own eyes. That was last Friday, Mr. Holmes, and I have never seen or heard anything since then to throw any light upon what became of him."

"It seems to me that you have been very shamefully treated," said Holmes.

"Oh, no, sir! He was too good and kind to leave me so. Why, all the morning he was saying to me that, whatever happened, I was to be true; and that even if something quite unforeseen occurred to separate us, I was always to remember that I was pledged to him, and that he would claim his pledge sooner or later. It seemed strange talk for a wedding morning, but what has happened since gives a meaning to it."

"Most certainly it does. Your own opinion is, then, that some unforeseen catastrophe has occurred to him?"

"Yes, sir. I believe that he foresaw some danger, or else he would not have talked so. And then I think that what he foresaw happened."

"But you have no notion as to what it could have been?"

"None."

"One more question. How did your mother take the matter?"

"She was angry, and said that I was never to speak of the matter again."

"And your father? Did you tell him?"

"Yes, and he seemed to think, with me, that something had happened, and that I should hear of Hosmer again. As he said, what interest could anyone have in bringing me to the door of the church, and then leaving me? Now, if he had borrowed my money, or if he had married me and got my money settled on him, there might be some reason; but Hosmer was very independent about money, and never would look at a shilling of mine. And yet what could have happened? And why could he not write? Oh! it drives me half mad to think of, and I can't sleep a wink at night." She pulled a little handkerchief out of her muff, and began to sob heavily into it.

"I shall glance into the case for you," said Holmes, rising, "and I have no doubt that we shall reach some definite result. Let the weight of the matter rest upon me now, and do not let your mind dwell upon it further. Above all, try to let Mr. Hosmer Angel vanish from your memory, as he has done from your life."

"Then you don't think I'll see him again?"

"I fear not."

"Then what has happened to him?"

"You will leave that question in my hands. I should like an accurate description of him, and any letters of his which you can spare."

"I advertised for him in last Saturday's Chronicle," said she. "Here is the slip, and here are four letters from him."

"Thank you. And your address?"

"No. 31 Lyon Place, Camberwell."

"Mr. Angel's address you never had, I understand. Where is your father's place of business?"

"He travels for Westhouse & Marbank, the great claret importers of Fenchurch Street."

"Thank you. You have made your statement very clearly. You will leave the papers here, and remember the advice which I have given you. Let the whole incident be a sealed book, and do not allow it to affect your life."

"You are very kind, Mr. Holmes, but I cannot do that. I shall be true to Hosmer. He shall find me ready when he comes back."

For all the preposterous hat and the vacuous face, there was something noble in the simple faith of our visitor which compelled our respect. She laid her little bundle of papers upon the table, and went her way, with a promise to come again whenever she might be summoned.

Sherlock Holmes sat silent for a few minutes with his finger tips still pressed together, his legs stretched out in front of him, and his gaze directed upward to the ceiling. Then he took down from the rack the old and oily clay pipe, which was to him as a counselor, and, having lighted it, he leaned back in his chair, with thick blue cloud wreaths spinning up from him, and a look of infinite languor in his face.

"Quite an interesting study, that maiden," he observed. "I found her more interesting than her little problem, which, by the way, is rather a trite one. You will find parallel cases, if you consult my index, in Andover in '77, and there was something of the sort at The Hague last year. Old as is the idea, however, there were one or two details which were new to me. But the maiden herself was most instructive."

"You appeared to read a good deal upon her which was quite invisible to me," I remarked.

"Not invisible, but unnoticed, Watson. You did not know where to look, and so you missed all that was important. I can never bring you to realize the importance of sleeves, the suggestiveness of thumb nails, or the great issues that may hang from a boot lace. Now, what did you gather from that woman's appearance? Describe it."

"Well, she had a slate-colored, broad-brimmed straw hat, with a feather of a brickish red. Her jacket was black, with black beads sewed upon it and a fringe of little black jet ornaments. Her dress was brown, rather darker than coffee color, with a little purple plush at the neck and sleeves. Her gloves were grayish, and were worn through at the right forefinger. Her boots I didn't observe. She had small round, hanging gold earrings, and a general air of being fairly well-to-do, in a vulgar, comfortable, easy-going way."

Sherlock Holmes clapped his hands softly together and chuckled.

"'Pon my word, Watson, you are coming along wonderfully. You have really done very well indeed. It is true that you have missed everything of importance, but you have hit upon the method, and you have a quick eye for color. Never trust to general impressions, my boy, but concentrate yourself upon details. My first glance is always at a woman's sleeve. In a man it is perhaps better first to take the knee of the trouser. As you observe, this woman had plush upon her sleeve, which is a most useful material for showing traces. The double line a little above the wrist, where the typewritist presses against the table, was beautifully defined. The sewing machine, of the hand type, leaves a similar mark, but only on the left arm, and on the side of it farthest from the thumb, instead of being right across the broadest part, as this was. I then glanced at her face, and observing the dint of a pince-nez at either side of her nose, I ventured a remark upon short sight and typewriting, which seemed to surprise her."

"It surprised me."

"But, surely, it was very obvious. I was then much surprised and interested on glancing down to observe that, though the boots which she was wearing were not unlike each other, they were really odd ones, the one having a slightly decorated toe cap and the other a plain one. One was buttoned only in the two lower buttons out of five, and the other at the first, third, and fifth. Now, when you see that a young lady, otherwise neatly dressed, has come away from home with odd boots, half-buttoned, it is no great deduction to say that she came away in a hurry."

"And what else?" I asked, keenly interested, as I always was, by my friend's incisive reasoning.

"I noted, in passing, that she had written a note before leaving home, but after being fully dressed. You observed that her right glove was torn at the forefinger, but you did not, apparently, see that both glove and finger were stained with violet ink. She had written in a hurry, and dipped her pen too deep. It must have been this morning, or the mark would not remain clear upon the finger. All this is amusing, though rather elementary, but I must go back to business, Watson. Would you mind reading me the advertised description of Mr. Hosmer Angel?"

I held the little printed slip to the light. "Missing," it said, "on the morning of the fourteenth, a gentleman named Hosmer Angel. About five feet seven inches in height; strongly built, sallow complexion, black hair, a little bald in the center, bushy black side-whiskers and mustache; tinted glasses; slight infirmity of speech. Was dressed, when last seen, in black frock-coat faced with silk, black waistcoat, gold Albert chain, and gray Harris tweed trousers, with brown gaiters over elastic-sided boots. Known to have been employed in an office in Leadenhall Street. Anybody bringing," etc., etc.

"That will do," said Holmes. "As to the letters," he continued, glancing over them, "they are very commonplace. Absolutely no clew in them to Mr. Angel, save that he quotes Balzac once. There is one remarkable point, however, which will no doubt strike you."

"They are typewritten," I remarked.

"Not only that, but the signature is typewritten. Look at the neat little 'Hosmer Angel' at the bottom. There is a date, you see, but no superscription except Leadenhall Street, which is rather vague. The point about the signature is very suggestive—in fact, we may call it conclusive."

"Of what?"

"My dear fellow, is it possible you do not see how strongly it bears upon the case?"

"I cannot say that I do, unless it were that he wished to be able to deny his signature if an action for breach of promise were instituted."

"No, that was not the point. However, I shall write two letters which should settle the matter. One is to a firm in the City, the other is to the young lady's stepfather, Mr. Windibank, asking him whether he could meet us here at six o'clock to-morrow evening. It is just as well that we should do business with the male relatives. And now, doctor, we can do nothing until the answers to those letters come, so we may put our little problem upon the shelf for the interim."

I had had so many reasons to believe in my friend's subtle powers of reasoning, and extraordinary energy in action, that I felt that he must have some solid grounds for the assured and easy demeanor with which he treated the singular mystery which he had been called upon to fathom. Once only had I known him to fail, in the case of the King of Bohemia and the Irene Adler photograph, but when I looked back to the weird business of the "Sign of the Four," and the extraordinary circumstances connected with the "Study in Scarlet," I felt that it would be a strange tangle indeed which he could not unravel.

I left him then, still puffing at his black clay pipe, with the conviction that when I came again on the next evening I would find that he held in his hands all the clews which would lead up to the identity of the disappearing bridegroom of Miss Mary Sutherland.

A professional case of great gravity was engaging my own attention at the time, and the whole of next day I was busy at the bedside of the sufferer. It was not until close upon six o'clock that I found myself free, and was able to spring into a hansom and drive to Baker Street, half afraid that I might be too late to assist at the dénouement of the little mystery. I found Sherlock Holmes alone, however, half asleep, with his long, thin form curled up in the recesses of his armchair. A formidable array of bottles and test-tubes, with the pungent, cleanly smell of hydrochloric acid, told me that he had spent his day in the chemical work which was so dear to him.

"Well, have you solved it?" I asked as I entered.

"Yes. It was the bisulphate of baryta."

"No, no; the mystery!" I cried.

"Oh, that! I thought of the salt that I have been working upon. There was never any mystery in the matter, though, as I said yesterday, some of the details are of interest. The only drawback is that there is no law, I fear, that can touch the scoundrel."

"Who was he, then, and what was his object in deserting Miss Sutherland?"

The question was hardly out of my mouth, and Holmes had not

75

yet opened his lips to reply, when we heard a heavy footfall in the passage, and a tap at the door.

"This is the girl's stepfather, Mr. James Windibank," said Holmes. "He has written to me to say that he would be here at six. Come in!"

The man who entered was a sturdy, middle-sized fellow, some thirty years of age, clean shaven, and sallow-skinned, with a bland, insinuating manner, and a pair of wonderfully sharp and penetrating gray eyes. He shot a questioning glance at each of us, placed his shiny top hat upon the sideboard, and, with a slight bow, sidled down into the nearest chair.

"Good evening, Mr. James Windibank," said Holmes. "I think this typewritten letter is from you, in which you made an appointment with me for six o'clock?"

"Yes, sir. I am afraid that I am a little late, but I am not quite my own master, you know. I am sorry that Miss Sutherland has troubled you about this little matter, for I think it is far better not to wash linen of the sort in public. It was quite against my wishes that she came, but she is a very excitable, impulsive girl, as you may have noticed, and she is not easily controlled when she has made up her mind on a point. Of course, I did not mind you so much, as you are not connected with the official police, but it is not pleasant to have a family misfortune like this noised abroad. Besides, it is a useless expense, for how could you possibly find this Hosmer Angel?"

"On the contrary," said Holmes, quietly, "I have every reason to believe that I will succeed in discovering Mr. Hosmer Angel."

Mr. Windibank gave a violent start, and dropped his gloves. "I am delighted to hear it," he said.

"It is a curious thing," remarked Holmes, "that a typewriter has really quite as much individuality as a man's handwriting. Unless they are quite new no two of them write exactly alike. Some letters get more worn than others, and some wear only on one side. Now, you remark in this note of yours, Mr. Windibank, that in every case there is some little slurring over the e, and a slight defect in the tail of the r. There are fourteen other characteristics, but those are the more obvious."

"We do all our correspondence with this machine at the office, and no doubt it is a little worn," our visitor answered, glancing keenly at Holmes with his bright little eyes.

"And now I will show you what is really a very interesting study, Mr. Windibank," Holmes continued. "I think of writing another little monograph some of these days on the typewriter and its relation to crime. It is a subject to which I have devoted some little attention. I have here four letters which purport to come from the missing man. They are all typewritten. In each case, not only are the e's slurred and the r's tailless, but you will observe, if you care to use my magnifying lens, that the fourteen other characteristics to which I have alluded are there as well."

Mr. Windibank sprung out of his chair, and picked up his hat. "I cannot waste time over this sort of fantastic talk, Mr. Holmes," he said. "If you can catch the man, catch him, and let me know when you have done it."

"Certainly," said Holmes, stepping over and turning the key in the door. "I let you know, then, that I have caught him!"

"What! where?" shouted Mr. Windibank, turning white to his lips, and glancing about him like a rat in a trap.

"Oh, it won't do—really it won't," said Holmes, suavely. "There is no possible getting out of it, Mr. Windibank. It is quite too transparent, and it was a very bad compliment when you said that it was impossible for me to solve so simple a question. That's right! Sit down, and let us talk it over."

Our visitor collapsed into a chair, with a ghastly face, and a glitter of moisture on his brow. "It—it's not actionable," he stammered.

"I am very much afraid that it is not; but between ourselves, Windibank, it was as cruel, and selfish, and heartless a trick in a petty way as ever came before me. Now, let me just run over the course of events, and you will contradict me if I go wrong."

The man sat huddled up in his chair, with his head sunk upon his breast, like one who is utterly crushed. Holmes stuck his feet up on the corner of the mantelpiece, and, leaning back with his hands in his pockets, began talking, rather to himself, as it seemed, than to us.

"The man married a woman very much older than himself for her money," said he, "and he enjoyed the use of the money of the daughter as long as she lived with them. It was a considerable sum, for people in their position, and the loss of it would have made a serious difference. It was worth an effort to preserve it. The daughter was of a good, amiable disposition, but affectionate and warm-hearted in her ways, so that it was evident that with her fair personal advantages, and her little income, she would not be allowed to remain single long. Now her marriage would mean, of course, the loss of a hundred a year, so what does her stepfather do to prevent it? He takes the obvious course of keeping her at home, and forbidding her to seek the company of people of her own age. But soon he found that that would not answer forever. She became restive, insisted upon her rights, and finally announced her positive intention of going to a certain ball. What does her clever stepfather do then? He conceives an idea more creditable to his head than to his heart. With the connivance and assistance of his wife, he disguised himself, covered those keen eyes with tinted glasses masked the face with a mustache and a pair of bushy whiskers, sunk that clear voice into an insinuating whisper, and doubly secure on account of the girl's short sight, he appears as Mr. Hosmer Angel, and keeps off other lovers by making love himself."

"It was only a joke at first," groaned our visitor. "We never thought that she would have been so carried away."

"Very likely not. However that may be, the young lady was very decidedly carried away, and having quite made up her mind that her stepfather was in France, the suspicion of treachery never for an instant entered her mind. She was flattered by the gentleman's attentions, and the effect was increased by the loudly expressed admiration of her mother. Then Mr. Angel began to call, for it was obvious that the matter should be pushed as far as if would go, if a real effect were to be produced. There were meetings, and an engagement, which would finally secure the girl's affections from turning toward anyone else. But the deception could not be kept up forever. These pretended journeys to France were rather cumbrous. The thing to do was clearly to bring the business to an end in such a dramatic manner that it would leave a permanent impression upon the young lady's mind, and prevent her from looking upon any other suitor for some time to come. Hence those vows of fidelity exacted upon a Testament, and hence also the allusions to a possibility of something happening on the very morning of the wedding. James Windibank wished Miss Sutherland to be so bound to Hosmer Angel, and so uncertain as to his fate, that for ten years to come, at any rate, she would not listen to another man. As far as the church door he brought her, and then, as he could go no farther, he conveniently vanished away by the old trick of stepping in at one door of a four-wheeler and out at the other. I think that that was the chain of events, Mr. Windibank!"

Our visitor had recovered something of his assurance while Holmes had been talking, and he rose from his chair now with a cold sneer upon his pale face.

"It may be so, or it may not, Mr. Holmes," said he; "but if you are so very sharp you ought to be sharp enough to know that it is you who are breaking the law now, and not me. I have done nothing actionable from the first, but as long as you keep that door locked you lay yourself open to an action for assault and illegal constraint."

"The law cannot, as you say, touch you," said Holmes, unlocking and throwing open the door, "yet there never was a man who deserved punishment more. If the young lady has a brother or a friend, he ought to lay a whip across your shoulders. By Jove!" he continued, flushing up at the sight of the bitter sneer upon the man's face, "it is not part of my duties to my client, but here's a hunting crop handy, and I think I shall just treat myself to—" He took two swift steps to the whip, but before he could grasp it there was a wild clatter of steps upon the stairs, the heavy hall door banged, and from the window we could see Mr. James Windibank running at the top of his speed down the road.

"There's a cold-blooded scoundrel!" said Holmes, laughing as he threw himself down into his chair once more. "That fellow will rise from crime to crime until he does something very bad and ends on a gallows. The case has, in some respects, been not entirely devoid of interest."

"I cannot now entirely see all the steps of your reasoning," I remarked.

"Well, of course it was obvious from the first that this Mr. Hosmer Angel must have some strong object for his curious conduct, and it was equally clear that the only man who really profited by the incident, as far as we could see, was the stepfather. Then the fact that the two men were never together, but that the one always appeared when the other was away, was suggestive. So were the tinted spectacles and the curious voice, which both hinted at a disguise, as did the bushy whiskers. My suspicions were all confirmed by his peculiar action in typewriting his signature, which, of course, inferred that his handwriting was so familiar to her that she would recognize even the smallest sample of it. You see all these isolated facts, together with many minor ones, all pointed in the same direction."

"And how did you verify them?"

"Having once spotted my man, it was easy to get corroboration. I knew the firm for which this man worked. Having taken the printed description, I eliminated everything from it which could be the result of a disguise,—the whiskers, the glasses, the voice,—and I sent it to the firm with a request that they would inform me whether it answered to the description of any of their travelers. I had already noticed the peculiarities of the typewriter, and I wrote to the man himself at his business address, asking him if he would come here. As I expected, his reply was typewritten, and revealed the same trivial but characteristic defects. The same post brought me a letter from Westhouse & Marbank, of Fenchurch Street, to say that the description tallied in every respect with that of their employee, James Windibank. Voilà tout!"

"And Miss Sutherland?"

"If I tell her she will not believe me. You may remember the old Persian saying, 'There is danger for him who taketh the tiger cub, and danger also for whoso snatcheth a delusion from a woman.' There is as much sense in Hafiz as in Horace, and as much knowledge of the world."

A SCANDAL IN BOHEMIA

I

To Sherlock Holmes she is always the woman. I have seldom heard him mention her under any other name. In his eyes she eclipses and predominates the whole of her sex. It was not that he felt any emotion akin to love for Irene Adler. All emotions, and that one particularly, were abhorrent to his cold, precise but admirably balanced mind. He was, I take it, the most perfect reasoning and observing machine that the world has seen; but as a lover, he would have placed himself in a false position. He never spoke of the softer passions, save with a gibe and a sneer. They were admirable things for the observer—excellent for drawing the veil from men's motives and actions. But for the trained reasoner to admit such intrusions into his own delicate and finely adjusted temperament was to introduce a distracting factor which might throw a doubt upon all his mental results. Grit in a sensitive instrument, or a crack in one of his own high-power lenses, would not be more disturbing that a strong emotion in a nature such as his. And yet there was but one woman to him, and that woman was the late Irene Adler, of dubious and questionable memory.

I had seen little of Holmes lately. My marriage had drifted us away from each other. My own complete happiness, and the home-centered interests which rise up around the man who first finds himself master of his own establishment, were sufficient to absorb all my attention; while Holmes, who loathed every form of society with his whole Bohemian soul, remained in our lodgings in Baker Street, buried among his old books, and alternating from week to week between cocaine and ambition, the drowsiness of the drug and the fierce energy of his own keen nature. He was still, as ever, deeply attracted by the study of crime, and occupied his immense faculties and extraordinary powers of observation in following out those clews, and clearing up those mysteries, which had been abandoned as hopeless by the official police. From time to time I heard some vague account of his doings; of his summons to Odessa in the case of the Trepoff murder, of his clearing up of the singular tragedy of the Atkinson brothers at Trincomalee, and finally of the mission which he had accomplished so delicately and successfully for the reigning family of Holland. Beyond these signs of his activity, however, which I merely shared with all the readers of the daily press, I knew little of my former friend and companion.

One night—it was on the 20th of March, 1888—I was returning

from a journey to a patient (for I had now returned to civil practice), when my way led me through Baker Street. As I passed the well-remembered door, which must always be associated in my mind with my wooing, and with the dark incidents of the Study in Scarlet, I was seized with a keen desire to see Holmes again, and to know how he was employing his extraordinary powers. His rooms were brilliantly lighted, and even as I looked up, I saw his tall, spare figure pass twice in a dark silhouette against the blind. He was pacing the room swiftly, eagerly, with his head sunk upon his chest, and his hands clasped behind him. To me, who knew his every mood and habit, his attitude and manner told their own story. He was at work again. He had risen out of his drug-created dreams, and was hot upon the scent of some new problem. I rang the bell, and was shown up to the chamber which had formerly been in part my own.

His manner was not effusive. It seldom was; but he was glad, I think, to see me. With hardly a word spoken, but with a kindly eye, he waved me to an armchair, threw across his case of cigars, and indicated a spirit case and a gasogene in the corner. Then he stood before the fire, and looked me over in his singular introspective fashion.

"Wedlock suits you," he remarked. "I think, Watson, that you have put on seven and a half pounds since I saw you."

"Seven," I answered.

"Indeed, I should have thought a little more. Just a trifle more, I fancy, Watson. And in practice again, I observe. You did not tell me that you intended to go into harness."

"Then how do you know?"

"I see it, I deduce it. How do I know that you have been getting yourself very wet lately, and that you have a most clumsy and careless servant girl?"

"My dear Holmes," said I, "this is too much. You would certainly have been burned had you lived a few centuries ago. It is true that I had a country walk on Thursday and came home in a dreadful mess; but as I have changed my clothes, I can't imagine how you deduce it. As to Mary Jane, she is incorrigible, and my wife has given her notice; but there again I fail to see how you work it out."

He chuckled to himself and rubbed his long nervous hands together.

"It is simplicity itself," said he, "my eyes tell me that on the inside of your left shoe, just where the firelight strikes it, the leather is scored by six almost parallel cuts. Obviously they have been caused by some one who has very carelessly scraped round the edges of the sole in order to remove crusted mud from it. Hence, you see, my double deduction that you had been out in vile weather, and that you had a particularly malignant boot-slicking specimen of the London slavey. As to your practice, if a gentleman walks into my rooms, smelling of iodoform, with a black mark of nitrate of silver upon his right

81

forefinger, and a bulge on the side of his top hat to show where he has secreted his stethoscope, I must be dull indeed if I do not pronounce him to be an active member of the medical profession."

I could not help laughing at the ease with which he, explained his process of deduction. "When I hear you give your reasons," I remarked, "the thing always appears to me so ridiculously simple that I could easily do it myself, though at each successive instance of your reasoning I am baffled, until you explain your process. And yet, I believe that my eyes are as good as yours."

"Quite so," he answered, lighting a cigarette, and throwing himself down into an armchair. "You see, but you do not observe. The distinction is clear. For example, you have frequently seen the steps which lead up from the hall to this room."

"Frequently."

"How often?"

"Well, some hundreds of times."

"Then how many are there?"

"How many? I don't know."

"Quite so! You have not observed. And yet you have seen. That is just my point. Now, I know there are seventeen steps, because I have both seen and observed. By the way, since you are interested in these little problems, and since you are good enough to chronicle one or two of my trifling experiences, you may be interested in this." He threw over a sheet of thick pink-tinted note paper which had been lying open upon the table. "It came by the last post," said he. "Read it aloud."

The note was undated, and without either signature or address.

"There will call upon you to-night, at a quarter to eight o'clock," it said, "a gentleman who desires to consult you upon a matter of the very deepest moment. Your recent services to one of the royal houses of Europe have shown that you are one who may safely be trusted with matters which are of an importance which can hardly be exaggerated. This account of you we have from all quarters received. Be in your chamber, then, at that hour, and do not take it amiss if your visitor wears a mask."

"This is indeed a mystery," I remarked. "What do you imagine that it means?"

"I have no data yet. It is a capital mistake to theorize before one has data. Insensibly one begins to twist facts to suit theories, instead of theories to suit facts. But the note itself—what do you deduce from it?"

I carefully examined the writing, and the paper upon which it was written.

"The man who wrote it was presumably well to do," I remarked, endeavoring to imitate my companion's processes. "Such paper could not be bought under half a crown a packet. It is peculiarly strong and stiff."

"Peculiar—that is the very word," said Holmes. "It is not an English paper at all. Hold it up to the light"

I did so, and saw a large E with a small g, a P and a large G with a small t woven into the texture of the paper.

"What do you make of that?" asked Holmes.

"The name of the maker, no doubt; or his monogram, rather."

"Not all. The G with the small t stands for 'Gesellschaft,' which is the German for 'Company.' It is a customary contraction like our 'Co.' P, of course, stands for 'Papier.' Now for the Eg. Let us glance at our 'Continental Gazetteer.'" He took down a heavy brown volume from his shelves. "Eglow, Eglonitz—here we are, Egria. It is in a German-speaking country—in Bohemia, not far from Carlsbad. 'Remarkable as being the scene of the death of Wallenstein, and for its numerous glass factories and paper mills.' Ha! ha! my boy, what do you make of that?" His eyes sparkled, and he sent up a great blue triumphant cloud from his cigarette.

"The paper was made in Bohemia," I said.

"Precisely. And the man who wrote the note is a German. Do you note the peculiar construction of the sentence—'This account of you we have from all quarters received'? A Frenchman or Russian could not have written that. It is the German who is so uncourteous to his verbs. It only remains, therefore, to discover what is wanted by this German who writes upon Bohemian paper, and prefers wearing a mask to showing his face. And here he comes, if I am not mistaken, to resolve all our doubts."

As he spoke there was the sharp sound of horses' hoofs and grating wheels against the curb, followed by a sharp pull at the bell. Holmes whistled.

"A pair, by the sound," said he. "Yes," he continued, glancing out of the window. "A nice little brougham and a pair of beauties. A hundred and fifty guineas apiece. There's money in this case, Watson, if there is nothing else."

"I think I had better go, Holmes."

"Not a bit, doctor. Stay where you are. I am lost without my Boswell. And this promises to be interesting. It would be a pity to miss it."

"But your client—"

"Never mind him. I may want your help, and so may he. Here he comes. Sit down in that armchair, doctor, and give us your best attention."

A slow and heavy step, which had been heard upon the stairs and in the passage, paused immediately outside the door. Then there was a loud and authoritative tap.

"Come in!" said Holmes.

A man entered who could hardly have been less than six feet six inches in height, with the chest and limbs of a Hercules. His dress was rich with a richness which would, in England, be looked upon as akin to bad taste. Heavy bands of astrakhan were slashed across the sleeves and front of his double-breasted coat, while the deep blue cloak which was thrown over his shoulders was lined with flame-colored silk, and secured at the neck with a brooch which consisted of a single flaming beryl. Boots which extended halfway up his calves, and which were trimmed at the tops with rich brown fur, completed the impression of barbaric opulence which was suggested by his whole appearance. He carried a broad-brimmed hat in his hand, while he wore across the upper part of his face, extending down past the cheek-bones, a black visard mask, which he had apparently adjusted that very moment, for his hand was still raised to it as he entered. From the lower part of the face he appeared to be a man of strong character, with a thick, hanging lip, and a long, straight chin, suggestive of resolution pushed to the length of obstinacy.

"You had my note?" he asked, with a deep, harsh voice and a strongly marked German accent. "I told you that I would call." He looked from one to the other of us, as if uncertain which to address.

"Pray take a seat," said Holmes. "This is my friend and colleague, Doctor Watson, who is occasionally good enough to help me in my cases. Whom have I the honor to address?"

"You may address me as the Count von Kramm, a Bohemian nobleman. I understand that this gentleman, your friend, is a man of honor and discretion, whom I may trust with a matter of the most extreme importance. If not, I should much prefer to communicate with you alone."

I rose to go, but Holmes caught me by the wrist and pushed me back into my chair. "It is both, or none," said he. "You may say before this gentleman anything which you may say to me."

The count shrugged his broad shoulders. "Then I must begin," said he, "by binding you both to absolute secrecy for two years; at the end of that time the matter will be of no importance. At present it is not too much to say that it is of such weight that it may have an influence upon European history."

"I promise," said Holmes.

"And I."

"You will excuse this mask," continued our strange visitor. "The august person who employs me wishes his agent to be unknown to you, and I may confess at once that the title by which I have just called myself is not exactly my own."

"I was aware of it," said Holmes, dryly.

"The circumstances are of great delicacy, and every precaution has to be taken to quench what might grow to be an immense scandal, and seriously compromise one of the reigning families of Europe. To speak plainly, the matter implicates the great House of Ormstein, hereditary kings of Bohemia."

84

"I was also aware of that," murmured Holmes, settling himself down in his armchair, and closing his eyes.

Our visitor glanced with some apparent surprise at the languid, lounging figure of the man who had been, no doubt, depicted to him as the most incisive reasoner and most energetic agent in Europe. Holmes slowly reopened his eyes and looked impatiently at his gigantic client.

"If your majesty would condescend to state your case," he remarked, "I should be better able to advise you."

The man sprung from his chair, and paced up and down the room in uncontrollable agitation. Then, with a gesture of desperation, he tore the mask from his face and hurled it upon the ground.

"You are right," he cried, "I am the king. Why should I attempt to conceal it?"

"Why, indeed?" murmured Holmes. "Your majesty had not spoken before I was aware that I was addressing Wilhelm Gottsreich Sigismond von Ormstein, Grand Duke of Cassel-Felstein, and hereditary King of Bohemia."

"But you can understand," said our strange visitor, sitting down once more and passing his hand over his high, white forehead, "you can understand that I am not accustomed to doing such business in my own person. Yet the matter was so delicate that I could not confide it to an agent without putting myself in his power. I have come incognito from Prague for the purpose of consulting you."

"Then, pray consult," said Holmes, shutting his eyes once more.

"The facts are briefly these: Some five years ago, during a lengthy visit to Warsaw, I made the acquaintance of the well-known adventuress Irene Adler. The name is no doubt familiar to you."

"Kindly look her up in my index, doctor," murmured Holmes, without opening his eyes. For many years he had adopted a system for docketing all paragraphs concerning men and things, so that it was difficult to name a subject or a person on which he could not at once furnish information. In this case I found her biography sandwiched in between that of a Hebrew rabbi and that of a staff commander who had written a monograph upon the deep-sea fishes.

"Let me see!" said Holmes. "Hum! Born in New Jersey in the year 1858. Contralto—hum! La Scala—hum! Prima donna Imperial Opera of Warsaw—yes! Retired from operatic stage—ha! Living in London—quite so! Your majesty, as I understand, became entangled with this young person, wrote her some compromising letters, and is now desirous of getting those letters back."

"Precisely so. But how—"

"Was there a secret marriage?"

"None."

"No legal papers or certificates?"

"None."

"Then I fail to follow your majesty. If this young person should produce her letters for blackmailing or other purposes, how is she to prove their authenticity?"

"There is the writing."

"Pooh-pooh! Forgery."

"My private note paper."

"Stolen."

"My own seal."

"Imitated."

"My photograph."

"Bought."

"We were both in the photograph."

"Oh, dear! That is very bad. Your majesty has indeed committed an indiscretion."

"I was mad—insane."

"You have compromised yourself seriously."

"I was only crown prince then. I was young. I am but thirty now."

"It must be recovered."

"We have tried and failed."

"Your majesty must pay. It must be bought."

"She will not sell."

"Stolen, then."

"Five attempts have been made. Twice burglars in my pay ransacked her house. Once we diverted her luggage when she traveled. Twice she has been waylaid. There has been no result."

"No sign of it?"

"Absolutely none."

Holmes laughed. "It is quite a pretty little problem," said he.

"But a very serious one to me," returned the king, reproachfully.

"Very, indeed. And what does she propose to do with the photograph?"

"To ruin me."

"But how?"

"I am about to be married."

"So I have heard."

"To Clotilde Lothman von Saxe-Meiningen, second daughter of the King of Scandinavia. You may know the strict principles of her family. She is herself the very soul of delicacy. A shadow of a doubt as to my conduct would bring the matter to an end."

"And Irene Adler?"

"Threatens to send them the photograph. And she will do it. I know that she will do it. You do not know her, but she has a soul of steel. She has the face of the most beautiful of women and the mind of the most resolute of men. Rather than I should marry another woman, there are no lengths to which she would not go—none."

"You are sure she has not sent it yet?"

"I am sure."

"And why?"

"Because she has said that she would send it on the day when the betrothal was publicly proclaimed. That will be next Monday."

"Oh, then we have three days yet," said Holmes, with a yawn. "That is very fortunate, as I have one or two matters of importance to look into just at present. Your majesty will, of course, stay in London for the present?"

"Certainly. You will find me at the Langham, under the name of the Count von Kramm."

"Then I shall drop you a line to let you know how we progress."

"Pray do so; I shall be all anxiety."

"Then, as to money?"

"You have carte blanche."

"Absolutely?"

"I tell you that I would give one of the provinces of my kingdom to have that photograph."

"And for present expenses?"

The king took a heavy chamois-leather bag from under his cloak, and laid it on the table.

"There are three hundred pounds in gold, and seven hundred in notes," he said.

Holmes scribbled a receipt upon a sheet of his notebook, and handed it to him.

"And mademoiselle's address?" he asked.

"Is Briony Lodge, Serpentine Avenue, St. John's Wood."

Holmes took a note of it. "One other question," said he, thoughtfully. "Was the photograph a cabinet?"

"It was."

"Then, good-night, your majesty, and I trust that we shall soon have some good news for you. And good-night, Watson," he added, as the wheels of the royal brougham rolled down the street. "If you will be good enough to call to-morrow afternoon, at three o'clock, I should like to chat this little matter over with you."

II

At three o'clock precisely I was at Baker Street, but Holmes had not yet returned. The landlady informed me that he had left the house shortly after eight o'clock in the morning. I sat down beside the fire, however, with the intention of awaiting him, however long he might be. I was already deeply interested in his inquiry, for, though it was surrounded by none of the grim and strange features which were associated with the two crimes which I have already recorded, still, the nature of the case and the exalted station of his client gave it a character of its own. Indeed, apart from the nature of the investigation which my friend had on hand, there was something in his masterly grasp of a situation, and his keen, incisive reasoning, which made it a pleasure to me to study his system of work, and to follow the quick, subtle methods by which he disentangled the most inextricable mysteries. So accustomed was I to his invariable success that the very possibility of his failing had ceased to enter into my head.

It was close upon four before the door opened, and a drunken-looking groom, ill-kempt and side-whiskered, with an inflamed face and disreputable clothes, walked into the room. Accustomed as I was to my friend's amazing powers in the use of disguises, I had to look three times before I was certain that it was indeed he. With a nod he vanished into the bedroom, whence he emerged in five minutes tweed-suited and respectable, as of old. Putting his hands into his pockets, he stretched out his legs in front of the fire, and laughed heartily for some minutes.

"Well, really!" he cried, and then he choked, and laughed again until he was obliged to lie back, limp and helpless, in the chair.

"What is it?"

"It's quite too funny. I am sure you could never guess how I employed my morning, or what I ended by doing."

"I can't imagine. I suppose that you have been watching the habits, and, perhaps, the house, of Miss Irene Adler."

"Quite so, but the sequel was rather unusual. I will tell you, however. I left the house a little after eight o'clock this morning in the character of a groom out of work. There is a wonderful sympathy and freemasonry among horsey men. Be one of them, and you will know all that there is to know. I soon found Briony Lodge. It is a bijou villa, with a garden at the back, but built out in the front right up to the road, two stories. Chubb lock to the door. Large sitting room on the right side, well furnished, with long windows almost to the floor, and those preposterous English window fasteners which a child could open. Behind there was nothing remarkable, save that the passage window could be reached from the top of the coach-house. I walked round it and examined it closely from every point of view, but without noting anything else of interest.

"I then lounged down the street, and found, as I expected, that there was a mews in a lane which runs down by one wall of the garden. I lent the hostlers a hand in rubbing down their horses, and I received in exchange twopence, a glass of half and half, two fills of shag tobacco, and as much information as I could desire about Miss Adler, to say nothing of half a dozen other people in the neighborhood, in whom I was not in the least interested, but whose biographies I was compelled to listen to."

"And what of Irene Adler?" I asked.

"Oh, she has turned all the men's heads down in that part. She is the daintiest thing under a bonnet on this planet. So say the Serpentine Mews, to a man. She lives quietly, sings at concerts, drives out at five every day, and returns at seven sharp for dinner. Seldom goes out at other times, except when she sings. Has only one male visitor, but a good deal of him. He is dark, handsome, and dashing; never calls less than once a day, and often twice. He is a Mr. Godfrey Norton of the Inner Temple. See the advantages of a cabman as a confidant. They had driven him home a dozen times from Serpentine Mews, and knew all about him. When I had listened to all that they had to tell, I began to walk up and down near Briony Lodge once more, and to think over my plan of campaign.

"This Godfrey Norton was evidently an important factor in the matter. He was a lawyer. That sounded ominous. What was the relation between them, and what the object of his repeated visits? Was she his client, his friend, or his mistress? If the former, she had probably transferred the photograph to his keeping. If the latter, it was less likely. On the issue of this question depended whether I should continue my work at Briony Lodge, or turn my attention to the gentleman's chambers in the Temple. It was a delicate point, and it widened the field of my inquiry. I fear that I bore you with these details, but I have to let you see my little difficulties, if you are to understand the situation."

"I am following you closely," I answered.

"I was still balancing the matter in my mind, when a hansom cab drove up to Briony Lodge, and a gentleman sprung out. He was a remarkably handsome man, dark, aquiline, and mustached—evidently the man of whom I had heard. He appeared to be in a great hurry, shouted to the cabman to wait, and brushed past the maid who opened the door, with the air of a man who was thoroughly at home.

"He was in the house about half an hour, and I could catch glimpses of him in the windows of the sitting room, pacing up and down, talking excitedly and waving his arms. Of her I could see nothing. Presently he emerged, looking even more flurried than before. As he stepped up to the cab, he pulled a gold watch from his pocket and looked at it earnestly. 'Drive like the devil!' he shouted, 'first to Gross & Hankey's in Regent Street, and then to the Church of St. Monica in the Edgeware Road. Half a guinea if you do it in twenty minutes!'

"Away they went, and I was just wondering whether I should not do well to follow them, when up the lane came a neat little landau, the coachman with his coat only half buttoned, and his tie under his ear, while all the tags of his harness were sticking out of the buckles. It hadn't pulled up before she shot out of the hall door and into it. I only caught a glimpse of her at the moment, but she was a lovely woman, with a face that a man might die for.

"'The Church of St. Monica, John,' she cried; 'and half a sovereign if you reach it in twenty minutes.'

"This was quite too good to lose, Watson. I was just balancing whether I should run for it, or whether I should perch behind her landau, when a cab came through the street. The driver looked twice at such a shabby fare; but I jumped in before he could object. 'The Church of St. Monica,' said I, 'and half a sovereign if you reach it in twenty minutes.' It was twenty-five minutes to twelve, and of course it was clear enough what was in the wind.

"My cabby drove fast. I don't think I ever drove faster, but the others were there before us. The cab and landau with their steaming horses were in front of the door when I arrived. I paid the man, and hurried into the church. There was not a soul there save the two whom I had followed, and a surpliced clergyman, who seemed to be expostulating with them. They were all three standing in a knot in front of the altar. I lounged up the side aisle like any other idler who has dropped into a church. Suddenly, to my surprise, the three at the altar faced round to me, and Godfrey Norton came running as hard as he could toward me.

"'Thank God!' he cried. 'You'll do. Come! Come!'

"'What then?' I asked.

"'Come, man, come; only three minutes, or it won't be legal.'

"I was half dragged up to the altar, and, before I knew where I was, I found myself mumbling responses which were whispered in my ear, and vouching for things of which I knew nothing, and generally assisting in the secure tying up of Irene Adler, spinster, to Godfrey Norton, bachelor. It was all done in an instant, and there was the gentleman thanking me on the one side and the lady on the other, while the clergyman beamed on me in front. It was the most preposterous position in which I ever found myself in my life, and it was the thought of it that started me laughing just now. It seems that there had been some informality about their license; that the clergyman absolutely refused to marry them without a witness of some sort, and that my lucky appearance saved the bridegroom from having to sally out into the streets in search of a best man. The bride gave me a sovereign, and I mean to wear it on my watch chain in memory of the occasion."

"This is a very unexpected turn of affairs," said I; "and what then?"

"Well, I found my plans very seriously menaced. It looked as if the pair might take an immediate departure, and so necessitate very prompt and energetic measures on my part. At the church door, however, they separated, he driving back to the Temple, and she to her own house. 'I shall drive out in the park at five as usual,' she said, as she left him. I heard no more. They drove away in different directions, and I went off to make my own arrangements."

"Which are?"

"Some cold beef and a glass of beer," he answered, ringing the bell. "I have been too busy to think of food, and I am likely to be busier still this evening. By the way, doctor, I shall want your cooperation."

"I shall be delighted."

"You don't mind breaking the law?"

"Not in the least."

"Nor running a chance of arrest?"

"Not in a good cause."

"Oh, the cause is excellent!"

"Then I am your man."

"I was sure that I might rely on you."

"But what is it you wish?"

"When Mrs. Turner has brought in the tray I will make it clear to you. Now," he said, as he turned hungrily on the simple fare that our landlady had provided, "I must discuss it while I eat, for I have not much time. It is nearly five now. In two hours we must be on the scene of action. Miss Irene, or Madame, rather, returns from her drive at seven. We must be at Briony Lodge to meet her."

"And what then?"

"You must leave that to me. I have already arranged what is to occur. There is only one point on which I must insist. You must not interfere, come what may. You understand?"

"I am to be neutral?"

"To do nothing whatever. There will probably be some small unpleasantness. Do not join in it. It will end in my being conveyed into the house. Four or five minutes afterwards the sitting-room window will open. You are to station yourself close to that open window."

"Yes."

"You are to watch me, for I will be visible to you."

"Yes."

"And when I raise my hand—so—you will throw into the room what I give you to throw, and will, at the same time, raise the cry of fire. You quite follow me?"

"Entirely."

"It is nothing very formidable," he said, taking a long, cigar-shaped roll from his pocket. "It is an ordinary plumber's smoke-rocket, fitted with a cap at either end, to make it self-lighting. Your task is confined to that. When you raise your cry of fire, it will be taken up by quite a number of people. You may then walk to the end of the street, and I will rejoin you in ten minutes. I hope that I have made myself clear?"

"I am to remain neutral, to get near the window, to watch you, and, at the signal, to throw in this object, then to raise the cry of fire and to wait you at the corner of the street."

"Precisely."

"Then you may entirely rely on me."

"That is excellent. I think, perhaps, it is almost time that I prepared for the new role I have to play."

He disappeared into his bedroom, and returned in a few minutes in the character of an amiable and simple-minded Nonconformist clergyman. His broad, black hat, his baggy trousers, his white tie, his sympathetic smile, and general look of peering and benevolent curiosity were such as Mr. John Hare alone could have equaled. It was not merely that Holmes changed his costume. His expression, his manner, his very soul seemed to vary with every fresh part that he assumed. The stage lost a fine actor, even as science lost an acute reasoner, when he became a specialist in crime.

It was a quarter past six when we left Baker Street, and it still wanted ten minutes to the hour when we found ourselves in Serpentine Avenue. It was already dusk, and the lamps were just being lighted as we paced up and down in front of Briony Lodge, waiting for the coming of its occupant. The house was just such as I had pictured it from Sherlock Holmes's succinct description, but the locality appeared to be less private than I expected. On the contrary, for a small street in a quiet neighborhood, it was remarkably animated. There was a group of shabbily dressed men smoking and laughing in a corner, a scissors grinder with his wheel, two guardsmen who were flirting with a nurse girl, and several well-dressed young men who were lounging up and down with cigars in their mouths.

"You see," remarked Holmes, as we paced to and fro in front of the house, "this marriage rather simplifies matters. The photograph becomes a double-edged weapon now. The chances are that she would be as averse to its being seen by Mr. Godfrey Norton as our client is to its coming to the eyes of his princess. Now the question is—where are we to find the photograph?"

"Where, indeed?"

"It is most unlikely that she carries it about with her. It is cabinet size. Too large for easy concealment about a woman's dress. She knows that the king is capable of having her waylaid and searched. Two attempts of the sort have already been made. We may take it, then, that she does not carry it about with her."

"Where, then?"

"Her banker or her lawyer. There is that double possibility. But I am inclined to think neither. Women are naturally secretive, and they like to do their own secreting. Why should she hand it over to anyone else? She could trust her own guardianship, but she could not tell what indirect or political influence might be brought to bear upon a business man. Besides, remember that she had resolved to use it within a few days. It must be where she can lay her hands upon it. It must be in her own house."

"But it has twice been burglarized."

"Pshaw! They did not know how to look."

"But how will you look?"

"I will not look."

"What then?"

"I will get her to show me."

"But she will refuse."

"She will not be able to. But I hear the rumble of wheels. It is her carriage. Now carry out my orders to the letter."

As he spoke, the gleam of the sidelights of a carriage came round the curve of the avenue. It was a smart little landau which rattled up to the door of Briony Lodge. As it pulled up one of the loafing men at the corner dashed forward to open the door in the hope of earning a copper, but was elbowed away by another loafer who had rushed up with the same intention. A fierce quarrel broke out which was increased by the two guardsmen, who took sides with one of the loungers, and by the scissors grinder, who was equally hot upon the other side. A blow was struck, and in an instant the lady, who had stepped from her carriage, was the center of a little knot of struggling men who struck savagely at each other with their fists and sticks. Holmes dashed into the crowd to protect the lady; but, just as he reached her, he gave a cry and dropped to the ground, with the blood running freely down his face. At his fall the guardsmen took to their heels in one direction and the loungers in the other, while a number of better-dressed people who had watched the scuffle without taking part in it crowded in to help the lady and to attend to the injured man. Irene Adler, as I will still call her, had hurried up the steps; but she stood at the top, with her superb figure outlined against the lights of the hall, looking back into the street.

"Is the poor gentleman much hurt?" she asked.

"He is dead," cried several voices.

"No, no, there's life in him," shouted another. "But he'll be gone before you can get him to the hospital."

"He's a brave fellow," said a woman. "They would have had the lady's purse and watch if it hadn't been for him. They were a gang, and a rough one, too. Ah! he's breathing now."

"He can't lie in the street. May we bring him in, marm?"

"Surely. Bring him into the sitting room. There is a comfortable sofa. This way, please." Slowly and solemnly he was borne into Briony Lodge, and laid out in the principal room, while I still observed the proceedings from my post by the window. The lamps had been lighted, but the blinds had not been drawn, so that I could see Holmes as he lay upon the couch. I do not know whether he was seized with compunction at that moment for the part he was playing, but I know that I never felt more heartily ashamed of myself in my life than when I saw the beautiful creature against whom I was conspiring, or the grace and kindliness with which she waited upon the injured man. And yet it

93

would be the blackest treachery to Holmes to draw back now from the part which he had intrusted to me. I hardened my heart, and took the smoke-rocket from under my ulster. After all, I thought, we are not injuring her. We are but preventing her from injuring another.

Holmes had sat upon the couch, and I saw him motion like a man who is in need of air. A maid rushed across and threw open the window. At the same instant I saw him raise his hand, and at the signal I tossed my rocket into the room with a cry of "Fire!" The word was no sooner out of my mouth than the whole crowd of spectators, well dressed and ill—gentlemen, hostlers, and servant maids—joined in a general shriek of "Fire!" Thick clouds of smoke curled through the room, and out at the open window. I caught a glimpse of rushing figures, and a moment later the voice of Holmes from within assuring them that it was a false alarm. Slipping through the shouting crowd, I made my way to the corner of the street, and in ten minutes was rejoiced to find my friend's arm in mine, and to get away from the scene of uproar. He walked swiftly and in silence for some few minutes, until we had turned down one of the quiet streets which led toward the Edgeware Road.

"You did it very nicely, doctor," he remarked. "Nothing could have been better. It is all right."

"You have the photograph?"

"I know where it is."

"And how did you find out?"

"She showed me, as I told you that she would."

"I am still in the dark."

"I do not wish to make a mystery," said he, laughing. "The matter was perfectly simple. You, of course, saw that everyone in the street was an accomplice. They were all engaged for the evening."

"I guessed as much."

"Then, when the row broke out, I had a little moist red paint in the palm of my hand. I rushed forward, fell down, clapped my hand to my face, and became a piteous spectacle. It is an old trick."

"That also I could fathom."

"Then they carried me in. She was bound to have me in. What else could she do? And into her sitting room, which was the very room which I suspected. It lay between that and her bedroom, and I was determined to see which. They laid me on a couch, I motioned for air, they were compelled to open the window, and you had your chance."

"How did that help you?"

"It was all-important. When a woman thinks that her house is on fire, her instinct is at once to rush to the thing which she values most. It is a perfectly overpowering impulse, and I have more than once taken advantage of it. In the case of the Darlington Substitution Scandal it was of use to me, and also in the Arnsworth Castle business. A married woman grabs at her baby—an unmarried one reaches for her jewel box.

94

Now it was clear to me that our lady of to-day had nothing in the house more precious to her than what we are in quest of. She would rush to secure it. The alarm of fire was admirably done. The smoke and shouting were enough to shake nerves of steel. She responded beautifully. The photograph is in a recess behind a sliding panel just above the right bell-pull. She was there in an instant, and I caught a glimpse of it as she drew it out. When I cried out that it was a false alarm, she replaced it, glanced at the rocket, rushed from the room, and I have not seen her since. I rose, and, making my excuses, escaped from the house. I hesitated whether to attempt to secure the photograph at once; but the coachman had come in, and as he was watching me narrowly, it seemed safer to wait. A little over-precipitance may ruin all."

"And now?" I asked.

"Our quest is practically finished. I shall call with the king to-morrow, and with you, if you care to come with us. We will be shown into the sitting room to wait for the lady, but it is probable that when she comes she may find neither us nor the photograph. It might be a satisfaction to his majesty to regain it with his own hands."

"And when will you call?"

"At eight in the morning. She will not be up, so that we shall have a clear field. Besides, we must be prompt, for this marriage may mean a complete change in her life and habits. I must wire to the king without delay."

We had reached Baker Street, and had stopped at the door. He was searching his pockets for the key, when some one passing said:

"Good night, Mister Sherlock Holmes."

There were several people on the pavement at the time, but the greeting appeared to come from a slim youth in an ulster who had hurried by.

"I've heard that voice before," said Holmes, staring down the dimly lighted street. "Now, I wonder who the deuce that could have been?"

III

I slept at Baker Street that night, and we were engaged upon our toast and coffee in the morning, when the King of Bohemia rushed into the room.

"You have really got it?" he cried, grasping Sherlock Holmes by either shoulder, and looking eagerly into his face.

"Not yet."

"But you have hopes?"

"I have hopes."

"Then come. I am all impatience to be gone."

"We must have a cab."

"No, my brougham is waiting."

"Then that will simplify matters." We descended, and started off once more for Briony Lodge.

"Irene Adler is married," remarked Holmes.

"Married! When?"

"Yesterday."

"But to whom?"

"To an English lawyer named Norton."

"But she could not love him."

"I am in hopes that she does."

"And why in hopes?"

"Because it would spare your majesty all fear of future annoyance. If the lady loves her husband, she does not love your majesty. If she does not love your majesty, there is no reason why she should interfere with your majesty's plan."

"It is true. And yet—Well, I wish she had been of my own station. What a queen she would have made!" He relapsed into a moody silence, which was not broken until we drew up in Serpentine Avenue.

The door of Briony Lodge was open, and an elderly woman stood upon the steps. She watched us with a sardonic eye as we stepped from the brougham.

"Mr. Sherlock Holmes, I believe?" said she.

"I am Mr. Holmes," answered my companion, looking at her with a questioning and rather startled gaze.

"Indeed! My mistress told me that you were likely to call. She left this morning, with her husband, by the 5:15 train from Charing Cross, for the Continent."

"What!" Sherlock Holmes staggered back, white with chagrin and surprise.

"Do you mean that she has left England?"

"Never to return."

"And the papers?" asked the king hoarsely. "All is lost!"

"We shall see." He pushed past the servant, and rushed into the drawing-room, followed by the king and myself. The furniture was scattered about in every direction, with dismantled shelves, and open drawers, as if the lady had hurriedly ransacked them before her flight. Holmes rushed at the bell-pull, tore back a small sliding shutter, and plunging in his hand, pulled out a photograph and a letter. The photograph was of Irene Adler herself in evening dress; the letter was superscribed to "Sherlock Holmes, Esq. To be left till called for." My friend tore it open, and we all three read it together. It was dated at midnight of the preceding night, and ran in this way:

"MY DEAR MR. SHERLOCK HOLMES,—You really did it very well. You took me in completely. Until after the alarm of the fire, I had not a suspicion. But then, when I found how I had betrayed myself, I began to think. I had been warned against you months ago. I had been told that if the king employed an agent, it would certainly be you. And your address had been given me. Yet, with all this, you made me reveal what you wanted to know. Even after I became suspicious, I found it hard to think evil of such a dear, kind old clergyman. But, you know, I have been trained as an actress myself. Male costume is nothing new to me. I often take advantage of the freedom which it gives. I sent John, the coachman, to watch you, ran upstairs, got into my walking clothes, as I call them, and came down just as you departed.

"Well, I followed you to the door, and so made sure that I was really an object of interest to the celebrated Mr. Sherlock Holmes. Then I, rather imprudently, wished you good night, and started for the Temple to see my husband.

"We both thought the best resource was flight when pursued by so formidable an antagonist; so you will find the nest empty when you call to-morrow. As to the photograph, your client may rest in peace. I love and am loved by a better man than he. The king may do what he will without hindrance from one whom he has cruelly wronged. I keep it only to safeguard myself, and preserve a weapon which will always secure me from any steps which he might take in the future. I leave a photograph which he might care to possess; and I remain, dear Mr. Sherlock Holmes, very truly yours,

"IRENE NORTON, née ADLER."

"What a woman—oh, what a woman!" cried the King of Bohemia, when we had all three read this epistle. "Did I not tell you how quick and resolute she was? Would she not have made an admirable queen? Is it not a pity that she was not on my level?"

"From what I have seen of the lady, she seems indeed to be on a very different level to your majesty," said Holmes coldly. "I am sorry that I have not been able to bring your majesty's business to a more successful conclusion."

"On the contrary, my dear sir," cried the king, "nothing could be more successful. I know that her word is inviolate. The photograph is now as safe as if it were in the fire."

"I am glad to hear your majesty say so."

"I am immensely indebted to you. Pray tell me in what way I can reward you. This ring—" He slipped an emerald snake ring from his finger, and held it out upon the palm of his hand.

97

"Your majesty has something which I should value even more highly," said Holmes.

"You have but to name it."

"This photograph!"

The king stared at him in amazement.

"Irene's photograph!" he cried. "Certainly, if you wish it."

"I thank your majesty. Then there is no more to be done in the matter. I have the honor to wish you a very good morning." He bowed, and turning away without observing the hand which the king had stretched out to him, he set off in my company for his chambers.

And that was how a great scandal threatened to affect the kingdom of Bohemia, and how the best plans of Mr. Sherlock Holmes were beaten by a woman's wit. He used to make merry over the cleverness of women, but I have not heard him do it of late. And when he speaks of Irene Adler, or when he refers to her photograph, it is always under the honorable title of the woman.

THE RED-HEADED LEAGUE

I had called upon my friend, Mr. Sherlock Holmes, one day in the autumn of last year, and found him in deep conversation with a very stout, florid-faced elderly gentleman, with fiery red hair. With an apology for my intrusion, I was about to withdraw, when Holmes pulled me abruptly into the room and closed the door behind me.

"You could not possibly have come at a better time, my dear Watson," he said, cordially.

"I was afraid that you were engaged."

"So I am. Very much so."

"Then I can wait in the next room."

"Not at all. This gentleman, Mr. Wilson, has been my partner and helper in many of my most successful cases, and I have no doubt that he will be of the utmost use to me in yours also."

The stout gentleman half rose from his chair and gave a bob of greeting, with a quick little questioning glance from his small, fat-encircled eyes.

"Try the settee," said Holmes, relapsing into his armchair, and putting his finger tips together, as was his custom when in judicial moods. "I know, my dear Watson, that you share my love of all that is bizarre and outside the conventions and humdrum routine of everyday life. You have shown your relish for it by the enthusiasm which has prompted you to chronicle, and, if you will excuse my saying so, somewhat to embellish so many of my own little adventures."

"Your cases have indeed been of the greatest interest to me," I observed.

"You will remember that I remarked the other day, just before we went into the very simple problem presented by Miss Mary Sutherland, that for strange effects and extraordinary combinations we must go to life itself, which is always far more daring than any effort of the imagination."

"A proposition which I took the liberty of doubting."

"You did, doctor, but none the less you must come round to my view, for otherwise I shall keep on piling fact upon fact on you, until your reason breaks down under them and acknowledge me to be right. Now, Mr. Jabez Wilson here has been good enough to call upon me this morning, and to begin a narrative which promises to be one of the most singular which I have listened to for some time. You have heard me remark that the strangest and most unique things are very often connected not with the larger but with the smaller crimes, and occasionally, indeed, where there is room for doubt whether any positive crime has been committed. As far as I have heard, it is impossible for me to say whether the present case is an instance of crime or not, but the course of events is certainly among the most singular that I have ever listened to. Perhaps, Mr. Wilson, you would have the great kindness to recommence your narrative. I ask you, not merely because my friend, Dr. Watson, has not heard the opening part, but also because the peculiar nature of the story makes me anxious to have every possible detail from your lips. As a rule, when I have heard some slight indication of the course of events I am able to guide myself by the thousands of other similar cases which occur to my memory. In the present instance I am forced to admit that the facts are, to the best of my belief, unique."

The portly client puffed out his chest with an appearance of some little pride, and pulled a dirty and wrinkled newspaper from the inside pocket of his greatcoat. As he glanced down the advertisement column, with his head thrust forward, and the paper flattened out upon his knee, I took a good look at the man, and endeavored, after the fashion of my companion, to read the indications which might be presented by his dress or appearance.

I did not gain very much, however, by my inspection. Our visitor bore every mark of being an average commonplace British tradesman, obese, pompous, and slow. He wore rather baggy gray shepherd's check trousers, a not overclean black frock coat, unbuttoned in the front, and a drab waistcoat with a heavy brassy Albert chain, and a square pierced bit of metal dangling down as an ornament. A frayed top hat and a faded brown overcoat with a wrinkled velvet collar lay upon a chair beside him. Altogether, look as I would, there was nothing remarkable about the man save his blazing red head and the expression of extreme chagrin and discontent upon his features.

Sherlock Holmes's quick eye took in my occupation, and he shook his head with a smile as he noticed my questioning glances. "Beyond the obvious facts that he has at some time done manual labor, that he takes snuff, that he is a Freemason, that he has been in China, and that he has done a considerable amount of writing lately, I can deduce nothing else."

Mr. Jabez Wilson started up in his chair, with his forefinger upon the paper, but his eyes upon my companion.

"How, in the name of good fortune, did you know all that, Mr. Holmes?" he asked. "How did you know, for example, that I did manual labor? It's as true as gospel, for I began as a ship's carpenter."

"Your hands, my dear sir. Your right hand is quite a size larger than your left. You have worked with it and the muscles are more developed."

"Well, the snuff, then, and the Freemasonry?"

"I won't insult your intelligence by telling you how I read that, especially as, rather against the strict rules of your order, you use an arc and compass breastpin."

"Ah, of course, I forgot that. But the writing?"

"What else can be indicated by that right cuff so very shiny for five inches, and the left one with the smooth patch near the elbow where you rest it upon the desk."

"Well, but China?"

"The fish which you have tattooed immediately above your wrist could only have been done in China. I have made a small study of tattoo marks, and have even contributed to the literature of the subject. That trick of staining the fishes' scales of a delicate pink is quite peculiar to China. When, in addition, I see a Chinese coin hanging from your watch chain, the matter becomes even more simple."

Mr. Jabez Wilson laughed heavily. "Well, I never!" said he. "I thought at first that you had done something clever, but I see that there was nothing in it after all."

"I begin to think, Watson," said Holmes, "that I make a mistake in explaining. 'Omne ignotom pro magnifico,' you know, and my poor little reputation, such as it is, will suffer shipwreck if I am so candid. Can you not find the advertisement, Mr. Wilson?"

"Yes, I have got it now," he answered, with his thick, red finger planted halfway down the column. "Here it is. This is what began it all. You just read it for yourself, sir."

I took the paper from him and read as follows:

"To the Red-headed League: On account of the bequest of the late Ezekiah Hopkins, of Lebanon, Pa., U.S.A., there is now another vacancy open which entitles a member of the

League to a salary of four pounds a week for purely nominal services. All red-headed men who are sound in body and mind and above the age of twenty-one years are eligible. Apply in person on Monday, at eleven o'clock, to Duncan Ross, at the offices of the League, 7 Pope's Court, Fleet Street."

"What on earth does this mean?" I ejaculated, after I had twice read over the extraordinary announcement.

Holmes chuckled and wriggled in his chair, as was his habit when in high spirits. "It is a little off the beaten track, isn't it?" said he. "And now, Mr. Wilson, off you go at scratch, and tell us all about yourself, your household, and the effect which this advertisement had upon your fortunes. You will first make a note, doctor, of the paper and the date."

"It is The Morning Chronicle of April 27, 1890. Just two months ago."

"Very good. Now, Mr. Wilson."

"Well, it is just as I have been telling you, Mr. Sherlock Holmes," said Jabez Wilson, mopping his forehead, "I have a small pawnbroker's business at Saxe-Coburg Square, near the City. It's not a very large affair, and of late years it has not done more than just give me a living. I used to be able to keep two assistants, but now I only keep one; and I would have a job to pay him but that he is willing to come for half wages, so as to learn the business."

"What is the name of this obliging youth?" asked Sherlock Holmes.

"His name is Vincent Spaulding, and he's not such a youth either. It's hard to say his age. I should not wish a smarter assistant, Mr. Holmes; and I know very well that he could better himself, and earn twice what I am able to give him. But, after all, if he is satisfied, why should I put ideas in his head?"

"Why, indeed? You seem most fortunate in having an employee who comes under the full market price. It is not a common experience among employers in this age. I don't know that your assistant is not as remarkable as your advertisement."

"Oh, he has his faults, too," said Mr. Wilson. "Never was such a fellow for photography. Snapping away with a camera when he ought to be improving his mind, and then diving down into the cellar like a rabbit into its hole to develop his pictures. That is his main fault; but, on the whole, he's a good worker. There's no vice in him."

"He is still with you, I presume?"

"Yes, sir. He and a girl of fourteen, who does a bit of simple cooking, and keeps the place clean—that's all I have in the house, for I am a widower, and never had any family. We live very quietly, sir, the three of us; and we keep a roof over our heads, and pay our debts, if we do nothing more.

"The first thing that put us out was that advertisement. Spaulding, he came down into the office just this day eight weeks, with this very paper in his hand, and he says:

"'I wish to the Lord, Mr. Wilson, that I was a red-headed man.'

"'Why that?' I asks.

"'Why,' says he, 'here's another vacancy on the League of the Red-headed Men. It's worth quite a little fortune to any man who gets it, and I understand that there are more vacancies than there are men, so that the trustees are at their wits' end what to do with the money. If my hair would only change color here's a nice little crib all ready for me to step into.'

"'Why, what is it, then?' I asked. You see, Mr. Holmes, I am a very stay-at-home man, and, as my business came to me instead of my having to go to it, I was often weeks on end without putting my foot over the door mat. In that way I didn't know much of what was going on outside, and I was always glad of a bit of news.

"'Have you never heard of the League of the Red-headed Men?' he asked, with his eyes open.

"'Never.'

"'Why, I wonder at that, for you are eligible yourself for one of the vacancies.'

"'And what are they worth?' I asked.

"'Oh, merely a couple of hundred a year, but the work is slight, and it need not interfere very much with one's other occupations.'

"Well, you can easily think that that made me prick up my ears, for the business has not been over good for some years, and an extra couple of hundred would have been very handy.

"'Tell me all about it,' said I.

"'Well,' said he, showing me the advertisement, 'you can see for yourself that the League has a vacancy, and there is the address where you should apply for particulars. As far as I can make out, the League was founded by an American millionaire, Ezekiah Hopkins, who was very peculiar in his ways. He was himself red-headed, and he had a great sympathy for all red-headed men; so, when he died, it was found that he had left his enormous fortune in the hands of trustees, with instructions to apply the interest to the providing of easy berths to men whose hair is of that color. From all I hear it is splendid pay, and very little to do.'

"'But,' said I, 'there would be millions of red-headed men who would apply.'

"'Not so many as you might think,' he answered. 'You see it is really confined to Londoners, and to grown men. This American had started from London when he was young, and he wanted to do the old town a good turn. Then, again, I have heard it is of no use your applying if your hair is light red, or dark red, or anything but real, bright, blazing, fiery red. Now, if you cared to apply, Mr. Wilson, you would just walk in; but perhaps it would hardly be worth your while to put yourself out of the way for the sake of a few hundred pounds.'

"Now it is a fact, gentlemen, as you may see for yourselves, that my hair is of a very full and rich tint, so that it seemed to me that, if there was to be any competition in the matter, I stood as good a chance as any man that I had ever met. Vincent Spaulding seemed to know so much about it that I thought he might prove useful, so I just ordered him to put up the shutters for the day, and to come right away with me. He was very willing to have a holiday, so we shut the business up, and started off for the address that was given us in the advertisement.

"I never hope to see such a sight as that again, Mr. Holmes. From north, south, east, and west every man who had a shade of red in his hair had tramped into the City to answer the advertisement. Fleet Street was choked with red-headed folk, and Pope's Court looked like a coster's orange barrow. I should not have thought there were so many in the whole country as were brought together by that single advertisement. Every shade of color they were—straw, lemon, orange, brick, Irish setter, liver, clay; but, as Spaulding said, there were not many who had the real vivid flame-colored tint. When I saw how many were waiting, I would have given it up in despair; but Spaulding would not hear of it. How he did it I could not imagine, but he pushed and pulled and butted until he got me through the crowd, and right up to the steps which led to the office. There was a double stream upon the stair, some going up in hope, and some coming back dejected; but we wedged in as well as we could, and soon found ourselves in the office."

"Your experience has been a most entertaining one," remarked Holmes, as his client paused and refreshed his memory with a huge pinch of snuff. "Pray continue your very interesting statement."

"There was nothing in the office but a couple of wooden chairs and a deal table, behind which sat a small man, with a head that was even redder than mine. He said a few words to each candidate as he came up, and then he always managed to find some fault in them which would disqualify them. Getting a vacancy did not seem to be such a very easy matter after all. However, when our turn came, the little man was much more favorable to me than to any of the others, and he closed the door as we entered, so that he might have a private word with us.

"'This is Mr. Jabez Wilson,' said my assistant, 'and he is willing to fill a vacancy in the League.'

"'And he is admirably suited for it,' the other answered. 'He has every requirement. I cannot recall when I have seen anything so fine.' He took a step backward, cocked his head on one side, and gazed at my hair until I felt quite bashful. Then suddenly he plunged forward, wrung my hand, and congratulated me warmly on my success.

103

"'It would be injustice to hesitate,' said he. 'You will, however, I am sure, excuse me for taking an obvious precaution.' With that he seized my hair in both his hands, and tugged until I yelled with the pain. 'There is water in your eyes,' said he, as he released me. 'I perceive that all is as it should be. But we have to be careful, for we have twice been deceived by wigs and once by paint. I could tell you tales of cobbler's wax which would disgust you with human nature.' He stepped over to the window and shouted through it at the top of his voice that the vacancy was filled. A groan of disappointment came up from below, and the folk all trooped away in different directions, until there was not a red head to be seen except my own and that of the manager.

"'My name,' said he, 'is Mr. Duncan Ross, and I am myself one of the pensioners upon the fund left by our noble benefactor. Are you a married man, Mr. Wilson? Have you a family?'

"I answered that I had not.

"His face fell immediately.

"'Dear me!' he said, gravely, 'that is very serious indeed! I am sorry to hear you say that. The fund was, of course, for the propagation and spread of the red heads as well as for their maintenance. It is exceedingly unfortunate that you should be a bachelor.'

"My face lengthened at this, Mr. Holmes, for I thought that I was not to have the vacancy after all; but, after thinking it over for a few minutes, he said that it would be all right.

"'In the case of another,' said he, 'the objection might be fatal, but we must stretch a point in favor of a man with such a head of hair as yours. When shall you be able to enter upon your new duties?'

"'Well, it is a little awkward, for I have a business already,' said I.

"'Oh, never mind about that, Mr. Wilson!' said Vincent Spaulding. 'I shall be able to look after that for you.'

"'What would be the hours?' I asked.

"'Ten to two.'

"Now a pawnbroker's business is mostly done of an evening, Mr. Holmes, especially Thursday and Friday evenings, which is just before pay day; so it would suit me very well to earn a little in the mornings. Besides, I knew that my assistant was a good man, and that he would see to anything that turned up.

"'That would suit me very well,' said I. 'And the pay?'

"'Is four pounds a week.'

"'And the work?'

"'Is purely nominal.'

"'What do you call purely nominal?'

"'Well, you have to be in the office, or at least in the building, the whole time. If you leave, you forfeit your whole position forever. The will is very clear upon that point. You don't comply with the conditions if you budge from the office during that time.'

"'It's only four hours a day, and I should not think of leaving,' said I.

"'No excuse will avail,' said Mr. Duncan Ross, 'neither sickness, nor business, nor anything else. There you must stay, or you lose your billet.'

"'And the work?'

"'Is to copy out the "Encyclopædia Britannica." There is the first volume of it in that press. You must find your own ink, pens, and blotting paper, but we provide this table and chair. Will you be ready to-morrow?'

"'Certainly,' I answered.

"'Then, good-by, Mr. Jabez Wilson, and let me congratulate you once more on the important position which you have been fortunate enough to gain.' He bowed me out of the room, and I went home with my assistant hardly knowing what to say or do, I was so pleased at my own good fortune.

"Well, I thought over the matter all day, and by evening I was in low spirits again; for I had quite persuaded myself that the whole affair must be some great hoax or fraud, though what its object might be I could not imagine. It seemed altogether past belief that anyone could make such a will, or that they would pay such a sum for doing anything so simple as copying out the 'Encyclopædia Britannica.' Vincent Spaulding did what he could to cheer me up, but by bed time I had reasoned myself out of the whole thing. However, in the morning I determined to have a look at it anyhow, so I bought a penny bottle of ink, and with a quill pen and seven sheets of foolscap paper I started off for Pope's Court.

"Well, to my surprise and delight everything was as right as possible. The table was set out ready for me, and Mr. Duncan Ross was there to see that I got fairly to work. He started me off upon the letter A, and then he left me; but he would drop in from time to time to see that all was right with me. At two o'clock he bade me good-day, complimented me upon the amount that I had written, and locked the door of the office after me.

"This went on day after day, Mr. Holmes, and on Saturday the manager came in and planked down four golden sovereigns for my week's work. It was the same next week, and the same the week after. Every morning I was there at ten, and every afternoon I left at two. By degrees Mr. Duncan Ross took to coming in only once of a morning, and then, after a time, he did not come in at all. Still, of course, I never dared to leave the room for an instant, for I was not sure when he might come, and the billet was such a good one, and suited me so well, that I would not risk the loss of it.

"Eight weeks passed away like this, and I had written about Abbots, and Archery, and Armor, and Architecture, and Attica, and hoped with diligence that I might get on to the Bs before very long. It

105

cost me something in foolscap, and I had pretty nearly filled a shelf with my writings. And then suddenly the whole business came to an end."

"To an end?"

"Yes, sir. And no later than this morning. I went to my work as usual at ten o'clock, but the door was shut and locked, with a little square of cardboard hammered onto the middle of the panel with a tack. Here it is, and you can read for yourself."

He held up a piece of white cardboard, about the size of a sheet of note paper. It read in this fashion:

"THE RED-HEADED LEAGUE IS DISSOLVED.

Oct. 9, 1890."

Sherlock Holmes and I surveyed this curt announcement and the rueful face behind it, until the comical side of the affair so completely overtopped every consideration that we both burst out into a roar of laughter.

"I cannot see that there is anything very funny," cried our client, flushing up to the roots of his flaming head. "If you can do nothing better than laugh at me, I can go elsewhere."

"No, no," cried Holmes, shoving him back into the chair from which he had half risen. "I really wouldn't miss your case for the world. It is most refreshingly unusual. But there is, if you will excuse my saying so, something just a little funny about it. Pray what steps did you take when you found the card upon the door?"

"I was staggered, sir. I did not know what to do. Then I called at the offices round, but none of them seemed to know anything about it. Finally, I went to the landlord, who is an accountant living on the ground floor, and I asked him if he could tell me what had become of the Red-headed League. He said that he had never heard of any such body. Then I asked him who Mr. Duncan Ross was. He answered that the name was new to him.

"'Well' said I, 'the gentleman at No. 4.'

"'What, the red-headed man?'

"'Yes.'

"'Oh,' said he, 'his name was William Morris. He was a solicitor, and was using my room as a temporary convenience until his new premises were ready. He moved out yesterday.'

"'Where could I find him?'

"'Oh, at his new offices. He did tell me the address. Yes, 17 King Edward Street, near St. Paul's.'

"I started off, Mr. Holmes, but when I got to that address it was a manufactory of artificial knee-caps, and no one in it had ever heard of either Mr. William Morris or Mr. Duncan Ross."

"And what did you do then?" asked Holmes.

"I went home to Saxe-Coburg Square, and I took the advice of my assistant. But he could not help me in any way. He could only say that if

106

I waited I should hear by post. But that was not quite good enough, Mr. Holmes. I did not wish to lose such a place without a struggle, so, as I had heard that you were good enough to give advice to poor folk who were in need of it, I came right away to you."

"And you did very wisely," said Holmes. "Your case is an exceedingly remarkable one, and I shall be happy to look into it. From what you have told me I think that it is possible that graver issues hang from it than might at first sight appear."

"Grave enough!" said Mr. Jabez Wilson. "Why, I have lost four pound a week."

"As far as you are personally concerned," remarked Holmes, "I do not see that you have any grievance against this extraordinary league. On the contrary, you are, as I understand, richer by some thirty pounds, to say nothing of the minute knowledge which you have gained on every subject which comes under the letter A. You have lost nothing by them."

"No, sir. But I want to find out about them, and who they are, and what their object was in playing this prank—if it was a prank—upon me. It was a pretty expensive joke for them, for it cost them two-and-thirty pounds."

"We shall endeavor to clear up these points for you. And, first, one or two questions, Mr. Wilson. This assistant of yours who first called your attention to the advertisement—how long had he been with you?"

"About a month then."

"How did he come?"

"In answer to an advertisement."

"Was he the only applicant?"

"No, I had a dozen."

"Why did you pick him?"

"Because he was handy and would come cheap."

"At half wages, in fact."

"Yes."

"What is he like, this Vincent Spaulding?"

"Small, stout-built, very quick in his ways, no hair on his face, though he's not short of thirty. Has a white splash of acid upon his forehead."

Holmes sat up in his chair in considerable excitement. "I thought as much," said he. "Have you ever observed that his ears are pierced for earrings?"

"Yes, sir. He told me that a gypsy had done it for him when he was a lad."

"Hum!" said Holmes, sinking back in deep thought. "He is still with you?"

"Oh, yes, sir; I have only just left him."

"And has your business been attended to in your absence?"

"Nothing to complain of, sir. There's never very much to do of a morning."

"That will do, Mr. Wilson. I shall be happy to give you an opinion upon the subject in the course of a day or two. To-day is Saturday, and I hope that by Monday we may come to a conclusion."

"Well, Watson," said Holmes, when our visitor had left us, "what do you make of it all?"

"I make nothing of it," I answered frankly. "It is a most mysterious business."

"As a rule," said Holmes, "the more bizarre a thing is the less mysterious it proves to be. It is your commonplace, featureless crimes which are really puzzling, just as a commonplace face is the most difficult to identify. But I must be prompt over this matter."

"What are you going to do, then?" I asked.

"To smoke," he answered. "It is quite a three-pipe problem, and I beg that you won't speak to me for fifty minutes." He curled himself up in his chair, with his thin knees drawn up to his hawklike nose, and there he sat with his eyes closed and his black clay pipe thrusting out like the bill of some strange bird. I had come to the conclusion that he had dropped asleep, and indeed was nodding myself, when he suddenly sprang out of his chair with the gesture of a man who has made up his mind, and put his pipe down upon the mantelpiece.

"Sarasate plays at St. James's Hall this afternoon," he remarked. "What do you think, Watson? Could your patients spare you for a few hours?"

"I have nothing to do to-day. My practice is never very absorbing."

"Then put on your hat and come. I am going through the City first, and we can have some lunch on the way. I observe that there is a good deal of German music on the programme, which is rather more to my taste than Italian or French. It is introspective, and I want to introspect. Come along!"

We traveled by the Underground as far as Aldersgate; and a short walk took us to Saxe-Coburg Square, the scene of the singular story which we had listened to in the morning. It was a poky, little, shabby-genteel place, where four lines of dingy, two-storied brick houses looked out into a small railed-in inclosure, where a lawn of weedy grass, and a few clumps of faded laurel bushes made a hard fight against a smoke-laden and uncongenial atmosphere. Three gilt balls and a brown board with JABEZ WILSON in white letters, upon a corner house, announced the place where our red-headed client carried on his business. Sherlock Holmes stopped in front of it with his head on one side, and looked it all over, with his eyes shining brightly between puckered lids. Then he walked slowly up the street, and then down again to the corner, still looking keenly at the houses. Finally he returned to the pawnbroker's and, having thumped vigorously upon the pavement with his stick two or three times, he went up to the door and knocked. It was instantly opened by a bright-looking, clean-shaven young fellow, who asked him to step in.

"Thank you," said Holmes, "I only wished to ask you how you would go from here to the Strand."

"Third right, fourth left," answered the assistant, promptly, closing the door.

"Smart fellow, that," observed Holmes as we walked away. "He is, in my judgment, the fourth smartest man in London, and for daring I am not sure that he has not a claim to be third. I have known something of him before."

"Evidently," said I, "Mr. Wilson's assistant counts for a good deal in this mystery of the Red-headed League. I am sure that you inquired your way merely in order that you might see him."

"Not him."

"What then?"

"The knees of his trousers."

"And what did you see?"

"What I expected to see."

"Why did you beat the pavement?"

"My dear doctor, this is a time for observation, not for talk. We are spies in an enemy's country. We know something of Saxe-Coburg Square. Let us now explore the parts which lie behind it."

The road in which we found ourselves as we turned round the corner from the retired Saxe-Coburg Square presented as great a contrast to it as the front of a picture does to the back. It was one of the main arteries which convey the traffic of the City to the north and west. The roadway was blocked with the immense stream of commerce flowing in a double tide inward and outward, while the footpaths were black with the hurrying swarm of pedestrians. It was difficult to realize, as we looked at the line of fine shops and stately business premises, that they really abutted on the other side upon the faded and stagnant square which we had just quitted.

"Let me see," said Holmes, standing at the corner, and glancing along the line, "I should like just to remember the order of the houses here. It is a hobby of mine to have an exact knowledge of London. There is Mortimer's, the tobacconist; the little newspaper shop, the Coburg branch of the City and Suburban Bank, the Vegetarian Restaurant, and McFarlane's carriage-building depot. That carries us right on to the other block. And now, doctor, we've done our work, so it's time we had some play. A sandwich and a cup of coffee, and then off to violin-land, where all is sweetness, and delicacy, and harmony, and there are no red-headed clients to vex us with their conundrums."

My friend was an enthusiastic musician, being himself not only a very capable performer, but a composer of no ordinary merit. All the afternoon he sat in the stalls wrapped in the most perfect happiness, gently waving his long thin fingers in time to the music, while his gently smiling face and his languid, dreamy eyes were as unlike those of Holmes the sleuth-hound, Holmes the relentless, keen-witted, ready-handed criminal agent, as it was possible to conceive. In his singular character the dual nature alternately asserted itself, and his extreme exactness and astuteness represented, as I have often thought, the reaction against the poetic and contemplative mood which occasionally predominated in him. The swing of his nature took him from extreme languor to devouring energy; and, as I knew well, he was never so truly formidable as when, for days on end, he had been lounging in his armchair amid his improvisations and his black-letter editions. Then it was that the lust of the chase would suddenly come upon him, and that his brilliant reasoning power would rise to the level of intuition, until those who were unacquainted with his methods would look askance at him as on a man whose knowledge was not that of other mortals. When I saw him that afternoon so enwrapped in the music at St. James's Hall, I felt that an evil time might be coming upon those whom he had set himself to hunt down.

"You want to go home, no doubt, doctor," he remarked, as we emerged.

"Yes, it would be as well."

"And I have some business to do which will take some hours. This business at Saxe-Coburg Square is serious."

"Why serious?"

"A considerable crime is in contemplation. I have every reason to believe that we shall be in time to stop it. But to-day being Saturday rather complicates matters. I shall want your help to-night."

"At what time?"

"Ten will be early enough."

"I shall be at Baker Street at ten."

"Very well. And, I say, doctor! there may be some little danger, so kindly put your army revolver in your pocket." He waved his hand, turned on his heel, and disappeared in an instant among the crowd.

I trust that I am not more dense than my neighbors, but I was always oppressed with a sense of my own stupidity in my dealings with Sherlock Holmes. Here I had heard what he had heard, I had seen what he had seen, and yet from his words it was evident that he saw clearly not only what had happened, but what was about to happen, while to me the whole business was still confused and grotesque. As I drove home to my house in Kensington I thought over it all, from the extraordinary story of the red-headed copier of the "Encyclopædia" down to the visit to Saxe-Coburg Square, and the ominous words with which he had parted from me. What was this nocturnal expedition, and why should I go armed? Where were we going, and what were we to do? I had the hint from Holmes that this smooth-faced pawnbroker's assistant was a formidable man—a man who might play a deep game. I tried to puzzle it out, but gave it up in despair, and set the matter aside until night should bring an explanation.

It was a quarter-past nine when I started from home and made my way across the Park, and so through Oxford Street to Baker Street. Two hansoms were standing at the door, and, as I entered the passage, I heard the sound of voices from above. On entering his room, I found Holmes in animated conversation with two men, one of whom I recognized as Peter Jones, the official police agent; while the other was a long, thin, sad-faced man, with a very shiny hat and oppressively respectable frock coat.

"Ha! our party is complete," said Holmes, buttoning up his pea-jacket, and taking his heavy hunting crop from the rack. "Watson, I think you know Mr. Jones, of Scotland Yard? Let me introduce you to Mr. Merryweather, who is to be our companion in to-night's adventure."

"We're hunting in couples again, doctor, you see," said Jones, in his consequential way. "Our friend here is a wonderful man for starting a chase. All he wants is an old dog to help him do the running down."

"I hope a wild goose may not prove to be the end of our chase," observed Mr. Merryweather gloomily.

"You may place considerable confidence in Mr. Holmes, sir," said the police agent loftily. "He has his own little methods, which are, if he won't mind my saying so, just a little too theoretical and fantastic, but he has the makings of a detective in him. It is not too much to say that once or twice, as in that business of the Sholto murder and the Agra treasure, he has been more nearly correct than the official force."

"Oh, if you say so, Mr. Jones, it is all right!" said the stranger, with deference. "Still, I confess that I miss my rubber. It is the first Saturday night for seven-and-twenty years that I have not had my rubber."

"I think you will find," said Sherlock Holmes, "that you will play for a higher stake to-night than you have ever done yet, and that the play will be more exciting. For you, Mr. Merryweather, the stake will be some thirty thousand pounds; and for you, Jones, it will be the man upon whom you wish to lay your hands."

"John Clay, the murderer, thief, smasher, and forger. He's a young man, Mr. Merryweather, but he is at the head of his profession, and I would rather have my bracelets on him than on any criminal in London. He's a remarkable man, is young John Clay. His grandfather was a Royal Duke, and he himself has been to Eton and Oxford. His brain is as cunning as his fingers, and though we meet signs of him at every turn, we never know where to find the man himself. He'll crack a crib in Scotland one week, and be raising money to build an orphanage in Cornwall the next. I've been on his track for years, and have never set eyes on him yet."

"I hope that I may have the pleasure of introducing you to-night.

I've had one or two little turns also with Mr. John Clay, and I agree with you that he is at the head of his profession. It is past ten, however, and quite time that we started. If you two will take the first hansom, Watson and I will follow in the second."

Sherlock Holmes was not very communicative during the long drive, and lay back in the cab humming the tunes which he had heard in the afternoon. We rattled through an endless labyrinth of gaslit streets until we emerged into Farringdon Street.

"We are close there now," my friend remarked. "This fellow Merryweather is a bank director and personally interested in the matter. I thought it as well to have Jones with us also. He is not a bad fellow, though an absolute imbecile in his profession. He has one positive virtue. He is as brave as a bulldog, and as tenacious as a lobster if he gets his claws upon anyone. Here we are, and they are waiting for us."

We had reached the same crowded thoroughfare in which we had found ourselves in the morning. Our cabs were dismissed, and following the guidance of Mr. Merryweather, we passed down a narrow passage, and through a side door which he opened for us. Within there was a small corridor, which ended in a very massive iron gate. This also was opened, and led down a flight of winding stone steps, which terminated at another formidable gate. Mr. Merryweather stopped to light a lantern, and then conducted us down a dark, earth-smelling passage, and so, after opening a third door, into a huge vault or cellar, which was piled all round with crates and massive boxes.

"You are not very vulnerable from above," Holmes remarked, as he held up the lantern and gazed about him.

"Nor from below," said Mr. Merryweather, striking his stick upon the flags which lined the floor. "Why, dear me, it sounds quite hollow!" he remarked, looking up in surprise.

"I must really ask you to be a little more quiet," said Holmes severely. "You have already imperiled the whole success of our expedition. Might I beg that you would have the goodness to sit down upon one of those boxes, and not to interfere?"

The solemn Mr. Merryweather perched himself upon a crate, with a very injured expression upon his face, while Holmes fell upon his knees upon the floor, and, with the lantern and a magnifying lens, began to examine minutely the cracks between the stones. A few seconds sufficed to satisfy him, for he sprang to his feet again, and put his glass in his pocket.

"We have at least an hour before us," he remarked, "for they can hardly take any steps until the good pawnbroker is safely in bed. Then they will not lose a minute, for the sooner they do their work the longer time they will have for their escape. We are at present, doctor—as no doubt you have divined—in the cellar of the City branch of one of the principal London banks. Mr. Merryweather is the chairman of directors, and he will explain to you that there are reasons why the more daring criminals of London should take a considerable interest in this cellar at present."

"It is our French gold," whispered the director. "We have had several warnings that an attempt might be made upon it."

"Your French gold?"

"Yes. We had occasion some months ago to strengthen our resources, and borrowed, for that purpose, thirty thousand napoleons from the Bank of France. It has become known that we have never had occasion to unpack the money, and that it is still lying in our cellar. The crate upon which I sit contains two thousand napoleons packed between layers of lead foil. Our reserve of bullion is much larger at present than is usually kept in a single branch office, and the directors have had misgivings upon the subject."

"Which were very well justified," observed Holmes.

"And now it is time that we arranged our little plans. I expect that within an hour matters will come to a head. In the meantime, Mr. Merryweather, we must put the screen over that dark lantern."

"And sit in the dark?"

"I am afraid so. I had brought a pack of cards in my pocket, and I thought that, as we were a partie carrée, you might have your rubber after all. But I see that the enemy's preparations have gone so far that we cannot risk the presence of a light. And, first of all, we must choose our positions. These are daring men, and, though we shall take them at a disadvantage, they may do us some harm, unless we are careful. I shall stand behind this crate, and do you conceal yourself behind those. Then, when I flash a light upon them, close in swiftly. If they fire, Watson, have no compunction about shooting them down."

I placed my revolver, cocked, upon the top of the wooden case behind which I crouched. Holmes shot the slide across the front of his lantern, and left us in pitch darkness—such an absolute darkness as I have never before experienced. The smell of hot metal remained to assure us that the light was still there, ready to flash out at a moment's notice. To me, with my nerves worked up to a pitch of expectancy, there was something depressing and subduing in the sudden gloom, and in the cold, dank air of the vault.

"They have but one retreat," whispered Holmes. "That is back through the house into Saxe-Coburg Square. I hope that you have done what I asked you, Jones?"

"I have an inspector and two officers waiting at the front door."

"Then we have stopped all the holes. And now we must be silent and wait."

What a time it seemed! From comparing notes afterwards, it was but an hour and a quarter, yet it appeared to me that the night must have almost gone, and the dawn be breaking above us. My limbs were weary and stiff, for I feared to change my position, yet my nerves were

113

worked up to the highest pitch of tension, and my hearing was so acute that I could not only hear the gentle breathing of my companions, but I could distinguish the deeper, heavier inbreath of the bulky Jones from the thin, sighing note of the bank director. From my position I could look over the case in the direction of the floor. Suddenly my eyes caught the glint of a light.

At first it was but a lurid spark upon the stone pavement. Then it lengthened out until it became a yellow line, and then, without any warning or sound, a gash seemed to open and a hand appeared, a white, almost womanly hand, which felt about in the center of the little area of light. For a minute or more the hand, with its writhing fingers, protruded out of the floor. Then it was withdrawn as suddenly as it appeared, and all was dark again save the single lurid spark, which marked a chink between the stones.

Its disappearance, however, was but momentary. With a rending, tearing sound, one of the broad white stones turned over upon its side, and left a square, gaping hole, through which streamed the light of a lantern. Over the edge there peeped a clean-cut, boyish face, which looked keenly about it, and then, with a hand on either side of the aperture, drew itself shoulder-high and waist-high, until one knee rested upon the edge. In another instant he stood at the side of the hole, and was hauling after him a companion, lithe and small like himself, with a pale face and a shock of very red hair.

"It's all clear," he whispered. "Have you the chisel and the bags? Great Scott! Jump, Archie, jump, and I'll swing for it!"

Sherlock Holmes had sprung out and seized the intruder by the collar. The other dived down the hole, and I heard the sound of rending cloth as Jones clutched at his skirts. The light flashed upon the barrel of a revolver, but Holmes's hunting crop came down on the man's wrist, and the pistol clinked upon the stone floor.

"It's no use, John Clay," said Holmes blandly, "you have no chance at all."

"So I see," the other answered, with the utmost coolness. "I fancy that my pal is all right, though I see you have got his coat-tails."

"There are three men waiting for him at the door," said Holmes.

"Oh, indeed. You seem to have done the thing very completely. I must compliment you."

"And I you," Holmes answered. "Your red-headed idea was very new and effective."

"You'll see your pal again presently," said Jones. "He's quicker at climbing down holes than I am. Just hold out while I fix the derbies."

"I beg that you will not touch me with your filthy hands," remarked our prisoner, as the handcuffs clattered upon his wrists. "You may not be aware that I have royal blood in my veins. Have the goodness also, when you address me, always to say 'sir' and 'please.'"

"All right," said Jones, with a stare and a snigger. "Well, would you please, sir, march upstairs where we can get a cab to carry your highness to the police station?"

"That is better," said John Clay serenely. He made a sweeping bow to the three of us, and walked quietly off in the custody of the detective.

"Really, Mr. Holmes," said Mr. Merryweather, as we followed them from the cellar, "I do not know how the bank can thank you or repay you. There is no doubt that you have detected and defeated in the most complete manner one of the most determined attempts at bank robbery, that have ever come within my experience."

"I have had one or two little scores of my own to settle with Mr. John Clay," said Holmes. "I have been at some small expense over this matter, which I shall expect the bank to refund, but beyond that I am amply repaid by having had an experience which is in many ways unique, and by hearing the very remarkable narrative of the Red-headed League."

"You see, Watson," he explained, in the early hours of the morning, as we sat over a glass of whisky and soda in Baker Street, "it was perfectly obvious from the first that the only possible object of this rather fantastic business of the advertisement of the League, and the copying of the 'Encyclopædia,' must be to get this not over-bright pawnbroker out of the way for a number of hours every day. It was a curious way of managing it, but really it would be difficult to suggest a better. The method was no doubt suggested to Clay's ingenious mind by the color of his accomplice's hair. The four pounds a week was a lure which must draw him, and what was it to them, who were playing for thousands? They put in the advertisement, one rogue has the temporary office, the other rogue incites the man to apply for it, and together they manage to secure his absence every morning in the week. From the time that I heard of the assistant having come for half wages, it was obvious to me that he had some strong motive for securing the situation."

"But how could you guess what the motive was?"

"Had there been women in the house, I should have suspected a mere vulgar intrigue. That, however, was out of the question. The man's business was a small one, and there was nothing in his house which could account for such elaborate preparations, and such an expenditure as they were at. It must then be something out of the house. What could it be? I thought of the assistant's fondness for photography, and his trick of vanishing into the cellar. The cellar! There was the end of this tangled clew. Then I made inquiries as to this mysterious assistant, and found that I had to deal with one of the coolest and most daring criminals in London. He was doing something in the cellar—something which took many hours a day for months on end. What could it be, once more? I could think of nothing save that he was running a tunnel to some other building.

115

"So far I had got when we went to visit the scene of action. I surprised you by beating upon the pavement with my stick. I was ascertaining whether the cellar stretched out in front or behind. It was not in front. Then I rang the bell, and, as I hoped, the assistant answered it. We have had some skirmishes, but we had never set eyes upon each other before. I hardly looked at his face. His knees were what I wished to see. You must yourself have remarked how worn, wrinkled, and stained they were. They spoke of those hours of burrowing. The only remaining point was what they were burrowing for. I walked round the corner, saw that the City and Suburban Bank abutted on our friend's premises, and felt that I had solved my problem. When you drove home after the concert I called upon Scotland Yard, and upon the chairman of the bank directors, with the result that you have seen."

"And how could you tell that they would make their attempt to-night?" I asked.

"Well, when they closed their League offices that was a sign that they cared no longer about Mr. Jabez Wilson's presence; in other words, that they had completed their tunnel. But it was essential that they should use it soon, as it might be discovered, or the bullion might be removed. Saturday would suit them better than any other day, as it would give them two days for their escape. For all these reasons I expected them to come to-night."

"You reasoned it out beautifully," I exclaimed, in unfeigned admiration. "It is so long a chain, and yet every link rings true."

"It saved me from ennui," he answered, yawning. "Alas! I already feel it closing in upon me. My life is spent in one long effort to escape from the commonplaces of existence. These little problems help me to do so."

"And you are a benefactor of the race," said I. He shrugged his shoulders. "Well, perhaps, after all, it is of some little use," he remarked. "'L'homme c'est rien—l'oeuvre c'est tout,' as Gustave Flaubert wrote to Georges Sands."

EGERTON CASTLE

THE BARON'S QUARRY

"Oh, no, I assure you, you are not boring Mr. Marshfield," said this personage himself in his gentle voice—that curious voice that could flow on for hours, promulgating profound and startling theories on every department of human knowledge or conducting paradoxical arguments without a single inflection or pause of hesitation. "I am, on the contrary, much interested in your hunting talk. To paraphrase a well-worn quotation somewhat widely, nihil humanum a me alienum est. Even hunting stories may have their point of biological interest; the philologist sometimes pricks his ear to the jargon of the chase; moreover, I am not incapable of appreciating the subject matter itself. This seems to excite some derision. I admit I am not much of a sportsman to look at, nor, indeed, by instinct, yet I have had some out-of-the-way experiences in that line—generally when intent on other pursuits. I doubt, for instance, if even you, Major Travers, notwithstanding your well-known exploits against man and beast, notwithstanding that doubtful smile of yours, could match the strangeness of a certain hunting adventure in which I played an important part."

The speaker's small, deep-set, black eyes, that never warmed to anything more human than a purely speculative scientific interest in his surroundings, here wandered round the skeptical yet expectant circle with bland amusement. He stretched out his bloodless fingers for another of his host's superfine cigars and proceeded, with only such interruptions as were occasioned by the lighting and careful smoking of the latter.

"I was returning home after my prolonged stay in Petersburg, intending to linger on my way and test with mine own ears certain among the many dialects of Eastern Europe—anent which there is a symmetrical little cluster of philological knotty points it is my modest intention one day to unravel. However, that is neither here nor there. On the road to Hungary I bethought myself opportunely of proving the once pressingly offered hospitality of the Baron Kossowski.

"You may have met the man, Major Travers; he was a tremendous sportsman, if you like. I first came across him at McNeil's place in remote Ireland. Now, being in Bukowina, within measurable

117

distance of his Carpathian abode, and curious to see a Polish lord at home, I remembered his invitation. It was already of long standing, but it had been warm, born in fact of a sudden fit of enthusiasm for me"— here a half-mocking smile quivered an instant under the speaker's black mustache—"which, as it was characteristic, I may as well tell you about.

"It was on the day of, or, rather, to be accurate, on the day after my arrival, toward the small hours of the morning, in the smoking room at Rathdrum. Our host was peacefully snoring over his empty pipe and his seventh glass of whisky, also empty. The rest of the men had slunk off to bed. The baron, who all unknown to himself had been a subject of most interesting observation to me the whole evening, being now practically alone with me, condescended to turn an eye, as wide awake as a fox's, albeit slightly bloodshot, upon the contemptible white-faced person who had preferred spending the raw hours over his papers, within the radius of a glorious fire's warmth, to creeping slyly over treacherous quagmires in the pursuit of timid bog creatures (snipe shooting had been the order of the day)-the baron, I say, became aware of my existence and entered into conversation with me.

"He would no doubt have been much surprised could he have known that he was already mapped out, craniologically and physiognomically, catalogued with care and neatly laid by in his proper ethnological box, in my private type museum; that, as I sat and examined him from my different coigns of vantage in library, in dining and smoking room that evening, not a look of his, not a gesture went forth but had significance for me.

"You, I had thought, with your broad shoulders and deep chest; your massive head that should have gone with a tall stature, not with those short sturdy limbs; with your thick red hair, that should have been black for that matter, as should your wide-set yellow eyes—you would be a real puzzle to one who did not recognize in you equal mixtures of the fair, stalwart and muscular Slav with the bilious-sanguine, thick-set, wiry Turanian. Your pedigree would no doubt bear me out: there is as much of the Magyar as of the Pole in your anatomy. Athlete, and yet a tangle of nerves; a ferocious brute at bottom, I dare say, for your broad forehead inclines to flatness; under your bristling beard your jaw must protrude, and the base of your skull is ominously thick. And, with all that, capable of ideal transports: when that girl played and sang to-night I saw the swelling of your eyelid veins, and how that small, tenacious, claw-like hand of yours twitched! You would be a fine leader of men—but God help the wretches in your power!

"So had I mused upon him. Yet I confess that when we came in closer contact with each other, even I was not proof against the singular courtesy of his manner and his unaccountable personal charm.

"Our conversation soon grew interesting; to me as a matter of course, and evidently to him also. A few general words led to interchange of remarks upon the country we were both visitors in and so to national characteristics—Pole and Irishman have not a few in common, both in their nature and history. An observation which he made, not without a certain flash in his light eyes and a transient uncovering of the teeth, on the Irish type of female beauty suddenly suggested to me a stanza of an ancient Polish ballad, very full of milk-and-blood imagery, of alternating ferocity and voluptuousness. This I quoted to the astounded foreigner in the vernacular, and this it was that metamorphosed his mere perfection of civility into sudden warmth, and, in fact, procured me the invitation in question.

"When I left Rathdrum the baron's last words to me were that if I ever thought of visiting his country otherwise than in books, he held me bound to make Yany, his Galician seat, my headquarters of study.

"From Czernowicz, therefore, where I stopped some time, I wrote, received in due time a few lines of prettily worded reply, and ultimately entered my sled in the nearest town to, yet at a most forbidding distance from, Yany, and started on my journey thither.

"The undertaking meant many long hours of undulation and skidding over the November snow, to the somniferous bell jangle of my dirty little horses, the only impression of interest being a weird gypsy concert I came in for at a miserable drinking-booth half buried in the snow where we halted for the refreshment of man and beast. Here, I remember, I discovered a very definite connection between the characteristic run of the tsimbol, the peculiar bite of the Zigeuner's bow on his fiddle-string, and some distinctive points of Turanian tongues. In other countries, in Spain, for instance, your gypsy speaks differently on his instrument. But, oddly enough, when I later attempted to put this observation on paper I could find no word to express it."

A few of our company evinced signs of sleepiness, but most of us who knew Marshfield, and that he could, unless he had something novel to say, be as silent and retiring as he now evinced signs of being copious, awaited further developments with patience. He has his own deliberate way of speaking, which he evidently enjoys greatly, though it be occasionally trying to his listeners.

"On the afternoon of my second day's drive, the snow, which till then had fallen fine and continuous, ceased, and my Jehu, suddenly interrupting himself in the midst of some exciting wolf story quite in keeping with the time of year and the wild surroundings, pointed to a distant spot against the gray sky to the northwest, between two wood-covered folds of ground—the first eastern spurs of the great Carpathian chain.

"'There stands Yany,' said he. I looked at my far-off goal with interest. As we drew nearer, the sinking sun, just dipping behind the hills, tinged the now distinct frontage with a cold copper-like gleam, but it was only for a minute; the next the building became nothing more to the eye than a black irregular silhouette against the crimson sky.

"Before we entered the long, steep avenue of poplars, the early winter darkness was upon us, rendered all the more depressing by gray mists which gave a ghostly aspect to such objects as the sheen of the snow rendered visible. Once or twice there were feeble flashes of light looming in iridescent halos as we passed little clusters of hovels, but for which I should have been induced to fancy that the great Hof stood alone in the wilderness, such was the deathly stillness around. But even as the tall, square building rose before us above the vapor, yellow lighted in various stories, and mighty in height and breadth, there broke upon my ear a deep-mouthed, menacing bay, which gave at once almost alarming reality to the eerie surroundings. 'His lordship's boar and wolf hounds,' quoth my charioteer calmly, unmindful of the regular pandemonium, of howls and barks which ensued as he skillfully turned his horses through the gateway and flogged the tired beasts into a sort of shambling canter that we might land with glory before the house door: a weakness common, I believe, to drivers of all nations.

"I alighted in the court of honor, and while awaiting an answer to my tug at the bell, stood, broken with fatigue, depressed, chilled and aching, questioning the wisdom of my proceedings and the amount of comfort, physical and moral, that was likely to await me in a tête-à-tête visit with a well-mannered savage in his own home.

"The unkempt tribe of stable retainers who began to gather round me and my rough vehicle in the gloom, with their evil-smelling sheepskins and their resigned, battered visages, were not calculated to reassure me. Yet when the door opened, there stood a smart chasseur and a solemn major-domo who might but just have stepped out of Mayfair; and there was displayed a spreading vista of warm, deep-colored halls, with here a statue and there a stuffed bear, and under foot pile carpets strewn with rarest skins.

"Marveling, yet comforted withal, I followed the solemn butler, who received me with the deference due to an expected guest and expressed the master's regret for his enforced absence till dinner time. I traversed vast rooms, each more sumptuous than the last, feeling the strangeness of the contrast between the outer desolation and this sybaritic excess of luxury growing ever more strongly upon me; caught a glimpse of a picture gallery, where peculiar yet admirably executed latter-day French pictures hung side by side with ferocious boar hunts of Snyder and such kin; and, at length, was ushered into a most cheerful room, modern to excess in its comfortable promise, where, in addition to the tall stove necessary for warmth, there burned on an open hearth a vastly pleasant fire of resinous logs, and where, on a low table, awaited me a dainty service of fragrant Russian tea.

"My impression of utter novelty seemed somehow enhanced by this unexpected refinement in the heart of the solitudes and in such a

120

rugged shell, and yet, when I came to reflect, it was only characteristic of my cosmopolitan host. But another surprise was in store for me.

"When I had recovered bodily warmth and mental equilibrium in my downy armchair, before the roaring logs, and during the delicious absorption of my second glass of tea, I turned my attention to the French valet, evidently the baron's own man, who was deftly unpacking my portmanteau, and who, unless my practiced eye deceived me, asked for nothing better than to entertain me with agreeable conversation the while.

"'Your master is out, then?' quoth I, knowing that the most trivial remark would suffice to start him.

"True, Monseigneur was out; he was desolated in despair (this with the national amiable and imaginative instinct); 'but it was doubtless important business. M. le Baron had the visit of his factor during the midday meal; had left the table hurriedly, and had not been seen since. Madame la Baronne had been a little suffering, but she would receive monsieur!'

"'Madame!' exclaimed I, astounded, 'is your master then married?—since when?'—visions of a fair Tartar, fit mate for my baron, immediately springing somewhat alluringly before my mental vision. But the answer dispelled the picturesque fancy.

"'Oh, yes,' said the man, with a somewhat peculiar expression. 'Yes, Monseigneur is married. Did Monsieur not know? And yet it was from England that Monseigneur brought back his wife.'

"'An Englishwoman!'

"My first thought was one of pity; an Englishwoman alone in this wilderness—two days' drive from even a railway station—and at the mercy of Kossowski! But the next minute I reversed my judgment. Probably she adored her rufous lord, took his veneer of courtesy—a veneer of the most exquisite polish, I grant you, but perilously thin—for the very perfection of chivalry. Or perchance it was his inner savageness itself that charmed her; the most refined women often amaze one by the fascination which the preponderance of the brute in the opposite sex seems to have for them.

"I was anxious to hear more.

"'Is it not dull for the lady here at this time of the year?'

"The valet raised his shoulders with a gesture of despair that was almost passionate.

"Dull! Ah, monsieur could not conceive to himself the dullness of it. That poor Madame la Baronne! not even a little child to keep her company on the long, long days when there was nothing but snow in the heaven and on the earth and the howling of the wind and the dogs to cheer her. At the beginning, indeed, it had been different; when the master first brought home his bride the house was gay enough. It was all redecorated and refurnished to receive her (monsieur should have seen it before, a mere rendezvous-de-chasse—for the matter of that so

121

were all the country houses in these parts). Ah, that was the good time! There were visits month after month; parties, sleighing, dancing, trips to St. Petersburg and Vienna. But this year it seemed they were to have nothing but boars and wolves. How madame could stand it—well, it was not for him to speak—and heaving a deep sigh he delicately inserted my white tie round my collar, and with a flourish twisted it into an irreproachable bow beneath my chin. I did not think it right to cross-examine the willing talker any further, especially as, despite his last asseveration, there were evidently volumes he still wished to pour forth; but I confess that, as I made my way slowly out of my room along the noiseless length of passage, I was conscious of an unwonted, not to say vulgar, curiosity concerning the woman who had captivated such a man as the Baron Kossowski.

"In a fit of speculative abstraction I must have taken the wrong turning, for I presently found myself in a long, narrow passage. I did not remember. I was retracing my steps when there came the sound of rapid footfalls upon stone flags; a little door flew open in the wall close to me, and a small, thick-set man, huddled in the rough sheepskin of the Galician peasant, with a mangy fur cap on his head, nearly ran headlong into my arms. I was about condescendingly to interpellate him in my best Polish, when I caught the gleam of an angry yellow eye and noted the bristle of a red beard—Kossowski!

"Amazed, I fell back a step in silence. With a growl like an uncouth animal disturbed, he drew his filthy cap over his brow with a savage gesture and pursued his way down the corridor at a sort of wild-boar trot.

"This first meeting between host and guest was so odd, so incongruous, that it afforded me plenty of food for a fresh line of conjecture as I traced my way back to the picture gallery, and from thence successfully to the drawing room, which, as the door was ajar, I could not this time mistake.

"It was large and lofty and dimly lit by shaded lamps; through the rosy gloom I could at first only just make out a slender figure by the hearth; but as I advanced, this was resolved into a singularly graceful woman in clinging, fur-trimmed velvet gown, who, with one hand resting on the high mantelpiece, the other hanging listlessly by her side, stood gazing down at the crumbling wood fire as if in a dream.

"My friends are kind enough to say that I have a cat-like tread; I know not how that may be; at any rate the carpet I was walking upon was thick enough to smother a heavier footfall: not until I was quite close to her did my hostess become aware of my presence. Then she started violently and looked over her shoulder at me with dilating eyes. Evidently a nervous creature, I saw the pulse in her throat, strained by her attitude, flutter like a terrified bird.

"The next instant she had stretched out her hand with sweet English words of welcome, and the face, which I had been comparing in

122

my mind to that of Guido's Cenci, became transformed by the arch and exquisite smile of a Greuse. For more than two years I had had no intercourse with any of my nationality. I could conceive the sound of his native tongue under such circumstances moving a man in a curious unexpected fashion.

"I babbled some commonplace reply, after which there was silence while we stood opposite each other, she looking at me expectantly. At length, with a sigh checked by a smile and an overtone of sadness in a voice that yet tried to be sprightly:

"'Am I then so changed, Mr. Marshfield?' she asked. And all at once I knew her: the girl whose nightingale throat had redeemed the desolation of the evenings at Rathdrum, whose sunny beauty had seemed (even to my celebrated cold-blooded æstheticism) worthy to haunt a man's dreams. Yes, there was the subtle curve of the waist, the warm line of throat, the dainty foot, the slender tip-tilted fingers—witty fingers, as I had classified them—which I now shook like a true Briton, instead of availing myself of the privilege the country gave me, and kissing her slender wrist.

"But she was changed; and I told her so with unconventional frankness, studying her closely as I spoke.

"'I am afraid,' I said gravely, 'that this place does not agree with you.'

"She shrank from my scrutiny with a nervous movement and flushed to the roots of her red-brown hair. Then she answered coldly that I was wrong, that she was in excellent health, but that she could not expect any more than other people to preserve perennial youth (I rapidly calculated she might be two-and-twenty), though, indeed, with a little forced laugh, it was scarcely flattering to hear one had altered out of all recognition. Then, without allowing me time to reply, she plunged into a general topic of conversation which, as I should have been obtuse indeed not to take the hint, I did my best to keep up.

"But while she talked of Vienna and Warsaw, of her distant neighbors, and last year's visitors, it was evident that her mind was elsewhere; her eye wandered, she lost the thread of her discourse, answered me at random, and smiled her piteous smile incongruously.

"However lonely she might be in her solitary splendor, the company of a countryman was evidently no such welcome diversion.

"After a little while she seemed to feel herself that she was lacking in cordiality, and, bringing her absent gaze to bear upon me with a puzzled strained look: 'I fear you will find it very dull,' she said, 'my husband is so wrapped up this winter in his country life and his sport. You are the first visitor we have had. There is nothing but guns and horses here, and you do not care for these things.'

"The door creaked behind us; and the baron entered, in faultless evening dress. Before she turned toward him I was sharp enough to catch again the upleaping of a quick dread in her eyes, not even so

123

much dread perhaps, I thought afterwards, as horror—the horror we notice in some animals at the nearing of a beast of prey. It was gone in a second, and she was smiling. But it was a revelation.

"Perhaps he beat her in Russian fashion, and she, as an Englishwoman, was narrow-minded enough to resent this; or perhaps, merely, I had the misfortune to arrive during a matrimonial misunderstanding.

"The baron would not give me leisure to reflect; he was so very effusive in his greeting—not a hint of our previous meeting—unlike my hostess, all in all to me; eager to listen, to reply; almost affectionate, full of references to old times and genial allusions. No doubt when he chose he could be the most charming of men; there were moments when, looking at him in his quiet smile and restrained gesture, the almost exaggerated politeness of his manner to his wife, whose fingers he had kissed with pretty, old-fashioned gallantry upon his entrance, I asked myself, Could that encounter in the passage have been a dream? Could that savage in the sheepskin be my courteous entertainer?

"Just as I came in, did I hear my wife say there was nothing for you to do in this place?" he said presently to me. Then, turning to her:

"You do not seem to know Mr. Marshfield. Wherever he can open his eyes there is for him something to see which might not interest other men. He will find things in my library which I have no notion of. He will discover objects for scientific observation in all the members of my household, not only in the good-looking maids—though he could, I have no doubt, tell their points as I could those of a horse. We have maidens here of several distinct races, Marshfield. We have also witches, and Jew leeches, and holy daft people. In any case, Yany, with all its dependencies, material, male and female, are at your disposal, for what you can make out of them.

"'It is good," he went on gayly, 'that you should happen to have this happy disposition, for I fear that, no later than to-morrow, I may have to absent myself from home. I have heard that there are news of wolves—they threaten to be a greater pest than usual this winter, but I am going to drive them on quite a new plan, and it will go hard with me if I don't come even with them. Well for you, by the way, Marshfield, that you did not pass within their scent to-day.' Then, musingly: 'I should not give much for the life of a traveler who happened to wander in these parts just now.' Here he interrupted himself hastily and went over to his wife, who had sunk back on her chair, livid, seemingly on the point of swooning.

"His gaze was devouring; so might a man look at the woman he adored, in his anxiety.

"'What! faint, Violet, alarmed!' His voice was subdued, yet there was an unmistakable thrill of emotion in it.

"'Pshaw!' thought I to myself, 'the man is a model husband.'

"She clinched her hands, and by sheer force of will seemed to

124

pull herself together. These nervous women have often an unexpected fund of strength.

"'Come, that is well,' said the baron with a flickering smile; 'Mr. Marshfield will think you but badly acclimatized to Poland if a little wolf scare can upset you. My dear wife is so soft-hearted,' he went on to me, 'that she is capable of making herself quite ill over the sad fate that might have, but has not, overcome you. Or, perhaps,' he added, in a still gentler voice, 'her fear is that I may expose myself to danger for the public weal.'

"She turned her head away, but I saw her set her teeth as if to choke a sob. The baron chuckled in his throat and seemed to luxuriate in the pleasant thought.

"At this moment folding doors were thrown open, and supper was announced. I offered my arm, she rose and took it in silence. This silence she maintained during the first part of the meal, despite her husband's brilliant conversation and almost uproarious spirits. But by and by a bright color mounted to her cheeks and luster to her eyes. I suppose you will think me horribly unpoetical if I add that she drank several glasses of champagne one after the other, a fact which perhaps may account for the change.

"At any rate she spoke and laughed and looked lovely, and I did not wonder that the baron could hardly keep his eyes off her. But whether it was her wifely anxiety or not—it was evident her mind was not at ease through it all, and I fancied that her brightness was feverish, her merriment slightly hysterical.

"After supper—an exquisite one it was—we adjourned together, in foreign fashion, to the drawing-room; the baron threw himself into a chair and, somewhat with the air of a pasha, demanded music. He was flushed; the veins of his forehead were swollen and stood out like cords; the wine drunk at table was potent: even through my phlegmatic frame it ran hotly.

"She hesitated a moment or two, then docilely sat down to the piano. That she could sing I have already made clear: how she could sing, with what pathos, passion, as well as perfect art, I had never realized before.

"When the song was ended she remained for a while, with eyes lost in distance, very still, save for her quick breathing. It was clear she was moved by the music; indeed she must have thrown her whole soul into it.

"At first we, the audience, paid her the rare compliment of silence. Then the baron broke forth into loud applause. 'Brava, brava! that was really said con amore. A delicious love song, delicious—but French! You must sing one of our Slav melodies for Marshfield before you allow us to go and smoke.'

"She started from her reverie with a flush, and after a pause struck slowly a few simple chords, then began one of those strangely

125

sweet, yet intensely pathetic Russian airs, which give one a curious revelation of the profound, endless melancholy lurking in the national mind.

"'What do you think of it?' asked the baron of me when it ceased.

"'What I have always thought of such music—it is that of a hopeless people; poetical, crushed, and resigned.'

"He gave a loud laugh. 'Hear the analyst, the psychologue—why, man, it is a love song! Is it possible that we, uncivilized, are truer realists than our hypercultured Western neighbors? Have we gone to the root of the matter, in our simple way?'

"The baroness got up abruptly. She looked white and spent; there were bister circles round her eyes.

"'I am tired,' she said, with dry lips. 'You will excuse me, Mr. Marshfield, I must really go to bed.'

"'Go to bed, go to bed,' cried her husband gayly. Then, quoting in Russian from the song she had just sung: 'Sleep, my little soft white dove: my little innocent tender lamb!' She hurried from the room. The baron laughed again, and, taking me familiarly by the arm, led me to his own set of apartments for the promised smoke. He ensconced me in an armchair, placed cigars of every description and a Turkish pipe ready to my hand, and a little table on which stood cut-glass flasks and beakers in tempting array.

"After I had selected my cigar with some precautions, I glanced at him over a careless remark, and was startled to see a sudden alteration in his whole look and attitude.

"'You will forgive me, Marshfield,' he said, as he caught my eye, speaking with spasmodic politeness. 'It is more than probable that I shall have to set out upon this chase I spoke of to-night, and I must now go and change my clothes, that I may be ready to start at any moment. This is the hour when it is most likely these hell beasts are to be got at. You have all you want, I hope,' interrupting an outbreak of ferocity by an effort after his former courtesy.

"It was curious to watch the man of the world struggling with the primitive man.

"'But, baron,' said I, 'I do not at all see the fun of sticking at home like this. You know my passion for witnessing everything new, strange, and outlandish. You will surely not refuse me such an opportunity for observation as a midnight wolf raid. I will do my best not to be in the way if you will take me with you.'

"At first it seemed as if he had some difficulty in realizing the drift of my words, he was so engrossed by some inner thought. But as I repeated them, he gave vent to a loud cachinnation.

"'By heaven! I like your spirit,' he exclaimed, clapping me strongly on the shoulder. 'Of course you shall come. You shall,' he repeated, 'and I promise you a sight, a hunt such as you never heard or dreamed of—you will be able to tell them in England the sort of thing

126

we can do here in that line—such wolves are rare quarry,' he added, looking slyly at me, 'and I have a new plan for getting at them.'

"There was a long pause, and then there rose in the stillness the unearthly howling of the baron's hounds, a cheerful sound which only their owner's somewhat loud converse of the evening had kept from becoming excessively obtrusive.

"'Hark at them—the beauties!' cried he, showing his short, strong teeth, pointed like a dog's in a wide grin of anticipative delight. 'They have been kept on pretty short commons, poor things! They are hungry. By the way, Marshfield, you can sit tight to a horse, I trust? If you were to roll off, you know, these splendid fellows—they would chop you up in a second. They would chop you up,' he repeated unctuously, 'snap, crunch, gobble, and there would be an end of you!'

"'If I could not ride a decent horse without being thrown,' I retorted, a little stung by his manner, 'after my recent three months' torture with the Guard Cossacks, I should indeed be a hopeless subject. Do not think of frightening me from the exploit, but say frankly if my company would be displeasing.'

"'Tut!' he said, waving his hand impatiently, 'it is your affair. I have warned you. Go and get ready if you want to come. Time presses.'

"I was determined to be of the fray; my blood was up. I have hinted that the baron's Tokay had stirred it.

"I went to my room and hurriedly donned clothes more suitable for rough night work. My last care was to slip into my pockets a brace of double-barreled pistols which formed part of my traveling kit. When I returned I found the baron already booted and spurred; this without metaphor. He was stretched full length on the divan, and did not speak as I came in, or even look at me. Chewing an unlit cigar, with eyes fixed on the ceiling, he was evidently following some absorbing train of ideas.

"The silence was profound; time went by; it grew oppressive; at length, wearied out, I fell, over my chibouque, into a doze filled with puzzling visions, out of which I was awakened with a start. My companion had sprung up, very lightly, to his feet. In his throat was an odd, half-suppressed cry, grewsome to hear. He stood on tiptoe, with eyes fixed, as though looking through the wall, and I distinctly saw his ears point in the intensity of his listening.

"After a moment, with hasty, noiseless energy, and without the slightest ceremony, he blew the lamps out, drew back the heavy curtains and threw the tall window wide open. A rush of icy air, and the bright rays of the moon—gibbous, I remember, in her third quarter—filled the room. Outside the mist had condensed, and the view was unrestricted over the white plains at the foot of the hill.

"The baron stood motionless in the open window, callous to the cold in which, after a minute, I could hardly keep my teeth from chattering, his head bent forward, still listening. I listened too, with 'all

127

my ears,' but could not catch a sound; indeed the silence over the great expanse of snow might have been called awful; even the dogs were mute.

"Presently, far, far away, came a faint tinkle of bells; so faint, at first, that I thought it was but fancy, then distincter. It was even more eerie than the silence, I thought, though I knew it could come but from some passing sleigh. All at once that ceased, and again my duller senses could perceive nothing, though I saw by my host's craning neck that he was more on the alert than ever. But at last I too heard once more, this time not bells, but as it were the tread of horses muffled by the snow, intermittent and dull, yet drawing nearer. And then in the inner silence of the great house it seemed to me I caught the noise of closing doors; but here the hounds, as if suddenly becoming alive to some disturbance, raised the same fearsome concert of yells and barks with which they had greeted my arrival, and listening became useless.

"I had risen to my feet. My host, turning from the window, seized my shoulder with a fierce grip, and bade me 'hold my noise'; for a second or two I stood motionless under his iron talons, then he released me with an exultant whisper: "Now for our chase!" and made for the door with a spring. Hastily gulping down a mouthful of arrack from one of the bottles on the table, I followed him, and, guided by the sound of his footsteps before me, groped my way through passages as black as Erebus.

"After a time, which seemed a long one, a small door was flung open in front, and I saw Kossowski glide into the moonlit courtyard and cross the square. When I too came out he was disappearing into the gaping darkness of the open stable door, and there I overtook him.

"A man who seemed to have been sleeping in a corner jumped up at our entrance, and led out a horse ready saddled. In obedience to a gruff order from his master, as the latter mounted, he then brought forward another which he had evidently thought to ride himself and held the stirrup for me.

"We came delicately forth, and the Cossack hurriedly barred the great door behind us. I caught a glimpse of his worn, scarred face by the moonlight, as he peeped after us for a second before shutting himself in; it was stricken with terror.

"The baron trotted briskly toward the kennels, from whence there was now issuing a truly infernal clangor, and, as my steed followed suit of his own accord, I could see how he proceeded dexterously to unbolt the gates without dismounting, while the beasts within dashed themselves against them and tore the ground in their fury of impatience.

"He smiled, as he swung back the barriers at last, and his 'beauties' came forth. Seven or eight monstrous brutes, hounds of a kind unknown to me: fulvous and sleek of coat, tall on their legs, square-headed, long-tailed, deep-chested; with terrible jaws slobbering

128

in eagerness. They leaped around and up at us, much to our horses' distaste. Kossowski, still smiling, lashed at them unsparingly with his hunting whip, and they responded, not with yells of pain, but with snarls of fury.

"Managing his restless steed and his cruel whip with consummate ease, my host drove the unruly crew before him out of the precincts, then halted and bent down from his saddle to examine some slight prints in the snow which led, not the way I had come, but toward what seemed another avenue. In a second or two the hounds were gathered round this spot, their great snake-like tails quivering, nose to earth, yelping with excitement. I had some ado to manage my horse, and my eyesight was far from being as keen as the baron's, but I had then no doubt he had come already upon wolf tracks, and I shuddered mentally, thinking of the sleigh bells.

"Suddenly Kossowski raised himself from his strained position; under his low fur cap his face, with its fixed smile, looked scarcely human in the white light: and then we broke into a hand canter just as the hounds dashed, in a compact body, along the trail.

"But we had not gone more than a few hundred yards before they began to falter, then straggled, stopped and ran back and about with dismal cries. It was clear to me they had lost the scent. My companion reined in his horse, and mine, luckily a well-trained brute, halted of himself.

"We had reached a bend in a broad avenue of firs and larches, and just where we stood, and where the hounds ever returned and met nose to nose in frantic conclave, the snow was trampled and soiled, and a little farther on planed in a great sweep, as if by a turning sleigh. Beyond was a double-furrowed track of skaits and regular hoof prints leading far away.

"Before I had time to reflect upon the bearing of this unexpected interruption, Kossowski, as if suddenly possessed by a devil, fell upon the hounds with his whip, flogging them upon the new track, uttering the while the most savage cries I have ever heard issue from human throat. The disappointed beasts were nothing loath to seize upon another trail; after a second of hesitation they had understood, and were off upon it at a tearing pace, we after them at the best speed of our horses.

"Some unformed idea that we were going to escort, or rescue, benighted travelers flickered dimly in my mind as I galloped through the night air; but when I managed to approach my companion and called out to him for explanation, he only turned half round and grinned at me.

"Before us lay now the white plain, scintillating under the high moon's rays. That light is deceptive; I could be sure of nothing upon the wide expanse but of the dark, leaping figures of the hounds already spread out in a straggling line, some right ahead, others just in front of us. In a short time also the icy wind, cutting my face mercilessly as we increased our pace, well nigh blinded me with tears of cold.

"I can hardly realize how long this pursuit after an unseen prey lasted; I can only remember that I was getting rather faint with fatigue, and ignominiously held on to my pommel, when all of a sudden the black outline of a sleigh merged into sight in front of us.

"I rubbed my smarting eyes with my benumbed hand; we were gaining upon it second by second; two of those hell hounds of the baron's were already within a few leaps of it.

"Soon I was able to make out two figures, one standing up and urging the horses on with whip and voice, the other clinging to the back seat and looking toward us in an attitude of terror. A great fear crept into my half-frozen brain—were we not bringing deadly danger instead of help to these travelers? Great God! did the baron mean to use them as a bait for his new method of wolf hunting?

"I would have turned upon Kossowski with a cry of expostulation or warning, but he, urging on his hounds as he galloped on their flank, howling and gesticulating like a veritable Hun, passed me by like a flash—and all at once I knew."

Marshfield paused for a moment and sent his pale smile round upon his listeners, who now showed no signs of sleepiness; he knocked the ash from his cigar, twisted the latter round in his mouth, and added dryly:

"And I confess it seemed to me a little strong even for a baron in the Carpathians. The travelers were our quarry. But the reason why the Lord of Yany had turned man-hunter I was yet to learn. Just then I had to direct my energies to frustrating his plans. I used my spurs mercilessly. While I drew up even with him I saw the two figures in the sleigh change places; he who had hitherto driven now faced back, while his companion took the reins, there was the pale blue sheen of a revolver barrel under the moonlight, followed by a yellow flash, and the nearest hound rolled over in the snow.

"With an oath the baron twisted round in his saddle to call up and urge on the remainder. My horse had taken fright at the report and dashed irresistibly forward, bringing me at once almost level with the fugitives, and the next instant the revolver was turned menacingly toward me. There was no time to explain; my pistol was already drawn, and as another of the brutes bounded up, almost under my horse's feet, I loosed it upon him. I must have let off both barrels at once, for the weapon flew out of my hand, but the hound's back was broken. I presume the traveler understood; at any rate, he did not fire at me.

"In moments of intense excitement like these, strangely enough, the mind is extraordinarily open to impressions. I shall never forget that man's countenance in the sledge, as he stood upright and defied us in his mortal danger; it was young, very handsome, the features not distorted, but set into a sort of desperate, stony calm, and I knew it,

130

beyond all doubt, for that of an Englishman. And then I saw his companion—it was the baron's wife. And I understood why the bells had been removed.

"It takes a long time to say this; it only required an instant to see it. The loud explosion of my pistol had hardly ceased to ring before the baron, with a fearful imprecation, was upon me. First he lashed at me with his whip as we tore along side by side, and then I saw him wind the reins round his off arm and bend over, and I felt his angry fingers close tightly on my right foot. The next instant I should have been lifted out of my saddle, but there came another shot from the sledge. The baron's horse plunged and stumbled, and the baron, hanging on to my foot with a fierce grip, was wrenched from his seat. His horse, however, was up again immediately, and I was released, and then I caught a confused glimpse of the frightened and wounded animal galloping wildly away to the right, leaving a black track of blood behind him in the snow, his master, entangled in the reins, running with incredible swiftness by his side and endeavoring to vault back into the saddle.

"And now came to pass a terrible thing which, in his savage plans, my host had doubtless never anticipated.

"One of the hounds that had during this short check recovered lost ground, coming across this hot trail of blood, turned away from his course, and with a joyous yell darted after the running man. In another instant the remainder of the pack was upon the new scent.

"As soon as I could stop my horse, I tried to turn him in the direction the new chase had taken, but just then, through the night air, over the receding sound of the horse's scamper and the sobbing of the pack in full cry, there came a long scream, and after that a sickening silence. And I knew that somewhere yonder, under the beautiful moonlight, the Baron Kossowski was being devoured by his starving dogs.

"I looked round, with the sweat on my face, vaguely, for some human being to share the horror of the moment, and I saw, gliding away, far away in the white distance, the black silhouette of the sledge."

"Well?" said we, in divers tones of impatience, curiosity, or horror, according to our divers temperaments, as the speaker uncrossed his legs and gazed at us in mild triumph, with all the air of having said his say, and satisfactorily proved his point.

"Well," repeated he, "what more do you want to know? It will interest you but slightly, I am sure, to hear how I found my way back to the Hof; or how I told as much as I deemed prudent of the evening's grewsome work to the baron's servants, who, by the way, to my amazement, displayed the profoundest and most unmistakable sorrow at the tidings, and sallied forth (at their head the Cossack who had seen us depart) to seek for his remains. Excuse the unpleasantness of the remark: I fear the dogs must have left very little of him, he had dieted them so carefully. However, since it was to have been a case of 'chop,

131

crunch, and gobble,' as the baron had it, I preferred that that particular fate should have overtaken him rather than me—or, for that matter, either of those two country people of ours in the sledge.

"Nor am I going to inflict upon you," continued Marshfield, after draining his glass, "a full account of my impressions when I found myself once more in that immense, deserted, and stricken house, so luxuriously prepared for the mistress who had fled from it; how I philosophized over all this, according to my wont; the conjectures I made as to the first acts of the drama; the untold sufferings my countrywoman must have endured from the moment her husband first grew jealous till she determined on this desperate step; as to how and when she had met her lover, how they communicated, and how the baron had discovered the intended flitting in time to concoct his characteristic revenge.

"One thing you may be sure of, I had no mind to remain at Yany an hour longer than necessary. I even contrived to get well clear of the neighborhood before the lady's absence was discovered. Luckily for me—or I might have been taxed with connivance, though indeed the simple household did not seem to know what suspicion was, and accepted my account with childlike credence—very typical, and very convenient to me at the same time."

"But how do you know," said one of us, "that the man was her lover? He might have been her brother or some other relative."

"That," said Marshfield, with his little flat laugh, "I happen to have ascertained—and, curiously enough, only a few weeks ago. It was at the play, between the acts, from my comfortable seat (the first row in the pit). I was looking leisurely round the house when I caught sight of a woman, in a box close by, whose head was turned from me, and who presented the somewhat unusual spectacle of a young neck and shoulders of the most exquisite contour—and perfectly gray hair; and not dull gray, but rather of a pleasing tint like frosted silver. This aroused my curiosity. I brought my glasses to a focus on her and waited patiently till she turned round. Then I recognized the Baroness Kassowski, and I no longer wondered at the young hair being white.

"Yet she looked placid and happy; strangely so, it seemed to me, under the sudden reviving in my memory of such scenes as I have now described. But presently I understood further: beside her, in close attendance, was the man of the sledge, a handsome fellow with much of a military air about him.

"During the course of the evening, as I watched, I saw a friend of mine come into the box, and at the end I slipped out into the passage to catch him as he came out.

"'Who is the woman with the white hair?' I asked. Then, in the fragmentary style approved of by ultra-fashionable young men—this earnest-languid mode of speech presents curious similarities in all languages—he told me: 'Most charming couple in London—awfully pretty, wasn't she?—he had been in the Guards—attaché at Vienna once—they adored each other. White hair, devilish queer, wasn't it? Suited her, somehow. And then she had been married to a Russian, or something, somewhere in the wilds, and their names were—' But do you know," said Marshfield, interrupting himself, "I think I had better let you find that out for yourselves, if you care."

STANLEY J. WEYMAN

THE FOWL IN THE POT

An Episode Adapted from the Memoirs of Maximilian de Bethune, Duke of Sully

What I am going to relate may seem to some merely to be curious and on a party with the diverting story of M. Boisrosé, which I have set down in an earlier part of my memoirs. But among the calumnies of those who have never ceased to attack me since the death of the late king, the statement that I kept from his majesty things which should have reached his ears has always had a prominent place, though a thousand times refuted by my friends, and those who from an intimate acquaintance with events could judge how faithfully I labored to deserve the confidence with which my master honored me. Therefore, I take it in hand to show by an example, trifling in itself, the full knowledge of affairs which the king had, and to prove that in many matters, which were never permitted to become known to the idlers of the court, he took a personal share, worthy as much of Haroun as of Alexander.

It was my custom, before I entered upon those negotiations with the Prince of Condé which terminated in the recovery of the estate of Villebon, where I now principally reside, to spend a part of the autumn and winter at Rosny. On these occasions I was in the habit of leaving Paris with a considerable train of Swiss, pages, valets, and grooms, together with the maids of honor and waiting women of the duchess. We halted to take dinner at Poissy, and generally contrived to reach Rosny toward nightfall, so as to sup by the light of flambeaux in a manner enjoyable enough, though devoid of that state which I have ever maintained, and enjoined upon my children, as at once the privilege and burden of rank.

At the time of which I am speaking I had for my favorite charger the sorrel horse which the Duke of Mercoeur presented to me with a view to my good offices at the time of the king's entry into Paris; and which I honestly transferred to his majesty in accordance with a principle laid down in another place. The king insisted on returning it to me, and for several years I rode it on these annual visits to Rosny. What was more remarkable was that on each of these occasions it cast a shoe about the middle of the afternoon, and always when we were within a short league of the village of Aubergenville. Though I never had with me less than half a score of led horses, I had such an affection for the sorrel that I preferred to wait until it was shod, rather than accommodate myself to a nag of less easy paces; and would allow my household to precede me, staying behind myself with at most a guard or two, my valet, and a page.

The forge at Aubergenville was kept by a smith of some skill, a cheerful fellow, whom I always remembered to reward, considering my own position rather than his services, with a gold livre. His joy at receiving what was to him the income of a year was great, and never failed to reimburse me; in addition to which I took some pleasure in unbending, and learning from this simple peasant and loyal man, what the taxpayers were saying of me and my reforms—a duty I always felt I owed to the king my master.

As a man of breeding it would ill become me to set down the homely truths I thus learned. The conversations of the vulgar are little suited to a nobleman's memoirs; but in this I distinguish between the Duke of Sully and the king's minister, and it is in the latter capacity that I relate what passed on these diverting occasions. "Ho, Simon," I would say, encouraging the poor man as he came bowing and trembling before me, "how goes it, my friend?"

"Badly," he would answer, "very badly until your lordship came this way."

"And how is that, little man?"

"Oh, it is the roads," he always replied, shaking his bald head as he began to set about his business. "The roads since your lordship became surveyor-general are so good that not one horse in a hundred casts a shoe; and then there are so few highwaymen now that not one robber's plates do I replace in a twelvemonth. There is where it is."

At this I was highly delighted.

"Still, since I began to pass this way times have not been so bad with you, Simon," I would answer.

Thereto he had one invariable reply.

"No; thanks to Ste. Geneviève and your lordship, whom we call in this village the poor man's friend, I have a fowl in the pot."

This phrase so pleased me that I repeated it to the king. It tickled his fancy also, and for some years it was a very common remark of that good and great ruler, that he hoped to live to see every peasant with a fowl in his pot.

"But why," I remember I once asked this honest fellow—it was on the last occasion of the sorrel falling lame there—"do you thank Ste. Geneviève?"

"She is my patron saint," he answered.

"Then you are a Parisian?"

"Your lordship is always right."

135

"But does her saintship do you any good?" I asked curiously.

"Certainly, by your lordship's leave. My wife prays to her and she loosens the nails in the sorrel's shoes."

"In fact she pays off an old grudge," I answered, "for there was a time when Paris liked me little; but hark ye, master smith, I am not sure that this is not an act of treason to conspire with Madame Geneviève against the comfort of the king's minister. What think you, you rascal; can you pass the justice elm without a shiver?"

This threw the simple fellow into a great fear, which the sight of the livre of gold speedily converted into joy as stupendous. Leaving him still staring at his fortune I rode away; but when we had gone some little distance, the aspect of his face, when I charged him with treason, or my own unassisted discrimination suggested a clew to the phenomenon.

"La Trape," I said to my valet—the same who was with me at Cahors—"what is the name of the innkeeper at Poissy, at whose house we are accustomed to dine?"

"Andrew, may it please your lordship."

"Andrew! I thought so!" I exclaimed, smiting my thigh. "Simon and Andrew his brother! Answer, knave, and, if you have permitted me to be robbed these many times, tremble for your ears. Is he not brother to the smith at Aubergenville who has just shod my horse?"

La Trape professed to be ignorant on this point, but a groom who had stayed behind with me, having sought my permission to speak, said it was so, adding that Master Andrew had risen in the world through large dealings in hay, which he was wont to take daily into Paris and sell, and that he did not now acknowledge or see anything of his brother the smith, though it was believed that he retained a sneaking liking for him.

On receiving this confirmation of my suspicions, my vanity as well as my sense of justice led me to act with the promptitude which I have exhibited in greater emergencies. I rated La Trape for his carelessness of my interests in permitting this deception to be practiced on me; and the main body of my attendants being now in sight, I ordered him to take two Swiss and arrest both brothers without delay. It wanted yet three hours of sunset, and I judged that, by hard riding, they might reach Rosny with their prisoners before bedtime.

I spent some time while still on the road in considering what punishment I should inflict on the culprits; and finally laid aside the purpose I had at first conceived of putting them to death—an infliction they had richly deserved—in favor of a plan which I thought might offer me some amusement. For the execution of this I depended upon Maignan, my equerry, who was a man of lively imagination, being the same who had of his own motion arranged and carried out the triumphal procession, in which I was borne to Rosny after the battle of Ivry. Before I sat down to supper I gave him his directions; and as I had expected, news was brought to me while I was at table that the prisoners had arrived.

Thereupon I informed the duchess and the company generally, for, as was usual, a number of my country neighbors had come to compliment me on my return, that there was some sport of a rare kind on foot; and we adjourned, Maignan, followed by four pages bearing lights, leading the way to that end of the terrace which abuts on the linden avenue. Here, a score of grooms holding torches aloft had been arranged in a circle so that the impromptu theater thus formed, which Maignan had ordered with much taste, was as light as in the day. On a sloping bank at one end seats had been placed for those who had supped at my table, while the rest of the company found such places of vantage as they could; their number, indeed, amounting, with my household, to two hundred persons. In the center of the open space a small forge fire had been kindled, the red glow of which added much to the strangeness of the scene; and on the anvil beside it were ranged a number of horses' and donkeys' shoes, with a full complement of the tools used by smiths. All being ready I gave the word to bring in the prisoners, and escorted by La Trape and six of my guards, they were marched into the arena. In their pale and terrified faces, and the shaking limbs which could scarce support them to their appointed stations, I read both the consciousness of guilt and the apprehension of immediate death; it was plain that they expected nothing less. I was very willing to play with their fears, and for some time looked at them in silence, while all wondered with lively curiosity what would ensue. I then addressed them gravely, telling the innkeeper that I knew well he had loosened each year a shoe of my horse, in order that his brother might profit by the job of replacing it; and went on to reprove the smith for the ingratitude which had led him to return my bounty by the conception of so knavish a trick.

Upon this they confessed their guilt, and flinging themselves upon their knees with many tears and prayers begged for mercy. This, after a decent interval, I permitted myself to grant. "Your lives, which are forfeited, shall be spared," I pronounced. "But punished you must be. I therefore ordain that Simon, the smith, at once fit, nail, and properly secure a pair of iron shoes to Andrew's heels, and that then Andrew, who by that time will have picked up something of the smith's art, do the same to Simon. So will you both learn to avoid such shoeing tricks for the future."

It may well be imagined that a judgment so whimsical, and so justly adapted to the offense, charmed all save the culprits; and in a hundred ways the pleasure of those present was evinced, to such a degree, indeed, that Maignan had some difficulty in restoring silence and gravity to the assemblage. This done, however, Master Andrew was taken in hand and his wooden shoes removed. The tools of his trade were placed before the smith, who cast glances so piteous, first at his brother's feet and then at the shoes on the anvil, as again gave rise to a prodigious amount of merriment, my pages in particular well-nigh forgetting my presence, and rolling about in a manner unpardonable at another time. However, I rebuked them sharply, and was about to order the sentence to be carried into effect, when the remembrance of the many pleasant simplicities which the smith had uttered to me, acting upon a natural disposition to mercy, which the most calumnious of my enemies have never questioned, induced me to give the prisoners a chance of escape. "Listen," I said, "Simon and Andrew. Your sentence has been pronounced, and will certainly be executed unless you can avail yourself of the condition I now offer. You shall have three minutes; if in that time either of you can make a good joke, he shall go free. If not, let a man attend to the bellows, La Trape!"

This added a fresh satisfaction to my neighbors, who were well assured now that I had not promised them a novel entertainment without good grounds; for the grimaces of the two knaves thus bidden to jest if they would save their skins, were so diverting they would have made a nun laugh. They looked at me with their eyes as wide as plates, and for the whole of the time of grace never a word could they utter save howls for mercy. "Simon," I said gravely, when the time was up, "have you a joke? No. Andrew, my friend, have you a joke? No. Then—"

I was going on to order the sentence to be carried out, when the innkeeper flung himself again upon his knees, and cried out loudly—as much to my astonishment as to the regret of the bystanders, who were bent on seeing so strange a shoeing feat—"One word, my lord; I can give you no joke, but I can do a service, an eminent service to the king. I can disclose a conspiracy!"

I was somewhat taken aback by this sudden and public announcement. But I had been too long in the king's employment not to have remarked how strangely things are brought to light. On hearing the man's words therefore—which were followed by a stricken silence— I looked sharply at the faces of such of those present as it was possible to suspect, but failed to observe any sign of confusion or dismay, or anything more particular than so abrupt a statement was calculated to produce. Doubting much whether the man was not playing with me, I addressed him sternly, warning him to beware, lest in his anxiety to save his heels by falsely accusing others, he should lose his head. For that if his conspiracy should prove to be an invention of his own, I should certainly consider it my duty to hang him forthwith.

He heard me out, but nevertheless persisted in his story, adding desperately, "It is a plot, my lord, to assassinate you and the king on the same day."

This statement struck me a blow; for I had good reason to know that at that time the king had alienated many by his infatuation for Madame de Verneuil; while I had always to reckon firstly with all who hated him, and secondly with all whom my pursuit of his interests injured, either in reality or appearance. I therefore immediately directed that the prisoners should be led in close custody to the chamber adjoining my private closet, and taking the precaution to call my guards about me, since I knew not what attempt despair might not breed, I withdrew myself, making such apologies to the company as the nature of the case permitted.

I ordered Simon the smith to be first brought to me, and in the presence of Maignan only, I severely examined him as to his knowledge of any conspiracy. He denied, however, that he had ever heard of the matters referred to by his brother, and persisted so firmly in the denial that I was inclined to believe him. In the end he was taken out and Andrew was brought in. The innkeeper's demeanor was such as I have often observed in intriguers brought suddenly to book. He averred the existence of the conspiracy, and that its objects were those which he had stated. He also offered to give up his associates, but conditioned that he should do this in his own way; undertaking to conduct me and one other person—but no more, lest the alarm should be given—to a place in Paris on the following night, where we could hear the plotters state their plans and designs. In this way only, he urged, could proof positive be obtained.

I was much startled by this proposal, and inclined to think it a trap; but further consideration dispelled my fears. The innkeeper had held no parley with anyone save his guards and myself since his arrest, and could neither have warned his accomplices, nor acquainted them with any design the execution of which should depend on his confession to me. I therefore accepted his terms—with a private reservation that I should have help at hand—and before daybreak next morning left Rosny, which I had only seen by torchlight, with my prisoner and a select body of Swiss. We entered Paris in the afternoon in three parties, with as little parade as possible, and went straight to the Arsenal, whence, as soon as evening fell, I hurried with only two armed attendants to the Louvre.

A return so sudden and unexpected was as great a surprise to the court as to the king, and I was not slow to mark with an inward smile the discomposure which appeared very clearly on the faces of several, as the crowd in the chamber fell back for me to approach my master. I was careful, however, to remember that this might arise from other causes than guilt. The king received me with his wonted affection; and divining at once that I must have something important to communicate, withdrew with me to the farther end of the chamber, where we were out of earshot of the court. I there related the story to his majesty, keeping back nothing.

He shook his head, saying merely: "The fish to escape the frying pan, grand master, will jump into the fire. And human nature, save in the case of you and me, who can trust one another, is very fishy."

I was touched by this gracious compliment, but not convinced.

139

"You have not seen the man, sire," I said, "and I have had that advantage."

"And believe him?"

"In part," I answered with caution. "So far at least as to be assured that he thinks to save his skin, which he will only do if he be telling the truth. May I beg you, sire," I added hastily, seeing the direction of his glance, "not to look so fixedly at the Duke of Epernon? He grows uneasy."

"Conscience makes—you know the rest."

"Nay, sire, with submission," I replied, "I will answer for him; if he be not driven by fear to do something reckless."

"Good! I take your warranty, Duke of Sully," the king said, with the easy grace which came so natural to him. "But now in this matter what would you have me do?"

"Double your guards, sire, for to-night—that is all. I will answer for the Bastile and the Arsenal; and holding these we hold Paris."

But thereupon I found that the king had come to a decision, which I felt it to be my duty to combat with all my influence. He had conceived the idea of being the one to accompany me to the rendezvous. "I am tired of the dice," he complained, "and sick of tennis, at which I know everybody's strength. Madame de Verneuil is at Fontainebleau, the queen is unwell. Ah, Sully, I would the old days were back when we had Nerac for our Paris, and knew the saddle better than the armchair!"

"A king must think of his people," I reminded him.

"The fowl in the pot? To be sure. So I will—to-morrow," he replied. And in the end he would be obeyed. I took my leave of him as if for the night, and retired, leaving him at play with the Duke of Epernon. But an hour later, toward eight o'clock, his majesty, who had made an excuse to withdraw to his closet, met me outside the eastern gate of the Louvre.

He was masked, and attended only by Coquet, his master of the household. I too wore a mask and was esquired by Maignan, under whose orders were four Swiss—whom I had chosen because they were unable to speak French—guarding the prisoner Andrew. I bade Maignan follow the innkeeper's directions, and we proceeded in two parties through the streets on the left bank of the river, past the Châtelet and Bastile, until we reached an obscure street near the water, so narrow that the decrepit wooden houses shut out well-nigh all view of the sky. Here the prisoner halted and called upon me to fulfill the terms of my agreement. I bade Maignan therefore to keep with the Swiss at a distance of fifty paces, but to come up should I whistle or otherwise give the alarm; and myself with the king and Andrew proceeded onward in the deep shadow of the houses. I kept my hand on my pistol, which I had previously shown to the prisoner, intimating that on the first sign of treachery I should blow out his brains.

However, despite precaution, I felt uncomfortable to the last degree. I blamed myself severely for allowing the king to expose himself and the country to this unnecessary danger; while the meanness of the locality, the fetid air, the darkness of the night, which was wet and tempestuous, and the uncertainty of the event lowered my spirits, and made every splash in the kennel and stumble on the reeking, slippery pavements—matters over which the king grew merry—seem no light troubles to me.

Arriving at a house, which, if we might judge in the darkness, seemed to be of rather greater pretensions than its fellows, our guide stopped, and whispered to us to mount some steps to a raised wooden gallery, which intervened between the lane and the doorway. On this, besides the door, a couple of unglazed windows looked out. The shutter of one was ajar, and showed us a large, bare room, lighted by a couple of rushlights. Directing us to place ourselves close to this shutter, the innkeeper knocked at the door in a peculiar fashion, and almost immediately entered, going at once into the lighted room. Peering cautiously through the window we were surprised to find that the only person within, save the newcomer, was a young woman, who, crouching over a smoldering fire, was crooning a lullaby while she attended to a large black pot.

"Good evening, mistress!" said the innkeeper, advancing to the fire with a fair show of nonchalance.

"Good evening, Master Andrew," the girl replied, looking up and nodding, but showing no sign of surprise at his appearance. "Martin is away, but he may return at any moment."

"Is he still of the same mind?"

"Quite."

"And what of Sully? Is he to die then?" he asked.

"They have decided he must," the girl answered gloomily. It may be believed that I listened with all my ears, while the king by a nudge in my side seemed to rally me on the destiny so coolly arranged for me. "Martin says it is no good killing the other unless he goes too—they have been so long together. But it vexes me sadly, Master Andrew," she added with a sudden break in her voice. "Sadly it vexes me. I could not sleep last night for thinking of it, and the risk Martin runs. And I shall sleep less when it is done."

"Pooh-pooh!" said that rascally innkeeper. "Think less about it. Things will grow worse and worse if they are let live. The King has done harm enough already. And he grows old besides."

"That is true!" said the girl. "And no doubt the sooner he is put out of the way the better. He is changed sadly. I do not say a word for him. Let him die. It is killing Sully that troubles me—that and the risk Martin runs."

At this I took the liberty of gently touching the king. He answered by an amused grimace; then by a motion of his hand he enjoined silence. We stooped still farther forward so as better to command the

141

room. The girl was rocking herself to and fro in evident distress of mind. "If we killed the King," she continued, "Martin declares we should be no better off, as long as Sully lives. Both or neither, he says. But I do not know. I cannot bear to think of it. It was a sad day when we brought Epernon here, Master Andrew; and one I fear we shall rue as long as we live."

It was now the king's turn to be moved. He grasped my wrist so forcibly that I restrained a cry with difficulty. "Epernon!" he whispered harshly in my ear. "They are Epernon's tools! Where is your guaranty now, Rosny?"

I confess that I trembled. I knew well that the king, particular in small courtesies, never forgot to call his servants by their correct titles, save in two cases; when he indicated by the seeming error, as once in Marshal Biron's affair, his intention to promote or degrade them; or when he was moved to the depths of his nature and fell into an old habit. I did not dare to reply, but listened greedily for more information.

"When is it to be done?" asked the innkeeper, sinking his voice and glancing round, as if he would call especial attention to this.

"That depends upon Master la Rivière," the girl answered. "Tomorrow night, I understand, if Master la Rivière can have the stuff ready."

I met the king's eyes. They shone fiercely in the faint light, which issuing from the window fell on him. Of all things he hated treachery most, and La Rivière was his first body physician, and at this very time, as I well knew, was treating him for a slight derangement which the king had brought upon himself by his imprudence. This doctor had formerly been in the employment of the Bouillon family, who had surrendered his services to the king. Neither I nor his majesty had trusted the Duke of Bouillon for the last year past, so that we were not surprised by this hint that he was privy to the design.

Despite our anxiety not to miss a word, an approaching step warned us at this moment to draw back. More than once before we had done so to escape the notice of a wayfarer passing up and down. But this time I had a difficulty in inducing the king to adopt the precaution. Yet it was well that I succeeded, for the person who came stumbling along toward us did not pass, but, mounting the steps, walked by within touch of us and entered the house.

"The plot thickens," muttered the king. "Who is this?"

At the moment he asked I was racking my brain to remember. I have a good eye and a fair recollection for faces, and this was one I had seen several times. The features were so familiar that I suspected the man of being a courtier in disguise, and I ran over the names of several persons whom I knew to be Bouillon's secret agents. But he was none of these, and obeying the king's gesture, I bent myself again to the task of listening.

142

The girl looked up on the man's entrance, but did not rise. "You are late, Martin," she said.

"A little," the newcomer answered. "How do you do, Master Andrew? What cheer? What, still vexing, mistress?" he added contemptuously to the girl. "You have too soft a heart for this business!"

She sighed, but made no answer.

"You have made up your mind to it, I hear?" said the innkeeper.

"That is it. Needs must when the devil drives!" replied the man jauntily. He had a downcast, reckless, luckless air, yet in his face I thought I still saw traces of a better spirit.

"The devil in this case was Epernon," quoth Andrew.

"Aye, curse him! I would I had cut his dainty throat before he crossed my threshold," cried the desperado. "But there, it is too late to say that now. What has to be done, has to be done."

"How are you going about it? Poison, the mistress says."

"Yes; but if I had my way," the man growled fiercely, "I would out one of these nights and cut the dogs' throats in the kennel!"

"You could never escape, Martin!" the girl cried, rising in excitement. "It would be hopeless. It would merely be throwing away your own life."

"Well, it is not to be done that way, so there is an end of it," quoth the man wearily. "Give me my supper. The devil take the king and Sully too! He will soon have them."

On this Master Andrew rose, and I took his movement toward the door for a signal for us to retire. He came out at once, shutting the door behind him as he bade the pair within a loud good night. He found us standing in the street waiting for him and forthwith fell on his knees in the mud and looked up at me, the perspiration standing thick on his white face. "My lord," he cried hoarsely, "I have earned my pardon!"

"If you go on," I said encouragingly, "as you have begun, have no fear." Without more ado I whistled up the Swiss and bade Maignan go with them and arrest the man and woman with as little disturbance as possible. While this was being done we waited without, keeping a sharp eye upon the informer, whose terror, I noted with suspicion, seemed to be in no degree diminished. He did not, however, try to escape, and Maignan presently came to tell us that he had executed the arrest without difficulty or resistance.

The importance of arriving at the truth before Epernon and the greater conspirators should take the alarm was so vividly present to the minds of the king and myself, that we did not hesitate to examine the prisoners in their house, rather than hazard the delay and observation which their removal to a more fit place must occasion. Accordingly, taking the precaution to post Coquet in the street outside, and to plant a burly Swiss in the doorway, the king and I entered. I removed my

143

mask as I did so, being aware of the necessity of gaining the prisoners' confidence, but I begged the king to retain his. As I had expected, the man immediately recognized me and fell on his knees, a nearer view confirming the notion I had previously entertained that his features were familiar to me, though I could not remember his name. I thought this a good starting-point for my examination, and bidding Maignan withdraw, I assumed an air of mildness and asked the fellow his name.

"Martin, only, please your lordship," he answered; adding, "once I sold you two dogs, sir, for the chase, and to your lady a lapdog called Ninette no larger than her hand."

I remembered the knave, then, as a fashionable dog dealer, who had been much about the court in the reign of Henry the Third and later; and I saw at once how convenient a tool he might be made, since he could be seen in converse with people of all ranks without arousing suspicion. The man's face as he spoke expressed so much fear and surprise that I determined to try what I had often found successful in the case of greater criminals, to squeeze him for a confession while still excited by his arrest, and before he should have had time to consider what his chances of support at the hands of his confederates might be. I charged him therefore solemnly to tell the whole truth as he hoped for the king's mercy. He heard me, gazing at me piteously; but his only answer, to my surprise, was that he had nothing to confess.

"Come, come," I replied sternly, "this will avail you nothing; if you do not speak quickly, rogue, and to the point, we shall find means to compel you. Who counseled you to attempt his majesty's life?"

On this he stared so stupidly at me, and exclaimed with so real an appearance of horror: "How? I attempt the king's life? God forbid!" that I doubted that we had before us a more dangerous rascal than I had thought, and I hastened to bring him to the point.

"What, then," I cried, frowning, "of the stuff Master la Rivière is to give you to take the king's life to-morrow night? Oh, we know something, I assure you; bethink you quickly, and find your tongue if you would have an easy death."

I expected to see his self-control break down at this proof of our knowledge of his design, but he only stared at me with the same look of bewilderment. I was about to bid them bring in the informer that I might see the two front to front, when the female prisoner, who had hitherto stood beside her companion in such distress and terror as might be expected in a woman of that class, suddenly stopped her tears and lamentations. It occurred to me that she might make a better witness. I turned to her, but when I would have questioned her she broke into a wild scream of hysterical laughter.

From that I remember that I learned nothing, though it greatly annoyed me. But there was one present who did—the king. He laid his hand on my shoulder, gripping it with a force that I read as a command to be silent.

"Where," he said to the man, "do you keep the King and Sully and Epernon, my friend?"

"The King and Sully—with the lordship's leave," said the man quickly, with a frightened glance at me—"are in the kennels at the back of the house, but it is not safe to go near them. The King is raving mad, and—and the other dog is sickening. Epernon we had to kill a month back. He brought the disease here, and I have had such losses through him as have nearly ruined me, please your lordship."

"Get up—get up, man!" cried the king, and tearing off his mask he stamped up and down the room, so torn by paroxysms of laughter that he choked himself when again and again he attempted to speak.

I too now saw the mistake, but I could not at first see it in the same light. Commanding myself as well as I could, I ordered one of the Swiss to fetch in the innkeeper, but to admit no one else.

The knave fell on his knees as soon as he saw me, his cheeks shaking like a jelly.

"Mercy, mercy!" was all he could say.

"You have dared to play with me?" I whispered.

"You bade me joke," he sobbed, "you bade me."

I was about to say that it would be his last joke in this world—for my anger was fully aroused—when the king intervened.

"Nay," he said, laying his hand softly on my shoulder. "It has been the most glorious jest. I would not have missed it for a kingdom. I command you, Sully, to forgive him."

Thereupon his majesty strictly charged the three that they should not on peril of their lives mention the circumstances to anyone. Nor to the best of my belief did they do so, being so shrewdly scared when they recognized the king that I verily think they never afterwards so much as spoke of the affair to one another. My master further gave me on his own part his most gracious promise that he would not disclose the matter even to Madame de Verneuil or the queen, and upon these representations he induced me freely to forgive the innkeeper. So ended this conspiracy, on the diverting details of which I may seem to have dwelt longer than I should; but alas! in twenty-one years of power I investigated many, and this one only can I regard with satisfaction. The rest were so many warnings and predictions of the fate which, despite all my care and fidelity, was in store for the great and good master I served.

WILKIE COLLINS

THE DREAM WOMAN

A MYSTERY IN FOUR NARRATIVES

THE FIRST NARRATIVE

INTRODUCTORY STATEMENT OF THE FACTS BY PERCY FAIRBANK

I

"Hullo, there! Hostler! Hullo-o-o!"

"My dear! why don't you look for the bell?"

"I have looked—there is no bell."

"And nobody in the yard. How very extraordinary! Call again, dear."

"Hostler! Hullo, there! Hostler-r-r!"

My second call echoes through empty space, and rouses nobody—produces, in short, no visible result. I am at the end of my resources—I don't know what to say or what to do next. Here I stand in the solitary inn yard of a strange town, with two horses to hold, and a lady to take care of. By way of adding to my responsibilities, it so happens that one of the horses is dead lame, and that the lady is my wife.

Who am I?—you will ask.

There is plenty of time to answer the question. Nothing happens; and nobody appears to receive us. Let me introduce myself and my wife.

I am Percy Fairbank—English gentleman—age (let us say) forty—no profession—moderate politics—middle height—fair complexion—easy character—plenty of money.

My wife is a French lady. She was Mademoiselle Clotilde Delorge—when I was first presented to her at her father's house in

146

France. I fell in love with her—I really don't know why. It might have been because I was perfectly idle, and had nothing else to do at the time. Or it might have been because all my friends said she was the very last woman whom I ought to think of marrying. On the surface, I must own, there is nothing in common between Mrs. Fairbank and me. She is tall; she is dark; she is nervous, excitable, romantic; in all her opinions she proceeds to extremes. What could such a woman see in me? what could I see in her? I know no more than you do. In some mysterious manner we exactly suit each other. We have been man and wife for ten years, and our only regret is, that we have no children. I don't know what you may think; I call that—upon the whole—a happy marriage.

So much for ourselves. The next question is—what has brought us into the inn yard? and why am I obliged to turn groom, and hold the horses?

We live for the most part in France—at the country house in which my wife and I first met. Occasionally, by way of variety, we pay visits to my friends in England. We are paying one of those visits now. Our host is an old college friend of mine, possessed of a fine estate in Somersetshire; and we have arrived at his house—called Farleigh Hall—toward the close of the hunting season.

On the day of which I am now writing—destined to be a memorable day in our calendar—the hounds meet at Farleigh Hall. Mrs. Fairbank and I are mounted on two of the best horses in my friend's stables. We are quite unworthy of that distinction; for we know nothing and care nothing about hunting. On the other hand, we delight in riding, and we enjoy the breezy Spring morning and the fair and fertile English landscape surrounding us on every side. While the hunt prospers, we follow the hunt. But when a check occurs—when time passes and patience is sorely tried; when the bewildered dogs run hither and thither, and strong language falls from the lips of exasperated sportsmen—we fail to take any further interest in the proceedings. We turn our horses' heads in the direction of a grassy lane, delightfully shaded by trees. We trot merrily along the lane, and find ourselves on an open common. We gallop across the common, and follow the windings of a second lane. We cross a brook, we pass through a village, we emerge into pastoral solitude among the hills. The horses toss their heads, and neigh to each other, and enjoy it as much as we do. The hunt is forgotten. We are as happy as a couple of children; we are actually singing a French song—when in one moment our merriment comes to an end. My wife's horse sets one of his forefeet on a loose stone, and stumbles. His rider's ready hand saves him from falling. But, at the first attempt he makes to go on, the sad truth shows itself—a tendon is strained; the horse is lame.

What is to be done? We are strangers in a lonely part of the country. Look where we may, we see no signs of a human habitation.

147

There is nothing for it but to take the bridle road up the hill, and try what we can discover on the other side. I transfer the saddles, and mount my wife on my own horse. He is not used to carry a lady; he misses the familiar pressure of a man's legs on either side of him; he fidgets, and starts, and kicks up the dust. I follow on foot, at a respectful distance from his heels, leading the lame horse. Is there a more miserable object on the face of creation than a lame horse? I have seen lame men and lame dogs who were cheerful creatures; but I never yet saw a lame horse who didn't look heartbroken over his own misfortune.

For half an hour my wife capers and curvets sideways along the bridle road. I trudge on behind her; and the heartbroken horse halts behind me. Hard by the top of the hill, our melancholy procession passes a Somersetshire peasant at work in a field. I summon the man to approach us; and the man looks at me stolidly, from the middle of the field, without stirring a step. I ask at the top of my voice how far it is to Farleigh Hall. The Somersetshire peasant answers at the top of his voice:

"Vourteen mile. Gi' oi a drap o' zyder."

I translate (for my wife's benefit) from the Somersetshire language into the English language. We are fourteen miles from Farleigh Hall; and our friend in the field desires to be rewarded, for giving us that information, with a drop of cider. There is the peasant, painted by himself! Quite a bit of character, my dear! Quite a bit of character!

Mrs. Fairbank doesn't view the study of agricultural human nature with my relish. Her fidgety horse will not allow her a moment's repose; she is beginning to lose her temper.

"We can't go fourteen miles in this way," she says. "Where is the nearest inn? Ask that brute in the field!"

I take a shilling from my pocket and hold it up in the sun. The shilling exercises magnetic virtues. The shilling draws the peasant slowly toward me from the middle of the field. I inform him that we want to put up the horses and to hire a carriage to take us back to Farleigh Hall. Where can we do that? The peasant answers (with his eye on the shilling):

"At Oonderbridge, to be zure." (At Underbridge, to be sure.)

"Is it far to Underbridge?"

The peasant repeats, "Var to Oonderbridge?"—and laughs at the question. "Hoo-hoo-hoo!" (Underbridge is evidently close by—if we could only find it.) "Will you show us the way, my man?" "Will you gi' oi a drap of zyder?" I courteously bend my head, and point to the shilling. The agricultural intelligence exerts itself. The peasant joins our melancholy procession. My wife is a fine woman, but he never once looks at my wife—and, more extraordinary still, he never even looks at the horses. His eyes are with his mind—and his mind is on the shilling.

148

We reach the top of the hill—and, behold on the other side, nestling in a valley, the shrine of our pilgrimage, the town of Underbridge! Here our guide claims his shilling, and leaves us to find out the inn for ourselves. I am constitutionally a polite man. I say "Good morning" at parting. The guide looks at me with the shilling between his teeth to make sure that it is a good one. "Marnin!" he says savagely—and turns his back on us, as if we had offended him. A curious product, this, of the growth of civilization. If I didn't see a church spire at Underbridge, I might suppose that we had lost ourselves on a savage island.

II

Arriving at the town, we had no difficulty in finding the inn. The town is composed of one desolate street; and midway in that street stands the inn—an ancient stone building sadly out of repair. The painting on the sign-board is obliterated. The shutters over the long range of front windows are all closed. A cock and his hens are the only living creatures at the door. Plainly, this is one of the old inns of the stage-coach period, ruined by the railway. We pass through the open arched doorway, and find no one to welcome us. We advance into the stable yard behind; I assist my wife to dismount—and there we are in the position already disclosed to view at the opening of this narrative. No bell to ring. No human creature to answer when I call. I stand helpless, with the bridles of the horses in my hand. Mrs. Fairbank saunters gracefully down the length of the yard and does—what all women do, when they find themselves in a strange place. She opens every door as she passes it, and peeps in. On my side, I have just recovered my breath, I am on the point of shouting for the hostler for the third and last time, when I hear Mrs. Fairbank suddenly call to me:

"Percy! come here!"

Her voice is eager and agitated. She has opened a last door at the end of the yard, and has started back from some sight which has suddenly met her view. I hitch the horses' bridles on a rusty nail in the wall near me, and join my wife. She has turned pale, and catches me nervously by the arm.

"Good heavens!" she cries; "look at that!"

I look—and what do I see? I see a dingy little stable, containing two stalls. In one stall a horse is munching his corn. In the other a man is lying asleep on the litter.

A worn, withered, woebegone man in a hostler's dress. His hollow wrinkled cheeks, his scanty grizzled hair, his dry yellow skin, tell their own tale of past sorrow or suffering. There is an ominous frown

149

on his eyebrows—there is a painful nervous contraction on the side of his mouth. I hear him breathing convulsively when I first look in; he shudders and sighs in his sleep. It is not a pleasant sight to see, and I turn round instinctively to the bright sunlight in the yard. My wife turns me back again in the direction of the stable door.

"Wait!" she says. "Wait! he may do it again."

"Do what again?"

"He was talking in his sleep, Percy, when I first looked in. He was dreaming some dreadful dream. Hush! he's beginning again."

I look and listen. The man stirs on his miserable bed. The man speaks in a quick, fierce whisper through his clinched teeth. "Wake up! Wake up, there! Murder!"

There is an interval of silence. He moves one lean arm slowly until it rests over his throat; he shudders, and turns on his straw; he raises his arm from his throat, and feebly stretches it out; his hand clutches at the straw on the side toward which he has turned; he seems to fancy that he is grasping at the edge of something. I see his lips begin to move again; I step softly into the stable; my wife follows me, with her hand fast clasped in mine. We both bend over him. He is talking once more in his sleep—strange talk, mad talk, this time.

"Light gray eyes" (we hear him say), "and a droop in the left eyelid—flaxen hair, with a gold-yellow streak in it—all right, mother! afair, white arms with a down on them—little, lady's hand, with a reddish look round the fingernails—the knife—the cursed knife—first on one side, then on the other—aha, you she-devil! where is the knife?"

He stops and grows restless on a sudden. We see him writhing on the straw. He throws up both his hands and gasps hysterically for breath. His eyes open suddenly. For a moment they look at nothing, with a vacant glitter in them—then they close again in deeper sleep. Is he dreaming still? Yes; but the dream seems to have taken a new course. When he speaks next, the tone is altered; the words are few— sadly and imploringly repeated over and over again. "Say you love me! I am so fond of you. Say you love me! say you love me!" He sinks into deeper and deeper sleep, faintly repeating those words. They die away on his lips. He speaks no more.

By this time Mrs. Fairbank has got over her terror; she is devoured by curiosity now. The miserable creature on the straw has appealed to the imaginative side of her character. Her illimitable appetite for romance hungers and thirsts for more. She shakes me impatiently by the arm.

"Do you hear? There is a woman at the bottom of it, Percy! There is love and murder in it, Percy! Where are the people of the inn? Go into the yard, and call to them again."

My wife belongs, on her mother's side, to the South of France. The South of France breeds fine women with hot tempers. I say no more. Married men will understand my position. Single men may need

150

to be told that there are occasions when we must not only love and honor—we must also obey—our wives.

I turn to the door to obey my wife, and find myself confronted by a stranger who has stolen on us unawares. The stranger is a tiny, sleepy, rosy old man, with a vacant pudding-face, and a shining bald head. He wears drab breeches and gaiters, and a respectable square-tailed ancient black coat. I feel instinctively that here is the landlord of the inn.

"Good morning, sir," says the rosy old man. "I'm a little hard of hearing. Was it you that was a-calling just now in the yard?"

Before I can answer, my wife interposes. She insists (in a shrill voice, adapted to our host's hardness of hearing) on knowing who that unfortunate person is sleeping on the straw. "Where does he come from? Why does he say such dreadful things in his sleep? Is he married or single? Did he ever fall in love with a murderess? What sort of a looking woman was she? Did she really stab him or not? In short, dear Mr. Landlord, tell us the whole story!"

Dear Mr. Landlord waits drowsily until Mrs. Fairbank has quite done—then delivers himself of his reply as follows:

"His name's Francis Raven. He's an Independent Methodist. He was forty-five year old last birthday. And he's my hostler. That's his story."

My wife's hot southern temper finds its way to her foot, and expresses itself by a stamp on the stable yard.

The landlord turns himself sleepily round, and looks at the horses. "A fine pair of horses, them two in the yard. Do you want to put 'em in my stables?" I reply in the affirmative by a nod. The landlord, bent on making himself agreeable to my wife, addresses her once more. "I'm a-going to wake Francis Raven. He's an Independent Methodist. He was forty-five year old last birthday. And he's my hostler. That's his story."

Having issued this second edition of his interesting narrative, the landlord enters the stable. We follow him to see how he will wake Francis Raven, and what will happen upon that. The stable broom stands in a corner; the landlord takes it—advances toward the sleeping hostler—and coolly stirs the man up with a broom as if he was a wild beast in a cage. Francis Raven starts to his feet with a cry of terror—looks at us wildly, with a horrid glare of suspicion in his eyes—recovers himself the next moment—and suddenly changes into a decent, quiet, respectable serving-man.

"I beg your pardon, ma'am. I beg your pardon, sir."

The tone and manner in which he makes his apologies are both above his apparent station in life. I begin to catch the infection of Mrs. Fairbank's interest in this man. We both follow him out into the yard to see what he will do with the horses. The manner in which he lifts the injured leg of the lame horse tells me at once that he understands his business. Quickly and quietly, he leads the animal into an empty stable; quickly and quietly, he gets a bucket of hot water, and puts the lame horse's leg into it. "The warm water will reduce the swelling, sir. I will bandage the leg afterwards." All that he does is done intelligently; all that he says, he says to the purpose.

Nothing wild, nothing strange about him now. Is this the same man whom we heard talking in his sleep?—the same man who woke with that cry of terror and that horrid suspicion in his eyes? I determine to try him with one or two questions.

III

"Not much to do here," I say to the hostler.

"Very little to do, sir," the hostler replies.

"Anybody staying in the house?"

"The house is quite empty, sir."

"I thought you were all dead. I could make nobody hear me."

"The landlord is very deaf, sir, and the waiter is out on an errand."

"Yes; and you were fast asleep in the stable. Do you often take a nap in the daytime?"

The worn face of the hostler faintly flushes. His eyes look away from my eyes for the first time. Mrs. Fairbank furtively pinches my arm. Are we on the eve of a discovery at last? I repeat my question. The man has no civil alternative but to give me an answer. The answer is given in these words:

"I was tired out, sir. You wouldn't have found me asleep in the daytime but for that."

"Tired out, eh? You had been hard at work, I suppose?"

"No, sir."

"What was it, then?"

He hesitates again, and answers unwillingly, "I was up all night."

"Up all night? Anything going on in the town?"

"Nothing going on, sir."

"Anybody ill?"

"Nobody ill, sir."

That reply is the last. Try as I may, I can extract nothing more from him. He turns away and busies himself in attending to the horse's leg. I leave the stable to speak to the landlord about the carriage which is to take us back to Farleigh Hall. Mrs. Fairbank remains with the hostler, and favors me with a look at parting. The look says plainly, "I mean to find out why he was up all night. Leave him to Me."

The ordering of the carriage is easily accomplished. The inn

152

possesses one horse and one chaise. The landlord has a story to tell of the horse, and a story to tell of the chaise. They resemble the story of Francis Raven—with this exception, that the horse and chaise belong to no religious persuasion. "The horse will be nine year old next birthday. I've had the shay for four-and-twenty year. Mr. Max, of Underbridge, he bred the horse; and Mr. Pooley, of Yeovil, he built the shay. It's my horse and my shay. And that's their story!" Having relieved his mind of these details, the landlord proceeds to put the harness on the horse. By way of assisting him, I drag the chaise into the yard. Just as our preparations are completed, Mrs. Fairbank appears. A moment or two later the hostler follows her out. He has bandaged the horse's leg, and is now ready to drive us to Farleigh Hall. I observe signs of agitation in his face and manner, which suggest that my wife has found her way into his confidence. I put the question to her privately in a corner of the yard. "Well? Have you found out why Francis Raven was up all night?"

Mrs. Fairbank has an eye to dramatic effect. Instead of answering plainly, Yes or No, she suspends the interest and excites the audience by putting a question on her side.

"What is the day of the month, dear?"

"The day of the month is the first of March."

"The first of March, Percy, is Francis Raven's birthday."

I try to look as if I was interested—and don't succeed.

"Francis was born," Mrs. Fairbank proceeds gravely, "at two o'clock in the morning."

I begin to wonder whether my wife's intellect is going the way of the landlord's intellect. "Is that all?" I ask.

"It is not all," Mrs. Fairbank answers. "Francis Raven sits up on the morning of his birthday because he is afraid to go to bed."

"And why is he afraid to go to bed?"

"Because he is in peril of his life."

"On his birthday?"

"On his birthday. At two o'clock in the morning. As regularly as the birthday comes round."

There she stops. Has she discovered no more than that? No more thus far. I begin to feel really interested by this time. I ask eagerly what it means? Mrs. Fairbank points mysteriously to the chaise—with Francis Raven (hitherto our hostler, now our coachman) waiting for us to get in. The chaise has a seat for two in front, and a seat for one behind. My wife casts a warning look at me, and places herself on the seat in front.

The necessary consequence of this arrangement is that Mrs. Fairbank sits by the side of the driver during a journey of two hours and more. Need I state the result? It would be an insult to your intelligence to state the result. Let me offer you my place in the chaise. And let Francis Raven tell his terrible story in his own words.

THE SECOND NARRATIVE

THE HOSTLER'S STORY.—TOLD BY HIMSELF

IV

It is now ten years ago since I got my first warning of the great trouble of my life in the Vision of a Dream.

I shall be better able to tell you about it if you will please suppose yourselves to be drinking tea along with us in our little cottage in Cambridgeshire, ten years since.

The time was the close of day, and there were three of us at the table, namely, my mother, myself, and my mother's sister, Mrs. Chance. These two were Scotchwomen by birth, and both were widows. There was no other resemblance between them that I can call to mind. My mother had lived all her life in England, and had no more of the Scotch brogue on her tongue than I have. My aunt Chance had never been out of Scotland until she came to keep house with my mother after her husband's death. And when she opened her lips you heard broad Scotch, I can tell you, if you ever heard it yet!

As it fell out, there was a matter of some consequence in debate among us that evening. It was this: whether I should do well or not to take a long journey on foot the next morning.

Now the next morning happened to be the day before my birthday; and the purpose of the journey was to offer myself for a situation as groom at a great house in the neighboring county to ours. The place was reported as likely to fall vacant in about three weeks' time. I was as well fitted to fill it as any other man. In the prosperous days of our family, my father had been manager of a training stable, and he had kept me employed among the horses from my boyhood upward. Please to excuse my troubling you with these small matters. They all fit into my story farther on, as you will soon find out. My poor mother was dead against my leaving home on the morrow.

"You can never walk all the way there and all the way back again by to-morrow night," she says. "The end of it will be that you will sleep away from home on your birthday. You have never done that yet, Francis, since your father's death, I don't like your doing it now. Wait a day longer, my son—only one day."

For my own part, I was weary of being idle, and I couldn't abide the notion of delay. Even one day might make all the difference. Some other man might take time by the forelock, and get the place.

"Consider how long I have been out of work," I says, "and don't

154

ask me to put off the journey. I won't fail you, mother. I'll get back by to-morrow night, if I have to pay my last sixpence for a lift in a cart."

My mother shook her head. "I don't like it, Francis—I don't like it!" There was no moving her from that view. We argued and argued, until we were both at a deadlock. It ended in our agreeing to refer the difference between us to my mother's sister, Mrs. Chance.

While we were trying hard to convince each other, my aunt Chance sat as dumb as a fish, stirring her tea and thinking her own thoughts. When we made our appeal to her, she seemed as it were to wake up. "Ye baith refer it to my puir judgment?" she says, in her broad Scotch. We both answered Yes. Upon that my aunt Chance first cleared the tea-table, and then pulled out from the pocket of her gown a pack of cards.

Don't run away, if you please, with the notion that this was done lightly, with a view to amuse my mother and me. My aunt Chance seriously believed that she could look into the future by telling fortunes on the cards. She did nothing herself without first consulting the cards. She could give no more serious proof of her interest in my welfare than the proof which she was offering now. I don't say it profanely; I only mention the fact—the cards had, in some incomprehensible way, got themselves jumbled up together with her religious convictions. You meet with people nowadays who believe in spirits working by way of tables and chairs. On the same principle (if there is any principle in it) my aunt Chance believed in Providence working by way of the cards.

"Whether you are right, Francie, or your mither—whether ye will do weel or ill, the morrow, to go or stay—the cairds will tell it. We are a' in the hands of Proavidence. The cairds will tell it."

Hearing this, my mother turned her head aside, with something of a sour look in her face. Her sister's notions about the cards were little better than flat blasphemy to her mind. But she kept her opinion to herself. My aunt Chance, to own the truth, had inherited, through her late husband, a pension of thirty pounds a year. This was an important contribution to our housekeeping, and we poor relations were bound to treat her with a certain respect. As for myself, if my poor father never did anything else for me before he fell into difficulties, he gave me a good education, and raised me (thank God) above superstitions of all sorts. However, a very little amused me in those days; and I waited to have my fortune told, as patiently as if I believed in it too!

My aunt began her hocus pocus by throwing out all the cards in the pack under seven. She shuffled the rest with her left hand for luck; and then she gave them to me to cut. "Wi' yer left hand, Francie. Mind that! Pet your trust in Proavidence—but dinna forget that your luck's in yer left hand!" A long and roundabout shifting of the cards followed, reducing them in number until there were just fifteen of them left, laid out neatly before my aunt in a half circle. The card which happened to lie outermost, at the right-hand end of the circle, was, according to rule in such cases, the card chosen to represent Me. By way of being appropriate to my situation as a poor groom out of employment, the card was—the King of Diamonds.

"I tak' up the King o' Diamants," says my aunt. "I count seven cairds fra' richt to left; and I humbly ask a blessing on what follows." My aunt shut her eyes as if she was saying grace before meat, and held up to me the seventh card. I called the seventh card—the Queen of Spades. My aunt opened her eyes again in a hurry, and cast a sly look my way. "The Queen o' Spades means a dairk woman. Ye'll be thinking in secret, Francie, of a dairk woman?"

When a man has been out of work for more than three months, his mind isn't troubled much with thinking of women—light or dark. I was thinking of the groom's place at the great house, and I tried to say so. My aunt Chance wouldn't listen. She treated my interpretation with contempt. "Hoot-toot! there's the caird in your hand! If ye're no thinking of her the day, ye'll be thinking of her the morrow. Where's the harm of thinking of a dairk woman! I was ance a dairk woman myself, before my hair was gray. Haud yer peace, Francie, and watch the cairds."

I watched the cards as I was told. There were seven left on the table. My aunt removed two from one end of the row and two from the other, and desired me to call the two outermost of the three cards now left on the table. I called the Ace of Clubs and the Ten of Diamonds. My aunt Chance lifted her eyes to the ceiling with a look of devout gratitude which sorely tried my mother's patience. The Ace of Clubs and the Ten of Diamonds, taken together, signified—first, good news (evidently the news of the groom's place); secondly, a journey that lay before me (pointing plainly to my journey to-morrow!); thirdly and lastly, a sum of money (probably the groom's wages!) waiting to find its way into my pockets. Having told my fortune in these encouraging terms, my aunt declined to carry the experiment any further. "Eh, lad! it's a clean tempting o' Proavidence to ask mair o' the cairds than the cairds have tauld us noo. Gae yer ways to-morrow to the great hoose. A dairk woman will meet ye at the gate; and she'll have a hand in getting ye the groom's place, wi' a' the gratifications and pairquisites appertaining to the same. And, mebbe, when yer poaket's full o' money, ye'll no' be forgetting yer aunt Chance, maintaining her ain unblemished widowhood—wi' Proavidence assisting—on thratty punds a year!"

I promised to remember my aunt Chance (who had the defect, by the way, of being a terribly greedy person after money) on the next happy occasion when my poor empty pockets were to be filled at last. This done, I looked at my mother. She had agreed to take her sister for umpire between us, and her sister had given it in my favor. She raised no more objections. Silently, she got on her feet, and kissed me, and sighed bitterly—and so left the room. My aunt Chance shook her head.

156

"I doubt, Francie, yer puir mither has but a heathen notion of the vairtue of the cairds!"

By daylight the next morning I set forth on my journey. I looked back at the cottage as I opened the garden gate. At one window was my mother, with her handkerchief to her eyes. At the other stood my aunt Chance, holding up the Queen of Spades by way of encouraging me at starting. I waved my hands to both of them in token of farewell, and stepped out briskly into the road. It was then the last day of February. Be pleased to remember, in connection with this, that the first of March was the day, and two o'clock in the morning the hour of my birth.

V

Now you know how I came to leave home. The next thing to tell is, what happened on the journey.

I reached the great house in reasonably good time considering the distance. At the very first trial of it, the prophecy of the cards turned out to be wrong. The person who met me at the lodge gate was not a dark woman—in fact, not a woman at all—but a boy. He directed me on the way to the servants' offices; and there again the cards were all wrong. I encountered, not one woman, but three—and not one of the three was dark. I have stated that I am not superstitious, and I have told the truth. But I must own that I did feel a certain fluttering at the heart when I made my bow to the steward, and told him what business had brought me to the house. His answer completed the discomfiture of aunt Chance's fortune-telling. My ill-luck still pursued me. That very morning another man had applied for the groom's place, and had got it.

I swallowed my disappointment as well as I could, and thanked the steward, and went to the inn in the village to get the rest and food which I sorely needed by this time.

Before starting on my homeward walk I made some inquiries at the inn, and ascertained that I might save a few miles, on my return, by following a new road. Furnished with full instructions, several times repeated, as to the various turnings I was to take, I set forth, and walked on till the evening with only one stoppage for bread and cheese. Just as it was getting toward dark, the rain came on and the wind began to rise; and I found myself, to make matters worse, in a part of the country with which I was entirely unacquainted, though I guessed myself to be some fifteen miles from home. The first house I found to inquire at, was a lonely roadside inn, standing on the outskirts of a thick wood. Solitary as the place looked, it was welcome to a lost man who was also hungry, thirsty, footsore, and wet. The landlord was civil and respectable-looking; and the price he asked for a bed was reasonable enough. I was grieved to disappoint my mother. But there was no conveyance to be had, and I could go no farther afoot that night. My weariness fairly forced me to stop at the inn.

I may say for myself that I am a temperate man. My supper simply consisted of some rashers of bacon, a slice of home-made bread, and a pint of ale. I did not go to bed immediately after this moderate meal, but sat up with the landlord, talking about my bad prospects and my long run of ill-luck, and diverging from these topics to the subjects of horse-flesh and racing. Nothing was said, either by myself, my host, or the few laborers who strayed into the tap-room, which could, in the slightest degree, excite my mind, or set my fancy—which is only a small fancy at the best of times—playing tricks with my common sense.

At a little after eleven the house was closed. I went round with the landlord, and held the candle while the doors and lower windows were being secured. I noticed with surprise the strength of the bolts, bars, and iron-sheathed shutters.

"You see, we are rather lonely here," said the landlord. "We never have had any attempts to break in yet, but it's always as well to be on the safe side. When nobody is sleeping here, I am the only man in the house. My wife and daughter are timid, and the servant girl takes after her missuses. Another glass of ale, before you turn in?—No!—Well, how such a sober man as you comes to be out of a place is more than I can understand for one.—Here's where you're to sleep. You're the only lodger to-night, and I think you'll say my missus has done her best to make you comfortable. You're quite sure you won't have another glass of ale?—Very well. Good night."

It was half-past eleven by the clock in the passage as we went upstairs to the bedroom. The window looked out on the wood at the back of the house.

I locked my door, set my candle on the chest of drawers, and wearily got me ready for bed. The bleak wind was still blowing, and the solemn, surging moan of it in the wood was very dreary to hear through the night silence. Feeling strangely wakeful, I resolved to keep the candle alight until I began to grow sleepy. The truth is, I was not quite myself. I was depressed in mind by my disappointment of the morning; and I was worn out in body by my long walk. Between the two, I own I couldn't face the prospect of lying awake in the darkness, listening to the dismal moan of the wind in the wood.

Sleep stole on me before I was aware of it; my eyes closed, and I fell off to rest, without having so much as thought of extinguishing the candle.

The next thing that I remember was a faint shivering that ran through me from head to foot, and a dreadful sinking pain at my heart, such as I had never felt before. The shivering only disturbed my slumbers—the pain woke me instantly. In one moment I passed from a state of sleep to a state of wakefulness—my eyes wide open—my mind

158

clear on a sudden as if by a miracle. The candle had burned down nearly to the last morsel of tallow, but the unsnuffed wick had just fallen off, and the light was, for the moment, fair and full.

Between the foot of the bed and the closet door, I saw a person in my room. The person was a woman, standing looking at me, with a knife in her hand. It does no credit to my courage to confess it—but the truth is the truth. I was struck speechless with terror. There I lay with my eyes on the woman; there the woman stood (with the knife in her hand) with her eyes on me.

She said not a word as we stared each other in the face; but she moved after a little—moved slowly toward the left-hand side of the bed.

The light fell full on her face. A fair, fine woman, with yellowish flaxen hair, and light gray eyes, with a droop in the left eyelid. I noticed these things and fixed them in my mind, before she was quite round at the side of the bed. Without saying a word; without any change in the stony stillness of her face; without any noise following her footfall, she came closer and closer; stopped at the bed-head; and lifted the knife to stab me. I laid my arm over my throat to save it; but, as I saw the blow coming, I threw my hand across the bed to the right side, and jerked my body over that way, just as the knife came down, like lightning, within a hair's breadth of my shoulder.

My eyes fixed on her arm and her hand—she gave me time to look at them as she slowly drew the knife out of the bed. A white, well-shaped arm, with a pretty down lying lightly over the fair skin. A delicate lady's hand, with a pink flush round the finger nails.

She drew the knife out, and passed back again slowly to the foot of the bed; she stopped there for a moment looking at me; then she came on without saying a word; without any change in the stony stillness of her face; without any noise following her footfall—came on to the side of the bed where I now lay.

Getting near me, she lifted the knife again, and I drew myself away to the left side. She struck, as before right into the mattress, with a swift downward action of her arm; and she missed me, as before; by a hair's breadth. This time my eyes wandered from her to the knife. It was like the large clasp knives which laboring men use to cut their bread and bacon with. Her delicate little fingers did not hide more than two thirds of the handle; I noticed that it was made of buckhorn, clean and shining as the blade was, and looking like new.

For the second time she drew the knife out of the bed, and suddenly hid it away in the wide sleeve of her gown. That done, she stopped by the bedside watching me. For an instant I saw her standing in that position—then the wick of the spent candle fell over into the socket. The flame dwindled to a little blue point, and the room grew dark.

A moment, or less, if possible, passed so—and then the wick flared up, smokily, for the last time. My eyes were still looking for her

159

over the right-hand side of the bed when the last flash of light came. Look as I might, I could see nothing. The woman with the knife was gone.

I began to get back to myself again. I could feel my heart beating; I could hear the woeful moaning of the wind in the wood; I could leap up in bed, and give the alarm before she escaped from the house. "Murder! Wake up there! Murder!"

Nobody answered to the alarm. I rose and groped my way through the darkness to the door of the room. By that way she must have got in. By that way she must have gone out.

The door of the room was fast locked, exactly as I had left it on going to bed! I looked at the window. Fast locked too!

Hearing a voice outside, I opened the door. There was the landlord, coming toward me along the passage, with his burning candle in one hand, and his gun in the other.

"What is it?" he says, looking at me in no very friendly way.

I could only answer in a whisper, "A woman, with a knife in her hand. In my room. A fair, yellow-haired woman. She jabbed at me with the knife, twice over."

He lifted his candle, and looked at me steadily from head to foot. "She seems to have missed you—twice over."

"I dodged the knife as it came down. It struck the bed each time. Go in, and see."

The landlord took his candle into the bedroom immediately. In less than a minute he came out again into the passage in a violent passion.

"The devil fly away with you and your woman with the knife! There isn't a mark in the bedclothes anywhere. What do you mean by coming into a man's place and frightening his family out of their wits by a dream?"

A dream? The woman who had tried to stab me, not a living human being like myself? I began to shake and shiver. The horrors got hold of me at the bare thought of it.

"I'll leave the house," I said. "Better be out on the road in the rain and dark, than back in that room, after what I've seen in it. Lend me the light to get my clothes by, and tell me what I'm to pay."

The landlord led the way back with his light into the bedroom. "Pay?" says he. "You'll find your score on the slate when you go downstairs. I wouldn't have taken you in for all the money you've got about you, if I had known your dreaming, screeching ways beforehand. Look at the bed—where's the cut of a knife in it? Look at the window— is the lock bursted? Look at the door (which I heard you fasten yourself)—is it broke in? A murdering woman with a knife in my house! You ought to be ashamed of yourself!"

My eyes followed his hand as it pointed first to the bed—then to the window—then to the door. There was no gainsaying it. The bed sheet was as sound as on the day it was made. The window was fast. The door hung on its hinges as steady as ever. I huddled my clothes on without speaking. We went downstairs together. I looked at the clock in the bar-room. The time was twenty minutes past two in the morning. I paid my bill, and the landlord let me out. The rain had ceased; but the night was dark, and the wind was bleaker than ever. Little did the darkness, or the cold, or the doubt about the way home matter to me. My mind was away from all these things. My mind was fixed on the vision in the bedroom. What had I seen trying to murder me? The creature of a dream? Or that other creature from the world beyond the grave, whom men call ghost? I could make nothing of it as I walked along in the night; I had made nothing by it by midday—when I stood at last, after many times missing my road, on the doorstep of home.

VI

My mother came out alone to welcome me back. There were no secrets between us two. I told her all that had happened, just as I have told it to you. She kept silence till I had done. And then she put a question to me.

"What time was it, Francis, when you saw the Woman in your Dream?"

I had looked at the clock when I left the inn, and I had noticed that the hands pointed to twenty minutes past two. Allowing for the time consumed in speaking to the landlord, and in getting on my clothes, I answered that I must have first seen the Woman at two o'clock in the morning. In other words, I had not only seen her on my birthday, but at the hour of my birth.

My mother still kept silence. Lost in her own thoughts, she took me by the hand, and led me into the parlor. Her writing-desk was on the table by the fireplace. She opened it, and signed to me to take a chair by her side.

"My son! your memory is a bad one, and mine is fast failing me. Tell me again what the Woman looked like. I want her to be as well known to both of us, years hence, as she is now."

I obeyed; wondering what strange fancy might be working in her mind. I spoke; and she wrote the words as they fell from my lips:

"Light gray eyes, with a droop in the left eyelid. Flaxen hair, with a golden-yellow streak in it. White arms, with a down upon them. Little, lady's hands, with a rosy-red look about the finger nails."

"Did you notice how she was dressed, Francis?"

"No, mother."

"Did you notice the knife?"

161

"Yes. A large clasp knife, with a buckhorn handle, as good as new."

My mother added the description of the knife. Also the year, month, day of the week, and hour of the day when the Dream-Woman appeared to me at the inn. That done, she locked up the paper in her desk.

"Not a word, Francis, to your aunt. Not a word to any living soul. Keep your Dream a secret between you and me."

The weeks passed, and the months passed. My mother never returned to the subject again. As for me, time, which wears out all things, wore out my remembrance of the Dream. Little by little, the image of the Woman grew dimmer and dimmer. Little by little, she faded out of my mind.

VII

The story of the warning is now told. Judge for yourself if it was a true warning or a false, when you hear what happened to me on my next birthday.

In the Summer time of the year, the Wheel of Fortune turned the right way for me at last. I was smoking my pipe one day, near an old stone quarry at the entrance to our village, when a carriage accident happened, which gave a new turn, as it were, to my lot in life. It was an accident of the commonest kind—not worth mentioning at any length. A lady driving herself; a runaway horse; a cowardly man-servant in attendance, frightened out of his wits; and the stone quarry too near to be agreeable—that is what I saw, all in a few moments, between two whiffs of my pipe. I stopped the horse at the edge of the quarry, and got myself a little hurt by the shaft of the chaise. But that didn't matter. The lady declared I had saved her life; and her husband, coming with her to our cottage the next day, took me into his service then and there. The lady happened to be of a dark complexion; and it may amuse you to hear that my aunt Chance instantly pitched on that circumstance as a means of saving the credit of the cards. Here was the promise of the Queen of Spades performed to the very letter, by means of "a dark woman," just as my aunt had told me. "In the time to come, Francis, beware o' pettin' yer ain blinded intairpretation on the cairds. Ye're ower ready, I trow, to murmur under dispensation of Proavidence that ye canna fathom—like the Eesraelites of auld. I'll say nae mair to ye. Mebbe when the mony's powering into yer poakets, ye'll no forget yer aunt Chance, left like a sparrow on the housetop, wi' a sma' annuitee o' thratty punds a year."

I remained in my situation (at the West-end of London) until the

Spring of the New Year. About that time, my master's health failed. The doctors ordered him away to foreign parts, and the establishment was broken up. But the turn in my luck still held good. When I left my place, I left it—thanks to the generosity of my kind master—with a yearly allowance granted to me, in remembrance of the day when I had saved my mistress's life. For the future, I could go back to service or not, as I pleased; my little income was enough to support my mother and myself.

My master and mistress left England toward the end of February. Certain matters of business to do for them detained me in London until the last day of the month. I was only able to leave for our village by the evening train, to keep my birthday with my mother as usual. It was bedtime when I got to the cottage; and I was sorry to find that she was far from well. To make matters worse, she had finished her bottle of medicine on the previous day, and had omitted to get it replenished, as the doctor had strictly directed. He dispensed his own medicines, and I offered to go and knock him up. She refused to let me do this; and, after giving me my supper, sent me away to my bed.

I fell asleep for a little, and woke again. My mother's bed-chamber was next to mine. I heard my aunt Chance's heavy footsteps going to and fro in the room, and, suspecting something wrong, knocked at the door. My mother's pains had returned upon her; there was a serious necessity for relieving her sufferings as speedily as possible, I put on my clothes, and ran off, with the medicine bottle in my hand, to the other end of the village, where the doctor lived. The church clock chimed the quarter to two on my birthday just as I reached his house. One ring of the night bell brought him to his bedroom window to speak to me. He told me to wait, and he would let me in at the surgery door. I noticed, while I was waiting, that the night was wonderfully fair and warm for the time of year. The old stone quarry where the carriage accident had happened was within view. The moon in the clear heavens lit it up almost as bright as day.

In a minute or two the doctor let me into the surgery. I closed the door, noticing that he had left his room very lightly clad. He kindly pardoned my mother's neglect of his directions, and set to work at once at compounding the medicine. We were both intent on the bottle; he filling it, and I holding the light—when we heard the surgery door suddenly opened from the street.

VIII

Who could possibly be up and about in our quiet village at the second hour of the morning?

163

The person who opened the door appeared within range of the light of the candle. To complete our amazement, the person proved to be a woman! She walked up to the counter, and standing side by side with me, lifted her veil. At the moment when she showed her face, I heard the church clock strike two. She was a stranger to me, and a stranger to the doctor. She was also, beyond all comparison, the most beautiful woman I have ever seen in my life.

"I saw the light under the door," she said. "I want some medicine."

She spoke quite composedly, as if there was nothing at all extraordinary in her being out in the village at two in the morning, and following me into the surgery to ask for medicine! The doctor stared at her as if he suspected his own eyes of deceiving him. "Who are you?" he asked. "How do you come to be wandering about at this time in the morning?"

She paid no heed to his questions. She only told him coolly what she wanted. "I have got a bad toothache. I want a bottle of laudanum."

The doctor recovered himself when she asked for the laudanum. He was on his own ground, you know, when it came to a matter of laudanum; and he spoke to her smartly enough this time.

"Oh, you have got the toothache, have you? Let me look at the tooth."

She shook her head, and laid a two-shilling piece on the counter. "I won't trouble you to look at the tooth," she said. "There is the money. Let me have the laudanum, if you please."

The doctor put the two-shilling piece back again in her hand. "I don't sell laudanum to strangers," he answered. "If you are in any distress of body or mind, that is another matter. I shall be glad to help you."

She put the money back in her pocket. "You can't help me," she said, as quietly as ever. "Good morning."

With that, she opened the surgery door to go out again into the street. So far, I had not spoken a word on my side. I had stood with the candle in my hand (not knowing I was holding it)—with my eyes fixed on her, with my mind fixed on her like a man bewitched. Her looks betrayed, even more plainly than her words, her resolution, in one way or another, to destroy herself. When she opened the door, in my alarm at what might happen I found the use of my tongue.

"Stop!" I cried out. "Wait for me. I want to speak to you before you go away." She lifted her eyes with a look of careless surprise and a mocking smile on her lips.

"What can you have to say to me?" She stopped, and laughed to herself. "Why not?" she said. "I have got nothing to do, and nowhere to go." She turned back a step, and nodded to me. "You're a strange man— I think I'll humor you—I'll wait outside." The door of the surgery closed on her. She was gone.

I am ashamed to own what happened next. The only excuse for me is that I was really and truly a man bewitched. I turned me round to follow her out, without once thinking of my mother. The doctor stopped me.

"Don't forget the medicine," he said. "And if you will take my advice, don't trouble yourself about that woman. Rouse up the constable. It's his business to look after her—not yours."

I held out my hand for the medicine in silence: I was afraid I should fail in respect if I trusted myself to answer him. He must have seen, as I saw, that she wanted the laudanum to poison herself. He had, to my mind, taken a very heartless view of the matter. I just thanked him when he gave me the medicine—and went out.

She was waiting for me as she had promised; walking slowly to and fro—a tall, graceful, solitary figure in the bright moonbeams. They shed over her fair complexion, her bright golden hair, her large gray eyes, just the light that suited them best. She looked hardly mortal when she first turned to speak to me.

"Well?" she said. "And what do you want?"

In spite of my pride, or my shyness, or my better sense—whichever it might me—all my heart went out to her in a moment. I caught hold of her by the hands, and owned what was in my thoughts, as freely as if I had known her for half a lifetime.

"You mean to destroy yourself," I said. "And I mean to prevent you from doing it. If I follow you about all night, I'll prevent you from doing it."

She laughed. "You saw yourself that he wouldn't sell me the laudanum. Do you really care whether I live or die?" She squeezed my hands gently as she put the question: her eyes searched mine with a languid, lingering look in them that ran through me like fire. My voice died away on my lips; I couldn't answer her.

She understood, without my answering. "You have given me a fancy for living, by speaking kindly to me," she said. "Kindness has a wonderful effect on women, and dogs, and other domestic animals. It is only men who are superior to kindness. Make your mind easy—I promise to take as much care of myself as if I was the happiest woman living! Don't let me keep you here, out of your bed. Which way are you going?"

Miserable wretch that I was, I had forgotten my mother—with the medicine in my hand! "I am going home," I said. "Where are you staying? At the inn?"

She laughed her bitter laugh, and pointed to the stone quarry. "There is my inn for to-night," she said. "When I got tired of walking about, I rested there."

We walked on together, on my way home. I took the liberty of asking her if she had any friends.

"I thought I had one friend left," she said, "or you would never

165

have met me in this place. It turns out I was wrong. My friend's door was closed in my face some hours since; my friend's servants threatened me with the police. I had nowhere else to go, after trying my luck in your neighborhood; and nothing left but my two-shilling piece and these rags on my back. What respectable innkeeper would take me into his house? I walked about, wondering how I could find my way out of the world without disfiguring myself, and without suffering much pain. You have no river in these parts. I didn't see my way out of the world, till I heard you ringing at the doctor's house. I got a glimpse at the bottles in the surgery, when he let you in, and I thought of the laudanum directly. What were you doing there? Who is that medicine for? Your wife?"

"I am not married!"

She laughed again. "Not married! If I was a little better dressed there might be a chance for ME. Where do you live? Here?"

We had arrived, by this time, at my mother's door. She held out her hand to say good-by. Houseless and homeless as she was, she never asked me to give her a shelter for the night. It was my proposal that she should rest, under my roof, unknown to my mother and my aunt. Our kitchen was built out at the back of the cottage: she might remain there unseen and unheard until the household was astir in the morning. I led her into the kitchen, and set a chair for her by the dying embers of the fire. I dare say I was to blame—shamefully to blame, if you like. I only wonder what you would have done in my place. On your word of honor as a man, would you have let that beautiful creature wander back to the shelter of the stone quarry like a stray dog? God help the woman who is foolish enough to trust and love you, if you would have done that!

I left her by the fire, and went to my mother's room.

IX

If you have ever felt the heartache, you will know what I suffered in secret when my mother took my hand, and said, "I am sorry, Francis, that your night's rest has been disturbed through me." I gave her the medicine; and I waited by her till the pains abated. My aunt Chance went back to her bed; and my mother and I were left alone. I noticed that her writing-desk, moved from its customary place, was on the bed by her side. She saw me looking at it. "This is your birthday, Francis," she said. "Have you anything to tell me?" I had so completely forgotten my Dream, that I had no notion of what was passing in her mind when she said those words. For a moment there was a guilty fear in me that she suspected something. I turned away my face, and said, "No, mother; I have nothing to tell." She signed to me to stoop down over the pillow and kiss her. "God bless you, my love!" she said; "and many happy returns of the day." She patted my hand, and closed her weary eyes, and, little by little, fell off peaceably into sleep.

I stole downstairs again. I think the good influence of my mother must have followed me down. At any rate, this is true: I stopped with my hand on the closed kitchen door, and said to myself: "Suppose I leave the house, and leave the village, without seeing her or speaking to her more?"

Should I really have fled from temptation in this way, if I had been left to myself to decide? Who can tell? As things were, I was not left to decide. While my doubt was in my mind, she heard me, and opened the kitchen door. My eyes and her eyes met. That ended it.

We were together, unsuspected and undisturbed, for the next two hours. Time enough for her to reveal the secret of her wasted life. Time enough for her to take possession of me as her own, to do with me as she liked. It is needless to dwell here on the misfortunes which had brought her low; they are misfortunes too common to interest anybody.

Her name was Alicia Warlock. She had been born and bred a lady. She had lost her station, her character, and her friends. Virtue shuddered at the sight of her; and Vice had got her for the rest of her days. Shocking and common, as I told you. It made no difference to me. I have said it already—I say it again—I was a man bewitched. Is there anything so very wonderful in that? Just remember who I was. Among the honest women in my own station in life, where could I have found the like of her? Could they walk as she walked? and look as she looked? When they gave me a kiss, did their lips linger over it as hers did? Had they her skin, her laugh, her foot, her hand, her touch? She never had a speck of dirt on her: I tell you her flesh was a perfume. When she embraced me, her arms folded round me like the wings of angels; and her smile covered me softly with its light like the sun in heaven. I leave you to laugh at me, or to cry over me, just as your temper may incline. I am not trying to excuse myself—I am trying to explain. You are gentle-folks; what dazzled and maddened me, is everyday experience to you. Fallen or not, angel or devil, it came to this—she was a lady; and I was a groom.

Before the house was astir, I got her away (by the workmen's train) to a large manufacturing town in our parts.

Here—with my savings in money to help her—she could get her outfit of decent clothes and her lodging among strangers who asked no questions so long as they were paid. Here—now on one pretense and now on another—I could visit her, and we could both plan together what our future lives were to be. I need not tell you that I stood pledged to make her my wife. A man in my station always marries a woman of her sort.

Do you wonder if I was happy at this time? I should have been perfectly happy but for one little drawback. It was this: I was never quite at my ease in the presence of my promised wife.

I don't mean that I was shy with her, or suspicious of her, or ashamed of her. The uneasiness I am speaking of was caused by a faint doubt in my mind whether I had not seen her somewhere, before the morning when we met at the doctor's house. Over and over again, I found myself wondering whether her face did not remind me of some other face—what other I never could tell. This strange feeling, this one question that could never be answered, vexed me to a degree that you would hardly credit. It came between us at the strangest times— oftenest, however, at night, when the candles were lit. You have known what it is to try and remember a forgotten name—and to fail, search as you may, to find it in your mind. That was my case. I failed to find my lost face, just as you failed to find your lost name.

In three weeks we had talked matters over, and had arranged how I was to make a clean breast of it at home. By Alicia's advice, I was to describe her as having been one of my fellow servants during the time I was employed under my kind master and mistress in London. There was no fear now of my mother taking any harm from the shock of a great surprise. Her health had improved during the three weeks' interval. On the first evening when she was able to take her old place at tea time, I summoned my courage, and told her I was going to be married. The poor soul flung her arms round my neck, and burst out crying for joy. "Oh, Francis!" she says, "I am so glad you will have somebody to comfort you and care for you when I am gone!" As for my aunt Chance, you can anticipate what she did, without being told. Ah, me! If there had really been any prophetic virtue in the cards, what a terrible warning they might have given us that night! It was arranged that I was to bring my promised wife to dinner at the cottage on the next day.

X

I own I was proud of Alicia when I led her into our little parlor at the appointed time. She had never, to my mind, looked so beautiful as she looked that day. I never noticed any other woman's dress—I noticed hers as carefully as if I had been a woman myself! She wore a black silk gown, with plain collar and cuffs, and a modest lavender-colored bonnet, with one white rose in it placed at the side. My mother, dressed in her Sunday best, rose up, all in a flutter, to welcome her daughter-in-law that was to be. She walked forward a few steps, half smiling, half in tears—she looked Alicia full in the face—and suddenly

168

stood still. Her cheeks turned white in an instant; her eyes stared in horror; her hands dropped helplessly at her sides. She staggered back, and fell into the arms of my aunt, standing behind her. It was no swoon—she kept her senses. Her eyes turned slowly from Alicia to me. "Francis," she said, "does that woman's face remind you of nothing?".

Before I could answer, she pointed to her writing-desk on the table at the fireside. "Bring it!" she cried, "bring it!".

At the same moment I felt Alicia's hand on my shoulder, and saw Alicia's face red with anger—and no wonder!

"What does this mean?" she asked. "Does your mother want to insult me?".

I said a few words to quiet her; what they were I don't remember—I was so confused and astonished at the time. Before I had done, I heard my mother behind me.

My aunt had fetched her desk. She had opened it; she had taken a paper from it. Step by step, helping herself along by the wall, she came nearer and nearer, with the paper in her hand. She looked at the paper—she looked in Alicia's face—she lifted the long, loose sleeve of her gown, and examined her hand and arm. I saw fear suddenly take the place of anger in Alicia's eyes. She shook herself free of my mother's grasp. "Mad!" she said to herself, "and Francis never told me!" With those words she ran out of the room.

I was hastening out after her, when my mother signed to me to stop. She read the words written on the paper. While they fell slowly, one by one, from her lips, she pointed toward the open door.

"Light gray eyes, with a droop in the left eyelid. Flaxen hair, with a gold-yellow streak in it. White arms, with a down upon them. Little, lady's hand, with a rosy-red look about the finger nails. The Dream Woman, Francis! The Dream Woman!"

Something darkened the parlor window as those words were spoken. I looked sidelong at the shadow. Alicia Warlock had come back! She was peering in at us over the low window blind. There was the fatal face which had first looked at me in the bedroom of the lonely inn. There, resting on the window blind, was the lovely little hand which had held the murderous knife. I had seen her before we met in the village. The Dream Woman! The Dream Woman!

XI

I expect nobody to approve of what I have next to tell of myself. In three weeks from the day when my mother had identified her with the Woman of the Dream, I took Alicia Warlock to church, and made her my wife. I was a man bewitched. Again and again I say it—I was a man bewitched!

During the interval before my marriage, our little household at the cottage was broken up. My mother and my aunt quarreled. My mother, believing in the Dream, entreated me to break off my engagement. My aunt, believing in the cards, urged me to marry.

This difference of opinion produced a dispute between them, in the course of which my aunt Chance—quite unconscious of having any superstitious feelings of her own—actually set out the cards which prophesied happiness to me in my married life, and asked my mother how anybody but "a blinded heathen could be fule enough, after seeing those cairds, to believe in a dream!" This was, naturally, too much for my mother's patience; hard words followed on either side; Mrs. Chance returned in dudgeon to her friends in Scotland. She left me a written statement of my future prospects, as revealed by the cards, and with it an address at which a post-office order would reach her. "The day was not that far off," she remarked, "when Francie might remember what he owed to his aunt Chance, maintaining her ain unbleemished widowhood on thratty punds a year."

Having refused to give her sanction to my marriage, my mother also refused to be present at the wedding, or to visit Alicia afterwards. There was no anger at the bottom of this conduct on her part. Believing as she did in this Dream, she was simply in mortal fear of my wife. I understood this, and I made allowances for her. Not a cross word passed between us. My one happy remembrance now—though I did disobey her in the matter of my marriage—is this: I loved and respected my good mother to the last.

As for my wife, she expressed no regret at the estrangement between her mother-in-law and herself. By common consent, we never spoke on that subject. We settled in the manufacturing town which I have already mentioned, and we kept a lodging-house. My kind master, at my request, granted me a lump sum in place of my annuity. This put us into a good house, decently furnished. For a while things went well enough. I may describe myself at this time of my life as a happy man.

My misfortunes began with a return of the complaint with which my mother had already suffered. The doctor confessed, when I asked him the question, that there was danger to be dreaded this time. Naturally, after hearing this, I was a good deal away at the cottage. Naturally also, I left the business of looking after the house, in my absence, to my wife. Little by little, I found her beginning to alter toward me. While my back was turned, she formed acquaintances with people of the doubtful and dissipated sort. One day, I observed something in her manner which forced the suspicion on me that she had been drinking. Before the week was out, my suspicion was a certainty. From keeping company with drunkards, she had grown to be a drunkard herself.

I did all a man could do to reclaim her. Quite useless! She had never really returned the love I felt for her: I had no influence; I could do nothing. My mother, hearing of this last worse trouble, resolved to try what her influence could do. Ill as she was, I found her one day dressed to go out.

"I am not long for this world, Francis," she said. "I shall not feel easy on my deathbed, unless I have done my best to the last to make you happy. I mean to put my own fears and my own feelings out of the question, and go with you to your wife, and try what I can do to reclaim her. Take me home with you, Francis. Let me do all I can to help my son, before it is too late."

How could I disobey her? We took the railway to the town: it was only half an hour's ride. By one o'clock in the afternoon we reached my house. It was our dinner hour, and Alicia was in the kitchen. I was able to take my mother quietly into the parlor and then to prepare my wife for the visit. She had drunk but little at that early hour; and, luckily, the devil in her was tamed for the time.

She followed me into the parlor, and the meeting passed off better than I had ventured to forecast; with this one drawback, that my mother—though she tried hard to control herself—shrank from looking my wife in the face when she spoke to her. It was a relief to me when Alicia began to prepare the table for dinner.

She laid the cloth, brought in the bread tray, and cut some slices for us from the loaf. Then she returned to the kitchen. At that moment, while I was still anxiously watching my mother, I was startled by seeing the same ghastly change pass over her face which had altered it in the morning when Alicia and she first met. Before I could say a word, she started up with a look of horror.

"Take me back!—home, home again, Francis! Come with me, and never go back more!"

I was afraid to ask for an explanation; I could only sign her to be silent, and help her quickly to the door. As we passed the bread tray on the table, she stopped and pointed to it.

"Did you see what your wife cut your bread with?" she asked.

"No, mother; I was not noticing. What was it?"

"Look!"

I did look. A new clasp knife, with a buckhorn handle, lay with the loaf in the bread tray. I stretched out my hand to possess myself of it. At the same moment, there was a noise in the kitchen, and my mother caught me by the arm.

"The knife of the Dream! Francis, I'm faint with fear—take me away before she comes back!"

I couldn't speak to comfort or even to answer her. Superior as I was to superstition, the discovery of the knife staggered me. In silence, I helped my mother out of the house; and took her home.

I held out my hand to say good-by. She tried to stop me.

"Don't go back, Francis! don't go back!".

"I must get the knife, mother. I must go back by the next train." I held to that resolution. By the next train I went back.

XII

My wife had, of course, discovered our secret departure from the house. She had been drinking. She was in a fury of passion. The dinner in the kitchen was flung under the grate; the cloth was off the parlor table. Where was the knife?

I was foolish enough to ask for it. She refused to give it to me. In the course of the dispute between us which followed, I discovered that there was a horrible story attached to the knife. It had been used in a murder—years since—and had been so skillfully hidden that the authorities had been unable to produce it at the trial. By help of some of her disreputable friends, my wife had been able to purchase this relic of a bygone crime. Her perverted nature set some horrid unacknowledged value on the knife. Seeing there was no hope of getting it by fair means, I determined to search for it, later in the day, in secret. The search was unsuccessful. Night came on, and I left the house to walk about the streets. You will understand what a broken man I was by this time, when I tell you I was afraid to sleep in the same room with her!

Three weeks passed. Still she refused to give up the knife; and still that fear of sleeping in the same room with her possessed me. I walked about at night, or dozed in the parlor, or sat watching by my mother's bedside. Before the end of the first week in the new month, the worst misfortune of all befell me—my mother died. It wanted then but a short time to my birthday. She had longed to live till that day. I was present at her death. Her last words in this world were addressed to me. "Don't go back, my son—don't go back!"

I was obliged to go back, if it was only to watch my wife. In the last days of my mother's illness she had spitefully added a sting to my grief by declaring she would assert her right to attend the funeral. In spite of all that I could do or say, she held to her word. On the day appointed for the burial she forced herself, inflamed and shameless with drink, into my presence, and swore she would walk in the funeral procession to my mother's grave.

This last insult—after all I had gone through already—was more than I could endure. It maddened me. Try to make allowances for a man beside himself. I struck her.

The instant the blow was dealt, I repented it. She crouched down, silent, in a corner of the room, and eyed me steadily. It was a look that

172

cooled my hot blood in an instant. There was no time now to think of making atonement. I could only risk the worst, and make sure of her till the funeral was over. I locked her into her bedroom.

When I came back, after laying my mother in the grave, I found her sitting by the bedside, very much altered in look and bearing, with a bundle on her lap. She faced me quietly; she spoke with a curious stillness in her voice—strangely and unnaturally composed in look and manner.

"No man has ever struck me yet," she said. "My husband shall have no second opportunity. Set the door open, and let me go."

She passed me, and left the room. I saw her walk away up the street. Was she gone for good?

All that night I watched and waited. No footstep came near the house. The next night, overcome with fatigue, I lay down on the bed in my clothes, with the door locked, the key on the table, and the candle burning. My slumber was not disturbed. The third night, the fourth, the fifth, the sixth, passed, and nothing happened. I lay down on the seventh night, still suspicious of something happening; still in my clothes; still with the door locked, the key on the table, and the candle burning.

My rest was disturbed. I awoke twice, without any sensation of uneasiness. The third time, that horrid shivering of the night at the lonely inn, that awful sinking pain at the heart, came back again, and roused me in an instant. My eyes turned to the left-hand side of the bed. And there stood, looking at me—

The Dream Woman again? No! My wife. The living woman, with the face of the Dream—in the attitude of the Dream—the fair arm up; the knife clasped in the delicate white hand.

I sprang upon her on the instant; but not quickly enough to stop her from hiding the knife. Without a word from me, without a cry from her, I pinioned her in a chair. With one hand I felt up her sleeve; and there, where the Dream Woman had hidden the knife, my wife had hidden it—the knife with the buckhorn handle, that looked like new.

What I felt when I made that discovery I could not realize at the time, and I can't describe now. I took one steady look at her with the knife in my hand. "You meant to kill me?" I said.

"Yes," she answered; "I meant to kill you." She crossed her arms over her bosom, and stared me coolly in the face. "I shall do it yet," she said. "With that knife."

I don't know what possessed me—I swear to you I am no coward; and yet I acted like a coward. The horrors got hold of me. I couldn't look at her—I couldn't speak to her. I left her (with the knife in my hand), and went out into the night.

There was a bleak wind abroad, and the smell of rain was in the air. The church clocks chimed the quarter as I walked beyond the last

173

house in the town. I asked the first policeman I met what hour that was, of which the quarter past had just struck.

The man looked at his watch, and answered, "Two o'clock." Two in the morning. What day of the month was this day that had just begun? I reckoned it up from the date of my mother's funeral. The horrid parallel between the dream and the reality was complete—it was my birthday!

Had I escaped, the mortal peril which the dream foretold? or had I only received a second warning? As that doubt crossed my mind I stopped on my way out of the town. The air had revived me—I felt in some degree like my own self again. After a little thinking, I began to see plainly the mistake I had made in leaving my wife free to go where she liked and to do as she pleased.

I turned instantly, and made my way back to the house. It was still dark. I had left the candle burning in the bedchamber. When I looked up to the window of the room now, there was no light in it. I advanced to the house door. On going away, I remembered to have closed it; on trying it now, I found it open.

I waited outside, never losing sight of the house till daylight. Then I ventured indoors—listened, and heard nothing—looked into the kitchen, scullery, parlor, and found nothing—went up at last into the bedroom. It was empty.

A picklock lay on the floor, which told me how she had gained entrance in the night. And that was the one trace I could find of the Dream Woman.

XIII

I waited in the house till the town was astir for the day, and then I went to consult a lawyer. In the confused state of my mind at the time, I had one clear notion of what I meant to do: I was determined to sell my house and leave the neighborhood. There were obstacles in the way which I had not counted on. I was told I had creditors to satisfy before I could leave—I, who had given my wife the money to pay my bills regularly every week! Inquiry showed that she had embezzled every farthing of the money I had intrusted to her. I had no choice but to pay over again.

Placed in this awkward position, my first duty was to set things right, with the help of my lawyer. During my forced sojourn in the town I did two foolish things. And, as a consequence that followed, I heard once more, and heard for the last time, of my wife.

In the first place, having got possession of the knife, I was rash enough to keep it in my pocket. In the second place, having something

174

of importance to say to my lawyer, at a late hour of the evening, I went to his house after dark—alone and on foot. I got there safely enough. Returning, I was seized on from behind by two men, dragged down a passage and robbed—not only of the little money I had about me, but also of the knife. It was the lawyer's opinion (as it was mine) that the thieves were among the disreputable acquaintances formed by my wife, and that they had attacked me at her instigation. To confirm this view I received a letter the next day, without date or address, written in Alicia's hand. The first line informed me that the knife was back again in her possession. The second line reminded me of the day when I struck her. The third line warned me that she would wash out the stain of that blow in my blood, and repeated the words, "I shall do it with the knife!"

These things happened a year ago. The law laid hands on the men who had robbed me; but from that time to this, the law has failed completely to find a trace of my wife.

My story is told. When I had paid the creditors and paid the legal expenses, I had barely five pounds left out of the sale of my house; and I had the world to begin over again. Some months since—drifting here and there—I found my way to Underbridge. The landlord of the inn had known something of my father's family in times past. He gave me (all he had to give) my food, and shelter in the yard. Except on market days, there is nothing to do. In the coming winter the inn is to be shut up, and I shall have to shift for myself. My old master would help me if I applied to him—but I don't like to apply: he has done more for me already than I deserve. Besides, in another year who knows but my troubles may all be at an end? Next winter will bring me nigh to my next birthday, and my next birthday may be the day of my death. Yes! it's true I sat up all last night; and I heard two in the morning strike: and nothing happened. Still, allowing for that, the time to come is a time I don't trust. My wife has got the knife—my wife is looking for me. I am above superstition, mind! I don't say I believe in dreams; I only say, Alicia Warlock is looking for me. It is possible I may be wrong. It is possible I may be right. Who can tell?

175

THE THIRD NARRATIVE

THE STORY CONTINUED BY PERCY FAIRBANK

XIV

We took leave of Francis Raven at the door of Farleigh Hall, with the understanding that he might expect to hear from us again.

The same night Mrs. Fairbank and I had a discussion in the sanctuary of our own room. The topic was "The Hostler's Story"; and the question in dispute between us turned on the measure of charitable duty that we owed to the hostler himself.

The view I took of the man's narrative was of the purely matter-of-fact kind. Francis Raven had, in my opinion, brooded over the misty connection between his strange dream and his vile wife, until his mind was in a state of partial delusion on that subject. I was quite willing to help him with a trifle of money, and to recommend him to the kindness of my lawyer, if he was really in any danger and wanted advice. There my idea of my duty toward this afflicted person began and ended.

Confronted with this sensible view of the matter, Mrs. Fairbank's romantic temperament rushed, as usual, into extremes. "I should no more think of losing sight of Francis Raven when his next birthday comes round," says my wife, "than I should think of laying down a good story with the last chapters unread. I am positively determined, Percy, to take him back with us when we return to France, in the capacity of groom. What does one man more or less among the horses matter to people as rich as we are?" In this strain the partner of my joys and sorrows ran on, perfectly impenetrable to everything that I could say on the side of common sense. Need I tell my married brethren how it ended? Of course I allowed my wife to irritate me, and spoke to her sharply.

Of course my wife turned her face away indignantly on the conjugal pillow, and burst into tears. Of course upon that, "Mr." made his excuses, and "Mrs." had her own way.

Before the week was out we rode over to Underbridge, and duly offered to Francis Raven a place in our service as supernumerary groom.

At first the poor fellow seemed hardly able to realize his own extraordinary good fortune. Recovering himself, he expressed his gratitude modestly and becomingly. Mrs. Fairbank's ready sympathies overflowed, as usual, at her lips. She talked to him about our home in France, as if the worn, gray-headed hostler had been a child. "Such a

176

dear old house, Francis; and such pretty gardens! Stables! Stables ten times as big as your stables here—quite a choice of rooms for you. You must learn the name of our house—Maison Rouge. Our nearest town is Metz. We are within a walk of the beautiful River Moselle. And when we want a change we have only to take the railway to the frontier, and find ourselves in Germany."

Listening, so far, with a very bewildered face, Francis started and changed color when my wife reached the end of her last sentence. "Germany?" he repeated.

"Yes. Does Germany remind you of anything?"

The hostler's eyes looked down sadly on the ground. "Germany reminds me of my wife," he replied.

"Indeed! How?"

"She once told me she had lived in Germany—long before I knew her—in the time when she was a young girl."

"Was she living with relations or friends?"

"She was living as governess in a foreign family."

"In what part of Germany?"

"I don't remember, ma'am. I doubt if she told me."

"Did she tell you the name of the family?"

"Yes, ma'am. It was a foreign name, and it has slipped my memory long since. The head of the family was a wine grower in a large way of business—I remember that."

"Did you hear what sort of wine he grew? There are wine growers in our neighborhood. Was it Moselle wine?"

"I couldn't say, ma'am, I doubt if I ever heard."

There the conversation dropped. We engaged to communicate with Francis Raven before we left England, and took our leave. I had made arrangements to pay our round of visits to English friends, and to return to Maison Rouge in the summer. On the eve of departure, certain difficulties in connection with the management of some landed property of mine in Ireland obliged us to alter our plans. Instead of getting back to our house in France in the Summer, we only returned a week or two before Christmas. Francis Raven accompanied us, and was duly established, in the nominal capacity of stable keeper, among the servants at Maison Rouge.

Before long, some of the objections to taking him into our employment, which I had foreseen and had vainly mentioned to my wife, forced themselves on our attention in no very agreeable form. Francis Raven failed (as I had feared he would) to get on smoothly with his fellow-servants They were all French; and not one of them understood English. Francis, on his side, was equally ignorant of French. His reserved manners, his melancholy temperament, his solitary ways—all told against him. Our servants called him "the English Bear." He grew widely known in the neighborhood under his nickname. Quarrels took place, ending once or twice in blows. It became plain, even to Mrs. Fairbank herself, that some wise change must be made. While we were still considering what the change was to be, the unfortunate hostler was thrown on our hands for some time to come by an accident in the stables. Still pursued by his proverbial ill-luck, the poor wretch's leg was broken by a kick from a horse.

He was attended to by our own surgeon, in his comfortable bedroom at the stables. As the date of his birthday drew near, he was still confined to his bed.

Physically speaking, he was doing very well. Morally speaking, the surgeon was not satisfied. Francis Raven was suffering under some mysterious mental disturbance, which interfered seriously with his rest at night. Hearing this, I thought it my duty to tell the medical attendant what was preying on the patient's mind. As a practical man, he shared my opinion that the hostler was in a state of delusion on the subject of his Wife and his Dream. "Curable delusion, in my opinion," the surgeon added, "if the experiment could be fairly tried."

"How can it be tried?" I asked. Instead of replying, the surgeon put a question to me, on his side.

"Do you happen to know," he said, "that this year is Leap Year?"

"Mrs. Fairbank reminded me of it yesterday," I answered. "Otherwise I might not have known it."

"Do you think Francis Raven knows that this year is Leap Year?"

(I began to see dimly what my friend was driving at.)

"It depends," I answered, "on whether he has got an English almanac. Suppose he has not got the almanac—what then?"

"In that case," pursued the surgeon, "Francis Raven is innocent of all suspicion that there is a twenty-ninth day in February this year. As a necessary consequence—what will he do? He will anticipate the appearance of the Woman with the Knife, at two in the morning of the twenty-ninth of February, instead of the first of March. Let him suffer all his superstitious terrors on the wrong day. Leave him, on the day that is really his birthday, to pass a perfectly quiet night, and to be as sound asleep as other people at two in the morning. And then, when he wakes comfortably in time for his breakfast, shame him out of his delusion by telling him the truth."

I agreed to try the experiment. Leaving the surgeon to caution Mrs. Fairbank on the subject of Leap Year, I went to the stables to see Mr. Raven.

XV

The poor fellow was full of forebodings of the fate in store for him on the ominous first of March. He eagerly entreated me to order one of the men servants to sit up with him on the birthday morning. In granting his request, I asked him to tell me on which day of the week his birthday fell. He reckoned the days on his fingers; and proved his innocence of all suspicion that it was Leap Year, by fixing on the twenty-ninth of February, in the full persuasion that it was the first of March. Pledged to try the surgeon's experiment, I left his error uncorrected, of course. In so doing, I took my first step blindfold toward the last act in the drama of the Hostler's Dream.

The next day brought with it a little domestic difficulty, which indirectly and strangely associated itself with the coming end.

My wife received a letter, inviting us to assist in celebrating the "Silver Wedding" of two worthy German neighbors of ours—Mr. and Mrs. Beldheimer. Mr. Beldheimer was a large wine grower on the banks of the Moselle. His house was situated on the frontier line of France and Germany; and the distance from our house was sufficiently considerable to make it necessary for us to sleep under our host's roof. Under these circumstances, if we accepted the invitation, a comparison of dates showed that we should be away from home on the morning of the first of March. Mrs. Fairbank—holding to her absurd resolution to see with her own eyes what might, or might not, happen to Francis Raven on his birthday—flatly declined to leave Maison Rouge. "It's easy to send an excuse," she said, in her off-hand manner.

I failed, for my part, to see any easy way out of the difficulty. The celebration of a "Silver Wedding" in Germany is the celebration of twenty-five years of happy married life; and the host's claim upon the consideration of his friends on such an occasion is something in the nature of a royal "command." After considerable discussion, finding my wife's obstinacy invincible, and feeling that the absence of both of us from the festival would certainly offend our friends, I left Mrs. Fairbank to make her excuses for herself, and directed her to accept the invitation so far as I was concerned. In so doing, I took my second step, blindfold, toward the last act in the drama of the Hostler's Dream.

A week elapsed; the last days of February were at hand. Another domestic difficulty happened; and, again, this event also proved to be strangely associated with the coming end.

My head groom at the stables was one Joseph Rigobert. He was an ill-conditioned fellow, inordinately vain of his personal appearance, and by no means scrupulous in his conduct with women. His one virtue consisted of his fondness for horses, and in the care he took of the animals under his charge. In a word, he was too good a groom to be easily replaced, or he would have quitted my service long since. On the occasion of which I am now writing, he was reported to me by my steward as growing idle and disorderly in his habits. The principal offense alleged against him was, that he had been seen that day in the city of Metz, in the company of a woman (supposed to be an Englishwoman), whom he was entertaining at a tavern, when he ought to have been on his way back to Maison Rouge. The man's defense was that "the lady" (as he called her) was an English stranger, unacquainted with the ways of the place, and that he had only shown her where she could obtain some refreshments at her own request. I administered the necessary reprimand, without troubling myself to inquire further into the matter. In failing to do this, I took my third step, blindfold, toward the last act in the drama of the Hostler's Dream.

On the evening of the twenty-eighth, I informed the servants at the stables that one of them must watch through the night by the Englishman's bedside. Joseph Rigobert immediately volunteered for the duty—as a means, no doubt, of winning his way back to my favor. I accepted his proposal.

That day the surgeon dined with us. Toward midnight he and I left the smoking room, and repaired to Francis Raven's bedside. Rigobert was at his post, with no very agreeable expression on his face. The Frenchman and the Englishman had evidently not got on well together so far. Francis Raven lay helpless on his bed, waiting silently for two in the morning and the Dream Woman.

"I have come, Francis, to bid you good night," I said, cheerfully. "To-morrow morning I shall look in at breakfast time, before I leave home on a journey."

"Thank you for all your kindness, sir. You will not see me alive to-morrow morning. She will find me this time. Mark my words—she will find me this time."

"My good fellow! she couldn't find you in England. How in the world is she to find you in France?"

"It's borne in on my mind, sir, that she will find me here. At two in the morning on my birthday I shall see her again, and see her for the last time."

"Do you mean that she will kill you?"

"I mean that, sir, she will kill me—with the knife."

"And with Rigobert in the room to protect you?"

"I am a doomed man. Fifty Rigoberts couldn't protect me."

"And you wanted somebody to sit up with you?"

"Mere weakness, sir. I don't like to be left alone on my deathbed."

I looked at the surgeon. If he had encouraged me, I should certainly, out of sheer compassion, have confessed to Francis Raven the trick that we were playing him. The surgeon held to his experiment; the surgeon's face plainly said—"No."

The next day (the twenty-ninth of February) was the day of the "Silver Wedding." The first thing in the morning, I went to Francis Raven's room. Rigobert met me at the door.

"How has he passed the night?" I asked.

"Saying his prayers, and looking for ghosts," Rigobert answered. "A lunatic asylum is the only proper place for him."

I approached the bedside. "Well, Francis, here you are, safe and sound, in spite of what you said to me last night."

His eyes rested on mine with a vacant, wondering look.

"I don't understand it," he said.

"Did you see anything of your wife when the clock struck two?"

"No, sir."

"Did anything happen?"

"Nothing happened, sir."

"Doesn't this satisfy you that you were wrong?"

His eyes still kept their vacant, wondering look. He only repeated the words he had spoken already: "I don't understand it."

I made a last attempt to cheer him. "Come, come, Francis! keep a good heart. You will be out of bed in a fortnight."

He shook his head on the pillow. "There's something wrong," he said. "I don't expect you to believe me, sir. I only say there's something wrong—and time will show it."

I left the room. Half an hour later I started for Mr. Beldheimer's house; leaving the arrangements for the morning of the first of March in the hands of the doctor and my wife.

XVI

The one thing which principally struck me when I joined the guests at the "Silver Wedding" is also the one thing which it is necessary to mention here. On this joyful occasion a noticeable lady present was out of spirits. That lady was no other than the heroine of the festival, the mistress of the house!

In the course of the evening I spoke to Mr. Beldheimer's eldest son on the subject of his mother. As an old friend of the family, I had a claim on his confidence which the young man willingly recognized.

"We have had a very disagreeable matter to deal with," he said; "and my mother has not recovered the painful impression left on her mind. Many years since, when my sisters were children, we had an English governess in the house. She left us, as we then understood, to be married. We heard no more of her until a week or ten days since, when my mother received a letter, in which our ex-governess described herself as being in a condition of great poverty and distress. After much hesitation she had ventured—at the suggestion of a lady who had been kind to her—to write to her former employers, and to appeal to their remembrance of old times. You know my mother: she is not only the most kind-hearted, but the most innocent of women—it is impossible to persuade her of the wickedness that there is in the world. She replied by return of post, inviting the governess to come here and see her, and

181

inclosing the money for her traveling expenses. When my father came home, and heard what had been done, he wrote at once to his agent in London to make inquiries, inclosing the address on the governess' letter. Before he could receive the agent's reply the governess, arrived. She produced the worst possible impression on his mind. The agent's letter, arriving a few days later, confirmed his suspicions. Since we had lost sight of her, the woman had led a most disreputable life. My father spoke to her privately: he offered—on condition of her leaving the house—a sum of money to take her back to England. If she refused, the alternative would be an appeal to the authorities and a public scandal. She accepted the money, and left the house. On her way back to England she appears to have stopped at Metz. You will understand what sort of woman she is when I tell you that she was seen the other day in a tavern, with your handsome groom, Joseph Rigobert."

While my informant was relating these circumstances, my memory was at work. I recalled what Francis Raven had vaguely told us of his wife's experience in former days as governess in a German family. A suspicion of the truth suddenly flashed across my mind. "What was the woman's name?" I asked.

Mr. Beldheimer's son answered: "Alicia Warlock."

I had but one idea when I heard that reply—to get back to my house without a moment's needless delay. It was then ten o'clock at night—the last train to Metz had left long since. I arranged with my young friend—after duly informing him of the circumstances—that I should go by the first train in the morning, instead of staying to breakfast with the other guests who slept in the house.

At intervals during the night I wondered uneasily how things were going on at Maison Rouge. Again and again the same question occurred to me, on my journey home in the early morning—the morning of the first of March. As the event proved, but one person in my house knew what really happened at the stables on Francis Raven's birthday. Let Joseph Rigobert take my place as narrator, and tell the story of the end to You—as he told it, in times past, to his lawyer and to Me.

182

FOURTH (AND LAST) NARRATIVE

STATEMENT OF JOSEPH RIGOBERT: ADDRESSED TO THE ADVOCATE WHO DEFENDED HIM AT HIS TRIAL

Respected Sir,—On the twenty-seventh of February I was sent, on business connected with the stables at Maison Rouge, to the city of Metz. On the public promenade I met a magnificent woman. Complexion, blond. Nationality, English. We mutually admired each other; we fell into conversation. (She spoke French perfectly—with the English accent.) I offered refreshment; my proposal was accepted. We had a long and interesting interview—we discovered that we were made for each other. So far, Who is to blame?

Is it my fault that I am a handsome man—universally agreeable as such to the fair sex? Is it a criminal offense to be accessible to the amiable weakness of love? I ask again, Who is to blame? Clearly, nature. Not the beautiful lady—not my humble self.

To resume. The most hard-hearted person living will understand that two beings made for each other could not possibly part without an appointment to meet again.

I made arrangements for the accommodation of the lady in the village near Maison Rouge. She consented to honor me with her company at supper, in my apartment at the stables, on the night of the twenty-ninth. The time fixed on was the time when the other servants were accustomed to retire—eleven o'clock.

Among the grooms attached to the stables was an Englishman, laid up with a broken leg. His name was Francis. His manners were repulsive; he was ignorant of the French language. In the kitchen he went by the nickname of the "English Bear." Strange to say, he was a great favorite with my master and my mistress. They even humored certain superstitious terrors to which this repulsive person was subject—terrors into the nature of which I, as an advanced freethinker, never thought it worth my while to inquire.

On the evening of the twenty-eighth the Englishman, being a prey to the terrors which I have mentioned, requested that one of his fellow servants might sit up with him for that night only. The wish that he expressed was backed by Mr. Fairbank's authority. Having already incurred my master's displeasure—in what way, a proper sense of my own dignity forbids me to relate—I volunteered to watch by the bedside of the English Bear. My object was to satisfy Mr. Fairbank that I bore no malice, on my side, after what had occurred between us. The wretched Englishman passed a night of delirium. Not understanding his barbarous language, I could only gather from his gesture that he

183

was in deadly fear of some fancied apparition at his bedside. From time to time, when this madman disturbed my slumbers, I quieted him by swearing at him. This is the shortest and best way of dealing with persons in his condition.

On the morning of the twenty-ninth, Mr. Fairbank left us on a journey. Later in the day, to my unspeakable disgust, I found that I had not done with the Englishman yet. In Mr. Fairbank's absence, Mrs. Fairbank took an incomprehensible interest in the question of my delirious fellow servant's repose at night. Again, one or the other of us was to watch at his bedside, and report it, if anything happened. Expecting my fair friend to supper, it was necessary to make sure that the other servants at the stables would be safe in their beds that night. Accordingly, I volunteered once more to be the man who kept watch. Mrs. Fairbank complimented me on my humanity. I possess great command over my feelings. I accepted the compliment without a blush.

Twice, after nightfall, my mistress and the doctor (the last staying in the house in Mr. Fairbank's absence) came to make inquiries. Once before the arrival of my fair friend—and once after. On the second occasion (my apartment being next door to the Englishman's) I was obliged to hide my charming guest in the harness room. She consented, with angelic resignation, to immolate her dignity to the servile necessities of my position. A more amiable woman (so far) I never met with!

After the second visit I was left free. It was then close on midnight. Up to that time there was nothing in the behavior of the mad Englishman to reward Mrs. Fairbank and the doctor for presenting themselves at his bedside. He lay half awake, half asleep, with an odd wondering kind of look in his face. My mistress at parting warned me to be particularly watchful of him toward two in the morning. The doctor (in case anything happened) left me a large hand bell to ring, which could easily be heard at the house.

Restored to the society of my fair friend, I spread the supper table. A pâté, a sausage, and a few bottles of generous Moselle wine, composed our simple meal. When persons adore each other, the intoxicating illusion of Love transforms the simplest meal into a banquet. With immeasurable capacities for enjoyment, we sat down to table. At the very moment when I placed my fascinating companion in a chair, the infamous Englishman in the next room took that occasion, of all others, to become restless and noisy once more. He struck with his stick on the floor; he cried out, in a delirious access of terror, "Rigobert! Rigobert!"

The sound of that lamentable voice, suddenly assailing our ears, terrified my fair friend. She lost all her charming color in an instant. "Good heavens!" she exclaimed. "Who is that in the next room?"

"A mad Englishman."

"An Englishman?"

184

"Compose yourself, my angel. I will quiet him."

The lamentable voice called out on me again, "Rigobert! Rigobert!"

My fair friend caught me by the arm. "Who is he?" she cried. "What is his name?"

Something in her face struck me as she put that question. A spasm of jealousy shook me to the soul. "You know him?" I said.

"His name!" she vehemently repeated; "his name!"

"Francis," I answered.

"Francis—what?"

I shrugged my shoulders. I could neither remember nor pronounce the barbarous English surname. I could only tell her it began with an "R."

She dropped back into the chair. Was she going to faint? No: she recovered, and more than recovered, her lost color. Her eyes flashed superbly. What did it mean? Profoundly as I understand women in general, I was puzzled by this woman!

"You know him?" I repeated.

She laughed at me. "What nonsense! How should I know him? Go and quiet the wretch."

My looking-glass was near. One glance at it satisfied me that no woman in her senses could prefer the Englishman to Me. I recovered my self-respect. I hastened to the Englishman's bedside.

The moment I appeared he pointed eagerly toward my room. He overwhelmed me with a torrent of words in his own language. I made out, from his gestures and his looks, that he had, in some incomprehensible manner, discovered the presence of my guest; and, stranger still, that he was scared by the idea of a person in my room. I endeavored to compose him on the system which I have already mentioned—that is to say, I swore at him in my language. The result not proving satisfactory, I own I shook my fist in his face, and left the bedchamber.

Returning to my fair friend, I found her walking backward and forward in a state of excitement wonderful to behold. She had not waited for me to fill her glass—she had begun the generous Moselle in my absence. I prevailed on her with difficulty to place herself at the table. Nothing would induce her to eat. "My appetite is gone," she said. "Give me wine."

The generous Moselle deserves its name—delicate on the palate, with prodigious "body." The strength of this fine wine produced no stupefying effect on my remarkable guest. It appeared to strengthen and exhilarate her—nothing more. She always spoke in the same low tone, and always, turn the conversation as I might, brought it back with the same dexterity to the subject of the Englishman in the next room. In any other woman this persistency would have offended me. My lovely guest was irresistible; I answered her questions with the docility

185

of a child. She possessed all the amusing eccentricity of her nation. When I told her of the accident which confined the Englishman to his bed, she sprang to her feet. An extraordinary smile irradiated her countenance. She said, "Show me the horse who broke the Englishman's leg! I must see that horse!" I took her to the stables. She kissed the horse—on my word of honor, she kissed the horse! That struck me. I said. "You do know the man; and he has wronged you in some way." No! she would not admit it, even then. "I kiss all beautiful animals," she said. "Haven't I kissed you?" With that charming explanation of her conduct, she ran back up the stairs. I only remained behind to lock the stable door again. When I rejoined her, I made a startling discovery. I caught her coming out of the Englishman's room.

"I was just going downstairs again to call you," she said. "The man in there is getting noisy once more."

The mad Englishman's voice assailed our ears once again. "Rigobert! Rigobert!"

He was a frightful object to look at when I saw him this time. His eyes were staring wildly; the perspiration was pouring over his face. In a panic of terror he clasped his hands; he pointed up to heaven. By every sign and gesture that a man can make, he entreated me not to leave him again. I really could not help smiling. The idea of my staying with him, and leaving my fair friend by herself in the next room!

I turned to the door. When the mad wretch saw me leaving him he burst out into a screech of despair—so shrill that I feared it might awaken the sleeping servants.

My presence of mind in emergencies is proverbial among those who know me. I tore open the cupboard in which he kept his linen—seized a handful of his handkerchiefs—gagged him with one of them, and secured his hands with the others. There was now no danger of his alarming the servants. After tying the last knot, I looked up.

The door between the Englishman's room and mine was open. My fair friend was standing on the threshold—watching him as he lay helpless on the bed; watching me as I tied the last knot.

"What are you doing there?" I asked. "Why did you open the door?"

She stepped up to me, and whispered her answer in my ear, with her eyes all the time upon the man on the bed:

"I heard him scream."

"Well?"

"I thought you had killed him."

I drew back from her in horror. The suspicion of me which her words implied was sufficiently detestable in itself. But her manner when she uttered the words was more revolting still. It so powerfully affected me that I started back from that beautiful creature as I might have recoiled from a reptile crawling over my flesh.

Before I had recovered myself sufficiently to reply, my nerves were assailed by another shock. I suddenly heard my mistress's voice calling to me from the stable yard.

There was no time to think—there was only time to act. The one thing needed was to keep Mrs. Fairbank from ascending the stairs, and discovering—not my lady guest only—but the Englishman also, gagged and bound on his bed. I instantly hurried to the yard. As I ran down the stairs I heard the stable clock strike the quarter to two in the morning.

My mistress was eager and agitated. The doctor (in attendance on her) was smiling to himself, like a man amused at his own thoughts. "Is Francis awake or asleep?" Mrs. Fairbank inquired.

"He has been a little restless, madam. But he is now quiet again. If he is not disturbed" (I added those words to prevent her from ascending the stairs), "he will soon fall off into a quiet sleep."

"Has nothing happened since I was here last?"

"Nothing, madam."

The doctor lifted his eyebrows with a comical look of distress. "Alas, alas, Mrs. Fairbank!" he said. "Nothing has happened! The days of romance are over!"

"It is not two o'clock yet," my mistress answered, a little irritably.

The smell of the stables was strong on the morning air. She put her handkerchief to her nose and led the way out of the yard by the north entrance—the entrance communicating with the gardens and the house. I was ordered to follow her, along with the doctor. Once out of the smell of the stables she began to question me again. She was unwilling to believe that nothing had occurred in her absence. I invented the best answers I could think of on the spur of the moment; and the doctor stood by laughing. So the minutes passed till the clock struck two. Upon that, Mrs. Fairbank announced her intention of personally visiting the Englishman in his room. To my great relief, the doctor interfered to stop her from doing this.

"You have heard that Francis is just falling asleep," he said. "If you enter his room you may disturb him. It is essential to the success of my experiment that he should have a good night's rest, and that he should own it himself, before I tell him the truth. I must request, madam, that you will not disturb the man. Rigobert will ring the alarm bell if anything happens."

My mistress was unwilling to yield. For the next five minutes, at least, there was a warm discussion between the two. In the end Mrs. Fairbank was obliged to give way—for the time. "In half an hour," she said, "Francis will either be sound asleep, or awake again. In half an hour I shall come back." She took the doctor's arm. They returned together to the house.

Left by myself, with half an hour before me, I resolved to take the Englishwoman back to the village—then, returning to the stables, to remove the gag and the bindings from Francis, and to let him screech to his heart's content. What would his alarming the whole establishment matter to me after I had got rid of the compromising presence of my guest?

Returning to the yard I heard a sound like the creaking of an open door on its hinges. The gate of the north entrance I had just closed with my own hand. I went round to the west entrance, at the back of the stables. It opened on a field crossed by two footpaths in Mr. Fairbank's grounds. The nearest footpath led to the village. The other led to the highroad and the river.

Arriving at the west entrance I found the door open—swinging to and fro slowly in the fresh morning breeze. I had myself locked and bolted that door after admitting my fair friend at eleven o'clock. A vague dread of something wrong stole its way into my mind. I hurried back to the stables.

I looked into my own room. It was empty. I went to the harness room. Not a sign of the woman was there. I returned to my room, and approached the door of the Englishman's bedchamber. Was it possible that she had remained there during my absence? An unaccountable reluctance to open the door made me hesitate, with my hand on the lock. I listened. There was not a sound inside. I called softly. There was no answer. I drew back a step, still hesitating. I noticed something dark moving slowly in the crevice between the bottom of the door and the boarded floor. Snatching up the candle from the table, I held it low, and looked. The dark, slowly moving object was a stream of blood!

That horrid sight roused me. I opened the door. The Englishman lay on his bed—alone in the room. He was stabbed in two places—in the throat and in the heart. The weapon was left in the second wound. It was a knife of English manufacture, with a handle of buckhorn as good as new.

I instantly gave the alarm. Witnesses can speak to what followed. It is monstrous to suppose that I am guilty of the murder. I admit that I am capable of committing follies: but I shrink from the bare idea of a crime. Besides, I had no motive for killing the man. The woman murdered him in my absence. The woman escaped by the west entrance while I was talking to my mistress. I have no more to say. I swear to you what I have here written is a true statement of all that happened on the morning of the first of March.

Accept, sir, the assurance of my sentiments of profound gratitude and respect.

JOSEPH RIGOBERT.

LAST LINES.—ADDED BY PERCY FAIRBANK

Tried for the murder of Francis Raven, Joseph Rigobert was found Not Guilty; the papers of the assassinated man presented ample evidence of the deadly animosity felt toward him by his wife.

The investigations pursued on the morning when the crime was committed showed that the murderess, after leaving the stable, had taken the footpath which led to the river. The river was dragged—without result. It remains doubtful to this day whether she died by drowning or not. The one thing certain is—that Alicia Warlock was never seen again.

So—beginning in mystery, ending in mystery—the Dream Woman passes from your view. Ghost; demon; or living human creature—say for yourselves which she is. Or, knowing what unfathomed wonders are around you, what unfathomed wonders are in you, let the wise words of the greatest of all poets be explanation enough:

> "We are such stuff
> As dreams are made of, and our little life
> Is rounded with, a sleep."

ANONYMOUS

THE LOST DUCHESS

I

"Has the duchess returned?"

"No, your grace."

Knowles came farther into the room. He had a letter on a salver. When the duke had taken it, Knowles still lingered. The duke glanced at him.

"Is an answer required?"

"No, your grace." Still Knowles lingered. "Something a little singular has happened. The carriage has returned without the duchess, and the men say that they thought her grace was in it."

"What do you mean?"

"I hardly understand myself, your grace. Perhaps you would like to see Barnes."

Barnes was the coachman.

"Send him up." When Knowles had gone, and he was alone, his grace showed signs of being slightly annoyed. He looked at his watch. "I told her she'd better be in by four. She says that she's not feeling well, and yet one would think that she was not aware of the fatigue entailed in having the prince come to dinner, and a mob of people to follow. I particularly wished her to lie down for a couple of hours."

Knowles ushered in not only Barnes, the coachman, but Moysey, the footman, too. Both these persons seemed to be ill at ease. The duke glanced at them sharply. In his voice there was a suggestion of impatience.

"What is the matter?"

Barnes explained as best he could.

"If you please, your grace, we waited for the duchess outside Cane and Wilson's, the drapers. The duchess came out, got into the carriage, and Moysey shut the door, and her grace said, 'Home!' and yet when we got home she wasn't there."

"She wasn't where?"

"Her grace wasn't in the carriage, your grace."

"What on earth do you mean?"

190

"Her grace did get into the carriage; you shut the door, didn't you?"

Barnes turned to Moysey. Moysey brought his hand up to his brow in a sort of military salute—he had been a soldier in the regiment in which, once upon a time, the duke had been a subaltern.

"She did. The duchess came out of the shop. She seemed rather in a hurry, I thought. She got into the carriage, and she said, 'Home, Moysey!' I shut the door, and Barnes drove straight home. We never stopped anywhere, and we never noticed nothing happen on the way; and yet when we got home the carriage was empty."

The duke started.

"Do you mean to tell me that the duchess got out of the carriage while you were driving full pelt through the streets without saying anything to you, and without you noticing it?"

"The carriage was empty when we got home, your grace."

"Was either of the doors open?"

"No, your grace."

"You fellows have been up to some infernal mischief. You have made a mess of it. You never picked up the duchess, and you're trying to palm this tale off on me to save yourselves."

Barnes was moved to adjuration:

"I'll take my Bible oath, your grace, that the duchess got into the carriage outside Cane and Wilson's."

Moysey seconded his colleague.

"I will swear to that, your grace. She got into that carriage, and I shut the door, and she said, 'Home, Moysey!'"

The duke looked as if he did not know what to make of the story and its tellers.

"What carriage did you have?"

"Her grace's brougham, your grace."

Knowles interposed:

"The brougham was ordered because I understood that the duchess was not feeling very well, and there's rather a high wind, your grace."

The duke snapped at him:

"What has that to do with it? Are you suggesting that the duchess was more likely to jump out of a brougham while it was dashing through the streets than out of any other kind of vehicle?"

The duke's glance fell on the letter which Knowles had brought him when he first had entered. He had placed it on his writing table. Now he took it up. It was addressed:

"To His Grace the Duke of Datchet.
Private!
VERY PRESSING!!!"

The name was written in a fine, clear, almost feminine hand. The words in the left-hand corner of the envelope were written in a different hand. They were large and bold; almost as though they had been painted with the end of the penholder instead of being written with the pen. The envelope itself was of an unusual size, and bulged out as though it contained something else besides a letter.

The duke tore the envelope open. As he did so something fell out of it on to the writing table. It looked as though it was a lock of a woman's hair. As he glanced at it the duke seemed to be a trifle startled. The duke read the letter:

"Your grace will be so good as to bring five hundred pounds in gold to the Piccadilly end of the Burlington Arcade within an hour of the receipt of this. The Duchess of Datchet has been kidnaped. An imitation duchess got into the carriage, which was waiting outside Cane and Wilson's, and she alighted on the road. Unless your grace does as you are requested, the Duchess of Datchet's left-hand little finger will be at once cut off, and sent home in time to receive the prince to dinner. Other portions of her grace will follow. A lock of her grace's hair is inclosed with this as an earnest of our good intentions.

"Before 5:30 p.m. your grace is requested to be at the Piccadilly end of the Burlington Arcade with five hundred pounds in gold. You will there be accosted by an individual in a white top hat, and with a gardenia in his buttonhole. You will be entirely at liberty to give him into custody, or to have him followed by the police, in which case the duchess's left arm, cut off at the shoulder, will be sent home for dinner—not to mention other extremely possible contingencies. But you are advised to give the individual in question the five hundred pounds in gold, because in that case the duchess herself will be home in time to receive the prince to dinner, and with one of the best stories with which to entertain your distinguished guests they ever heard.

"Remember! not later than 5:30, unless you wish to receive her grace's little finger."

The duke stared at this amazing epistle when he had read it as though he found it difficult to believe the evidence of his eyes. He was not a demonstrative person, as a rule, but this little communication astonished even him. He read it again. Then his hands dropped to his sides, and he swore.

He took up the lock of hair which had fallen out of the envelope. Was it possible that it could be his wife's, the duchess? Was it possible that a Duchess of Datchet could be kidnaped, in broad daylight, in the heart of London, and be sent home, as it were, in pieces? Had sacrilegious hands already been playing pranks with that great lady's hair? Certainly, that hair was so like her hair that the mere resemblance made his grace's blood run cold. He turned on Messrs. Barnes and Moysey as though he would have liked to rend them.

"You scoundrels!"

He moved forward as though the intention had entered his ducal heart to knock his servants down. But, if that were so, he did not act quite up to his intention. Instead, he stretched out his arm, pointing at them as if he were an accusing spirit:

"Will you swear that it was the duchess who got into the carriage outside Cane and Wilson's?"

Barnes began to stammer:

"I'll swear, your grace, that I—I thought—"

The duke stormed an interruption:

"I don't ask what you thought. I ask you, will you swear it was?"

The duke's anger was more than Barnes could face. He was silent. Moysey showed a larger courage.

"I could have sworn that it was at the time, your grace. But now it seems to me that it's a rummy go."

"A rummy go!" The peculiarity of the phrase did not seem to strike the duke just then—at least, he echoed it as if it didn't. "You call it a rummy go! Do you know that I am told in this letter that the woman who entered the carriage was not the duchess? What you were thinking about, or what case you will be able to make out for yourselves, you know better than I; but I can tell you this—that in an hour you will leave my service, and you may esteem yourselves fortunate if, to-night, you are not both of you sleeping in jail."

One might almost have suspected that the words were spoken in irony. But before they could answer, another servant entered, who also brought a letter for the duke. When his grace's glance fell on it he uttered an exclamation. The writing on the envelope was the same writing that had been on the envelope which had contained the very singular communication—like it in all respects, down to the broomstick-end thickness of the "Private!" and "Very pressing!!!" in the corner.

"Who brought this?" stormed the duke.

The servant appeared to be a little startled by the violence of his grace's manner.

"A lady—or, at least, your grace, she seemed to be a lady."

"Where is she?"

"She came in a hansom, your grace. She gave me that letter, and said, 'Give that to the Duke of Datchet at once—without a moment's delay!' Then she got into the hansom again, and drove away."

"Why didn't you stop her?"

"Your grace!"

The man seemed surprised, as though the idea of stopping chance visitors to the ducal mansion vi et armis had not, until that moment, entered into his philosophy. The duke continued to regard the man as if he could say a good deal, if he chose. Then he pointed to the door. His lips said nothing, but his gesture much. The servant vanished.

"Another hoax!" the duke said grimly, as he tore the envelope open.

This time the envelope contained a sheet of paper, and in the sheet of paper another envelope. The duke unfolded the sheet of paper. On it some words were written. These:

"The duchess appears so particularly anxious to drop you a line, that one really hasn't the heart to refuse her.

"Her grace's communication—written amidst blinding tears!— you will find inclosed with this."

"Knowles," said the duke, in a voice which actually trembled, "Knowles, hoax or no hoax, I will be even with the gentleman who wrote that."

Handing the sheet of paper to Mr. Knowles, his grace turned his attention to the envelope which had been inclosed. It was a small, square envelope, of the finest quality, and it reeked with perfume. The duke's countenance assumed an added frown—he had no fondness for envelopes which were scented. In the center of the envelope were the words, "To the Duke of Datchet," written in the big, bold, sprawling hand which he knew so well.

"Mabel's writing," he said, half to himself, as, with shaking fingers, he tore the envelope open.

The sheet of paper which he took out was almost as stiff as cardboard. It, too, emitted what his grace deemed the nauseous odors of the perfumer's shop. On it was written this letter:

"MY DEAR HEREWARD—For Heaven's sake do what these people require! I don't know what has happened or where I am, but I am nearly distracted! They have already cut off some of my hair, and they tell me that, if you don't let them have five hundred pounds in gold by half-past five, they will cut off my little finger too. I would sooner die than lose my little finger—and—I don't know what else besides.

"By the token which I send you, and which has never, until now, been off my breast, I conjure you to help me.

"Hereward—help me!"

When he read that letter the duke turned white—very white, as white as the paper on which it was written. He passed the epistle on to Knowles.

"I suppose that also is a hoax?"

Mr. Knowles was silent. He still yielded to his constitutional disrelish to commit himself. At last he asked:

"What is it that your grace proposes to do?"

The duke spoke with a bitterness which almost suggested a personal animosity toward the inoffensive Mr. Knowles.

194

"I propose, with your permission, to release the duchess from the custody of my estimable correspondent. I propose—always with your permission—to comply with his modest request, and to take him his five hundred pounds in gold." He paused, then continued in a tone which, coming from him, meant volumes: "Afterwards, I propose to cry quits with the concocter of this pretty little hoax, even if it costs me every penny I possess. He shall pay more for that five hundred pounds than he supposes."

II

The Duke of Datchet, coming out of the bank, lingered for a moment on the steps. In one hand he carried a canvas bag which seemed well weighted. On his countenance there was an expression which to a casual observer might have suggested that his grace was not completely at his ease. That casual observer happened to come strolling by. It took the form of Ivor Dacre.

Mr. Dacre looked the Duke of Datchet up and down in that languid way he has. He perceived the canvas bag. Then he remarked, possibly intending to be facetious:

"Been robbing the bank? Shall I call a cart?"

Nobody minds what Ivor Dacre says. Besides, he is the duke's own cousin. Perhaps a little removed; still, there it is. So the duke smiled a sickly smile, as if Mr. Dacre's delicate wit had given him a passing touch of indigestion.

Mr. Dacre noticed that the duke looked sallow, so he gave his pretty sense of humor another airing.

"Kitchen boiler burst? When I saw the duchess just now I wondered if it had."

His grace distinctly started. He almost dropped the canvas bag.

"You saw the duchess just now, Ivor! When?"

The duke was evidently moved. Mr. Dacre was stirred to languid curiosity. "I can't say I clocked it. Perhaps half an hour ago; perhaps a little more."

"Half an hour ago! Are you sure? Where did you see her?"

Mr. Dacre wondered. The Duchess of Datchet could scarcely have been eloping in broad daylight. Moreover, she had not yet been married a year. Everyone knew that she and the duke were still as fond of each other as if they were not man and wife. So, although the duke, for some cause or other, was evidently in an odd state of agitation, Mr. Dacre saw no reason why he should not make a clean breast of all he knew.

"She was going like blazes in a hansom cab."

195

"In a hansom cab? Where?"

"Down Waterloo Place."

"Was she alone?"

Mr. Dacre reflected. He glanced at the duke out of the corners of his eyes. His languid utterance became a positive drawl.

"I rather fancy that she wasn't."

"Who was with her?"

"My dear fellow, if you were to offer me the bank I couldn't tell you."

"Was it a man?"

Mr. Dacre's drawl became still more pronounced.

"I rather fancy that it was."

Mr. Dacre expected something. The duke was so excited. But he by no means expected what actually came.

"Ivor, she's been kidnaped!"

Mr. Dacre did what he had never been known to do before within the memory of man—he dropped his eyeglass.

"Datchet!"

"She has! Some scoundrel has decoyed her away, and trapped her. He's already sent me a lock of her hair, and he tells me that if I don't let him have five hundred pounds in gold by half-past five he'll let me have her little finger."

Mr. Dacre did not know what to make of his grace at all. He was a sober man—it couldn't be that! Mr. Dacre felt really concerned.

"I'll call a cab, old man, and you'd better let me see you home."

Mr. Dacre half raised his stick to hail a passing hansom. The duke caught him by the arm.

"You ass! What do you mean? I am telling you the simple truth. My wife's been kidnaped."

Mr. Dacre's countenance was a thing to be seen—and remembered.

"Oh! I hadn't heard that there was much of that sort of thing about just now. They talk of poodles being kidnaped, but as for duchesses—You'd really better let me call that cab."

"Ivor, do you want me to kick you? Don't you see that to me it's a question of life and death? I've been in there to get the money." His grace motioned toward the bank. "I'm going to take it to the scoundrel who has my darling at his mercy. Let me but have her hand in mine again, and he shall continue to pay for every sovereign with tears of blood until he dies."

"Look here, Datchet, I don't know if you're having a joke with me, or if you're not well—"

The duke stepped impatiently into the roadway.

"Ivor, you're a fool! Can't you tell jest from earnest, health from disease? I'm off! Are you coming with me? It would be as well that I should have a witness."

"Where are you off to?"

"To the other end of the Arcade."

"Who is the gentleman you expect to have the pleasure of meeting there?"

"How should I know?" The duke took a letter from his pocket—it was the letter which had just arrived. "The fellow is to wear a white top hat, and a gardenia in his buttonhole."

"What is it you have there?"

"It's the letter which brought the news—look for yourself and see; but, for God's sake, make haste!" His grace glanced at his watch. "It's already twenty after five."

"And do you mean to say that on the strength of a letter such as this you are going to hand over five hundred pounds to—"

The duke cut Mr. Dacre short.

"What are five hundred pounds to me? Besides, you don't know all. There is another letter. And I have heard from Mabel. But I will tell you all about it later. If you are coming, come!"

Folding up the letter, Mr. Dacre returned it to the duke.

"As you say, what are five hundred pounds to you? It's as well they are not as much to you as they are to me, or I'm afraid—"

"Hang it, Ivor, do prose afterwards!"

The duke hurried across the road. Mr. Dacre hastened after him. As they entered the Arcade they passed a constable. Mr. Dacre touched his companion's arm.

"Don't you think we'd better ask our friend in blue to walk behind us? His neighborhood might be handy."

"Nonsense!" The duke stopped short. "Ivor, this is my affair, not yours. If you are not content to play the part of silent witness, be so good as to leave me."

"My dear Datchet, I'm entirely at your service. I can be every whit as insane as you, I do assure you."

Side by side they moved rapidly down the Burlington Arcade. The duke was obviously in a state of the extremest nervous tension. Mr. Dacre was equally obviously in a state of the most supreme enjoyment. People stared as they rushed past. The duke saw nothing. Mr. Dacre saw everything, and smiled.

When they reached the Piccadilly end of the Arcade the duke pulled up. He looked about him. Mr. Dacre also looked about him.

"I see nothing of your white-hatted and gardenia-buttonholed friend," said Ivor.

The duke referred to his watch.

"It's not yet half-past five. I'm up to time."

Mr. Dacre held his stick in front of him and leaned on it. He indulged himself with a beatific smile.

"It strikes me, my dear Datchet, that you've been the victim of one of the finest things in hoaxes—"

197

"I hope I haven't kept you waiting."

The voice which interrupted Mr. Dacre came from the rear. While they were looking in front of them some one approached them from behind, apparently coming out of the shop which was at their backs.

The speaker looked a gentleman. He sounded like one, too. Costume, appearance, manner, were beyond reproach—even beyond the criticism of two such keen critics as were these. The glorious attire of a London dandy was surmounted with a beautiful white top hat. In his buttonhole was a magnificent gardenia.

In age the stranger was scarcely more than a boy, and a sunny-faced, handsome boy at that. His cheeks were hairless, his eyes were blue. His smile was not only innocent, it was bland. Never was there a more conspicuous illustration of that repose which stamps the caste of Vere de Vere.

The duke looked at him and glowered. Mr. Dacre looked at him and smiled.

"Who are you?" asked the duke.

"Ah—that is the question!" The newcomer's refined and musical voice breathed the very soul of affability. "I am an individual who is so unfortunate as to be in want of five hundred pounds."

"Are you the scoundrel who sent me that infamous letter?"

The charming stranger never turned a hair.

"I am the scoundrel mentioned in that infamous letter who wants to accost you at the Piccadilly end of the Burlington Arcade before half-past five—as witness my white hat and my gardenia."

"Where's my wife?"

The stranger gently swung his stick in front of him with his two hands. He regarded the duke as a merry-hearted son might regard his father. The thing was beautiful!

"Her grace will be home almost as soon as you are—when you have given me the money which I perceive you have all ready for me in that scarcely elegant-looking canvas bag." He shrugged his shoulders quite gracefully. "Unfortunately, in these matters one has no choice— one is forced to ask for gold."

"And suppose, instead of giving you what is in this canvas bag, I take you by the throat and choke the life right out of you?"

"Or suppose," amended Mr. Dacre, "that you do better, and commend this gentleman to the tender mercies of the first policeman we encounter."

The stranger turned to Mr. Dacre. He condescended to become conscious of his presence.

"Is this gentleman your grace's friend? Ah—Mr. Dacre, I perceive! I have the honor of knowing Mr. Dacre, though, possibly, I am unknown to him."

"You were—until this moment."

With an airy little laugh the stranger returned to the duke. He brushed an invisible speck of dust off the sleeve of his coat.

"As has been intimated in that infamous letter, his grace is at perfect liberty to give me into custody—why not? Only"—he said it with his boyish smile—"if a particular communication is not received from me in certain quarters within a certain time the Duchess of Datchet's beautiful white arm will be hacked off at the shoulder."

"You hound!"

The duke would have taken the stranger by the throat, and have done his best to choke the life right out of him then and there, if Mr. Dacre had not intervened.

"Steady, old man!" Mr. Dacre turned to the stranger. "You appear to be a pretty sort of a scoundrel."

The stranger gave his shoulders that almost imperceptible shrug.

"Oh, my dear Dacre, I am in want of money! I believe that you sometimes are in want of money, too."

Everybody knows that nobody knows where Ivor Dacre gets his money from, so the allusion must have tickled him immensely.

"You're a cool hand," he said.

"Some men are born that way."

"So I should imagine. Men like you must be born, not made."

"Precisely—as you say!" The stranger turned, with his graceful smile, to the duke: "But are we not wasting precious time? I can assure your grace that, in this particular matter, moments are of value."

Mr. Dacre interposed before the duke could answer.

"If you take my strongly urged advice, Datchet, you will summon this constable who is now coming down the Arcade, and hand this gentleman over to his keeping. I do not think that you need fear that the duchess will lose her arm, or even her little finger. Scoundrels of this one's kidney are most amenable to reason when they have handcuffs on their wrists."

The duke plainly hesitated. He would—and he would not. The stranger, as he eyed him, seemed much amused.

"My dear duke, by all means act on Mr. Dacre's valuable suggestion. As I said before, why not? It would at least be interesting to see if the duchess does or does not lose her arm—almost as interesting to you as to Mr. Dacre. Those blackmailing, kidnaping scoundrels do use such empty menaces. Besides, you would have the pleasure of seeing me locked up. My imprisonment for life would recompense you even for the loss of her grace's arm. And five hundred pounds is such a sum to have to pay—merely for a wife! Why not, therefore, act on Mr. Dacre's suggestion? Here comes the constable." The constable referred to was advancing toward them—he was not a dozen yards away. "Let me beckon to him—I will with pleasure." He took out his watch—a gold chronograph repeater. "There are scarcely ten minutes left during which it will be possible for me to send the communication which I spoke of, so that it may arrive in time. As it will then be too late, and the instruments are already prepared for the little operation which her grace is eagerly anticipating, it would, perhaps, be as well, after all, that you should give me into charge. You would have saved your five hundred pounds, and you would, at any rate, have something in exchange for her grace's mutilated limb. Ah, here is the constable! Officer!"

The stranger spoke with such a pleasant little air of easy geniality that it was impossible to tell if he were in jest or in earnest. This fact impressed the duke much more than if he had gone in for a liberal indulgence of the—under the circumstances—orthodox melodramatic scowling. And, indeed, in the face of his own common sense, it impressed Mr. Ivor Dacre too.

This well-bred, well-groomed youth was just the being to realize—aux bouts des ongles—a modern type of the devil, the type which depicts him as a perfect gentleman, who keeps smiling all the time.

The constable whom this audacious rogue had signaled approached the little group. He addressed the stranger:

"Do you want me, sir?"

"No, I do not want you. I think it is the Duke of Datchet."

The constable, who knew the duke very well by sight, saluted him as he turned to receive instructions.

The duke looked white, even savage. There was not a pleasant look in his eyes and about his lips. He appeared to be endeavoring to put a great restraint upon himself. There was a momentary silence. Mr. Dacre made a movement as if to interpose. The duke caught him by the arm.

He spoke: "No, constable, I do not want you. This person is mistaken."

The constable looked as if he could not quite make out how such a mistake could have arisen, hesitated, then, with another salute, he moved away.

The stranger was still holding his watch in his hand.

"Only eight minutes," he said.

The duke seemed to experience some difficulty in giving utterance to what he had to say.

"If I give you this five hundred pounds, you—you—"

As the duke paused, as if at a loss for language which was strong enough to convey his meaning, the stranger laughed.

"Let us take the adjectives for granted. Besides, it is only boys who call each other names—men do things. If you give me the five hundred sovereigns, which you have in that bag, at once—in five minutes it will be too late—I will promise—I will not swear; if you do not credit my simple promise, you will not believe my solemn affirmation—I will promise that, possibly within an hour, certainly

200

within an hour and a half, the Duchess of Datchet shall return to you absolutely uninjured—except, of course, as you are already aware, with regard to a few of the hairs of her head. I will promise this on the understanding that you do not yourself attempt to see where I go, and that you will allow no one else to do so." This with a glance at Ivor Dacre. "I shall know at once if I am followed. If you entertain such intentions, you had better, on all accounts, remain in possession of your five hundred pounds."

The duke eyed him very grimly.

"I entertain no such intentions—until the duchess returns."

Again the stranger indulged in that musical laugh of his.

"Ah, until the duchess returns! Of course, then the bargain's at an end. When you are once more in the enjoyment of her grace's society, you will be at liberty to set all the dogs in Europe at my heels. I assure you I fully expect that you will do so—why not?" The duke raised the canvas bag. "My dear duke, ten thousand thanks! You shall see her grace at Datchet House, 'pon my honor, probably within the hour."

"Well," commented Ivor Dacre, when the stranger had vanished, with the bag, into Piccadilly, and as the duke and himself moved toward Burlington Gardens, "if a gentleman is to be robbed, it is as well that he should have another gentleman rob him."

III

Mr. Dacre eyed his companion covertly as they progressed. His Grace of Datchet appeared to have some fresh cause for uneasiness. All at once he gave it utterance, in a tone of voice which was extremely somber:

"Ivor, do you think that scoundrel will dare to play me false?"

"I think," murmured Mr. Dacre, "that he has dared to play you pretty false already."

"I don't mean that. But I mean how am I to know, now that he has his money, that he will still not keep Mabel in his clutches?"

There came an echo from Mr. Dacre.

"Just so—how are you to know?"

"I believe that something of this sort has been done in the States."

"I thought that there they were content to kidnap them after they were dead. I was not aware that they had, as yet, got quite so far as the living."

"I believe that I have heard of something just like this."

"Possibly; they are giants over there."

"And in that case the scoundrels, when their demands were met, refused to keep to the letter of their bargain and asked for more."

The duke stood still. He clinched his fists, and swore:

"Ivor, if that—villain doesn't keep his word, and Mabel isn't home within the hour, by—I shall go mad!"

"My dear Datchet"—Mr. Dacre loved strong language as little as he loved a scene—"let us trust to time and, a little, to your white-hatted and gardenia-buttonholed friend's word of honor. You should have thought of possible eventualities before you showed your confidence—really. Suppose, instead of going mad, we first of all go home?"

A hansom stood waiting for a fare at the end of the Arcade. Mr. Dacre had handed the duke into it before his grace had quite realized that the vehicle was there.

"Tell the fellow to drive faster." That was what the duke said when the cab had started.

"My dear Datchet, the man's already driving his geerage off its legs. If a bobby catches sight of him he'll take his number."

A moment later, a murmur from the duke:

"I don't know if you're aware that the prince is coming to dinner?"

"I am perfectly aware of it."

"You take it uncommonly cool. How easy it is to bear our brother's burdens! Ivor, if Mabel doesn't turn up I shall feel like murder."

"I sympathize with you, Datchet, with all my heart, though, I may observe, parenthetically, that I very far from realize the situation even yet. Take my advice. If the duchess does not show quite as soon as we both of us desire, don't make a scene; just let me see what I can do."

Judging from the expression of his countenance, the duke was conscious of no overwhelming desire to witness an exhibition of Mr. Dacre's prowess.

When the cab reached Datchet House his grace dashed up the steps three at a time. The door flew open.

"Has the duchess returned?"

"Hereward!"

A voice floated downward from above. Some one came running down the stairs. It was her Grace of Datchet.

"Mabel!"

She actually rushed into the duke's extended arms. And he kissed her, and she kissed him—before the servants.

"So you're not quite dead?" she cried.

"I am almost," he said.

She drew herself a little away from him.

"Hereward, were you seriously hurt?"

"Do you suppose that I could have been otherwise than seriously hurt?"

"My darling! Was it a Pickford's van?"

The duke stared.

"A Pickford's van? I don't understand. But come in here. Come along, Ivor. Mabel, you don't see Ivor."

"How do you do, Mr. Dacre?"

Then the trio withdrew into a little anteroom; it was really time. Even then the pair conducted themselves as if Mr. Dacre had been nothing and no one. The duke took the lady's two hands in his. He eyed her fondly.

"So you are uninjured, with the exception of that lock of hair. Where did the villain take it from?"

The lady looked a little puzzled.

"What lock of hair?"

From an envelope which he took from his pocket the duke produced a shining tress. It was the lock of hair which had arrived in the first communication. "I will have it framed."

"You will have what framed?" The duchess glanced at what the duke was so tenderly caressing, almost, as it seemed, a little dubiously. "Whatever is it you have there?"

"It is the lock of hair which that scoundrel sent me." Something in the lady's face caused him to ask a question; "Didn't he tell you he had sent it to me?"

"Hereward!"

"Did the brute tell you that he meant to cut off your little finger?"

A very curious look came into the lady's face. She glanced at the duke as if she, all at once, was half afraid of him. She cast at Mr. Dacre what really seemed to be a look of inquiry. Her voice was tremulously anxious.

"Hereward, did—did the accident affect you mentally?"

"How could it not have affected me mentally? Do you think that my mental organization is of steel?"

"But you look so well."

"Of course I look well, now that I have you back again. Tell me, darling, did that hound actually threaten you with cutting off your arm? If he did, I shall feel half inclined to kill him yet."

The duchess seemed positively to shrink from her better half's near neighborhood.

"Hereward, was it a Pickford's van?"

The duke seemed puzzled. Well he might be.

"Was what a Pickford's van?"

The lady turned to Mr. Dacre. In her voice there was a ring of anguish.

"Mr. Dacre, tell me, was it a Pickford's van?"

Ivor could only imitate his relative's repetition of her inquiry.

"I don't quite catch you—was what a Pickford's van?"

The duchess clasped her hands in front of her.

"What is it you are keeping from me? What is it you are trying to hide? I implore you to tell me the worst, whatever it may be! Do not keep me any longer in suspense; you do not know what I already have endured. Mr. Dacre, is my husband mad?"

One need scarcely observe that the lady's amazing appeal to Mr. Dacre as to her husband's sanity was received with something like surprise. As the duke continued to stare at her, a dreadful fear began to loom in his brain.

"My darling, your brain is unhinged!"

He advanced to take her two hands again in his; but, to his unmistakable distress, she shrank away from him.

"Hereward—don't touch me. How is it that I missed you? Why did you not wait until I came?"

"Wait until you came?"

The duke's bewilderment increased.

"Surely, if your injuries turned out, after all, to be slight, that was all the more reason why you should have waited, after sending for me like that."

"I sent for you—I?" The duke's tone was grave. "My darling, perhaps you had better come upstairs."

"Not until we have had an explanation. You must have known that I should come. Why did you not wait for me after you had sent me that?"

The duchess held out something to the duke. He took it. It was a card—his own visiting card. Something was written on the back of it. He read aloud what was written.

"Mabel, come to me at once with the bearer. They tell me that they cannot take me home." It looks like my own writing."

"Looks like it! It is your writing."

"It looks like it—and written with a shaky pen."

"My dear child, one's hand would shake at such a moment as that."

"Mabel, where did you get this?"

"It was brought to me in Cane and Wilson's."

"Who brought it?"

"Who brought it? Why, the man you sent."

"The man I sent!" A light burst upon the duke's brain. He fell back a pace. "It's the decoy!"

Her grace echoed the words:

"The decoy?"

"The scoundrel! To set a trap with such a bait! My poor innocent darling, did you think it came from me? Tell me, Mabel, where did he cut off your hair?"

"Cut off my hair?"

Her grace put her hand to her head as if to make sure that her hair was there.

"Where did he take you to?"

"He took me to Draper's Buildings."

"Draper's Buildings?"

"I have never been in the City before, but he told me it was Draper's Buildings. Isn't that near the Stock Exchange?"

"Near the Stock Exchange?"

It seemed rather a curious place to which to take a kidnaped victim. The man's audacity!

"He told me that you were coming out of the Stock Exchange when a van knocked you over. He said that he thought it was a Pickford's van—was it a Pickford's van?"

"No, it was not a Pickford's van. Mabel, were you in Draper's Buildings when you wrote that letter?"

"Wrote what letter?"

"Have you forgotten it already? I do not believe that there is a word in it which will not be branded on my brain until I die."

"Hereward! What do you mean?"

"Surely you cannot have written me such a letter as that, and then have forgotten it already?"

He handed her the letter which had arrived in the second communication. She glanced at it, askance. Then she took it with a little gasp.

"Hereward, if you don't mind, I think I'll take a chair." She took a chair. "Whatever—whatever's this?" As she read the letter the varying expressions which passed across her face were, in themselves, a study in psychology. "Is it possible that you can imagine that, under any conceivable circumstances, I could have written such a letter as this?"

"Mabel!"

She rose to her feet with emphasis.

"Hereward, don't say that you thought this came from me!"

"Not from you?" He remembered Knowles's diplomatic reception of the epistle on its first appearance. "I suppose that you will say next that this is not a lock of your hair?"

"My dear child, what bee have you got in your bonnet? This a lock of my hair! Why, it's not in the least bit like my hair!"

Which was certainly inaccurate. As far as color was concerned it was an almost perfect match. The duke turned to Mr. Dacre.

"Ivor, I've had to go through a good deal this afternoon. If I have to go through much more, something will crack!" He touched his forehead. "I think it's my turn to take a chair." Not the one which the duchess had vacated, but one which faced it. He stretched out his legs in front of him; he thrust his hands into his trousers pockets; he said, in a tone which was not gloomy but absolutely grewsome:

"Might I ask, Mabel, if you have been kidnaped?"

"Kidnaped?"

205

"The word I used was 'kidnaped.' But I will spell it if you like. Or I will get a dictionary, that you may see its meaning."

The duchess looked as if she was beginning to be not quite sure if she was awake or sleeping. She turned to Ivor.

"Mr. Dacre, has the accident affected Hereward's brain?"

The duke took the words out of his cousin's mouth.

"On that point, my dear, let me ease your mind. I don't know if you are under the impression that I should be the same shape after a Pickford's van had run over me as I was before; but, in any case, I have not been run over by a Pickford's van. So far as I am concerned there has been no accident. Dismiss that delusion from your mind."

"Oh!"

"You appear surprised. One might even think that you were sorry. But may I now ask what you did when you arrived at Draper's Buildings?"

"Did! I looked for you!"

"Indeed! And when you had looked in vain, what was the next item in your programme?"

The lady shrank still farther from him.

"Hereward, have you been having a jest at my expense? Can you have been so cruel?" Tears stood in her eyes.

Rising, the duke laid his hand upon her arm.

"Mabel, tell me—what did you do when you had looked for me in vain?"

"I looked for you upstairs and downstairs and everywhere. It was quite a large place, it took me ever such a time. I thought that I should go distracted. Nobody seemed to know anything about you, or even that there had been an accident at all—it was all offices. I couldn't make it out in the least, and the people didn't seem to be able to make me out either. So when I couldn't find you anywhere I came straight home again."

The duke was silent for a moment. Then with funereal gravity he turned to Mr. Dacre. He put to him this question:

"Ivor, what are you laughing at?"

Mr. Dacre drew his hand across his mouth with rather a suspicious gesture.

"My dear fellow, only a smile!"

The duchess looked from one to the other.

"What have you two been doing? What is the joke?"

With an air of preternatural solemnity the duke took two letters from the breast pocket of his coat.

"Mabel, you have already seen your letter. You have already seen the lock of your hair. Just look at this—and that."

He gave her the two very singular communications which had arrived in such a mysterious manner, and so quickly one after the other. She read them with wide-open eyes.

206

"Hereward! Wherever did these come from?"

The duke was standing with his legs apart, and his hands in his trousers pockets. "I would give—I would give another five hundred pounds to know. Shall I tell you, madam, what I have been doing? I have been presenting five hundred golden sovereigns to a perfect stranger, with a top hat, and a gardenia in his buttonhole."

"Whatever for?"

"If you have perused those documents which you have in your hand, you will have some faint idea. Ivor, when it's your funeral, I'll smile. Mabel, Duchess of Datchet, it is beginning to dawn upon the vacuum which represents my brain that I've been the victim of one of the prettiest things in practical jokes that ever yet was planned. When that fellow brought you that card at Cane and Wilson's—which, I need scarcely tell you, never came from me—some one walked out of the front entrance who was so exactly like you that both Barnes and Moysey took her for you. Moysey showed her into the carriage, and Barnes drove her home. But when the carriage reached home it was empty. Your double had got out upon the road."

The duchess uttered a sound which was half gasp, half sigh.

"Hereward!"

"Barnes and Moysey, with beautiful and childlike innocence, when they found that they had brought the thing home empty, came straightway and told me that you had jumped out of the brougham while it had been driving full pelt through the streets. While I was digesting that piece of information there came the first epistle, with the lock of your hair. Before I had time to digest that there came the second epistle, with yours inside."

"It seems incredible!"

"It sounds incredible; but unfathomable is the folly of man, especially of a man who loves his wife." The duke crossed to Mr. Dacre. "I don't want, Ivor, to suggest anything in the way of bribery and corruption, but if you could keep this matter to yourself, and not mention it to your friends, our white-hatted and gardenia-buttonholed acquaintance is welcome to his five hundred pounds, and—Mabel, what on earth are you laughing at?"

The duchess appeared, all at once, to be seized with inextinguishable laughter.

"Hereward," she cried, "just think how that man must be laughing at you!"

And the Duke of Datchet thought of it.

THE MINOR CANON

It was Monday, and in the afternoon, as I was walking along the High Street of Marchbury, I was met by a distinguished-looking person whom I had observed at the services in the cathedral on the previous day. Now it chanced on that Sunday that I was singing the service. Properly speaking, it was not my turn; but, as my brother minor canons were either away from Marchbury or ill in bed, I was the only one left to perform the necessary duty. The distinguished-looking person was a tall, big man with a round fat face and small features. His eyes, his hair and mustache (his face was bare but for a small mustache) were quite black, and he had a very pleasant and genial expression. He wore a tall hat, set rather jauntily on his head, and he was dressed in black with a long frock coat buttoned across the chest and fitting him close to the body. As he came, with a half saunter, half swagger, along the street, I knew him again at once by his appearance; and, as he came nearer, I saw from his manner that he was intending to stop and speak to me, for he slightly raised his hat and in a soft, melodious voice with a colonial "twang" which was far from being disagreeable, and which, indeed, to my ear gave a certain additional interest to his remarks, he saluted me with "Good day, sir!"

"Good day," I answered, with just a little reserve in my tone.

"I hope, sir," he began, "you will excuse my stopping you in the street, but I wish to tell you how very much I enjoyed the music at your cathedral yesterday. I am an Australian, sir, and we have no such music in my country."

"I suppose not," I said.

"No, sir," he went on, "nothing nearly so fine. I am very fond of music, and as my business brought me in this direction, I thought I would stop at your city and take the opportunity of paying a visit to your grand cathedral. And I am delighted I came; so pleased, indeed, that I should like to leave some memorial of my visit behind me. I should like, sir, to do something for your choir."

"I am sure it is very kind of you," I replied.

"Yes, I should certainly be glad if you could suggest to me something I might do in this way. As regards money, I may say that I have plenty of it. I am the owner of a most valuable property. My business relations extend throughout the world, and if I am as fortunate in the projects of the future as I have been in the past, I shall probably one day achieve the proud position of being the richest man in the world."

I did not like to undertake myself the responsibility of advising or suggesting, so I simply said:

"I cannot venture to say, offhand, what would be the most

acceptable way of showing your great kindness and generosity, but I should certainly recommend you to put yourself in communication with the dean."

"Thank you, sir," said my Australian friend, "I will do so. And now, sir," he continued, "let me say how much I admire your voice. It is, without exception, the very finest and clearest voice I have ever heard."

"Really," I answered, quite overcome with such unqualified praise, "really it is very good of you to say so."

"Ah, but I feel it, my dear sir. I have been round the world, from Sydney to Frisco, across the continent of America" (he called it Amerrker) "to New York City, then on to England, and to-morrow I shall leave your city to continue my travels. But in all my experience I have never heard so grand a voice as your own."

This and a great deal more he said in the same strain, which modesty forbids me to reproduce.

Now I am not without some knowledge of the world outside the close of Marchbury Cathedral, and I could not listen to such a "flattering tale" without having my suspicions aroused. Who and what is this man? thought I. I looked at him narrowly. At first the thought flashed across me that he might be a "swell mobsman." But no, his face was too good for that; besides, no man with that huge frame, that personality so marked and so easily recognizable, could be a swindler; he could not escape detection a single hour. I dismissed the ungenerous thought. Perhaps he is rich, as he says. We do hear of munificent donations by benevolent millionaires now and then. What if this Australian, attracted by the glories of the old cathedral, should now appear as a deus ex machina to reëndow the choir, or to found a musical professoriate in connection with the choir, appointing me the first occupant of the professorial chair?

These thoughts flashed across my mind in the momentary pause of his fluent tongue.

"As for yourself, sir," he began again, "I have something to propose which I trust may not prove unwelcome. But the public street is hardly a suitable place to discuss my proposal. May I call upon you this evening at your house in the close? I know which it is, for I happened to see you go into it yesterday after the morning service."

"I shall be very pleased to see you," I replied. "We are going out to dinner this evening, but I shall be at home and disengaged till about seven."

"Thank you very much. Then I shall do myself the pleasure of calling upon you about six o'clock. Till then, farewell!" A graceful wave of the hand, and my unknown friend had disappeared round the corner of the street.

Now at last, I thought, something is going to happen in my uneventful life—something to break the monotony of existence. Of course, he must have inquired my name—he could get that from any of the cathedral vergers—and, as he said, he had observed whereabouts in the close I lived. What is he coming to see me for? I wondered. I spent the rest of the afternoon in making the wildest surmises. I was castle-building in Spain at a furious rate. At one time I imagined that this faithful son of the church—as he appeared to me—was going to build and endow a grand cathedral in Australia on condition that I should be appointed dean at a yearly stipend of, say, ten thousand pounds. Or perhaps, I said to myself, he will beg me to accept a sum of money—I never thought of it as less than a thousand pounds—as a slight recognition of and tribute to my remarkable vocal ability.

I took a long, lonely walk into the country to correct these ridiculous fancies and to steady my mind, and when I reached home and had refreshed myself with a quiet cup of afternoon tea, I felt I was morally and physically prepared for my interview with the opulent stranger.

Punctually as the cathedral clock struck six there was a ring at the visitor's bell. In a moment or two my unknown friend was shown into the drawing-room, which he entered with the easy air of a man of the world. I noticed he was carrying a small black bag.

"How do you do again, Mr. Dale?" he said as though we were old acquaintances; "you see I have come sharp to my time."

"Yes," I answered, "and I am pleased to see you; do sit down." He sank into my best armchair, and placed his bag on the floor beside him.

"Since we met in the afternoon," he said, "I have written a letter to your dean, expressing the great pleasure I felt in listening to your choir, and at the same time I inclosed a five-pound note, which I begged him to divide among the choir boys and men, from Alexander Poulter, Esq., of Poulter's Pills. You have of course heard of the world-renowned Poulter's Pills. I am Poulter!"

Poulter of Poulter's Pills! My heart sank within me! A five-pound note! My airy castles were tottering!

"I also sent him a couple of hundred of my pamphlets, which I said I trusted he would be so kind as to distribute in the close."

I was aghast!

"And now, with regard to the special object of my call, Mr. Dale. If you will allow me to say so, you are not making the most of that grand voice of yours; you are hidden under an ecclesiastical bushel here—lost to the world. You are wasting your vocal strength and sweetness on the desert air, so to speak. Why, if I may hazard a guess, I don't suppose you make five hundred a year here, at the outside?"

I could say nothing.

"Well, now, I can put you into the way of making at least three or four times as much as that. Listen! I am Alexander Poulter, of Poulter's Pills. I have a proposal to make to you. The scheme is bound to succeed, but I want your help. Accept my proposal and your fortune's made. Did you ever hear Moody and Sankey?" he asked abruptly.

The man is an idiot, thought I; he is now fairly carried away with his particular mania. Will it last long? Shall I ring?

"Novelty, my dear sir," he went on, "is the rule of the day; and there must be novelty in advertising, as in everything else, to catch the public interest. So I intend to go on a tour, lecturing on the merits of Poulter's Pills in all the principal halls of all the principal towns all over the world. But I have been delayed in carrying out my idea till I could associate myself with a gentleman such as yourself. Will you join me? I should be the Moody of the tour; you would be its Sankey. I would speak my patter, and you would intersperse my orations with melodious ballads bearing upon the virtues of Poulter's Pills. The ballads are all ready!"

So saying, he opened that bag and drew forth from its recesses nothing more alarming than a thick roll of manuscript music.

"The verses are my own," he said, with a little touch of pride; "and as for the music, I thought it better to make use of popular melodies, so as to enable an audience to join in the chorus. See, here is one of the ballads: 'Darling, I am better now.' It describes the woes of a fond lover, or rather his physical ailments, until he went through a course of Poulter. Here's another: 'I'm ninety-five! I'm ninety-five!' You catch the drift of that, of course—a healthy old age, secured by taking Poulter's Pills. Ah! what's this? 'Little sister's last request.' I fancy the idea of that is to beg the family never to be without Poulter's Pills. Here again: 'Then you'll remember me!' I'm afraid that title is not original; never mind, the song is. And here is—but there are many more, and I won't detain you with them now." He saw, perhaps, I was getting impatient. Thank Heaven, however, he was no escaped lunatic. I was safe!

"Mr. Poulter," said I, "I took you this afternoon for a disinterested and philanthropic millionaire; you take me for—for—something different from what I am. We have both made mistakes. In a word, it is impossible for me to accept your offer!"

"Is that final?" asked Poulter.

"Certainly," said I.

Poulter gathered his manuscripts together and replaced them in the bag, and got up to leave the room.

"Good evening, Mr. Dale," he said mournfully, as I opened the door of the room. "Good evening"—he kept on talking till he was fairly out of the house—"mark my words, you'll be sorry—very sorry—one day that you did not fall in with my scheme. Offers like mine don't come every day, and you will one day regret having refused it."

With these words he left the house.

I had little appetite for my dinner that evening.

THE PIPE

"RANDOLPH CRESCENT, N.W.
"MY DEAR PUGH—I hope you will like the pipe which I
send with this. It is rather a curious example of a certain
school of Indian carving. And is a present from
"Yours truly, Joseph Tress."

It was really very handsome of Tress—very handsome! The more
especially as I was aware that to give presents was not exactly in Tress's
line. The truth is that when I saw what manner of pipe it was I was
amazed. It was contained in a sandalwood box, which was itself
illustrated with some remarkable specimens of carving. I use the word
"remarkable" advisedly, because, although the workmanship was
undoubtedly, in its way, artistic, the result could not be described as
beautiful. The carver had thought proper to ornament the box with
some of the ugliest figures I remember to have seen. They appeared to
me to be devils. Or perhaps they were intended to represent deities
appertaining to some mythological system with which, thank goodness,
I am unacquainted. The pipe itself was worthy of the case in which it
was contained. It was of meerschaum, with an amber mouthpiece. It
was rather too large for ordinary smoking. But then, of course, one
doesn't smoke a pipe like that. There are pipes in my collection which I
should as soon think of smoking as I should of eating. Ask a china
maniac to let you have afternoon tea out of his Old Chelsea, and you
will learn some home truths as to the durability of human friendships.
The glory of the pipe, as Tress had suggested, lay in its carving. Not that
I claim that it was beautiful, any more than I make such a claim for the
carving on the box, but, as Tress said in his note, it was curious.

The stem and the bowl were quite plain, but on the edge of the
bowl was perched some kind of lizard. I told myself it was an octopus
when I first saw it, but I have since had reason to believe that it was
some almost unique member of the lizard tribe. The creature was
represented as climbing over the edge of the bowl down toward the
stem, and its legs, or feelers, or tentacula, or whatever the things are
called, were, if I may use a vulgarism, sprawling about "all over the
place." For instance, two or three of them were twined about the bowl,
two or three of them were twisted round the stem, and one, a
particularly horrible one, was uplifted in the air, so that if you put the
pipe in your mouth the thing was pointing straight at your nose.

Not the least agreeable feature about the creature was that it was
hideously lifelike. It appeared to have been carved in amber, but some
coloring matter must have been introduced, for inside the amber the
creature was of a peculiarly ghastly green. The more I examined the

212

pipe the more amazed I was at Tress's generosity. He and I are rival collectors. I am not going to say, in so many words, that his collection of pipes contains nothing but rubbish, because, as a matter of fact, he has two or three rather decent specimens. But to compare his collection to mine would be absurd. Tress is conscious of this, and he resents it. He resents it to such an extent that he has been known, at least on one occasion, to declare that one single pipe of his—I believe he alluded to the Brummagem relic preposterously attributed to Sir Walter Raleigh—was worth the whole of my collection put together. Although I have forgiven this, as I hope I always shall forgive remarks made when envious passions get the better of our nobler nature, even of a Joseph Tress, it is not to be supposed that I have forgotten it. He was, therefore, not at all the sort of person from whom I expected to receive a present. And such a present! I do not believe that he himself had a finer pipe in his collection. And to have given it to me! I had misjudged the man. I wondered where he had got it from. I had seen his pipes; I knew them off by heart—and some nice trumpery he has among them, too! but I had never seen that pipe before. The more I looked at it, the more my amazement grew. The beast perched upon the edge of the bowl was so lifelike. Its two bead-like eyes seemed to gleam at me with positively human intelligence. The pipe fascinated me to such an extent that I actually resolved to—smoke it!

I filled it with Perique. Ordinarily I use Birdseye, but on those very rare occasions on which I use a specimen I smoke Perique. I lit up with quite a small sensation of excitement. As I did so I kept my eyes perforce fixed upon the beast. The beast pointed its upraised tentacle directly at me. As I inhaled the pungent tobacco that tentacle impressed me with a feeling of actual uncanniness. It was broad daylight, and I was smoking in front of the window, yet to such an extent was I affected that it seemed to me that the tentacle was not only vibrating, which, owing to the peculiarity of its position, was quite within the range of probability, but actually moving, elongating—stretching forward, that is, farther toward me, and toward the tip of my nose. So impressed was I by this idea that I took the pipe out of my mouth and minutely examined the beast. Really, the delusion was excusable. So cunningly had the artist wrought that he succeeded in producing a creature which, such was its uncanniness, I could only hope had no original in nature.

Replacing the pipe between my lips I took several whiffs. Never had smoking had such an effect on me before. Either the pipe, or the creature on it, exercised some singular fascination. I seemed, without an instant's warning, to be passing into some land of dreams. I saw the beast, which was perched upon the bowl, writhe and twist. I saw it lift itself bodily from the meerschaum.

II

"Feeling better now?"

I looked up. Joseph Tress was speaking.

"What's the matter? Have I been ill?"

"You appear to have been in some kind of swoon."

Tress's tone was peculiar, even a little dry.

"Swoon! I never was guilty of such a thing in my life."

"Nor was I, until I smoked that pipe."

I sat up. The act of sitting up made me conscious of the fact that I had been lying down. Conscious, too, that I was feeling more than a little dazed. It seemed as though I was waking out of some strange, lethargic sleep—a kind of feeling which I have read of and heard about, but never before experienced.

"Where am I?"

"You're on the couch in your own room. You were on the floor; but I thought it would be better to pick you up and place you on the couch—though no one performed the same kind office to me when I was on the floor."

Again Tress's tone was distinctly dry.

"How came you here?"

"Ah, that's the question." He rubbed his chin—a habit of his which has annoyed me more than once before. "Do you think you're sufficiently recovered to enable you to understand a little simple explanation?" I stared at him, amazed. He went on stroking his chin. "The truth is that when I sent you the pipe I made a slight omission."

"An omission?"

"I omitted to advise you not to smoke it."

"And why?"

"Because—well, I've reason to believe the thing is drugged."

"Drugged!"

"Or poisoned."

"Poisoned!" I was wide awake enough then. I jumped off the couch with a celerity which proved it.

"It is this way. I became its owner in rather a singular manner." He paused, as if for me to make a remark; but I was silent. "It is not often that I smoke a specimen, but, for some reason, I did smoke this. I commenced to smoke it, that is. How long I continued to smoke it is more than I can say. It had on me the same peculiar effect which it appears to have had on you. When I recovered consciousness I was lying on the floor."

"On the floor?"

"On the floor. In about as uncomfortable a position as you can easily conceive. I was lying face downward, with my legs bent under me. I was never so surprised in my life as I was when I found myself

214

where I was. At first I supposed that I had had a stroke. But by degrees it dawned upon me that I didn't feel as though I had had a stroke." Tress, by the way, has been an army surgeon. "I was conscious of distinct nausea. Looking about, I saw the pipe. With me it had fallen on to the floor. I took it for granted, considering the delicacy of the carving, that the fall had broken it. But when I picked it up I found it quite uninjured. While I was examining it a thought flashed to my brain. Might it not be answerable for what had happened to me? Suppose, for instance, it was drugged? I had heard of such things. Besides, in my case were present all the symptoms of drug poisoning, though what drug had been used I couldn't in the least conceive. I resolved that I would give the pipe another trial."

"On yourself? or on another party, meaning me?"

"On myself, my dear Pugh—on myself! At that point of my investigations I had not begun to think of you. I lit up and had another smoke."

"With what result?"

"Well, that depends on the standpoint from which you regard the thing. From one point of view the result was wholly satisfactory—I proved that the thing was drugged, and more."

"Did you have another fall?"

"I did. And something else besides."

"On that account, I presume, you resolved to pass the treasure on to me?"

"Partly on that account, and partly on another."

"On my word, I appreciate your generosity. You might have labeled the thing as poison."

"Exactly. But then you must remember how often you have told me that you never smoke your specimens."

"That was no reason why you shouldn't have given me a hint that the thing was more dangerous than dynamite."

"That did occur to me afterwards. Therefore I called to supply the slight omission."

"Slight omission, you call it! I wonder what you would have called it if you had found me dead."

"If I had known that you intended smoking it I should not have been at all surprised if I had."

"Really, Tress, I appreciate your kindness more and more! And where is this example of your splendid benevolence? Have you pocketed it, regretting your lapse into the unaccustomed paths of generosity? Or is it smashed to atoms?"

"Neither the one nor the other. You will find the pipe upon the table. I neither desire its restoration nor is it in any way injured. It is merely an expression of personal opinion when I say that I don't believe that it could be injured. Of course, having discovered its deleterious properties, you will not want to smoke it again. You will therefore be able to enjoy the consciousness of being the possessor of what I honestly believe to be the most remarkable pipe in existence. Good day, Pugh."

He was gone before I could say a word. I immediately concluded, from the precipitancy of his flight, that the pipe was injured. But when I subjected it to close examination I could discover no signs of damage. While I was still eying it with jealous scrutiny the door reopened, and Tress came in again.

"By the way, Pugh, there is one thing I might mention, especially as I know it won't make any difference to you."

"That depends on what it is. If you have changed your mind, and want the pipe back again, I tell you frankly that it won't. In my opinion, a thing once given is given for good."

"Quite so; I don't want it back again. You may make your mind easy on that point. I merely wanted to tell you why I gave it you."

"You have told me that already."

"Only partly, my dear Pugh—only partly. You don't suppose I should have given you such a pipe as that merely because it happened to be drugged? Scarcely! I gave it you because I discovered from indisputable evidence, and to my cost, that it was haunted."

"Haunted?"

"Yes, haunted. Good day."

He was gone again. I ran out of the room, and shouted after him down the stairs. He was already at the bottom of the flight.

"Tress! Come back! What do you mean by talking such nonsense?"

"Of course it's only nonsense. We know that that sort of thing always is nonsense. But if you should have reason to suppose that there is something in it besides nonsense, you may think it worth your while to make inquiries of me. But I won't have that pipe back again in my possession on any terms—mind that!"

The bang of the front door told me that he had gone out into the street. I let him go. I laughed to myself as I reëntered the room. Haunted! That was not a bad idea of his. I saw the whole position at a glance. The truth of the matter was that he did regret his generosity, and he was ready to go any lengths if he could only succeed in cajoling me into restoring his gift. He was aware that I have views upon certain matters which are not wholly in accordance with those which are popularly supposed to be the views of the day, and particularly that on the question of what are commonly called supernatural visitations I have a standpoint of my own. Therefore, it was not a bad move on his part to try to make me believe that about the pipe on which he knew I had set my heart there was something which could not be accounted for by ordinary laws. Yet, as his own sense would have told him it would do, if he had only allowed himself to reflect for a moment, the move failed. Because I am not yet so far gone as to suppose that a pipe, a thing of meerschaum and of amber, in the sense in which I understand the word, could be haunted—a pipe, a mere pipe.

"Hollo! I thought the creature's legs were twined right round the bowl!"

I was holding the pipe in my hand, regarding it with the affectionate eyes with which a connoisseur does regard a curio, when I was induced to make this exclamation. I was certainly under the impression that, when I first took the pipe out of the box, two, if not three of the feelers had been twined about the bowl—twined tightly, so that you could not see daylight between them and it. Now they were almost entirely detached, only the tips touching the meerschaum, and those particular feelers were gathered up as though the creature were in the act of taking a spring. Of course I was under a misapprehension: the feelers couldn't have been twined; a moment before I should have been ready to bet a thousand to one that they were. Still, one does make mistakes, and very egregious mistakes, at times. At the same time, I confess that when I saw that dreadful-looking animal poised on the extreme edge of the bowl, for all the world as though it were just going to spring at me, I was a little startled. I remembered that when I was smoking the pipe I did think I saw the uplifted tentacle moving, as though it were reaching out to me. And I had a clear recollection that just as I had been sinking into that strange state of unconsciousness, I had been under the impression that the creature was writhing and twisting, as though it had suddenly become instinct with life. Under the circumstances, these reflections were not pleasant. I wished Tress had not talked that nonsense about the thing being haunted. It was surely sufficient to know that it was drugged and poisonous, without anything else.

I replaced it in the sandalwood box. I locked the box in a cabinet. Quite apart from the question as to whether that pipe was or was not haunted, I know it haunted me. It was with me in a figurative—which was worse than actual—sense all the day. Still worse, it was with me all the night. It was with me in my dreams. Such dreams! Possibly I had not yet wholly recovered from the effects of that insidious drug, but, whether or no, it was very wrong of Tress to set my thoughts into such a channel. He knows that I am of a highly imaginative temperament, and that it is easier to get morbid thoughts into my mind than to get them out again. Before that night was through I wished very heartily that I had never seen the pipe! I woke from one nightmare to fall into another. One dreadful dream was with me all the time—of a hideous, green reptile which advanced toward me out of some awful darkness, slowly, inch by inch, until it clutched me round the neck, and, gluing its lips to mine, sucked the life's blood out of my veins as it embraced me with a slimy kiss. Such dreams are not restful. I woke anything but refreshed when the morning came. And when I got up and dressed I felt that, on the whole, it would perhaps have been better if I never had

217

gone to bed. My nerves were unstrung, and I had that generally tremulous feeling which is, I believe, an inseparable companion of the more advanced stages of dipsomania. I ate no breakfast. I am no breakfast eater as a rule, but that morning I ate absolutely nothing.

"If this sort of thing is to continue, I will let Tress have his pipe again. He may have the laugh of me, but anything is better than this."

It was with almost funereal forebodings that I went to the cabinet in which I had placed the sandalwood box. But when I opened it my feelings of gloom partially vanished. Of what phantasies had I been guilty! It must have been an entire delusion on my part to have supposed that those tentacula had ever been twined about the bowl. The creature was in exactly the same position in which I had left it the day before—as, of course, I knew it would be—poised, as if about to spring. I was telling myself how foolish I had been to allow myself to dwell for a moment on Tress's words, when Martin Brasher was shown in.

Brasher is an old friend of mine. We have a common ground— ghosts. Only we approach them from different points of view. He takes the scientific—psychological—inquiry side. He is always anxious to hear of a ghost, so that he may have an opportunity of "showing it up."

"I've something in your line here," I observed, as he came in.

"In my line? How so? I'm not pipe mad."

"No; but you're ghost mad. And this is a haunted pipe."

"A haunted pipe! I think you're rather more mad about ghosts, my dear Pugh, than I am."

Then I told him all about it. He was deeply interested, especially when I told him that the pipe was drugged. But when I repeated Tress's words about its being haunted, and mentioned my own delusion about the creature moving, he took a more serious view of the case than I had expected he would do.

"I propose that we act on Tress's suggestion, and go and make inquiries of him."

"But you don't really think that there is anything in it?"

"On these subjects I never allow myself to think at all. There are Tress's words, and there is your story. It is agreed on all hands that the pipe has peculiar properties. It seems to me that there is a sufficient case here to merit inquiry."

He persuaded me. I went with him. The pipe, in the sandalwood box, went too. Tress received us with a grin—a grin which was accentuated when I placed the sandalwood box on the table.

"You understand," he said, "that a gift is a gift. On no terms will I consent to receive that pipe back in my possession."

I was rather nettled by his tone.

"You need be under no alarm. I have no intention of suggesting anything of the kind."

"Our business here," began Brasher—I must own that his manner is a little ponderous—"is of a scientific, I may say also, and at the same time, of a judicial nature. Our object is the Pursuit of Truth and the Advancement of Inquiry."

"Have you been trying another smoke?" inquired Tress, nodding his head toward me.

Before I had time to answer, Brasher went droning on:

"Our friend here tells me that you say this pipe is haunted."

"I say it is haunted because it is haunted."

I looked at Tress. I half suspected that he was poking fun at us. But he appeared to be serious enough.

"In these matters," remarked Brasher, as though he were giving utterance to a new and important truth, "there is a scientific and nonscientific method of inquiry. The scientific method is to begin at the beginning. May I ask how this pipe came into your possession?"

Tress paused before he answered.

"You may ask." He paused again. "Oh, you certainly may ask. But it doesn't follow that I shall tell you."

"Surely your object, like ours, can be but the Spreading About of the Truth?"

"I don't see it at all. It is possible to imagine a case in which the spreading about of the truth might make me look a little awkward."

"Indeed!" Brasher pursed up his lips. "Your words would almost lead one to suppose that there was something about your method of acquiring the pipe which you have good and weighty reasons for concealing."

"I don't know why I should conceal the thing from you. I don't suppose either of you is any better than I am. I don't mind telling you how I got the pipe. I stole it."

"Stole it!"

Brasher seemed both amazed and shocked. But I, who had previous experience of Tress's methods of adding to his collection, was not at all surprised. Some of the pipes which he calls his, if only the whole truth about them were publicly known, would send him to jail.

"That's nothing!" he continued. "All collectors steal! The eighth commandment was not intended to apply to them. Why, Pugh there has 'conveyed' three fourths of the pipes which he flatters himself are his."

I was so dumfounded by the charge that it took my breath away. I sat in astounded silence. Tress went raving on:

"I was so shy of this particular pipe when I had obtained it, that I put it away for quite three months. When I took it out to have a look at it something about the thing so tickled me that I resolved to smoke it. Owing to peculiar circumstances attending the manner in which the thing came into my possession, and on which I need not dwell—you don't like to dwell on those sort of things, do you, Pugh?—I knew really nothing about the pipe. As was the case with Pugh, one peculiarity I learned from actual experience. It was also from actual experience that I learned that the thing was—well, I said haunted, but you may use any other word you like."

"Tell us, as briefly as possible, what it was you really did discover."

"Take the pipe out of the box!" Brasher took the pipe out of the box and held it in his hand. "You see that creature on it. Well, when I first had it it was underneath the pipe."

"How do you mean that it was underneath the pipe?"

"It was bunched together underneath the stem, just at the end of the mouthpiece, in the same way in which a fly might be suspended from the ceiling. When I began to smoke the pipe I saw the creature move."

"But I thought that unconsciousness immediately followed."

"It did follow, but not before I saw that the thing was moving. It was because I thought that I had been, in a way, a victim of delirium that I tried the second smoke. Suspecting that the thing was drugged I swallowed what I believed would prove a powerful antidote. It enabled me to resist the influence of the narcotic much longer than before, and while I still retained my senses I saw the creature crawl along under the stem and over the bowl. It was that sight, I believe, as much as anything else, which sent me silly. When I came to I then and there decided to present the pipe to Pugh. There is one more thing I would remark. When the pipe left me the creature's legs were twined about the bowl. Now they are withdrawn. Possibly you, Pugh, are able to cap my story with a little one which is all your own."

"I certainly did imagine that I saw the creature move. But I supposed that while I was under the influence of the drug imagination had played me a trick."

"Not a bit of it! Depend upon it, the beast is bewitched. Even to my eye it looks as though it were, and to a trained eye like yours, Pugh! You've been looking for the devil a long time, and you've got him at last."

"I—I wish you wouldn't make those remarks, Tress. They jar on me."

"I confess," interpolated Brasher—I noticed that he had put the pipe down on the table as though he were tired of holding it—"that, to my thinking, such remarks are not appropriate. At the same time what you have told us is, I am bound to allow, a little curious. But of course what I require is ocular demonstration. I haven't seen the movement myself."

"No, but you very soon will do if you care to have a pull at the pipe on your own account. Do, Brasher, to oblige me! There's a dear!"

"It appears, then, that the movement is only observable when the pipe is smoked. We have at least arrived at step No. 1."

"Here's a match, Brasher! Light up, and we shall have arrived at step No. 2."

Tress lit a match and held it out to Brasher. Brasher retreated from its neighborhood.

"Thank you, Mr. Tress, I am no smoker, as you are aware. And I have no desire to acquire the art of smoking by means of a poisoned pipe."

Tress laughed. He blew out the match and threw it into the grate.

"Then I tell you what I'll do—I'll have up Bob."

"Bob—why Bob?"

"Bob"—whose real name was Robert Haines, though I should think he must have forgotten the fact, so seldom was he addressed by it—was Tress's servant. He had been an old soldier, and had accompanied his master when he left the service. He was as depraved a character as Tress himself. I am not sure even that he was not worse than his master. I shall never forget how he once behaved toward myself. He actually had the assurance to accuse me of attempting to steal the Wardour Street relic which Tress fondly deludes himself was once the property of Sir Walter Raleigh. The truth is that I had slipped it with my handkerchief into my pocket in a fit of absence of mind. A man who could accuse me of such a thing would be guilty of anything. I was therefore quite at one with Brasher when he asked what Bob could possibly be wanted for. Tress explained.

"I'll get him to smoke the pipe," he said.

Brasher and I exchanged glances, but we refrained from speech.

"It won't do him any harm," said Tress.

"What—not a poisoned pipe?" asked Brasher.

"It's not poisoned—it's only drugged."

"Only drugged!"

"Nothing hurts Bob. He is like an ostrich. He has digestive organs which are peculiarly his own. It will only serve him as it served me—and Pugh—it will knock him over. It is all done in the Pursuit of Truth and for the Advancement of Inquiry."

I could see that Brasher did not altogether like the tone in which Tress repeated his words. As for me, it was not to be supposed that I should put myself out in a matter which in no way concerned me. If Tress chose to poison the man, it was his affair, not mine. He went to the door and shouted:

"Bob! Come here, you scoundrel!"

That is the way in which he speaks to him. No really decent servant would stand it. I shouldn't care to address Nalder, my servant, in such a way. He would give me notice on the spot. Bob came in. He is a great hulking fellow who is always on the grin. Tress had a decanter of brandy in his hand. He filled a tumbler with the neat spirit.

"Bob, what would you say to a glassful of brandy—the real thing—my boy?"

221

"Thank you, sir."

"And what would you say to a pull at a pipe when the brandy is drunk!"

"A pipe?" The fellow is sharp enough when he likes. I saw him look at the pipe upon the table, and then at us, and then a gleam of intelligence came into his eyes. "I'd do it for a dollar, sir."

"A dollar, you thief?"

"I meant ten shillings, sir."

"Ten shillings, you brazen vagabond?"

"I should have said a pound."

"A pound! Was ever the like of that! Do I understand you to ask a pound for taking a pull at your master's pipe?"

"I'm thinking that I'll have to make it two."

"The deuce you are! Here, Pugh, lend me a pound."

"I'm afraid I've left my purse behind."

"Then lend me ten shillings—Ananias!"

"I doubt if I have more than five."

"Then give me the five. And, Brasher, lend me the other fifteen."

Brasher lent him the fifteen. I doubt if we shall either of us ever see our money again. He handed the pound to Bob.

"Here's the brandy—drink it up!" Bob drank it without a word, draining the glass of every drop. "And here's the pipe."

"Is it poisoned, sir?"

"Poisoned, you villain! What do you mean?"

"It isn't the first time I've seen your tricks, sir—is it now? And you're not the one to give a pound for nothing at all. If it kills me you'll send my body to my mother—she'd like to know that I was dead."

"Send your body to your grandmother! You idiot, sit down and smoke!"

Bob sat down. Tress had filled the pipe, and handed it, with a lighted match, to Bob. The fellow declined the match. He handled the pipe very gingerly, turning it over and over, eying it with all his eyes.

"Thank you, sir—I'll light up myself if it's the same to you. I carry matches of my own. It's a beautiful pipe, entirely. I never see the like of it for ugliness. And what's the slimy-looking varmint that looks as though it would like to have my life? Is it living, or is it dead?"

"Come, we don't want to sit here all day, my man!"

"Well, sir, the look of this here pipe has quite upset my stomach. I'd like another drop of liquor, if it's the same to you."

"Another drop! Why, you've had a tumblerful already! Here's another tumblerful to put on top of that. You won't want the pipe to kill you—you'll be killed before you get to it."

"And isn't it better to die a natural death?"

Bob emptied the second tumbler of brandy as though it were water. I believe he would empty a hogshead without turning a hair! Then he gave another look at the pipe. Then, taking a match from his

222

waistcoat pocket, he drew a long breath, as though he were resigning himself to fate. Striking the match on the seat of his trousers, while, shaded by his hand, the flame was gathering strength, he looked at each of us in turn. When he looked at Tress I distinctly saw him wink his eye. What my feelings would have been if a servant of mine had winked his eye at me I am unable to imagine! The match was applied to the tobacco, a puff of smoke came through his lips—the pipe was alight!

During this process of lighting the pipe we had sat—I do not wish to use exaggerated language, but we had sat and watched that alcoholic scamp's proceedings as though we were witnessing an action which would leave its mark upon the age. When we saw the pipe was lighted we gave a simultaneous start. Brasher put his hands under his coat tails and gave a kind of hop. I raised myself a good six inches from my chair, and Tress rubbed his palms together with a chuckle. Bob alone was calm.

"Now," cried Tress, "you'll see the devil moving."

Bob took the pipe from between his lips.

"See what?" he said.

"Bob, you rascal, put that pipe back into your mouth, and smoke it for your life!"

Bob was eying the pipe askance.

"I dare say, but what I want to know is whether this here varmint's dead or whether he isn't. I don't want to have him flying at my nose—and he looks vicious enough for anything."

"Give me back that pound, you thief, and get out of my house, and bundle."

"I ain't going to give you back no pound."

"Then smoke that pipe!"

"I am smoking it, ain't I?"

With the utmost deliberation Bob returned the pipe to his mouth. He emitted another whiff or two of smoke.

"Now—now!" cried Tress, all excitement, and wagging his hand in the air.

We gathered round. As we did so Bob again withdrew the pipe.

"What is the meaning of all this here? I ain't going to have you playing none of your larks on me. I know there's something up, but I ain't going to throw my life away for twenty shillings—not quite I ain't."

Tress, whose temper is not at any time one of the best, was seized with quite a spasm of rage.

"As I live, my lad, if you try to cheat me by taking that pipe from between your lips until I tell you, you leave this room that instant, never again to be a servant of mine."

I presume the fellow knew from long experience when his master meant what he said, and when he didn't. Without an attempt at remonstrance he replaced the pipe. He continued stolidly to puff away. Tress caught me by the arm.

223

"What did I tell you? There—there! That tentacle is moving."

The uplifted tentacle was moving. It was doing what I had seen it do, as I supposed, in my distorted imagination—it was reaching forward. Undoubtedly Bob saw what it was doing; but, whether in obedience to his master's commands, or whether because the drug was already beginning to take effect, he made no movement to withdraw the pipe. He watched the slowly advancing tentacle, coming closer and closer toward his nose, with an expression of such intense horror on his countenance that it became quite shocking. Farther and farther the creature reached forward, until on a sudden, with a sort of jerk, the movement assumed a downward direction, and the tentacle was slowly lowered until the tip rested on the stem of the pipe. For a moment the creature remained motionless. I was quieting my nerves with the reflection that this thing was but some trick of the carver's art, and that what we had seen we had seen in a sort of nightmare, when the whole hideous reptile was seized with what seemed to be a fit of convulsive shuddering. It seemed to be in agony. It trembled so violently that I expected to see it loosen its hold of the stem and fall to the ground. I was sufficiently master of myself to steal a glance at Bob. We had had an inkling of what might happen. He was wholly unprepared. As he saw that dreadful, human-looking creature, coming to life, as it seemed, within an inch or two of his nose, his eyes dilated to twice their usual size. I hoped, for his sake, that unconsciousness would supervene, through the action of the drug, before through sheer fright his senses left him. Perhaps mechanically he puffed steadily on.

The creature's shuddering became more violent. It appeared to swell before our eyes. Then, just as suddenly as it began, the shuddering ceased. There was another instant of quiescence. Then the creature began to crawl along the stem of the pipe! It moved with marvelous caution, the merest fraction of an inch at a time. But still it moved! Our eyes were riveted on it with a fascination which was absolutely nauseous. I am unpleasantly affected even as I think of it now. My dreams of the night before had been nothing to this.

Slowly, slowly, it went, nearer and nearer to the smoker's nose. Its mode of progression was in the highest degree unsightly. It glided, never, so far as I could see, removing its tentacles from the stem of the pipe. It slipped its hindmost feelers onward until they came up to those which were in advance. Then, in their turn, it advanced those which were in front. It seemed, too, to move with the utmost labor, shuddering as though it were in pain.

We were all, for our parts, speechless. I was momentarily hoping that the drug would take effect on Bob. Either his constitution enabled him to offer a strong resistance to narcotics, or else the large quantity of neat spirit which he had drunk acted—as Tress had malevolently intended that it should—as an antidote. It seemed to me that he would never succumb. On went the creature—on, and on, in its infinitesimal progression. I was spellbound. I would have given the world to scream, to have been able to utter a sound. I could do nothing else but watch.

The creature had reached the end of the stem. It had gained the amber mouthpiece. It was within an inch of the smoker's nose. Still on it went. It seemed to move with greater freedom on the amber. It increased its rate of progress. It was actually touching the foremost feature on the smoker's countenance. I expected to see it grip the wretched Bob, when it began to oscillate from side to side. Its oscillations increased in violence. It fell to the floor. That same instant the narcotic prevailed. Bob slipped sideways from the chair, the pipe still held tightly between his rigid jaws.

We were silent. There lay Bob. Close beside him lay the creature. A few more inches to the left, and he would have fallen on and squashed it flat. It had fallen on its back. Its feelers were extended upward. They were writhing and twisting and turning in the air.

Tress was the first to speak.

"I think a little brandy won't be amiss." Emptying the remainder of the brandy into a glass, he swallowed it at a draught. "Now for a closer examination of our friend." Taking a pair of tongs from the grate he nipped the creature between them. He deposited it upon the table. "I rather fancy that this is a case for dissection."

He took a penknife from his waistcoat pocket. Opening the large blade, he thrust its point into the object on the table. Little or no resistance seemed to be offered to the passage of the blade, but as it was inserted the tentacula simultaneously began to writhe and twist. Tress withdrew the knife.

"I thought so!" He held the blade out for our inspection. The point was covered with some viscid-looking matter. "That's blood! The thing's alive!"

"Alive!"

"Alive! That's the secret of the whole performance!"

"But—"

"But me no buts, my Pugh! The mystery's exploded! One more ghost is lost to the world! The person from whom I obtained that pipe was an Indian juggler—up to many tricks of the trade. He, or some one for him, got hold of this sweet thing in reptiles—and a sweeter thing would, I imagine, be hard to find—and covered it with some preparation of, possibly, gum arabic. He allowed this to harden. Then he stuck the thing—still living, for those sort of gentry are hard to kill— to the pipe. The consequence was that when anyone lit up, the warmth was communicated to the adhesive agent—again some preparation of gum, no doubt—it moistened it, and the creature, with infinite difficulty, was able to move. But I am open to lay odds with any gentleman of sporting tastes that this time the creature's traveling days are done. It has given me rather a larger taste of the horrors than is good for my digestion."

225

With the aid of the tongs he removed the creature from the table. He placed it on the hearth. Before Brasher or I had a notion of what it was he intended to do he covered it with a heavy marble paper weight. Then he stood upon the weight, and between the marble and the hearth he ground the creature flat.

While the execution was still proceeding, Bob sat up upon the floor.

"Hollo!" he asked, "what's happened?"

"We've emptied the bottle, Bob," said Tress. "But there's another where that came from. Perhaps you could drink another tumblerful, my boy?"

Bob drank it!

THE PUZZLE

I

Pugh came into my room holding something wrapped in a piece of brown paper.

"Tress, I have brought you something on which you may exercise your ingenuity." He began, with exasperating deliberation, to untie the string which bound his parcel; he is one of those persons who would not cut a knot to save their lives. The process occupied him the better part of a quarter of an hour. Then he held out the contents of the paper.

"What do you think of that?" he asked. I thought nothing of it, and I told him so. "I was prepared for that confession. I have noticed, Tress, that you generally do think nothing of an article which really deserves the attention of a truly thoughtful mind. Possibly, as you think so little of it, you will be able to solve the puzzle."

I took what he held out to me. It was an oblong box, perhaps seven inches long by three inches broad.

"Where's the puzzle?" I asked.

"If you will examine the lid of the box, you will see."

I turned it over and over; it was difficult to see which was the lid. Then I perceived that on one side were printed these words:

"PUZZLE: TO OPEN THE BOX"

The words were so faintly printed that it was not surprising that I had not noticed them at first. Pugh explained.

"I observed that box on a tray outside a second-hand furniture shop. It struck my eye. I took it up. I examined it. I inquired of the proprietor of the shop in what the puzzle lay. He replied that that was more than he could tell me. He himself had made several attempts to open the box, and all of them had failed. I purchased it. I took it home. I have tried, and I have failed. I am aware, Tress, of how you pride yourself upon your ingenuity. I cannot doubt that, if you try, you will not fail."

While Pugh was prosing, I was examining the box. It was at least well made. It weighed certainly under two ounces. I struck it with my knuckles; it sounded hollow. There was no hinge; nothing of any kind to show that it ever had been opened, or, for the matter of that, that it ever could be opened. The more I examined the thing, the more it whetted my curiosity. That it could be opened, and in some ingenious manner, I made no doubt—but how?

The box was not a new one. At a rough guess I should say that it had been a box for a good half century; there were certain signs of age

227

about it which could not escape a practiced eye. Had it remained unopened all that time? When opened, what would be found inside? It sounded hollow; probably nothing at all—who could tell?

It was formed of small pieces of inlaid wood. Several woods had been used; some of them were strange to me. They were of different colors; it was pretty obvious that they must all of them have been hard woods. The pieces were of various shapes—hexagonal, octagonal, triangular, square, oblong, and even circular. The process of inlaying them had been beautifully done. So nicely had the parts been joined that the lines of meeting were difficult to discover with the naked eye; they had been joined solid, so to speak. It was an excellent example of marquetry. I had been over-hasty in my deprecation; I owed as much to Pugh.

"This box of yours is better worth looking at than I first supposed. Is it to be sold?"

"No, it is not to be sold. Nor"—he "fixed" me with his spectacles—"is it to be given away. I have brought it to you for the simple purpose of ascertaining if you have ingenuity enough to open it."

"I will engage to open it in two seconds—with a hammer."

"I dare say. I will open it with a hammer. The thing is to open it without."

"Let me see." I began, with the aid of a microscope, to examine the box more closely. "I will give you one piece of information, Pugh. Unless I am mistaken, the secret lies in one of these little pieces of inlaid wood. You push it, or you press it, or something, and the whole affair flies open."

"Such was my own first conviction. I am not so sure of it now. I have pressed every separate piece of wood; I have tried to move each piece in every direction. No result has followed. My theory was a hidden spring."

"But there must be a hidden spring of some sort, unless you are to open it by a mere exercise of force. I suppose the box is empty."

"I thought it was at first, but now I am not so sure of that either. It all depends on the position in which you hold it. Hold it in this position—like this—close to your ear. Have you a small hammer?" I took a small hammer. "Tap it softly, with the hammer. Don't you notice a sort of reverberation within?"

Pugh was right, there certainly was something within; something which seemed to echo back my tapping, almost as if it were a living thing. I mentioned this to Pugh.

"But you don't think that there is something alive inside the box? There can't be. The box must be air-tight, probably as much air-tight as an exhausted receiver."

"How do we know that? How can we tell that no minute interstices have been left for the express purpose of ventilation?" I continued tapping with the hammer. I noticed one peculiarity, that it

228

was only when I held the box in a particular position, and tapped at a certain spot, there came the answering taps from within. "I tell you what it is, Pugh, what I hear is the reverberation of some machinery."

"Do you think so?"

"I'm sure of it."

"Give the box to me." Pugh put the box to his ear. He tapped. "It sounds to me like the echoing tick, tick of some great beetle; like the sort of noise which a deathwatch makes, you know."

Trust Pugh to find a remarkable explanation for a simple fact; if the explanation leans toward the supernatural, so much the more satisfactory to Pugh. I knew better.

"The sound which you hear is merely the throbbing or the trembling of the mechanism with which it is intended that the box should be opened. The mechanism is placed just where you are tapping it with the hammer. Every tap causes it to jar."

"It sounds to me like the ticking of a deathwatch. However, on such subjects, Tress, I know what you are."

"My dear Pugh, give it an extra hard tap, and you will see."

He gave it an extra hard tap. The moment he had done so, he started.

"I've done it now."

"What have you done?"

"Broken something, I fancy." He listened intently, with his ear to the box. "No—it seems all right. And yet I could have sworn I had damaged something; I heard it smash."

"Give me the box." He gave it me. In my turn, I listened. I shook the box. Pugh must have been mistaken. Nothing rattled; there was not a sound; the box was as empty as before. I gave a smart tap with the hammer, as Pugh had done. Then there certainly was a curious sound. To my ear, it sounded like the smashing of glass. "I wonder if there is anything fragile inside your precious puzzle, Pugh, and, if so, if we are shivering it by degrees?"

II

"What is that noise?"

I lay in bed in that curious condition which is between sleep and waking. When, at last, I knew that I was awake, I asked myself what it was that had woke me. Suddenly I became conscious that something was making itself audible in the silence of the night. For some seconds I lay and listened. Then I sat up in bed.

"What is that noise?"

It was like the tick, tick of some large and unusually clear-toned clock. It might have been a clock, had it not been that the sound was varied, every half dozen ticks or so, by a sort of stifled screech, such as might have been uttered by some small creature in an extremity of anguish. I got out of bed; it was ridiculous to think of sleep during the continuation of that uncanny shrieking. I struck a light. The sound seemed to come from the neighborhood of my dressing-table. I went to the dressing-table, the lighted match in my hand, and, as I did so, my eyes fell on Pugh's mysterious box. That same instant there issued, from the bowels of the box, a more uncomfortable screech than any I had previously heard. It took me so completely by surprise that I let the match fall from my hand to the floor. The room was in darkness. I stood, I will not say trembling, listening—considering their volume—to the eeriest shrieks I ever heard. All at once they ceased. Then came the tick, tick, tick again. I struck another match and lit the gas.

Pugh had left his puzzle box behind him. We had done all we could, together, to solve the puzzle. He had left it behind to see what I could do with it alone. So much had it engrossed my attention that I had even brought it into my bedroom, in order that I might, before retiring to rest, make a final attempt at the solution of the mystery. Now what possessed the thing?

As I stood, and looked, and listened, one thing began to be clear to me, that some sort of machinery had been set in motion inside the box. How it had been set in motion was another matter. But the box had been subjected to so much handling, to such pressing and such hammering, that it was not strange if, after all, Pugh or I had unconsciously hit upon the spring which set the whole thing going. Possibly the mechanism had got so rusty that it had refused to act at once. It had hung fire, and only after some hours had something or other set the imprisoned motive power free.

But what about the screeching? Could there be some living creature concealed within the box? Was I listening to the cries of some small animal in agony? Momentary reflection suggested that the explanation of the one thing was the explanation of the other. Rust!— there was the mystery. The same rust which had prevented the mechanism from acting at once was causing the screeching now. The uncanny sounds were caused by nothing more nor less than the want of a drop or two of oil. Such an explanation would not have satisfied Pugh, it satisfied me.

Picking up the box, I placed it to my ear.

"I wonder how long this little performance is going to continue. And what is going to happen when it is good enough to cease? I hope"— an uncomfortable thought occurred to me—"I hope Pugh hasn't picked up some pleasant little novelty in the way of an infernal machine. It would be a first-rate joke if he and I had been endeavoring to solve the puzzle of how to set it going."

I don't mind owning that as this reflection crossed my mind I replaced Pugh's puzzle on the dressing-table. The idea did not commend itself to me at all. The box evidently contained some curious mechanism. It might be more curious than comfortable. Possibly some agreeable little device in clockwork. The tick, tick, tick suggested clockwork which had been planned to go a certain time, and then—then, for all I knew, ignite an explosive, and—blow up. It would be a charming solution to the puzzle if it were to explode while I stood there, in my nightshirt, looking on. It is true that the box weighed very little. Probably, as I have said, the whole affair would not have turned the scale at a couple of ounces. But then its very lightness might have been part of the ingenious inventor's little game. There are explosives with which one can work a very satisfactory amount of damage with considerably less than a couple of ounces.

While I was hesitating—I own it!—whether I had not better immerse Pugh's puzzle in a can of water, or throw it out of the window, or call down Bob with a request to at once remove it to his apartment, both the tick, tick, tick, and the screeching ceased, and all within the box was still. If it was going to explode, it was now or never. Instinctively I moved in the direction of the door.

I waited with a certain sense of anxiety. I waited in vain. Nothing happened, not even a renewal of the sound.

"I wish Pugh had kept his precious puzzle at home. This sort of thing tries one's nerves."

When I thought that I perceived that nothing seemed likely to happen, I returned to the neighborhood of the table. I looked at the box askance. I took it up gingerly. Something might go off at any moment for all I knew. It would be too much of a joke if Pugh's precious puzzle exploded in my hand. I shook it doubtfully; nothing rattled. I held it to my ear. There was not a sound. What had taken place? Had the clockwork run down, and was the machine arranged with such a diabolical ingenuity that a certain, interval was required, after the clockwork had run down, before an explosion could occur? Or had rust caused the mechanism to again hang fire?

"After making all that commotion the thing might at least come open." I banged the box viciously against the corner of the table. I felt that I would almost rather that an explosion should take place than that nothing should occur. One does not care to be disturbed from one's sound slumber in the small hours of the morning for a trifle.

"I've half a mind to get a hammer, and try, as they say in the cookery books, another way."

Unfortunately I had promised Pugh to abstain from using force. I might have shivered the box open with my hammer, and then explained that it had fallen, or got trod upon, or sat upon, or something, and so got shattered, only I was afraid that Pugh would not believe me. The man is himself such an untruthful man that he is in a chronic state of suspicion about the truthfulness of others.

"Well, if you're not going to blow up, or open, or something, I'll say good night."

I gave the box a final rap with my knuckles and a final shake, replaced it on the table, put out the gas, and returned to bed.

I was just sinking again into slumber, when that box began again. It was true that Pugh had purchased the puzzle, but it was evident that the whole enjoyment of the purchase was destined to be mine. It was useless to think of sleep while that performance was going on. I sat up in bed once more.

"It strikes me that the puzzle consists in finding out how it is possible to go to sleep with Pugh's purchase in your bedroom. This is far better than the old-fashioned prescription of cats on the tiles."

It struck me the noise was distinctly louder than before; this applied both to the tick, tick, tick, and the screeching.

"Possibly," I told myself, as I relighted the gas, "the explosion is to come off this time."

I turned to look at the box. There could be no doubt about it; the noise was louder. And, if I could trust my eyes, the box was moving—giving a series of little jumps. This might have been an optical delusion, but it seemed to me that at each tick the box gave a little bound. During the screeches—which sounded more like the cries of an animal in an agony of pain even than before—if it did not tilt itself first on one end, and then on another, I shall never be willing to trust the evidence of my own eyes again. And surely the box had increased in size; I could have sworn not only that it had increased, but that it was increasing, even as I stood there looking on. It had grown, and still was growing, both broader, and longer, and deeper. Pugh, of course, would have attributed it to supernatural agency; there never was a man with such a nose for a ghost. I could picture him occupying my position, shivering in his nightshirt, as he beheld that miracle taking place before his eyes. The solution which at once suggested itself to me—and which would never have suggested itself to Pugh!—was that the box was fashioned, as it were, in layers, and that the ingenious mechanism it contained was forcing the sides at once both upward and outward. I took it in my hand. I could feel something striking against the bottom of the box, like the tap, tap, tapping of a tiny hammer.

"This is a pretty puzzle of Pugh's. He would say that that is the tapping of a deathwatch. For my part I have not much faith in deathwatches, et hoc genus omne, but it certainly is a curious tapping; I wonder what is going to happen next?"

Apparently nothing, except a continuation of those mysterious sounds. That the box had increased in size I had, and have, no doubt whatever. I should say that it had increased a good inch in every direction, at least half an inch while I had been looking on. But while I stood looking its growth was suddenly and perceptibly stayed; it ceased to move. Only the noise continued.

"I wonder how long it will be before anything worth happening does happen! I suppose something is going to happen; there can't be all this to-do for nothing. If it is anything in the infernal machine line, and there is going to be an explosion, I might as well be here to see it. I think I'll have a pipe."

I put on my dressing-gown. I lit my pipe. I sat and stared at the box. I dare say I sat there for quite twenty minutes when, as before, without any sort of warning, the sound was stilled. Its sudden cessation rather startled me.

"Has the mechanism again hung fire? Or, this time, is the explosion coming off?" It did not come off; nothing came off. "Isn't the box even going to open?"

It did not open. There was simply silence all at once, and that was all. I sat there in expectation for some moments longer. But I sat for nothing. I rose. I took the box in my hand. I shook it.

"This puzzle is a puzzle." I held the box first to one ear, then to the other. I gave it several sharp raps with my knuckles. There was not an answering sound, not even the sort of reverberation which Pugh and I had noticed at first. It seemed hollower than ever. It was as though the soul of the box was dead. "I suppose if I put you down, and extinguish the gas and return to bed, in about half an hour or so, just as I am dropping off to sleep, the performance will be recommenced. Perhaps the third time will be lucky."

But I was mistaken—there was no third time. When I returned to bed that time I returned to sleep, and I was allowed to sleep; there was no continuation of the performance, at least so far as I know. For no sooner was I once more between the sheets than I was seized with an irresistible drowsiness, a drowsiness which so mastered me that I—I imagine it must have been instantly—sank into slumber which lasted till long after day had dawned. Whether or not any more mysterious sounds issued from the bowels of Pugh's puzzle is more than I can tell. If they did, they did not succeed in rousing me.

And yet, when at last I did awake, I had a sort of consciousness that my waking had been caused by something strange. What it was I could not surmise. My own impression was that I had been awakened by the touch of a person's hand. But that impression must have been a mistaken one, because, as I could easily see by looking round the room, there was no one in the room to touch me.

It was broad daylight. I looked at my watch; it was nearly eleven o'clock. I am a pretty late sleeper as a rule, but I do not usually sleep as late as that. That scoundrel Bob would let me sleep all day without thinking it necessary to call me. I was just about to spring out of bed with the intention of ringing the bell so that I might give Bob a piece of my mind for allowing me to sleep so late, when my glance fell on the

233

dressing-table on which, the night before, I had placed Pugh's puzzle. It had gone!

Its absence so took me by surprise that I ran to the table. It had gone. But it had not gone far; it had gone to pieces! There were the pieces lying where the box had been. The puzzle had solved itself. The box was open, open with a vengeance, one might say. Like that unfortunate Humpty Dumpty, who, so the chroniclers tell us, sat on a wall, surely "all the king's horses and all the king's men" never could put Pugh's puzzle together again!

The marquetry had resolved itself into its component parts. How those parts had ever been joined was a mystery. They had been laid upon no foundation, as is the case with ordinary inlaid work. The several pieces of wood were not only of different shapes and sizes, but they were as thin as the thinnest veneer; yet the box had been formed by simply joining them together. The man who made that box must have been possessed of ingenuity worthy of a better cause.

I perceived how the puzzle had been worked. The box had contained an arrangement of springs, which, on being released, had expanded themselves in different directions until their mere expansion had rent the box to pieces. There were the springs, lying amid the ruin they had caused.

There was something else amid that ruin besides those springs; there was a small piece of writing paper. I took it up. On the reverse side of it was written in a minute, crabbed hand: "A Present For You." What was a present for me? I looked, and, not for the first time since I had caught sight of Pugh's precious puzzle, could scarcely believe my eyes.

There, poised between two upright wires, the bent ends of which held it aloft in the air, was either a piece of glass or—a crystal. The scrap of writing paper had exactly covered it. I understood what it was, when Pugh and I had tapped with the hammer, had caused the answering taps to proceed from within. Our taps caused the wires to oscillate, and in these oscillations the crystal, which they held suspended, had touched the side of the box.

I looked again at the piece of paper. "A Present For You." Was this the present—this crystal? I regarded it intently.

"It can't be a diamond."

The idea was ridiculous, absurd. No man in his senses would place a diamond inside a twopenny-halfpenny puzzle box. The thing was as big as a walnut! And yet—I am a pretty good judge of precious stones—if it was not an uncut diamond it was the best imitation I had seen. I took it up. I examined it closely. The more closely I examined it, the more my wonder grew.

"It is a diamond!"

And yet the idea was too preposterous for credence. Who would present a diamond as big as a walnut with a trumpery puzzle? Besides, all the diamonds which the world contains of that size are almost as well known as the Koh-i-noor.

"If it is a diamond, it is worth—it is worth—Heaven only knows what it isn't worth if it's a diamond."

I regarded it through a strong pocket lens. As I did so I could not restrain an exclamation.

"The world to a China orange, it is a diamond!"

The words had scarcely escaped my lips than there came a tapping at the door.

"Come in!" I cried, supposing it was Bob. It was not Bob, it was Pugh. Instinctively I put the lens and the crystal behind my back. At sight of me in my nightshirt Pugh began to shake his head.

"What hours, Tress, what hours! Why, my dear Tress, I've breakfasted, read the papers and my letters, came all the way from my house here, and you're not up!"

"Don't I look as though I were up?"

"Ah, Tress! Tress!" He approached the dressing-table. His eye fell upon the ruins. "What's this?"

"That's the solution to the puzzle."

"Have you—have you solved it fairly, Tress?"

"It has solved itself. Our handling, and tapping, and hammering must have freed the springs which the box contained, and during the night, while I slept, they have caused it to come open."

"While you slept? Dear me! How strange! And—what are these?"

He had discovered the two upright wires on which the crystal had been poised.

"I suppose they're part of the puzzle."

"And was there anything in the box? What's this?" He picked up the scrap of paper; I had left it on the table. He read what was written on it: "'A Present For You.' What's it mean? Tress, was this in the box?"

"It was."

"What's it mean about a present? Was there anything in the box besides?"

"Pugh, if you will leave the room I shall be able to dress; I am not in the habit of receiving quite such early calls, or I should have been prepared to receive you. If you will wait in the next room, I will be with you as soon as I'm dressed. There is a little subject in connection with the box which I wish to discuss with you."

"A subject in connection with the box? What is the subject?"

"I will tell you, Pugh, when I have performed my toilet."

"Why can't you tell me now?"

"Do you propose, then, that I should stand here shivering in my shirt while you are prosing at your ease? Thank you; I am obliged, but I decline. May I ask you once more, Pugh, to wait for me in the adjoining apartment?"

He moved toward the door. When he had taken a couple of steps, he halted.

"I—I hope, Tress, that you're—you're going to play no tricks on me?"

"Tricks on you! Is it likely that I am going to play tricks upon my oldest friend?"

When he had gone—he vanished, it seemed to me, with a somewhat doubtful visage—I took the crystal to the window. I drew the blind. I let the sunshine fall on it. I examined it again, closely and minutely, with the aid of my pocket lens. It was a diamond; there could not be a doubt of it. If, with my knowledge of stones, I was deceived, then I was deceived as never man had been deceived before. My heart beat faster as I recognized the fact that I was holding in my hand what was, in all probability, a fortune for a man of moderate desires. Of course, Pugh knew nothing of what I had discovered, and there was no reason why he should know. Not the least! The only difficulty was that if I kept my own counsel, and sold the stone and utilized the proceeds of the sale, I should have to invent a story which would account for my sudden accession to fortune. Pugh knows almost as much of my affairs as I do myself. That is the worst of these old friends!

When I joined Pugh I found him dancing up and down the floor like a bear upon hot plates. He scarcely allowed me to put my nose inside the door before attacking me.

"Tress, give me what was in the box."

"My dear Pugh, how do you know that there was something in the box to give you?"

"I know there was!"

"Indeed! If you know that there was something in the box, perhaps you will tell me what that something was."

He eyed me doubtfully. Then, advancing, he laid upon my arm a hand which positively trembled.

"Tress, you—you wouldn't play tricks on an old friend."

"You are right, Pugh, I wouldn't, though I believe there have been occasions on which you have had doubts upon the subject. By the way, Pugh, I believe that I am the oldest friend you have."

"I—I don't know about that. There's—there's Brasher."

"Brasher! Who's Brasher? You wouldn't compare my friendship to the friendship of such a man as Brasher? Think of the tastes we have in common, you and I. We're both collectors."

"Ye-es, we're both collectors."

"I make my interests yours, and you make your interests mine. Isn't that so, Pugh?"

"Tress, what—what was in the box?"

"I will be frank with you, Pugh. If there had been something in the box, would you have been willing to go halves with me in my discovery?"

"Go halves! In your discovery, Tress! Give me what is mine!"

"With pleasure, Pugh, if you will tell me what is yours."

"If—if you don't give me what was in the box I'll—I'll send for the police."

"Do! Then I shall be able to hand to them what was in the box in order that it may be restored to its proper owner."

"Its proper owner! I'm its proper owner!"

"Excuse me, but I don't understand how that can be; at least, until the police have made inquiries. I should say that the proper owner was the person from whom you purchased the box, or, more probably, the person from whom he purchased it, and by whom, doubtless, it was sold in ignorance, or by mistake. Thus, Pugh, if you will only send for the police, we shall earn the gratitude of a person of whom we never heard in our lives—I for discovering the contents of the box, and you for returning them."

As I said this, Pugh's face was a study. He gasped for breath. He actually took out his handkerchief to wipe his brow.

"Tress, I—I don't think you need to use a tone like that to me. It isn't friendly. What—what was in the box?"

"Let us understand each other, Pugh. If you don't hand over what was in the box to the police, I go halves."

Pugh began to dance about the floor.

"What a fool I was to trust you with the box! I knew I couldn't trust you." I said nothing. I turned and rang the bell. "What's that for?"

"That, my dear Pugh, is for breakfast, and, if you desire it, for the police. You know, although you have breakfasted, I haven't. Perhaps while I am breaking my fast, you would like to summon the representatives of law and order." Bob came in. I ordered breakfast. Then I turned to Pugh. "Is there anything you would like?"

"No, I—I've breakfasted."

"It wasn't of breakfast I was thinking. It was of—something else. Bob is at your service, if, for instance, you wish to send him on an errand."

"No, I want nothing. Bob can go." Bob went. Directly he was gone, Pugh turned to me. "You shall have half. What was in the box?"

"I shall have half?"

"You shall!"

"I don't think it is necessary that the terms of our little understanding should be expressly embodied in black and white. I fancy that, under the circumstance, I can trust you, Pugh. I believe that I am capable of seeing that, in this matter, you don't do me. That was in the box."

I held out the crystal between my finger and thumb.

"What is it?"

"That is what I desire to learn."

"Let me look at it."

"You are welcome to look at it where it is. Look at it as long as you like, and as closely."

Pugh leaned over my hand. His eyes began to gleam. He is himself not a bad judge of precious stones, is Pugh.

"It's—it's—Tress!—is it a diamond?"

"That question I have already asked myself."

"Let me look at it! It will be safe with me! It's mine!"

I immediately put the thing behind my back.

"Pardon me, it belongs neither to you nor to me. It belongs, in all probability, to the person who sold that puzzle to the man from whom you bought it—perhaps some weeping widow, Pugh, or hopeless orphan—think of it. Let us have no further misunderstanding upon that point, my dear old friend. Still, because you are my dear old friend, I am willing to trust you with this discovery of mine, on condition that you don't attempt to remove it from my sight, and that you return it to me the moment I require you."

"You're—you're very hard on me." I made a movement toward my waistcoat pocket. "I'll return it to you!"

I handed him the crystal, and with it I handed him my pocket lens.

"With the aid of that glass I imagine that you will be able to subject it to a more acute examination, Pugh."

He began to examine it through the lens. Directly he did so, he gave an exclamation. In a few moments he looked up at me. His eyes were glistening behind his spectacles. I could see he trembled.

"Tress, it's—it's a diamond, a Brazil diamond. It's worth a fortune!"

"I'm glad you think so."

"Glad I think so! Don't you think that it's a diamond?"

"It appears to be a diamond. Under ordinary conditions I should say, without hesitation, that it was a diamond. But when I consider the circumstances of its discovery, I am driven to doubts. How much did you give for that puzzle, Pugh?"

"Ninepence; the fellow wanted a shilling, but I gave him ninepence. He seemed content."

"Ninepence! Does it seem reasonable that we should find a diamond, which, if it is a diamond, is the finest stone I ever saw and handled, in a ninepenny puzzle? It is not as though it had got into the thing by accident, it had evidently been placed there to be found, and, apparently, by anyone who chanced to solve the puzzle; witness the writing on the scrap of paper."

Pugh reexamined the crystal.

"It is a diamond! I'll stake my life that it's a diamond!"

"Still, though it be a diamond, I smell a rat!"

"What do you mean?"

"I strongly suspect that the person who placed that diamond

238

inside that puzzle intended to have a joke at the expense of the person who discovered it. What was to be the nature of the joke is more than I can say at present, but I should like to have a bet with you that the man who compounded that puzzle was an ingenious practical joker. I may be wrong, Pugh; we shall see. But, until I have proved the contrary, I don't believe that the maddest man that ever lived would throw away a diamond worth, apparently, shall we say a thousand pounds?"

"A thousand pounds! This diamond is worth a good deal more than a thousand pounds."

"Well, that only makes my case the stronger; I don't believe that the maddest man that ever lived would throw away a diamond worth more than a thousand pounds with such utter wantonness as seems to have characterized the action of the original owner of the stone which I found in your ninepenny puzzle, Pugh."

"There have been some eccentric characters in the world, some very eccentric characters. However, as you say, we shall see. I fancy that I know somebody who would be quite willing to have such a diamond as this, and who, moreover, would be willing to pay a fair price for its possession; I will take it to him and see what he says."

"Pugh, hand me back that diamond."

"My dear Tress, I was only going—"

Bob came in with the breakfast tray.

"Pugh, you will either hand me that at once, or Bob shall summon the representatives of law and order."

He handed me the diamond. I sat down to breakfast with a hearty appetite. Pugh stood and scowled at me.

"Joseph Tress, it is my solemn conviction, and I have no hesitation in saying so in plain English, that you're a thief."

"My dear Pugh, it seems to me that we show every promise of becoming a couple of thieves."

"Don't bracket me with you!"

"Not at all, you are worse than I. It is you who decline to return the contents of the box to its proper owner. Put it to yourself, you have some common sense, my dear old friend!—do you suppose that a diamond worth more than a thousand pounds is to be honestly bought for ninepence?"

He resumed his old trick of dancing about the room.

"I was a fool ever to let you have the box! I ought to have known better than to have trusted you; goodness knows you have given me sufficient cause to mistrust you! Over and over again! Your character is only too notorious! You have plundered friend and foe alike—friend and foe alike! As for the rubbish which you call your collection, nine tenths of it, I know as a positive fact, you have stolen out and out."

"Who stole my Sir Walter Raleigh pipe? Wasn't it a man named Pugh?"

"Look here, Joseph Tress!"

239

"I'm looking."

"Oh, it's no good talking to you, not the least! You're—you're dead to all the promptings of conscience! May I inquire, Mr. Tress, what it is you propose to do?"

"I propose to do nothing, except summon the representatives of law and order. Failing that, my dear Pugh, I had some faint, vague, very vague idea of taking the contents of your ninepenny puzzle to a certain firm in Hatton Garden, who are dealers in precious stones, and to learn from them if they are disposed to give anything for it, and if so, what."

"I shall come with you."

"With pleasure, on condition that you pay the cab."

"I pay the cab! I will pay half."

"Not at all. You will either pay the whole fare, or else I will have one cab and you shall have another. It is a three-shilling cab fare from here to Hatton Garden. If you propose to share my cab, you will be so good as to hand over that three shillings before we start."

He gasped, but he handed over the three shillings. There are few things I enjoy so much as getting money out of Pugh!

On the road to Hatton Garden we wrangled nearly all the way. I own that I feel a certain satisfaction in irritating Pugh, he is such an irritable man. He wanted to know what I thought we should get for the diamond.

"You can't expect to get much for the contents of a ninepenny puzzle, not even the price of a cab fare, Pugh."

He eyed me, but for some minutes he was silent. Then he began again.

"Tress, I don't think we ought to let it go for less than—than five thousand pounds."

"Seriously, Pugh, I doubt whether, when the whole affair is ended, we shall get five thousand pence for it, or, for the matter of that, five thousand farthings."

"But why not? Why not? It's a magnificent stone—magnificent! I'll stake my life on it."

I tapped my breast with the tips of my fingers.

"There's a warning voice within my breast that ought to be in yours, Pugh! Something tells me, perhaps it is the unusually strong vein of common sense which I possess, that the contents of your ninepenny puzzle will be found to be a magnificent do—an ingenious practical joke, my friend."

"I don't believe it."

But I think he did; at any rate, I had unsettled the foundations of his faith.

We entered the Hatton Garden office side by side; in his anxiety not to let me get before him, Pugh actually clung to my arm. The office was divided into two parts by a counter which ran from wall to wall. I advanced to a man who stood on the other side of this counter.

"I want to sell you a diamond."

"We want to sell you a diamond," interpolated Pugh.

I turned to Pugh. I "fixed" him with my glance.

"I want to sell you a diamond. Here it is. What will you give me for it?"

Taking the crystal from my waistcoat pocket I handed it to the man on the other side of the counter. Directly, he got it between his fingers, and saw that it was that he had got, I noticed a sudden gleam come into his eyes.

"This is—this is rather a fine stone."

Pugh nudged my arm.

"I told you so." I paid no attention to Pugh. "What will you give me for it?"

"Do you mean, what will I give you for it cash down upon the nail?"

"Just so—what will you give me for it cash down upon the nail?"

The man turned the crystal over and over in his fingers.

"Well, that's rather a large order. We don't often get a chance of buying such a stone as this across the counter. What do you say to—well—to ten thousand pounds?"

Ten thousand pounds! It was beyond my wildest imaginings. Pugh gasped. He lurched against the counter.

"Ten thousand pounds!" he echoed.

The man on the other side glanced at him, I thought, a little curiously.

"If you can give me references, or satisfy me in any way as to your bona fides, I am prepared to give you for this diamond an open check for ten thousand pounds, or if you prefer it, the cash instead."

I stared; I was not accustomed to see business transacted on quite such lines as those.

"We'll take it," murmured Pugh; I believe he was too much overcome by his feelings to do more than murmur. I interposed.

"My dear sir, you will excuse my saying that you arrive very rapidly at your conclusions. In the first place, how can you make sure that it is a diamond?"

The man behind the counter smiled.

"I should be very ill-fitted for the position which I hold if I could not tell a diamond directly I get a sight of it, especially such a stone as this."

"But have you no tests you can apply?"

"We have tests which we apply in cases in which doubt exists, but in this case there is no doubt whatever. I am as sure that this is a diamond as I am sure that it is air I breathe. However, here is a test."

There was a wheel close by the speaker. It was worked by a treadle. It was more like a superior sort of traveling-tinker's grindstone than anything else. The man behind the counter put his foot upon the

241

treadle. The wheel began to revolve. He brought the crystal into contact with the swiftly revolving wheel. There was a s—s—sh! And, in an instant, his hand was empty; the crystal had vanished into air.

"Good heavens!" he gasped. I never saw such a look of amazement on a human countenance before. "It's splintered!"

POSTSCRIPT

It was a diamond, although it had splintered. In that fact lay the point of the joke. The man behind the counter had not been wrong; examination of such dust as could be collected proved that fact beyond a doubt. It was declared by experts that the diamond, at some period of its history, had been subjected to intense and continuing heat. The result had been to make it as brittle as glass.

There could be no doubt that its original owner had been an expert too. He knew where he got it from, and he probably knew what it had endured. He was aware that, from a mercantile point of view, it was worthless; it could never have been cut. So, having a turn for humor of a peculiar kind, he had devoted days, and weeks, and possibly months, to the construction of that puzzle. He had placed the diamond inside, and he had enjoyed, in anticipation and in imagination, the Alnaschar visions of the lucky finder.

Pugh blamed me for the catastrophe. He said, and still says, that if I had not, in a measure, and quite gratuitously, insisted on a test, the man behind the counter would have been satisfied with the evidence of his organs of vision, and we should have been richer by ten thousand pounds. But I satisfy my conscience with the reflection that what I did at any rate was honest, though, at the same time, I am perfectly well aware that such a reflection gives Pugh no sort of satisfaction.

242

THE GREAT VALDEZ SAPPHIRE

I know more about it than anyone else in the world, its present owner not excepted. I can give its whole history, from the Cingalese who found it, the Spanish adventurer who stole it, the cardinal who bought it, the Pope who graciously accepted it, the favored son of the Church who received it, the gay and giddy duchess who pawned it, down to the eminent prelate who now holds it in trust as a family heirloom.

It will occupy a chapter to itself in my forthcoming work on "Historic Stones," where full details of its weight, size, color, and value may be found. At present I am going to relate an incident in its history which, for obvious reasons, will not be published—which, in fact, I trust the reader will consider related in strict confidence.

I had never seen the stone itself when I began to write about it, and it was not till one evening last spring, while staying with my nephew, Sir Thomas Acton, that I came within measurable distance of it. A dinner party was impending, and, at my instigation, the Bishop of Northchurch and Miss Panton, his daughter and heiress, were among the invited guests.

The dinner was a particularly good one, I remember that distinctly. In fact, I felt myself partly responsible for it, having engaged the new cook—a talented young Italian, pupil of the admirable old chef at my club. We had gone over the menu carefully together, with a result refreshing in its novelty, but not so daring as to disturb the minds of the innocent country guests who were bidden thereto.

The first spoonful of soup was reassuring, and I looked to the end of the table to exchange a congratulatory glance with Leta. What was amiss? No response. Her pretty face was flushed, her smile constrained, she was talking with quite unnecessary empressement to her neighbor, Sir Harry Landor, though Leta is one of those few women who understand the importance of letting a man settle down tranquilly and with an undisturbed mind to the business of dining, allowing no topic of serious interest to come on before the relevés, and reserving mere conversational brilliancy for the entremets.

Guests all right? No disappointments? I had gone through the list with her, selecting just the right people to be asked to meet the Landors, our new neighbors. Not a mere cumbrous county gathering, nor yet a showy imported party from town, but a skillful blending of both. Had anything happened already? I had been late for dinner and missed the arrivals in the drawing-room. It was Leta's fault. She has got into a way of coming into my room and putting the last touches to my toilet. I let her, for I am doubtful of myself nowadays after many years' dependence on the best of valets. Her taste is generally beyond dispute, but to-day she had indulged in a feminine vagary that provoked me and made me late for dinner.

"Are you going to wear your sapphire, Uncle Paul!" she cried in a tone of dismay. "Oh, why not the ruby?"

"You would have your way about the table decorations," I gently reminded her. "With that service of Crown Derby repoussé and orchids, the ruby would look absolutely barbaric. Now if you would have had the Limoges set, white candles, and a yellow silk center—"

"Oh, but—I'm so disappointed—I wanted the bishop to see your ruby—or one of your engraved gems—"

"My dear, it is on the bishop's account I put this on. You know his daughter is heiress of the great Valdez sapphire—"

"Of course she is, and when he has the charge of a stone three times as big as yours, what's the use of wearing it? The ruby, dear Uncle Paul, please!"

She was desperately in earnest I could see, and considering the obligations which I am supposed to be under to her and Tom, it was but a little matter to yield, but it involved a good deal of extra trouble. Studs, sleeve-links, watch-guard, all carefully selected to go with the sapphire, had to be changed, the emerald which I chose as a compromise requiring more florid accompaniments of a deeper tone of gold; and the dinner hour struck as I replaced my jewel case, the one relic left me of a once handsome fortune, in my fireproof safe.

The emerald looked very well that evening, however. I kept my eyes upon it for comfort when Miss Panton proved trying.

She was a lean, yellow, dictatorial young person with no conversation. I spoke of her father's celebrated sapphires. "My sapphires," she amended sourly; "though I am legally debarred from making any profitable use of them." She furthermore informed me that she viewed them as useless gauds, which ought to be disposed of for the benefit of the heathen. I gave the subject up, and while she discoursed of the work of the Blue Ribbon Army among the Bosjesmans I tried to understand a certain dislocation in the arrangement of the table. Surely we were more or less in number than we should be? Opposite side all right. Who was extra on ours? I leaned forward. Lady Landor on one side of Tom, on the other who? I caught glimpses of plumes pink and green nodding over a dinner plate, and beneath them a pink nose in a green visage with a nutcracker chin altogether unknown to me. A sharp gray eye shot a sideway glance down the table and caught me peeping, and I retreated, having only marked in addition two clawlike hands, with pointed ruffles and a mass of brilliant rings, making good play with a knife and fork. Who was she? At intervals a high acid voice could be heard addressing Tom, and a laugh that made me shudder; it had the quality of the scream of a bird of prey or the yell of a jackal. I had heard that sort of laugh before, and it always made me feel like a defenseless rabbit. Every time it sounded I saw Leta's fan flutter more furiously and her manner grow more nervously animated. Poor dear girl! I never in all my recollection wished a dinner at an end so earnestly so as to assure her of my support and sympathy, though without the faintest conception why either should be required.

The ices at last. A menu card folded in two was laid beside me. I read it unobserved. "Keep the B. from joining us in the drawing-room." The B.? The bishop, of course. With pleasure. But why? And how? That's the question, never mind "why." Could I lure him into the library—the billiard room—the conservatory? I doubted it, and I doubted still more what I should do with him when I got him there.

The bishop is a grand and stately ecclesiastic of the mediæval type, broad-chested, deep-voiced, martial of bearing. I could picture him charging mace in hand at the head of his vassals, or delivering over a dissenter of the period to the rack and thumbscrew, but not pottering among rare editions, tall copies and Grolier bindings, nor condescending to a quiet cigar among the tree ferns and orchids. Leta must and should be obeyed, I swore, nevertheless, even if I were driven to lock the door in the fearless old fashion of a bygone day, and declare I'd shoot any man who left while a drop remained in the bottles.

The ladies were rising. The lady at the head of the line smirked and nodded her pink plumes coquettishly at Tom, while her hawk's eyes roved keen and predatory over us all. She stopped suddenly, creating a block and confusion.

"Ah, the dear bishop! You there, and I never saw you! You must come and have a nice long chat presently. By-by—!" She shook her fan at him over my shoulder and tripped off. Leta, passing me last, gave me a look of profound despair.

"Lady Carwitchet!" somebody exclaimed. "I couldn't believe my eyes."

"Thought she was dead or in penal servitude. Never should have expected to see her here," said some one else behind me confidentially.

"What Carwitchet? Not the mother of the Carwitchet who—"

"Just so. The Carwitchet who—" Tom assented with a shrug. "We needn't go farther, as she's my guest. Just my luck. I met them at Buxton, thought them uncommonly good company—in fact, Carwitchet laid me under a great obligation about a horse I was nearly let in for buying—and gave them a general invitation here, as one does, you know. Never expected her to turn up with her luggage this afternoon just before dinner, to stay a week, or a fortnight if Carwitchet can join her." A groan of sympathy ran round the table. "It can't be helped. I've told you this just to show that I shouldn't have asked you here to meet this sort of people of my own free will; but, as it is, please say no more about them." The subject was not dropped by any means, and I took care that it should not be. At our end of the table one story after another went buzzing round—sotto voce, out of deference to Tom—but perfectly audible.

"Carwitchet? Ah, yes. Mixed up in that Rawlings divorce case, wasn't he? A bad lot. Turned out of the Dragoon Guards for cheating at cards, or picking pockets, or something—remember the row at the Cerulean Club? Scandalous exposure—and that forged letter business— oh, that was the mother—prosecution hushed up somehow. Ought to be serving her fourteen years—and that business of poor Farrars, the banker—got hold of some of his secrets and blackmailed him till he blew his brains out—"

It was so exciting that I clean forgot the bishop, till a low gasp at my elbow startled me. He was lying back in his chair, his mighty shaven jowl a ghastly white, his fierce imperious eyebrows drooping limp over his fishlike eyes, his splendid figure shrunk and contracted. He was trying with a shaken hand to pour out wine. The decanter clattered against the glass and the wine spilled on the cloth.

"I'm afraid you find the room too warm. Shall we go into the library?"

He rose hastily and followed me like a lamb.

He recovered himself once we got into the hall, and affably rejected all my proffers of brandy and soda—medical advice— everything else my limited experience could suggest. He only demanded his carriage "directly" and that Miss Panton should be summoned forthwith.

I made the best use I could of the time left me.

"I'm uncommonly sorry you do not feel equal to staying a little longer, my lord. I counted on showing you my few trifles of precious stones, the salvage from the wreck of my possessions. Nothing in comparison with your own collection."

The bishop clasped his hand over his heart. His breath came short and quick.

"A return of that dizziness," he explained with a faint smile. "You are thinking of the Valdez sapphire, are you not? Some day," he went on with forced composure, "I may have the pleasure of showing it to you. It is at my banker's just now."

Miss Panton's steps were heard in the hall. "You are well known as a connoisseur, Mr. Acton," he went on hurriedly. "Is your collection valuable? If so, keep it safe; don't trust a ring off your hand, or the key of your jewel case out of your pocket till the house is clear again." The words rushed from his lips in an impetuous whisper, he gave me a meaning glance, and departed with his daughter. I went back to the drawing-room, my head swimming with bewilderment.

"What! The dear bishop gone!" screamed Lady Carwitchet from the central ottoman where she sat, surrounded by most of the gentlemen, all apparently well entertained by her conversation. "And I wanted to talk over old times with him so badly. His poor wife was my greatest friend. Mira Montanaro, daughter of the great banker, you know. It's not possible that that miserable little prig is my poor Mira's girl. The heiress of all the Montanaros in a black lace gown worth twopence! When I think of her mother's beauty and her toilets! Does she ever wear the sapphires? Has anyone ever seen her in them? Eleven large stones in a lovely antique setting, and the great Valdez sapphire—worth thousands and thousands—for the pendant." No one replied. "I wanted to get a rise out of the bishop to-night. It used to make him so mad when I wore this."

She fumbled among the laces at her throat, and clawed out a pendant that hung to a velvet band around her neck. I fairly gasped when she removed her hand. A sapphire of irregular shape flashed out its blue lightning on us. Such a stone! A true, rich, cornflower blue even by that wretched artificial light, with soft velvety depths of color and dazzling clearness of tint in its lights and shades—a stone to remember! I stretched out my hand involuntarily, but Lady Carwitchet drew back with a coquettish squeal. "No! no! You mustn't look any closer. Tell me what you think of it now. Isn't it pretty?"

"Superb!" was all I could ejaculate, staring at the azure splendor of that miraculous jewel in a sort of trance.

She gave a shrill cackling laugh of mockery.

"The great Mr. Acton taken in by a bit of Palais Royal gimcrackery! What an advertisement for Bogaerts et Cie! They are perfect artists in frauds. Don't you remember their stand at the first Paris Exhibition? They had imitation there of every celebrated stone; but I never expected anything made by man could delude Mr. Acton, never!" And she went off into another mocking cackle, and all the idiots round her haw-hawed knowingly, as if they had seen the joke all along. I was too bewildered to reply, which was on the whole lucky. "I suppose I mustn't tell why I came to give quite a big sum in francs for this?" she went on, tapping her closed lips with her closed fan, and cocking her eye at us all like a parrot wanting to be coaxed to talk. "It's a queer story."

I didn't want to hear her anecdote, especially as I saw she wanted to tell it. What I did want was to see that pendant again. She had thrust it back among her laces, only the loop which held it to the velvet being visible. It was set with three small sapphires, and even from a distance I clearly made them out to be imitations, and poor ones. I felt a queer thrill of self-mistrust. Was the large stone no better? Could I, even for an instant, have been dazzled by a sham, and a sham of that quality? The events of the evening had flurried and confused me. I wished to think them over in quiet. I would go to bed.

My rooms at the Manor are the best in the house. Leta will have it so. I must explain their position for a reason to be understood later. My bedroom is in the southeast angle of the house; it opens on one side into a sitting-room in the east corridor, the rest of which is taken up by the suite of rooms occupied by Tom and Leta; and on the other side into my bathroom, the first room in the south corridor, where the principal guest chambers are, to one of which it was originally the dressing-room. Passing this room I noticed a couple of housemaids preparing it for the night, and discovered with a shiver that Lady Carwitchet was to be my next-door neighbor. It gave me a turn.

The bishop's strange warning must have unnerved me. I was perfectly safe from her ladyship. The disused door into her room was locked, and the key safe on the housekeeper's bunch. It was also undiscoverable on her side, the recess in which it stood being completely filled by a large wardrobe. On my side hung a thick sound-proof portière. Nevertheless, I resolved not to use that room while she inhabited the next one. I removed my possessions, fastened the door of communication with my bedroom, and dragged a heavy ottoman across it.

Then I stowed away my emerald in my strong-box. It is built into the wall of my sitting-room, and masked by the lower part of an old carved oak bureau. I put away even the rings I wore habitually, keeping out only an inferior cat's-eye for workaday wear. I had just made all safe when Leta tapped at the door and came in to wish me good night. She looked flushed and harassed and ready to cry. "Uncle Paul," she began, "I want you to go up to town at once, and stay away till I send for you."

"My dear—!" I was too amazed to expostulate.

"We've got a—a pestilence among us," she declared, her foot tapping the ground angrily, "and the least we can do is to go into quarantine. Oh, I'm so sorry and so ashamed! The poor bishop! I'll take good care that no one else shall meet that woman here. You did your best for me, Uncle Paul, and managed admirably, but it was all no use. I hoped against hope that what between the dusk of the drawing-room before dinner, and being put at opposite ends of the table, we might get through without a meeting—"

"But, my dear, explain. Why shouldn't the bishop and Lady Carwitchet meet? Why is it worse for him than anyone else?"

"Why? I thought everybody had heard of that dreadful wife of his who nearly broke his heart. If he married her for her money it served him right, but Lady Landor says she was very handsome and really in love with him at first. Then Lady Carwitchet got hold of her and led her into all sorts of mischief. She left her husband—he was only a rector with a country living in those days—and went to live in town, got into a horrid fast set, and made herself notorious. You must have heard of her."

"I heard of her sapphires, my dear. But I was in Brazil at the time."

"I wish you had been at home. You might have found her out. She was furious because her husband refused to let her wear the great Valdez sapphire. It had been in the Montanaro family for some generations, and her father settled it first on her and then on her little

248

girl—the bishop being trustee. He felt obliged to take away the little girl, and send her off to be brought up by some old aunts in the country, and he locked up the sapphire. Lady Carwitchet tells as a splendid joke how they got the copy made in Paris, and it did just as well for the people to stare at. No wonder the bishop hates the very name of the stone."

"How long will she stay here?" I asked dismally.

"Till Lord Carwitchet can come and escort her to Paris to visit some American friends. Goodness knows when that will be! Do go up to town, Uncle Paul!"

I refused indignantly. The very least I could do was to stand by my poor young relatives in their troubles and help them through. I did so. I wore that inferior cat's eye for six weeks!

It is a time I cannot think of even now without a shudder. The more I saw of that terrible old woman the more I detested her, and we saw a very great deal of her. Leta kept her word, and neither accepted nor gave invitations all that time. We were cut off from all society but that of old General Fairford, who would go anywhere and meet anyone to get a rubber after dinner; the doctor, a sporting widower; and the Duberlys, a giddy, rather rackety young, couple who had taken the Dower House for a year. Lady Carwitchet seemed perfectly content. She reveled in the soft living and good fare of the Manor House, the drives in Leta's big barouche, and Domenico's dinners, as one to whom short commons were not unknown. She had a hungry way of grabbing and grasping at everything she could—the shillings she won at whist, the best fruit at dessert, the postage stamps in the library inkstand—that was infinitely suggestive. Sometimes I could have pitied her, she was so greedy, so spiteful, so friendless. She always made me think of some wicked old pirate putting into a peaceful port to provision and repair his battered old hulk, obliged to live on friendly terms with the natives, but his piratical old nostrils asniff for plunder and his piratical old soul longing to be off marauding once more. When would that be? Not till the arrival in Paris of her distinguished American friends, of whom we heard a great deal. "Charming people, the Bokums of Chicago, the American branch of the English Beauchamps, you know!" They seemed to be taking an unconscionable time to get there. She would have insisted on being driven over to Northchurch to call at the palace, but that the bishop was understood to be holding confirmations at the other end of the diocese.

I was alone in the house one afternoon sitting by my window, toying with the key of my safe, and wondering whether I dare treat myself to a peep at my treasures, when a suspicious movement in the park below caught my attention. A black figure certainly dodged from behind one tree to the next, and then into the shadow of the park paling instead of keeping to the footpath. It looked queer. I caught up my field glass and marked him at one point where he was bound to come into the open for a few steps. He crossed the strip of turf with giant strides and got into cover again, but not quick enough to prevent me recognizing him. It was—great heavens!—the bishop! In a soft hat pulled over his forehead, with a long cloak and a big stick, he looked like a poacher.

Guided by some mysterious instinct I hurried to meet him. I opened the conservatory door, and in he rushed like a hunted rabbit. Without explanation I led him up the wide staircase to my room, where he dropped into a chair and wiped his face.

"You are astonished, Mr. Acton," he panted. "I will explain directly. Thanks." He tossed off the glass of brandy I had poured out without waiting for the qualifying soda, and looked better.

"I am in serious trouble. You can help me. I've had a shock to-day—a grievous shock." He stopped and tried to pull himself together. "I must trust you implicitly, Mr. Acton, I have no choice. Tell me what you think of this." He drew a case from his breast pocket and opened it. "I promised you should see the Valdez sapphire. Look there!"

The Valdez sapphire! A great big shining lump of blue crystal—flawless and of perfect color—that was all. I took it up, breathed on it, drew out my magnifier, looked at it in one light and another. What was wrong with it? I could not say. Nine experts out of ten would undoubtedly have pronounced the stone genuine. I, by virtue of some mysterious instinct that has hitherto always guided me aright, was the unlucky tenth. I looked at the bishop. His eyes met mine. There was no need of spoken word between us.

"Has Lady Carwitchet shown you her sapphire?" was his most unexpected question. "She has? Now, Mr. Acton, on your honor as a connoisseur and a gentleman, which of the two is the Valdez?"

"Not this one." I could say naught else.

"You were my last hope." He broke off, and dropped his face on his folded arms with a groan that shook the table on which he rested, while I stood dismayed at myself for having let so hasty a judgment escape me. He lifted a ghastly countenance to me. "She vowed she would see me ruined and disgraced. I made her my enemy by crossing some of her schemes once, and she never forgives. She will keep her word. I shall appear before the world as a fraudulent trustee. I can neither produce the valuable confided to my charge nor make the loss good. I have only an incredible story to tell," he dropped his head and groaned again. "Who will believe me?"

"I will, for one."

"Ah, you? Yes, you know her. She took my wife from me, Mr. Acton. Heaven only knows what the hold was that she had over poor Mira. She encouraged her to set me at defiance and eventually to leave me. She was answerable for all the scandalous folly and extravagance of poor Mira's life in Paris—spare me the telling of the story. She left her at last to die alone and uncared for. I reached my wife to find her dying

250

of a fever from which Lady Carwitchet and her crew had fled. She was raving in delirium, and died without recognizing me. Some trouble she had been in which I must never know oppressed her. At the very last she roused from a long stupor and spoke to the nurse. 'Tell him to get the sapphire back—she stole it. She has robbed my child.' Those were her last words. The nurse understood no English, and treated them as wandering; but I heard them, and knew she was sane when she spoke."

"What did you do?"

"What could I? I saw Lady Carwitchet, who laughed at me, and defied me to make her confess or disgorge. I took the pendant to more than one eminent jeweler on pretense of having the setting seen to, and all have examined and admired without giving a hint of there being anything wrong. I allowed a celebrated mineralogist to see it; he gave no sign—"

"Perhaps they are right and we are wrong."

"No, no. Listen. I heard of an old Dutchman celebrated for his imitations. I went to him, and he told me at once that he had been allowed by Montanaro to copy the Valdez—setting and all—for the Paris Exhibition. I showed him this, and he claimed it for his own work at once, and pointed out his private mark upon it. You must take your magnifier to find it; a Greek Beta. He also told me that he had sold it to Lady Carwitchet more than a year ago."

"It is a terrible position."

"It is. My co-trustee died lately. I have never dared to have another appointed. I am bound to hand over the sapphire to my daughter on her marriage, if her husband consents to take the name of Montanaro."

The bishop's face was ghastly pale, and the moisture started on his brow. I racked my brain for some word of comfort.

"Miss Panton may never marry."

"But she will!" he shouted. "That is the blow that has been dealt me to-day. My chaplain—actually, my chaplain—tells me that he is going out as a temperance missionary to equatorial Africa, and has the assurance to add that he believes my daughter is not indisposed to accompany him!" His consummating wrath acted as a momentary stimulant. He sat upright, his eyes flashing and his brow thunderous. I felt for that chaplain. Then he collapsed miserably. "The sapphires will have to be produced, identified, revalued. How shall I come out of it? Think of the disgrace, the ripping up of old scandals! Even if I were to compound with Lady Carwitchet, the sum she hinted at was too monstrous. She wants more than my money. Help me, Mr. Acton! For the sake of your own family interests, help me!"

"I beg your pardon—family interests? I don't understand."

"If my daughter is childless, her next of kin is poor Marmaduke Panton, who is dying at Cannes, not married, or likely to marry; and failing him, your nephew, Sir Thomas Acton, succeeds."

251

My nephew Tom! Leta, or Leta's baby, might come to be the possible inheritor of the great Valdez sapphire! The blood rushed to my head as I looked at the great shining swindle before me. "What diabolic jugglery was at work when the exchange was made?" I demanded fiercely.

"It must have been on the last occasion of her wearing the sapphires in London. I ought never to have let her out of my sight."

"You must put a stop to Miss Panton's marriage in the first place," I pronounced as autocratically as he could have done himself.

"Not to be thought of," he admitted helplessly. "Mira has my force of character. She knows her rights, and she will have her jewels. I want you to take charge of the—thing for me. If it's in the house she'll make me produce it. She'll inquire at the banker's. If you have it we can gain time, if but for a day or two." He broke off. Carriage wheels were crashing on the gravel outside. We looked at one another in consternation. Flight was imperative. I hurried him downstairs and out of the conservatory just as the door bell rang. I think we both lost our heads in the confusion. He shoved the case into my hands, and I pocketed it, without a thought of the awful responsibility I was incurring, and saw him disappear into the shelter of the friendly night.

When I think of what my feelings were that evening—of my murderous hatred of that smirking, jesting Jezebel who sat opposite me at dinner, my wrathful indignation at the thought of the poor little expected heir defrauded ere his birth; of the crushing contempt I felt for myself and the bishop as a pair of witless idiots unable to see our way out of the dilemma; all this boiling and surging through my soul, I can only wonder—Domenico having given himself a holiday, and the kitchen maid doing her worst and wickedest—that gout or jaundice did not put an end to this story at once.

"Uncle Paul!" Leta was looking her sweetest when she tripped into my room next morning. "I've news for you. She," pointing a delicate forefinger in the direction of the corridor, "is going! Her Bokums have reached Paris at last, and sent for her to join them at the Grand Hotel."

I was thunderstruck. The longed-for deliverance had but come to remove hopelessly and forever out of my reach Lady Carwitchet and the great Valdez sapphire.

"Why, aren't you overjoyed? I am. We are going to celebrate the event by a dinner party. Tom's hospitable soul is vexed by the lack of entertainment we had provided her. We must ask the Brownleys some day or other, and they will be delighted to meet anything in the way of a ladyship, or such smart folks as the Duberly-Parkers. Then we may as well have the Blomfields, and air that awful modern Sèvres dessert service she gave us when we were married." I had no objection to make, and she went on, rubbing her soft cheek against my shoulder like the purring little cat she was: "Now I want you to do something to please

252

me—and Mrs. Blomfield. She has set her heart on seeing your rubies, and though I know you hate her about as much as you do that Sèvres china—"

"What! Wear my rubies with that! I won't. I'll tell you what I will do, though. I've got some carbuncles as big as prize gooseberries, a whole set. Then you have only to put those Bohemian glass vases and candelabra on the table, and let your gardener do his worst with his great forced, scentless, vulgar blooms, and we shall all be in keeping." Leta pouted. An idea struck me. "Or I'll do as you wish, on one condition. You get Lady Carwitchet to wear her big sapphire, and don't tell her I wish it."

I lived through the next few days as one in some evil dream. The sapphires, like twin specters, haunted me day and night. Was ever man so tantalized? To hold the shadow and see the substance dangled temptingly within reach. The bishop made no sign of ridding me of my unwelcome charge, and the thought of what might happen in a case of burglary—fire—earthquake—made me start and tremble at all sorts of inopportune moments.

I kept faith with Leta, and reluctantly produced my beautiful rubies on the night of her dinner party. Emerging from my room I came full upon Lady Carwitchet in the corridor. She was dressed for dinner, and at her throat I caught the blue gleam of the great sapphire. Leta had kept faith with me. I don't know what I stammered in reply to her ladyship's remarks; my whole soul was absorbed in the contemplation of the intoxicating loveliness of the gem. That a Palais Royal deception! Incredible! My fingers twitched, my breath came short and fierce with the lust of possession. She must have seen the covetous glare in my eyes. A look of gratified spiteful complacency overspread her features, as she swept on ahead and descended the stairs before me. I followed her to the drawing-room door. She stopped suddenly, and murmuring something unintelligible hurried back again.

Everybody was assembled there that I expected to see, with an addition. Not a welcome one by the look on Tom's face. He stood on the hearthrug conversing with a great hulking, high-shouldered fellow, sallow-faced, with a heavy mustache and drooping eyelids, from the corners of which flashed out a sudden suspicious look as I approached, which lighted up into a greedy one as it rested on my rubies, and seemed unaccountably familiar to me, till Lady Carwitchet tripping past me exclaimed:

"He has come at last! My naughty, naughty boy! Mr. Acton, this is my son, Lord Carwitchet!"

I broke off short in the midst of my polite acknowledgments to stare blankly at her. The sapphire was gone! A great gilt cross, with a Scotch pebble like an acid drop, was her sole decoration.

"I had to put my pendant away," she explained confidentially; "the clasp had got broken somehow." I didn't believe a word.

Lord Carwitchet contributed little to the general entertainment at dinner, but fell into confidential talk with Mrs. Duberly-Parker. I caught a few unintelligible remarks across the table. They referred, I subsequently discovered, to the lady's little book on Northchurch races, and I recollected that the Spring Meeting was on, and to-morrow "Cup Day." After dinner there was great talk about getting up a party to go on General Fairford's drag. Lady Carwitchet was in ecstasies and tried to coax me into joining. Leta declined positively. Tom accepted sulkily.

The look in Lord Carwitchet's eye returned to my mind as I locked up my rubies that night. It made him look so like his mother! I went round my fastenings with unusual care. Safe and closets and desk and doors, I tried them all. Coming at last to the bathroom, it opened at once. It was the housemaid's doing. She had evidently taken advantage of my having abandoned the room to give it "a thorough spring cleaning," and I anathematized her. The furniture was all piled together and veiled with sheets, the carpet and felt curtain were gone, there were new brooms about. As I peered around, a voice close at my ear made me jump—Lady Carwitchet's!

"I tell you I have nothing, not a penny! I shall have to borrow my train fare before I can leave this. They'll be glad enough to lend it."

Not only had the portière been removed, but the door behind it had been unlocked and left open for convenience of dusting behind the wardrobe. I might as well have been in the bedroom.

"Don't tell me," I recognized Carwitchet's growl. "You've not been here all this time for nothing. You've been collecting for a Kilburn cot or getting subscriptions for the distressed Irish landlords. I know you. Now I'm not going to see myself ruined for the want of a paltry hundred or so. I tell you the colt is a dead certainty. If I could have got a thousand or two on him last week, we might have ended our dog days millionaires. Hand over what you can. You've money's worth, if not money. Where's that sapphire you stole?"

"I didn't. I can show you the receipted bill. All I possess is honestly come by. What could you do with it, even if I gave it you? You couldn't sell it as the Valdez, and you can't get it cut up as you might if it were real."

"If it's only bogus, why are you always in such a flutter about it? I'll do something with it, never fear. Hand over."

"I can't. I haven't got it. I had to raise something on it before I left town."

"Will you swear it's not in that wardrobe? I dare say you will. I mean to see. Give me those keys."

I heard a struggle and a jingle, then the wardrobe door must have been flung open, for a streak of light struck through a crack in the wood of the back. Creeping close and peeping through, I could see an awful sight. Lady Carwitchet in a flannel wrapper, minus hair, teeth, complexion, pointing a skinny forefinger that quivered with rage at her son, who was out of the range of my vision.

"Stop that, and throw those keys down here directly, or I'll rouse the house. Sir Thomas is a magistrate, and will lock you up as soon as look at you." She clutched at the bell rope as she spoke. "I'll swear I'm in danger of my life from you and give you in charge. Yes, and when you're in prison I'll keep you there till you die. I've often thought I'd do it. How about the hotel robberies last summer at Cowes, eh? Mightn't the police be grateful for a hint or two? And how about—"

The keys fell with a crash on the bed, accompanied by some bad language in an apologetic tone, and the door slammed to. I crept trembling to bed.

This new and horrible complication of the situation filled me with dismay. Lord Carwitchet's wolfish glance at my rubies took a new meaning. They were safe enough, I believed—but the sapphire! If he disbelieved his mother, how long would she be able to keep it from his clutches? That she had some plot of her own of which the bishop would eventually be the victim I did not doubt, or why had she not made her bargain with him long ago? But supposing she took fright, lost her head, allowed her son to wrest the jewel from her, or gave consent to its being mutilated, divided! I lay in a cold perspiration till morning.

My terrors haunted me all day. They were with me at breakfast time when Lady Carwitchet, tripping in smiling, made a last attempt to induce me to accompany her and keep her "bad, bad boy" from getting among "those horrid betting men."

They haunted me through the long peaceful day with Leta and the tête-à-tête dinner, but they swarmed around and beset me sorest when, sitting alone over my sitting-room fire, I listened for the return of the drag party. I read my newspaper and brewed myself some hot strong drink, but there comes a time of night when no fire can warm and no drink can cheer. The bishop's despairing face kept me company, and his troubles and the wrongs of the future heir took possession of me. Then the uncanny noises that make all old houses ghostly during the small hours began to make themselves heard. Muffled footsteps trod the corridor, stopping to listen at every door, door latches gently clicked, boards creaked unreasonably, sounds of stealthy movements came from the locked-up bathroom. The welcome crash of wheels at last, and the sound of the front-door bell. I could hear Lady Carwitchet making her shrill adieux to her friends and her steps in the corridor. She was softly humming a little song as she approached. I heard her unlock her bedroom door before she entered—an odd thing to do. Tom came sleepily stumbling to his room later. I put my head out. "Where is Lord Carwitchet?"

"Haven't you seen him? He left us hours ago. Not come home, eh? Well, he's welcome to stay away. I don't want to see more of him." Tom's brow was dark and his voice surly. "I gave him to understand as

255

much." Whatever had happened, Tom was evidently too disgusted to explain just then.

I went back to my fire unaccountably relieved, and brewed myself another and a stronger brew. It warmed me this time, but excited me foolishly. There must be some way out of the difficulty. I felt now as if I could almost see it if I gave my mind to it. Why—suppose—there might be no difficulty after all! The bishop was a nervous old gentleman. He might have been mistaken all through, Bogaerts might have been mistaken, I might—no. I could not have been mistaken—or I thought not. I fidgeted and fumed and argued with myself till I found I should have no peace of mind without a look at the stone in my possession, and I actually went to the safe and took the case out.

The sapphire certainly looked different by lamplight. I sat and stared, and all but overpersuaded my better judgment into giving it a verdict. Bogaerts's mark—I suddenly remembered it. I took my magnifier and held the pendant to the light. There, scratched upon the stone, was the Greek Beta! There came a tap on my door, and before I could answer, the handle turned softly and Lord Carwitchet stood before me. I whipped the case into my dressing-gown pocket and stared at him. He was not pleasant to look at, especially at that time of night. He had a disheveled, desperate air, his voice was hoarse, his red-rimmed eyes wild.

"I beg your pardon," he began civilly enough. "I saw your light burning, and thought, as we go by the early train to-morrow, you might allow me to consult you now on a little business of my mother's." His eyes roved about the room. Was he trying to find the whereabouts of my safe? "You know a lot about precious stones, don't you?"

"So my friends are kind enough to say. Won't you sit down? I have unluckily little chance of indulging the taste on my own account," was my cautious reply.

"But you've written a book about them, and know them when you see them, don't you? Now my mother has given me something, and would like you to give a guess at its value. Perhaps you can put me in the way of disposing of it?"

"I certainly can do so if it is worth anything. Is that it?" I was in a fever of excitement, for I guessed what was clutched in his palm. He held out to me the Valdez sapphire.

How it shone and sparkled like a great blue star! I made myself a deprecating smile as I took it from him, but how dare I call it false to its face? As well accuse the sun in heaven of being a cheap imitation. I faltered and prevaricated feebly. Where was my moral courage, and where was the good, honest, thumping lie that should have aided me? "I have the best authority for recognizing this as a very good copy of a famous stone in the possession of the Bishop of Northchurch." His scowl grew so black that I saw he believed me, and I went on more cheerily: "This was manufactured by Johannes Bogaerts—I can give you his address, and you can make inquiries yourself—by special permission of the then owner, the late Leone Montanaro."

"Hand it back!" he interrupted (his other remarks were outrageous, but satisfactory to hear); but I waved him off. I couldn't give it up. It fascinated me. I toyed with it, I caressed it. I made it display its different tones of color. I must see the two stones together. I must see it outshine its paltry rival. It was a whimsical frenzy that seized me—I can call it by no other name.

"Would you like to see the original? Curiously enough, I have it here. The bishop has left it in my charge."

The wolfish light flamed up in Carwitchet's eyes as I drew forth the case. He laid the Valdez down on a sheet of paper, and I placed the other, still in its case, beside it. In that moment they looked identical, except for the little loop of sham stones, replaced by a plain gold band in the bishop's jewel. Carwitchet leaned across the table eagerly, the table gave a lurch, the lamp tottered, crashed over, and we were left in semidarkness.

"Don't stir!" Carwitchet shouted. "The paraffin is all over the place!" He seized my sofa blanket, and flung it over the table while I stood helpless. "There, that's safe now. Have you candles on the chimney-piece? I've got matches."

He looked very white and excited as he lit up. "Might have been an awkward job with all that burning paraffin, running about," he said quite pleasantly. "I hope no real harm is done." I was lifting the rug with shaking hands. The two stones lay as I had placed them. No! I nearly dropped it back again. It was the stone in the case that had the loop with the three sham sapphires!

Carwitchet picked the other up hastily. "So you say this is rubbish?" he asked, his eyes sparkling wickedly, and an attempt at mortification in his tone.

"Utter rubbish!" I pronounced, with truth and decision, snapping up the case and pocketing it. "Lady Carwitchet must have known it."

"Ah, well, it's disappointing, isn't it? Good-by, we shall not meet again."

I shook hands with him most cordially. "Good-by, Lord Carwitchet. So glad to have met you and your mother. It has been a source of the greatest pleasure, I assure you."

I have never seen the Carwitchets since. The bishop drove over next day in rather better spirits. Miss Panton had refused the chaplain.

"It doesn't matter, my lord," I said to him heartily. "We've all been under some strange misconception. The stone in your possession is the veritable one. I could swear to that anywhere. The sapphire Lady Carwitchet wears is only an excellent imitation, and—I have seen it with my own eyes—is the one bearing Bogaerts's mark, the Greek Beta."